THE RIM OF THE PRAIRIE

The Rim of the Prairie

by

Bess Streeter Aldrich

UNIVERSITY OF NEBRASKA PRESS • LINCOLN/LONDON

First Bison Book printing October, 1966

Most recent printing shown by first digit below:

6   7   8   9   10

Bison Book edition published by arrangement with the Meredith Publishing Co. in behalf of D. Appleton and Company.

CONTENTS

FOREWORD

Nebraska is only the state of my adoption but I am sure that I feel all the loyalty for it which the native-born bears. My own people came into Iowa in its early days. My father came with his parents in 1852. My grandfather Streeter, who bore the ponderous name of Zimri, represented Blackhawk County in the first Iowa legislature where he was affectionately known as "old Blackhawk." Mother, at eighteen, driving a team of horses the entire way from Lockport, Illinois, accompanied by five young brothers and sisters and her widowed mother, came in 1854.

The home of mother's family during the construction of their own cabin in the timberland was a sheep-shed which had been cleaned out for their coming and before whose entrance quilts were hung in lieu of a door. A far cry to the heat-regulated, button-pressing, faucet-turning, telephone-connected, radio-fitted homes of that mother's children!

Mother taught one of the first log-cabin schools in that part of the state, receiving twenty dollars for a three-months term and "boarding around." She and my father were married on New Year's Day of 1855, in a log-cabin out of which the humble furniture had been set in order to make room for the guests. There was music at the wedding and because fashions run in cycles, some of the tunes which the fiddler used that day have recently come into vogue. Mother came down the stairs at the appointed time, although the stairway was a ladder from the loft which she shakily descended backwards. To make up for this seeming discrepancy she had a most elaborate trousseau consisting of two new dresses and a silk shawl which had been sent out from Chicago by ox-team.

And so, while I am not a native Nebraskan, the blood of the midwestern pioneer runs in my veins and I come rightly by my love for the Nebraska pioneer and admiration for the courage and fortitude which he displayed in the early days of the state's history. After having made my home in Nebraska for seventeen years and feeling as I did that I was as proud of her heritage as were the children of the pioneers who bequeathed it, I tried to do my bit in helping preserve a little of the spirit of these pioneers in fiction.

It seems to be characteristic of the amateur to write of things beyond his horizon. There is no doubt a psychological reason for this. Be that as it may, the young writer will find eventually that he can work with truth and sincerity only on the material with which he is familiar. One of my early stories concerned itself with a millionaire's wife sojourning in the hills of Vermont. Now I have never been in the hills of Vermont although I am going there some day to see if by any chance I happened to describe them correctly. And my first-hand knowledge of millionaires' wives has been somewhat limited. After many unsatisfactory trips, the story was purchased by a third-rate magazine which was more than the hollow tale deserved. I had not then learned the lesson which the experience of later years brought; that a story rings most true when it is drawn from material within the limitations of our geographical, mental, or emotional boundaries.

Bess Streeter Aldrich

[*From an article in* Prairie Schooner, *January, 1927, the first issue of the literary quarterly sponsored by the University of Nebraska's Department of English.*]

Maple City is in Nebraska. It is far enough from the Missouri River to be out of the high bluff region. It is near enough to lie among the low rolling hills that rise and dip like solidified waves of the sea.

Wheat fields, corn fields, meadows, apple orchards, country roads . . . these frame Maple City. They not only frame it but they wander through it. Maple City children play in half-block pastures of timothy and bluegrass; gnarled old Ben Davis trees straggle down alleys; paved Main Street is but the continuation of a dusty highway which was once a buffalo trail; and, save at the more pretentious homes, plebeian corn patches flourish boldly in back yards.

Small and midwestern is Maple City, which in the eyes of many modernists is synonymous for all that is hideous and cramping. A handful of people, they say we are, knotted together like roots in the darkness. Blind souls, they call us—struggling spirits who can never find deliverance from sordid surroundings. Poor thinkers! Not to know that from tangled roots shimmering growth may spring to the light in beautiful winged release.

This is the story of a group of people in Maple City— "tangled roots" if you will, but roots from which grew the fragrant flower of romance.

THE RIM OF THE PRAIRIE

CHAPTER I

THE RETURN

O N the second Friday in September the evening passenger train from the East pulled into the Maple City station. a little late as usual, like an old man with a chronic complaint which he accepts stoically.

There was the customary stir around the station to greet this event. The drayman noisily backed his team into the platform. The agent came importantly out of the ticket office. A fat boy hurried along to get the mail sacks. A group of idlers pressed forward with a feeble show of animation. The brakeman swung down from the Pullman with a flourish of arms. It was almost a ridiculous anticlimax that after all this commotion only one passenger alighted . . . a young woman in her early twenties.

She wore a trim dark suit, a close-fitting hat and a fur, which gave her an appearance of slim daintiness. She gave no glance toward the people on the platform, but turned abruptly to her right and walked quickly past the baggage room and freight shed where a great pile of chicken crates gave forth feathery rustling sounds. The drayman, watching the stranger, made a half movement toward going after her and explaining that Main Street was up the other way, thought better of it and let her go.

The girl turned up a grassy side street without walks and hurried along in the soft dusk. She continued to walk

1

rapidly, looking neither to the right nor the left, as though she wanted no one to speak to her. By this out-of-the-way route she reached Main Street near its end and crossed the railroad tracks where the pavement abruptly changed to gravel road. Only there did she stop in her swift walk, turn and look back toward the business part of town.

She saw a few new store buildings and a stone court house replacing the old brick one of her childhood. But to her searching eyes everything else seemed the same and yet paradoxically different. The street that had been so wide years before was not of unusual width. Buildings that had seemed huge were dwarfed. Far back up Main Street through the trees she could see the old Baldwin home that had once been the show place of the town. To her surprise the vast conservatory with its multitude of long paneled glass panes was merely a big double bay window. And she had once wondered whether there could be any other place in the world in which so much glass was assembled! It made her chuckle . . . to think how Time, the careless laundryman, shrinks many of our ideals.

If the Baldwin place had once been the show place of the town it was evidently no longer so, for up on the hill where formerly there had been only rank undergrowth, stood a new house, wonderfully fine and artistic for Maple City. Whose could it be? The girl, who had seen Italian architecture in its native setting, recognized it as belonging to the Renaissance period. There was something out of place about it here overlooking the sleepy maple-and-elm-bordered streets of the old midwestern town. It looked supercilious above the comfortable brick and frame houses, a little like a sophisticated alien among provincial natives.

She turned and walked to the bridge over Tinkling Creek. For a moment she loitered, seeing in memory the little girl who was herself drop a bent pin and line over its railing.

She recalled skating under it, too, with Walt Thomas, while a team and wagon rumbled and crashed over their heads. She had shivered and clung to Walt with, "What if it'd *bust* through?"

This was fun. She was enjoying herself . . . was glad she had decided to make the trip. She passed the creamery with its peculiar odor, half sour and half sweet, and the little cottages near it. She came to the Carlsons' home and from the number of children in the yard decided that the family had been increasing with its old-time regularity. In the dusk she recognized the mother, Jen Carlson, on her front steps, but not wanting to talk to her, she hurried along, ostrich-like.

She had left the town behind now and was out on the highway heading for the east. Night was beginning to settle down comfortably over the country. There was a hush on the twilight fields. It looked peaceful. But the girl knew that peace is a matter of heart and mind and not of location.

She passed the cemetery. There was no fear within her to be out on the country road. The way was too familiar and homelike to call forth any forebodings.

Several times cars passed her. When she saw their head-lights coming she would slip farther up into the friendly shadow of the cottonwoods and Lombardy poplars that lined some of the pastures. The corn rustled eerily, its long brown fingers beckoning to her, its low sibilant voices whispering to her.

The moon swung up from the east and scattered white magic over the fields. It made the Lombardys look like the mosque towers from which the Muezzin cries the call to prayer. Those on the right of the road cast ridiculously long minaret-like shadows toward the northwest.

She passed the mile corner. As she walked she threw

back her head and breathed deeply of the night odor, that peculiar mid-west combination of loam and subsoil, corn and apple trees and clover bloom.

Toward the end of the second mile, Tinkling Creek, a gypsy stream that seemed to wander where it desired, swung across her path again. Frogs were croaking below its banks. A clammy dampness hung over it like a tangible thing. She crossed the white-railed bridge.

There was the Thomas place now on her right. She took the opposite side of the road under the Lombardys. If Walt's mother, Mattie Thomas, should see her, the whole countryside would know of her arrival.

There it was . . . on the left. . . . Uncle Jud Moore's place behind the cottonwoods. They did not know she was coming, did not believe that she would ever come again.

Now that she was so near she began, for the first time, to question her impulsive decision to come; questioned, too, the possibility of their still being there, whether in fact they were living. Aunt Biny especially, always frail, might not have lived through these years. The girl's heart was pounding tumultuously. Four years is a long time. If they were dead. . . . Quite suddenly the trouble she had given them seemed larger and more cruel.

She stood for a moment by the gate with its clanking chain on which a horseshoe swung. In the moon shadows nothing seemed changed unless there was a dwarfed crumbling look about the buildings as though Time had leaned heavily upon them.

There was a light in the middle room of the house and another one out in the cabin that had once been her playhouse.

She walked up the grassy path between the petunias. She knew that the blossoms were pink and lavender but, in the half dusk, half moonlight, they were all white. There was that same odor again . . . the mingling of loam, alfalfa, dust, petunias, apple trees. . . .

She placed her bag quietly by the steps and walked to the sitting-room window. She had not dreamed that she would feel such fear and agitation, such hope that everything was as it had been.

There they were. Two old people sat by a red-covered, drop-leaf table. The old man, huge of body, gaunt framed, gray bearded, was reading a paper. The old lady, gentle looking, white haired, a crutch by her side, was darning a stocking. A swift flash of tears swept the girl's brown eyes and she put her hand to her throat to stop its quivering. Why, how *old* they looked! They had seemed only middle-aged the day she went away.

She lingered for a few moments as though she could not bear to leave the picture. Then she took off her hat and dropped it by her bag. Everything hung on her reception. There would be no middle ground of welcome. Either they would be quite beside themselves with joy or . . . shut the door upon her.

She stepped up on the porch and with infinite care to be quiet lay down at the very threshold of the door and curled herself into a ball. Then, trembling with the import of the decision, she reached up and knocked sharply.

She could hear the creaking of a chair, a heavy shuffling and the door above her opening. The old man looked out and then down at the girl by his feet. In a high squeaky voice that shook a little in spite of its brave attempt at fun, she said, "Baby on your doorstep."

There was a long moment in which she scarcely breathed. The old man seemed dazed as though the faculties of his mind could not adjust themselves to the peculiar situation. And then quite suddenly comprehending, he opened his bearded mouth and roared, great enormous laughter, and slapped his knee. The girl looked up impishly. "I didn't really *darken* your doorway, Uncle Jud, did I?" Then she jumped up and threw her arms around him.

The old lady who had been coming forward slowly on her crutch, and peering curiously at the two, suddenly realized the truth and put out her hands. "Oh, my dear . . . my dear . . ." she said brokenly, her withered cheek against the fresh one. "My dear. . . ."

They stood in a little group together with some laughter and some tears. And because people do not say all that is in their hearts there were no apologies and no forgiveness, no questions and no answers. Only tears! And laughter! And home!

And then Uncle Jud Moore, whose idea of hospitality was to make the house very hot, was stuffing cottonwood chunks into the kitchen range. And Aunt Biny, her gentle face aglow, her worn crutch thumping over the scrubbed bareness of the kitchen floor, was getting a bite for the wayfarer to eat.

The girl curled up in a deep chintz-covered chair and took in the scene. The long narrow room, a combination kitchen and dining room, was spotless. In the dining-room end where she sat, rag rugs lay over the slate-colored painted floor. There were geraniums in the window and a little Black Prince fuchsia that looked as gentle and frail as Aunt Biny. The table was set with a white cloth and shining heavy dishes. In the kitchen end the huge range and wood-box, piled high with dried chunks, took up the width of the room. It was an old-fashioned room, not very convenient and not at all artistic, but to the girl it seemed peaceful, homelike, and because she was troubled, a haven.

There was much to say. Aunt Biny could not seem to get lunch for stopping to take in the fragrant slender charm of the girl curled up in the big chair. Uncle Jud asked multitudinous questions, ending each one with a split stick for the range, like so many cottonwood interrogation points.

"Yes, I'm going to stay six weeks or two months."

"Only two months! That ain't half long enough."

"Oh, *why* such a short time?" Now that she was home it seemed that it must be for always.

"I have to go back to my wedding," she said unconcernedly. "They quite insist that I shall attend it."

Aunt Biny on her crutch came up to the chintz-covered chair and put her hand on the girl's brown head.

"And so you've met a man you love?" she said gently.

The girl reached up and patted the worn old fingers. "Well'. . ." she threw out her own hand in a little characteristic gesture, "I've met *a man*. . . ."

It hurt Aunt Biny. It did not sound right. There was a note missing from the girl's voice . . . a note that should have been there.

Both of the old folks questioned her further until, quite abruptly, she changed the subject.

"Do you have hired help living in the old cabin, Uncle Jud? I saw a light there when I came."

Uncle Jud roared and slapped his knee. "Help? Lord, no. A feller's out there writin'. Rented it for a week to write in. Writes all day and all night and tramps down the cockleburrs in Tinklin' Creek when he ain't. Works over in town in the First National Bank. This is his vacation. Lord!" He slapped his knee again in the ecstasy of the joke. "Think of puttin' in your vacation writin'! Name's Field. . . . Warner Field."

The girl stared at him. "Warner Field?" she repeated it questioningly as though she had not heard right. There was surprise and incredulity in her tone, and something that might have been either interest or pleasure. But old Jud Moore was not subtle. He did not concern himself with the

nuances of the human voice. And there were more important things to explain to the girl while she ate, the taxes for
the new graveled road, the cow that had twin calves, the
muskrat catch of the winter before with two minks thrown
in for good measure.

After the three had talked for a long time, Aunt Biny
said happily that they must all go to bed, that there would
be a lot of to-morrows in which to visit. The girl took a
lamp from a high shelf in the kitchen, lighted its clean
wick, gave each of the old folks an impetuous kiss and went
up the narrow built-in stairway. Straight to the south bedroom she went, opened the door and stepped inside. The
room was neat and clean. The single bed was made up with
a white spread and a fat pillow standing upright in its
starched case. On the high bureau were a gay scarf and
many girlish trinkets. A small writing desk stood in the
curve of the south windows. The chairs, the pictures, the
cedar chest, were all in their old places. Through the open
closet door she could see a few out-of-date dresses and a sun-
hat hanging limply on their hooks. Everything was just as
she had left it. Nothing of hers had been changed. With the
lamp still in her hand she stood for some time just inside the
doorway and took in the picture of the old-fashioned room.
It was not true that environment made any difference with
one's personality but, if it were so, it would account for the
feeling of tranquillity that possessed her, the witchery of the
place that enveloped her. For a whimsical moment she had
the sensation that the girl who climbed the stairs had been
met at the door of the bedroom by another and, crossing the
threshold, had become that one.

> *God send us a little home*
> *To come back to when we roam.*
> *Red firelight and deep chairs*
> *And a small white bed upstairs.*

CHAPTER II

WARNER FIELD

THE telling of a story is necessarily as flat as the paper on which it is penned. It has no third dimension. Like a picture on canvas there is no back side to it. And for that reason it will never show life in its completeness. For in reality while one thing is taking place a dozen small events are transpiring elsewhere to influence or change that particular act. If one could only walk around back of it and see these other incidents that are happening simultaneously, the story would become more complete and real, would take upon itself depth as well as length and breadth.

That one may know why Warner Field was spending a week in a cabin on old Jud Moore's farm, it becomes necessary, then, to walk around behind the story to the Sunday noon before the girl's arrival.

On that second Sunday noon in September, Warner Field turned in at the old Baldwin house, once Maple City's most select home, but now its most select boarding house. Warner Field was not quite thirty but he walked laggingly like a man from whom the energy of youth had fled.

Houses have personality. Have you never seen a dignified house looking disdainfully, critically down upon its frivolous bungalow neighbors? Or an old weather-beaten one trying to appear debonair in new shingles like a withered old woman in a wig?

The old Baldwin house—nicknamed "The Bee-House" by the boarders—had personality. It stood on the corner of

9

Main and Tenth Streets just far enough back in the maples and elms to give an impression of exclusiveness. It was large and solid, built of red brick and white sandstone, with a three-storied tower on one corner which, if detached from the rest of the house, would have made a substantial silo.

A porch ran from the tower corner on the left around to the right side of the house where it ended rather foolishly in the windowless brick wall. There were double bay windows and gingerbread cornices, small glass panes in all the colors of the spectrum, and the word "Baldwin" picked out in pebbles on the top step. Old-fashioned it may have been but it was dignified. Fussy it may have looked but it had gentility. It said, "Of the modern young people who come in and out, I take no notice. Calm and reserved I sit here in the sun and the wind and the rain, like an old man, dreaming my dreams and counting my memories of the time when I was the show place of the town and all the country side came to look and exclaim."

There was a driveway which turned in from the Tenth Street side, ran under a porte-cochère (which no one in Maple City had ever had the temerity to pronounce) and ended in a barn built to match the house: red brick and sandstone, dormer windows and gimcracks. At least a barn it had been in Judge Baldwin's day, housing a pair of portly asthmatic horses, a surrey and a phaëton, to say nothing of a spotted pony and cart for the children. And now two of those little girls, who had driven around town years before, clean and stiff in their starched white dresses and broad brimmed hats tied under plump chins, were keeping boarders in the aristocratic old house which sat dozing and dreaming behind the maples. And the barn was a garage in which two of the boarders ran their cars up to the mangers where the spirits of the fat old horses stood munching ghost hay all night long.

No one could remember who started calling it "The Bee-House" and neither was any one definitely sure whether "B" stood for "Baldwin" or "Boarding" or for that type of Apis insect which has gone down in history with a reputation for improving each shining hour. If the last, it was aptly named, for all the boarders belonged to the class of American young people that earns its salt by the sweat of its brain.

The two little girls who had grown up to keep boarders were now Miss Ann and Miss Rilla. Twins! While quite easily distinguishable they were very similar in appearance: heavy, erect, gray-haired and pink-cheeked. Rather childishly they still dressed alike. Round china-blue eyes gave them an added touch of similarity. But where Miss Rilla's mouth turned up, Miss Ann's turned down. This point was characteristic of their dispositions. Miss Rilla was emotional. Any passing remark which touched upon joy, sorrow or sympathy set her tear ducts to working. Miss Ann was cold-hearted. Any passing remark which touched upon joy, sorrow or sympathy left her impassive, callous, questioning its motive. Miss Rilla was diplomatic. Miss Ann was blunt. "I'm fifty-four," Miss Ann would say frankly. And as everybody knows that things which are equal to the same thing are equal to each other, it followed that poor Miss Rilla, who thought her age her own business, was also fifty-four.

If Miss Rilla was full of sentiment, Miss Ann was businesslike. If Miss Rilla thought with her heart, Miss Ann used her head. Indeed, each one's attitude toward the boarders was typical of herself. To Miss Rilla the boarders were so many personalities. To Miss Ann the boarders were so many portions.

Because of the stern masculine quality in Miss Ann's make-up she naturally assumed the dictatorship and no

Worthy Patron or Illustrious Potentate was more chary of the reputations of his lodge candidates than Miss Ann of the boarders. To all applicants she presented an imposing and impenetrable front if it happened that she knew little about them. "We are full to-day," she would announce as firmly as though she possessed no more leaves for her table. "I'll let you know this evening."

Warner Field, however, had not found it difficult to gain admittance to the elect. When he arrived in Maple City to take a position in the First National Bank, O. J. Rineland, the president, had called up Miss Ann to engage a room for the newcomer.

For eight months now he had been living at the "Bee-House." Two-thirds of a year he had spent in Maple City and yet he felt no more an integral part of it than when he had first come. These months had been crowded with mental upheaval. Although he had given himself diligently to his new task, there had been neither buoyancy nor keen interest in it. In his unsettled condition he seemed to be two men; one who worked doggedly on, infinitely painstaking, habitually courteous; and one who was dissatisfied with his environment, critical of the community, deeply disgusted with himself.

Just now he went up the walk where leaf shadows from the elms lay thick under the September sun, entered the "Bee-House," and hung his hat in the vestibule. There was no one in the reception hall with its inlaid floor and fireplace, no one at least but old Judge Baldwin, who seemed a living personality looking pompously down upon the intruder from his heavy gilt frame.

Warner passed on to the dining room at the left. It was a long, narrow room, the result of the original dining room and old Mrs. Baldwin's bedroom having been thrown together after her death. A table with many people around it was in the long room with its curving archway. Miss Rilla sat at the north end and Miss Ann at the south end, which gave each half of the table the uncanny sensation of seeing its own reflection in a glass. Warner Field sat down at the left of Miss Rilla. He had been the last comer so that the table now carried its full quota of twelve.

The nine other boarders were of the type to be found in a small town's best boarding house. By reason of age, dignity and priority of residence, Major Slack, an old bachelor real estate agent, sat next to Miss Ann. One gathered from the florid, well-groomed, self-satisfied Major Slack that he had been responsible for the relatively quick decision of the Spanish-American War. Whatever he said carried weight. The merest statement, that salmon was better than trout, or that springtime in the mid-west was more delightful than fall, was weighted with a brick of finality so that when it fell into the conversation there was a dull thud intended to close the argument for all time. It was as though he challenged one to say more. All well-known statements quite readily traceable to their origin, became the Major's own as he uttered them. "Honesty is the best policy" and "Virtue is its own reward" were given with the stamp of authorship.

At the Major's right sat young Martin Spencer, a bookkeeper in the First National Bank. Marty was the self-appointed table wit. He prepared a new story or two for each meal with the regularity with which he washed his hands for it. "Have you heard this one?" or "I read a good one to-day—" was his idea of enlightening dinner conversation.

Then came Miss Sarah Gunn, principal of the Whittier School. Miss Gunn was nothing if not sensible. A facetious person would say she never went off half-cocked. Life to Miss Gunn was divided systematically. She weighed everything carefully: her speech, her actions, her food. She ate so-many proteids and so-many carbohydrates. She spent so-many hours in exercise and so-many in study. She believed that part of life was meant for work and part for fun, the only discrepancy in her philosophy being that she thought the first half was for the work and the last half for the fun. Poor lady . . . not to know that the two should be so intermingled that no one knows where the one leaves off and the other begins.

Next to Miss Gunn sat Helen Blakely, whose life work was an attempt to teach high-school boys and girls to speak English instead of American. To this end she, herself, spoke with the same pure diction to be found in Blackstone's *Commentaries.* She was a nice girl with a quite definite desire to seem still nicer in the eyes of Dr. Pearson, who sat across the table from her, and who, on occasion, thought no more of removing an appendix than his hat.

George and Genevieve Kendall sat side by side, a living illustration that love dies early and easily. Seven years before, George Kendall had married Genevieve with high hopes and the nest-building instinct. For that period of time he had now to show: the same job with the same furnace company, a childless wife with a recognized genius for bridge and mah jongg, and a second-floor back room at the "Bee-House." As for Genevieve Kendall, her brain, so far as it functioned, told her that from what it had heard, it was a horrible experience to have a child, that boarding was easier than keeping house and that George might better be sure of that check every month than to risk starting out for himself with no telling what sort of luck.

Next to the Kendalls was Mary Mae Gates, a vocal teacher who realized fully that she was made of finer, more artistic, less dusty dust, as it were, than other people. She was habitually tired, the inference being that her services in the musical world were so sought after that it kept her in a state of perpetual exhaustion.

At Miss Rilla's right sat Ambrose Jones, a clerk in a dry-goods store. He had a white-livered, parchmentlike look which came from long years of confinement. He said little but had a foolish way of darting his head here and there as though overly interested in everyone's most trivial statement. In all he was as amusing as a bolt of toweling, as entertaining as a box of darning cotton.

The girl who waited on the table answered to the name of Essie Carlson, a neat, washed-out nonentity with pale moist hair in a state of perpetual crimpiness.

These were Warner Field's associates of eight months but they seemed alien, people apart. He was out of tune with them, with Maple City, with life itself. But with a pleasant word of greeting from that outer man who bore himself creditably, he took his napkin and looked about the table as he silently appraised the diners. There they sat, eating, talking, bound up in their own small lives . . . little cars on narrow-gauge tracks, running around in circles, always ending at the place they started . . . themselves. He was half angry, wholly irritated with them and with himself that he should feel this way toward them. They were getting on his nerves. Why was he here? Well, one had to be somewhere.

As he sat at the table on this September Sunday it occurred to him that if he would pull away altogether, get out into the country away from this eternal irritation, perhaps he could accomplish something. It had been that way with him for months . . . a desire to get away from everybody and everything. He was restless . . . seeking . . . seeking . . . the thing he had lost.

All through the dinner hour he held himself to his habitual courtesy and later even made himself stop for a

few moments with the others in the big reception hall where
the old Judge scowled down at the usurping tenants like
some baron of feudal days. Then he slipped out to the
garage and ran his roadster out. A dormant conscience
roused to tap him on the shoulder and remind him that one
of the fellows like Marty Spencer who had no car, or that
old bore, Ambrose Jones, would enjoy a country drive in
the lazy September air, but he let that vague organ go on
tapping unanswered, and pulled out by himself.

He turned east on Main and headed for the country where
he felt the open spaces might help to clarify his vision.
And driving so, he came to the top of the hill where the
Rineland home, the modern show place of the town, sat up
on three terraces like a lady with her skirts pulled up from
the commonness of Main Street. For a brief moment he
was undecided, then suddenly swung up into the sloping
asphalt drive.

The Rineland house had none of the gingerbread fussi-
ness, nor did it have any of the friendly look which the
"Bee-House" held with its tree-filled yard and its ample
porches. It was plain, chaste, and porchless, save for the
small formal entrance. In its discreet, retiring way it said:
"We do not flaunt our family life on a veranda where all
may see. We carry it on behind rose draperies." During
its construction, its Italian Renaissance architecture had not
met with approval in the community. Old Jud Moore,
bringing a load of wood to town, had spat over the wheel
as he rendered his verdict: "Eyetalian? Gosh A'mighty.
. . . Eyetalian things don't belong on the prairie. They
belong where the Dagos live," a weighty remark that had
made the younger Walt Thomas riding with him rock with
glee.

When Warner Field touched the gondola-shaped knocker,
Alice Rineland came to the door. At the sight of Warner,

she flushed a little and a warm flood of pleasure swept her gray-blue eyes. With a friendly if detached greeting to the girl, Warner said: "I wonder if I could see your father for a few minutes."

She took Warner into a long living room, a little over-furnished and overstuffed in mulberry and taupe. "I'll call Papa," she said in a soft, clinging voice. She went into another room but she did not call him. When she came back she sat down in a corner of the big mulberry daven-port. She looked womanly, soft and gentle, quite lovely in rather a pale way. Against the mulberry of the background her face stood out like a purely cut cameo.

Her eyes, that had changed from cold gray to warm blue when Warner entered, swept him now with an enfolding look. "What have you been doing all week?" she asked. In the question there might have been the faint deft touch of reproof.

They spoke of local subjects for a time until Alice, sens-ing that Warner's attention was slipping, went after her father. He came in almost immediately, a small, dapper man, gray haired, efficient-looking, cordial.

The call was not long. After the short interview with Mr. Rineland, Warner rose to go. As he was leaving, it occurred to him that he ought to ask Alice to drive with him. Vaguely he sensed that it was what she was wanting. But he did not ask her. He felt like being alone. He wanted to go over the ground again and think the thing out.

So he drove alone through the Sunday afternoon quiet of the country. The interview had turned out just as he had expected. Mr. Rineland had told him to go ahead and take his week's vacation. He had said that he did not really deserve one, having been there less than a year, but Mr. Rineland had waved that aside. From the decision of taking the coming week off from his bank work, Warner's mind went once more to the same old worry. The Debt! That debt was like the terrible old man of the sea which Sindbad had encountered on one of his journeys. Would he ever be able to shake him off?

There was a slight breeze springing up now so that the leaves on the Lombardy poplars and cottonwoods which lined many of the farmyards were twinkling, little Pierrots, dancing in the sunshine. Coming out of that black mental swamp into which he was so constantly plunging, Warner gave a few moments' thought to the beauty of the panorama before him. He had that same feeling he had experienced on other occasions . . . that the whole countryside was a huge chessboard with many-colored squares. There were the dark green squares of alfalfa ready for the third cutting, pale yellow squares of wheat stubble, light tan squares of maturing corn fields, black squares where the fall plowing had been done and a half dozen shades in the pastures. Between masses of the squares wound brown ribbon roads, symmetrically dividing the country into blocks of six hundred and forty acres. Yes, it was a chessboard and the people were pawns being moved from square to square. He, himself, was a pawn, to be swept, when the game was over and the chessboard closed, into the box of oblivion. Warner Field's stock in himself that summer was quite below par.

At the two-mile corner he came to the bridge across Tinkling Creek. In a hastily formed desire to plunge into the tangled thicket that followed the little stream, he left the car under the cottonwoods at the side of the road and walked down to the creek bed. The sumac was beginning to show a faint touch of pink on the tips of the leaves, preparatory to kindling the fires of October. There was goldenrod everywhere, as though many knights in driving by had dropped their plumes. In the thicket of wild plums a catbird sang like a mocking bird and then, grotesquely, in a very parody of its other song, gave out its raucous clown call. Elderberries spilled the last of their great flat trays of seedy food.

Simultaneously with Warner's arrival an old man with a fishpole in his hand broke through the bushes and came down to the edge of the creek. Warner recognized him as one of the bank's customers. It had been hard for him to get acquainted with the farmers. Their overalls and un-shaven faces gave them a sort of made-in-a-mold look like the muddy little cars in which the majority of them came to town. The man was Jud Moore, a big-boned creature, gray, weather-beaten, one of the old settlers. His skin lay in loose wrinkles above his whitening beard, as though a size too large for the flesh.

Warner spoke to him. Jud Moore's salutation was clipped to " 'Do, sir."

"Fishing?" Warner had that exterior interest in people which he had trained himself to feel.

"No, sir. *'N I ain't goin' to.* Sundays I come down here 'n take my pole out that hollow tree. Start to throw in the line. Somethin' keeps me from it. It's Ma. Thinks it's wicked. Hurts her feelin's if I fish on Sunday. Women's funny, ain't they? Can do most any darn fool thing but hurt Ma."

It amused Warner. His interest was not so forced. The two men sat down under the cottonwoods. That mellowness of the day soothed Warner a little. The lush warmth, the suggestion of fall in the presence of the goldenrod and gentians, the call of wild free things all leagued together to entice him.

"Rather nice here," was his friendly comment.

"Lord, yes. Best place on earth. Know every hump in

the ground 'n every bush. Never could see how any one could work indoors. Wouldn't be no bankers or merchants in the world if they was all like me." He talked in crisp blunt sentences. There was something expressive about the way he clipped them out.

For some time the two sat, commenting on various agricultural subjects. If he was going to stay in a country bank forever, make it his life work, Warner thought, he might as well knuckle down to get the farmers' viewpoint of life. When at last he rose, the sun's rays were sloping through the clump of wild plums. The old man rose, too, unfolding his gaunt form like a camel. "Come on up to the house. Meet Ma," he invited.

Warner was just on the verge of thanking him and refusing when that slight interest which the old man had kindled in an uninteresting time turned the answer. The house was visible through the trees, a plain boxlike structure with a straight porch across the front and a queer bay window above it.

The man's wife was lame. She was tall and stooped, her crutch apparently a little too short for her. Her hair was snow white and neatly parted.

"Ma, . . . Mr. Field. One I told you was workin' in the old First National. Used to live in Omaha. Been back East the last few years afore he come here."

The woman took Warner's hand and said gently: "I know about you. You were very sick just before you came. Rilla Baldwin told me."

For the first time since coming to Maple City Warner had a boyish warmth of feeling toward a human, the peculiar sensation that here was the first person in the community to whom he would like to tell all the trouble of the past year. To his surprise she was asking him to stay to supper. He thanked her and said he thought he had better get back to the "Bee-House." But when he sensed that she was feeling he did not think the meal worth staying to, he stayed.

As soon as "Ma" had gone to start the supper the old man slapped his knee in silent mirth: "Glad you're stayin'. Every Sunday night Ma has cornmeal mush 'n milk. Don't like the darn stuff but Ma does. Won't tell her so. Wouldn't cook it if she knew what a hard time I have gettin' it down. When anybody else is here she gets somethin' else. Glad you're stayin'."

During the simple meal, served in the dining-room end of the kitchen, Jud Moore expressed himself in that blunt fashion on many subjects. But under all the rough exterior Warner could see the devotion he gave to the gentle lame woman. "Pa! Pa!" she would admonish him soothingly when he became too vehement.

It was when she was clearing away the plain heavy dishes, that she suddenly called "Pa!" from the doorway. She was colorless and her hand was at her heart. "Call Doc Minnish," the old man ordered Warner sharply, fear in his voice. He hurried to his wife and assisted her to a big chintz-covered chair near the bay window. In a moment he was dropping out medicine for her with huge shaking hands.

Warner rang for the old doctor, hearing, as he waited, the click, click of the receivers on the party line being removed from their hooks. The telephone is the daily newspaper in many a country home. Dr. Minnish was not in, so Warner took things in his own hands and called young Dr. Pearson from the "Bee-House," who arrived in an amazingly short space of time. Helen Blakely, the high-school English teacher, was with him, trying not to look important. Almost simultaneously a middle-aged woman and a young man arrived in the yard in a little rattling car to see what was the matter and to proffer their aid. Warner had his first glimpse of the way a country community looks out for its own. This is called neighborliness or curiosity, depending entirely on the viewpoint of the observer.

The woman was a mound of quivering fat that seemed to have been slipped out of some human-shaped gelatine mold. But she climbed spryly out of the car and walked up to the porch as lightly as an inflated balloon. Warner had never seen a fat woman walk so springily. "Aunt Biny got a spell?" she asked.

Old Jud Moore addressed the big woman as "Mattie" and presented her as "Mis' Thomas" to Warner, the inference being that Warner was the more important of the two. The young man in his early twenties was her son Walt.

While the others were attending to Aunt Biny, Warner and Helen Blakely walked around the picketed yard. On the north there was a windbreak of huge maple trees. A row of cottonwoods followed a lane south to meet the cotton-woods that lined the main highway. In the yard there were several outbuildings. One of these little structures, a two-roomed dwelling, was located near the orchard on a rise of land behind which flowed Tinkling Creek. "The old folks' first house," Warner guessed. It had been painted white but the various coats had peeled off and hung in gray dingy blisters. Both the front and back doors were closed, but womanlike, Helen Blakely looked in at the window. "See how cozy it is inside," she called to Warner, "and as clean as can be."

"Ready for hired help, I expect," Warner told her.

When Aunt Biny was easy again and Dr. Pearson and Helen Blakely had left, old Doc Minnish, whose call had not been canceled, arrived. He was an old man, grizzled and slouchy. His shoes were mud-caked. His hands had axle-grease on them. He had been known to carry tablets loose in his coat pocket and to turn them out on the table along with a collection of oats and buttons. But he fought Death like Achilles fought Hector and only occasionally was he worsted.

"Look Ma over," Jud Moore told him. "Don't have much faith in these spick and span young fries." With the return of color to his wife's face, Jud Moore's bluntness and bluffness had returned. It was as though he slipped a garment over his emotion.

After Doc Minnish had gone and Aunt Biny, with pillows at her back, was talking comfortably from the big chair, Warner put the question for whose answer he had waited: "You folks wouldn't want to rent me that little house out there for a week, would you? I'm to have a few days' vacation and I've taken a notion that maybe it would be just the place for what I want to do."

The old man's astonishment was genuine. "What in tunkit would you do there?"

"I used to . . ." Warner found himself hesitating to explain to the blunt old farmer, "do some writing. I've rather fallen out of the way of it in the last year. I thought perhaps if I could get completely away from people I might try my hand at it again."

"Do it for a livin'?"

Warner had to smile. "Yes. Pushing an adding machine hasn't exactly been my line. But . . . some things happened so that I've not been writing."

Aunt Biny said weakly from her chair, "I always wished I could write. I have, too . . . lots of things. But they're not like I want them. I feel them all in my heart . . . beautiful things that sing. But when I want to put them down on paper, it seems they're like little wild things . . . they're gone."

"I don't see any argyment agin' this here new tenant, do you, Ma?" Ma saw none either.

"You're scarcely well enough for me to take my meals with you?" Warner asked.

Aunt Biny thought not, but she called Mattie Thomas in from the kitchen with "Mattie, could you feed Mr. Field over at your place for a week?"

Mattie came bouncing in with that astonishing rubber-ball movement. Her small eyes above the inflated cheeks shone at the prospect. She was like a race horse awaiting the signal. "If he thinks he can put up with my plain kind of cookin'."

She was one of the best cooks in the community and no one knew it better than she, but she liked to pose as a servant unworthy of his hire.

So Warner left with "Then I'll see you people again to-morrow."

On his way into town as he passed the Rineland home sitting upon three terraces he could hear the lovely strains of Wagner's "Evening Star" from Alice's piano. No one in Maple City could play like Alice Rineland.

At the "Bee-House" supper was over. The boarders were out on the wide porch when Warner put up his car. He joined them, not from any special desire, but because he did not want to seem too stand-offish.

There was the customary varying and unrelated conversation. Miss Gunn had been improving her mind with a little light review of feudalism from the time of the Carlovingians up to the Crusades. Marty Spencer's heaviest literary research of the afternoon had concerned itself with one Andy Gump.

"Hasn't the day been lovely?" Miss Rilla, with moist eyes, asked the others.

"Anybody but a witless person ought to know it's been too hot," Miss Ann gave forth sourly.

"September is inferior to October," Major Slack laid it

down definitely. It was as though he had made the months and knew whereof he spoke.

Mary Mae Gates was languid as one who has almost sung away her life. "It seems impossible for a Maple City church service to take place without some solo work from *me*. I guess if I should go to Omaha they would *have* to get along without me."

Ambrose Jones, the bore, darted his head foolishly here and there as though afraid he might miss something. Only the two Kendalls were not talking. George did not know just why Genevieve was in one of her frigid moods but, if she chose to be so, he guessed he could manufacture some chemical ice himself.

Warner Field looked on at the little people playing their little parts in the little town and felt critical, aloof, exiled.

CHAPTER III

THE DIARIES

WHEN morning came the renting of the old house seemed foolish to Warner Field. His own room on the second floor of the "Bee-House" was quiet enough, for that matter. There was nothing wrong with the place. It was all with him. One could write anywhere if one had anything to say. He himself had written in busy offices and on an ocean liner. Some of his best work had been scribbled on the elevated. If only he applied himself, he could get down to business.

Mechanically he went about his packing. He threw some things into a bag and sat down to clean the typewriter. It was like an old friend with an alien, unfriendly look on its face. For the first time since his arrival he noticed that things in his room were dusty. Mrs. Carlson, the mother of Essie, the waitress, usually came in to clean for Miss Ann, but she couldn't come any more for a while. One would think that a man like Gus Carlson could support his family without letting his wife go out to work at such a time.

When he had finished cleaning the machine, he packed it into the car with a few clothes, some toilet articles, a book or two and a box of paper. The whole thing had flattened out a little since his first impulse.

Out at the farm he ran his car under an old shed. When he came out Jud Moore in work clothes had come into the yard with Aunt Biny on her crutch not far behind. "Mattie's waitin' for you," was the old man's terse greeting. "She's all ready to set up."

Warner looked at his watch. "Lunch so soon? I wonder, then, when she has dinner."

"Just right plum on the tick o' the clock at *noon*," Jud Moore said crossly. "There ain't no such thing as dinner at night. I bet I could find them very words in the Bible if I set out to hunt: 'Breakfast, dinner and *supper* created He them.'"

"Pa! Pa!" Aunt Biny remonstrated. It did not bother her in the least excepting as she feared its misinterpretation by a stranger. For a half century that rough fretting and fuming and roaring laughter had been as the wind in the maples to her.

Warner ran his car out again and went immediately to the Thomas farm, which was west of the Moores' but on the opposite side of the road. The three sat down together, Mattie and her son Walt and Warner. Walt seemed about twenty-two or three, a big awkward fellow with a good face. Warner liked him at once, even though there was something distant about his quietness. It was not sullenness, certainly not sulkiness. Warner could not know that it was a touch of envy, that the young man was resenting the cut of the boarder's summer flannels and the ease with which he did things.

To Mattie Thomas earth held no sorrow that food could not heal. In consequence the meal was a gourmand's meal: chicken, dumplings, a half dozen vegetables, a salad, two kinds of pie. Warner ate more heartily than he had done for months. There was a flavor about everything that not even so good a place as the "Bee-House" gave.

"Please don't cook so much again," he said with his slow ingratiating smile. So seldom did he smile these days. Mattie was swollen with pride. It was all she needed to urge her on to greater effort. Already she was planning a supper of soda biscuits, creamed chicken, cabbage slaw, angel food cake and maple ice cream.

Warner was as torpid as an alligator when he went back to the little house. The two rooms had evidently been rescrubbed for they still bore a clean moist smell. The bed was made up with a quilt of green stars on a pink calico background. There were two chairs, a table and a clean rag rug on the floor. At one end of the room a cupboard was built in the wall. Warner put his typewriter on the stand, unpacked the things in his bag and walked over to put them in the built-in drawer under the cupboard. But the drawer was locked. He turned the wooden button of the cupboard and by means of the spool which served as a knob opened the pine doors. To his surprise the cupboard was not empty. The three shelves were well filled. An old-fashioned stiff-looking china doll stared at him with painted eyes. There were pine cones, some miniature dishes, a box of shells and many books. Evidently they were the treasures of a little girl. That she had lived many years before was apparent, for the doll, the dishes, the books, everything seemed to look ancient.

He reached to the second shelf for one of the books. On a flyleaf in tipsy, heavily-pressed print it said "Nancy Moore, aged six." There were other books: *Lady of the Lake, Rollo in Switzerland, Elsie Dinsmore,* a tiny Bible . . . old things with their ownership established on each flyleaf as Nancy Moore's, aged twelve or seven or fourteen. The little girl of Old Jud Moore, Warner thought. Dead, he imagined, or if living, at least middle-aged. A grandmother, now, no doubt. These country girls married young. The old folks evidently had kept the keepsakes in the first house for reasons of sentiment. Tragedy and pathos were in the little things even though the girl did not die.

Change! Change was the most heartbreaking thing in the world. In front of the cupboard with its hoard of ancient treasures he dropped into one of those moods of deep depression which met him so frequently. Change! That was why he was here. Change! That was why his father had done what he did. Change! Warner shuddered. It was the most terrifying word in the language.

On the lowest shelf was an old photograph of a young slip of a girl with a sweet, if scared, expression. Her hands were crossed demurely in her lap and there was a wreath of flowers in her hair. On the back was written, "Nancy Moore on her 15th birthday."

Warner put the picture carefully back, closed the door and threw his own articles back into the bag.

He pulled the typewriter a little closer to the open window and sat down. Through the window he could see the bank of Tinkling Creek with its fringe of wild plum and elderberry, cottonwood and sumac. To the north the old apple orchard stood, heavy boughed, with its offerings of Ben Davis and Golden Glow, Jonathans and Winesaps. Warner was almost trembling as he ran the paper in the machine. So much hung on the moment.

For an hour or two he wrote haltingly, in an agony of effort. At the end of that time he read it all over carefully. A great depression seized him. He had been a fool to think the setting of the peaceful farming country could make any difference. It would not come. The whole thing lacked something. To his critical mind it sounded amateurish, insipid. He told himself a callow freshman might have used it in his theme class. He had lost it . . . the knack. For a long time he sat slumped down in his chair. Old Jud Moore brought the cows up through the lane, their great bags bulging. Aunt Biny Moore limped from chicken house to straw stack gathering the eggs. The sun slipped toward the rim of the prairie. The waters of Tinkling Creek ran on under the road bridge. Empty birds' nests swung in the huge maples. Over in the cupboard was Nancy Moore in the gay toggery of her birthday apparel, fresh flowers in her hair, the glow of youth in her face. Change!

He sat crumpled down before his typewriter until Jud Moore came to the door. "Hey . . . you Nathaniel Hawthorne Longfeller, Mattie's called up to see if her cookin' clean killed you off."

Warner jumped up with an embarrassed laugh. "Tell her I'll be right over."

After the evening meal he went back to the Moore place but he did not go to the cabin. He sat down on a grassy hillock at the edge of the orchard. He heard the evening train whistle in, saw it crawling, toylike, across the prairie, a light in each miniature window. A star shot across the night. Where did it go? And why? The great eternal questions. He seemed so small in the gigantic scheme of things . . . so insignificant . . . his life so unnecessary. Back to his troubles he went like a dog worrying a rat. Not by anything in his education, his sophistication or his philosophy could he shake off those great black engulfing clouds. Around in circles went his thoughts, always back to the Debt . . . that clinging, slimy octopus. Was he to live out his life here among these circumscribed, provincial people? There was no one toward whom he felt any special warmth of friendship but the Rinelands whom he had known when he was a small boy and they had visited his father's home in Omaha. Alice . . . ! He wondered vaguely whether he ought to drop in there so much. The thing was getting a little obvious, wasn't it? Or was she merely kind because she sensed his loneliness? He put the question aside in favor of the latter decision. At least with his other faults, he was not weighted with ego.

The mood stayed with him for hours. He was not in deep anguish. Rather was he in a state of lethargy. There is an element of activity in deep groveling anguish. But this worry was old . . . and his mental processes seemed dulled.

He pulled himself up and went into the little house where he lighted an evil-smelling kerosene lamp with a red flannel in the oil. Vaguely he wondered why the red flannel? He opened the door of the little cupboard and, ashamed at what he took to be the weakness of his groping, picked up the little leather Bible and opened it. It opened to the book of Job. He grinned sardonically. Job! Pretty good that was! Job was the duffer with the thousand miseries. His grim humor, that was not humor at all, faded. He looked down at the fine print of the tissuelike page. As though it were a personal message an underlined passage stared back at him:

That which I see not, teach Thou me.

For some time he stood at the cupboard before the keepsakes of the ancient little girl. Then he put the book back and turned the wooden button.

On Tuesday he tried writing again with that same disheartening success. In the afternoon he tramped through the fields and along Tinkling Creek where the dragonflies darted up from the half-dried bed. Always he seemed searching for something lost. Once life had been good and now it was stale. Once he was young but now he felt old.

The little cupboard with its musty odor fascinated him. He let it play on his emotions, the aliveness of the little girl who was dead to youth if not in reality. When he returned from his tramp he opened the pine doors again. The top shelf was packed with cheap little note books. Thinking they were her school work, half curiously he reached up for

one. They had been old account books, evidently, for across
the top of the first page in a masculine hand was written:
"In account with Jonathan Fair . . . 1 keg nails." This
had been crossed out and underneath in the little girl's
handwriting it said: "The apple blossoms are all out to-day.
The orchard looks as though the clouds had fallen and
spattered over the trees and fences. When you're walking
down the rows under the boughs it seems as though you are
walking in an enchanted land where everything is pink and
white. When you shut your eyes you're drowning in per-
fume and when you open them you're drowning in color."

Warner smiled involuntarily. The little girl had the soul
of a poet. The late afternoon sun penetrated the open door
and window and made odd-shaped flickering shadows over
the book. He turned the page. It said: "In account with
Jonathan Fair . . . 10 lbs. sugar. I have tried to decide
which I like best, yellow dandelions, white daisies or lavender crocuses. The yellow dandelions are gay cheerful
people who are full of jokes. The daisies are girls in
white hats standing by the roadside to see the parade go by.
The lavender crocuses are vain satiny old women who like
to dress up just as much as they did when they were girls."

Warner smiled again at the whimsical thought of the
ancient little girl and placed the cheap gray account book
upon its shelf.

On Wednesday he worked at his writing, painfully, laboriously. He tried different types of work. Nothing satisfied
him. At the close of the afternoon when he had finished
the labored task he came back to the cupboard and took
down one of the diaries. No events seemed chronicled.
They were merely fanciful imaginings . . . the child's innermost thoughts. He told himself if there had been personalities, any story of human contact, he would not have
read them. But they were so impersonal . . . and so

ancient. It was as though he reached up and took down from the shelf the memoirs of Napoleon's Josephine or Mary Queen of Scots. And they seemed to bring near to him, in their freshness, the little prairie girl of long ago, to recreate the vision of her, old-fashioned, dainty, elusive.

On Thursday his interest had not waned and he closed the day with the reading of a whole volume of her childish sentiments.

Friday was cloudy and cool with a promise of autumn in the air. All afternoon he kept at his self-appointed task with no return of his old-time enthusiasm. Doggedly he stayed by it with the hope that by such persistent labor he could feel the old zest for it. As he had done on the other days when he stopped working, he took down one of the diaries and ran through the pages with their girlish freshness of vision. In this volume the handwriting was firmer, more mature. He turned back to the first page. It said, "Nancy Moore, aged seventeen." Instinct and training told him that to read the childish thoughts of a little girl was one thing . . . to deliberately walk uninvited into the mind of a young woman of that age was another.

Almost before he was aware, he read: "Love comes into my thoughts now when the leaves dance on the cottonwoods and when the moon shines down through the maples and when the robins sing after the rain. Lately I know what the man I shall love is going to look like. I mean I almost do but not quite. I can see his shoulders and the back of his head and how tall he is, but, try as hard as I can to see it, his face stays dim and blurred. But of one thing I am sure . . . he is *somewhere* and when I see him I shall know him."

Warner Field laughed. "Dear little unsophisticated Nancy Moore," he said to himself. "I hope that long ago you knew him when you saw him."

Still smiling, he turned the page. It looked broken, blurred, erased, in sharp contrast to the neatness of the other pages. "In account with Jonathan Fair . . . 10 lbs. codfish. I am eighteen to-day. Something has happened . . . something terrible. My mind is crowded with a thousand things to write. But I shall never write in you again. Good-by, little diaries. Good-by, thrushes and lilacs and orchard and Tinkling Creek. Good-by, my prairie. And most of all, good-by, Nancy Moore. Oh, Nancy Moore, I loved you. Good-by."

Warner hastily turned the page. But only the account of Jonathan Fair in regard to six yards of calico met him. For the rest of the pages the blankness of gray-white paper stared back at him. For the rest of the merry-hearted little Nancy Moore's life . . . nothing. She had gone.

He went back and read over the closing pages. What was it? Had they sent her away? Had she died? Had she been married to some one against her will? What had happened to her? For heaven's sake, what ever became of her? One thing was certain; up to the day of her last writing, when some crashing thing had happened, she had been sweet and lovely and happy.

All the rest of the day the thing hung over him. It obsessed him. It was like the bad ending of a play, the distressing finish of a book. But it was more than those. He could have thrown those off but this held him. With mind occupied with the tragedy . . . if tragedy it really was . . . he walked out through the orchard . . . Nancy Moore's orchard, long grown hoary with many years of blossoming and bearing, and down by Tinkling Creek . . . Nancy Moore's creek in which the water was still running on to the sea.

At the supper table he put it half haltingly to Walt and Mattie. "Did the old folks . . . the Moores . . . ever have any children?" It was as though he did not want to hear.

"One girl," Mattie, who was usually so voluble, said tersely. "She died when she was two. They raised their niece. Won't you have some more potatoes, Mr. Field?"

Walt reddened to the ears, a dull brick color.

Their attitude intrigued his interest the more. What mystery was this? Had some dramatic thing happened on the edge of this prosaic mid-west town? Did some tragedy lie buried among the cornfields and apple trees? He would ask Miss Rilla Baldwin when he went back to town, or Mr. Rineland.

After supper, drawn back to it like a needle to a magnet, he got out that last diary and read it again. She was acting, pretending something that was not so. No, that broken, blurred page was life itself, not imagery. Well, it was all ages ago, years before he was born. But the thing haunted him, the personality of the little girl who had been happy and was happy no more. He experienced the sense of a personal loss. He felt deprived of another thing, disappointed again. He read over what he had written that day. When he had finished he tore it up. It was rottenly constructed and it was not true.

He sat out on the knoll near the orchard again and watched the evening train creep across the prairie. How people rushed futilely about like ants with their tiny crumbs! There were people on that train whose entire lives were to be changed by journeying on the little crawling lighted toy. And Warner Field's life was to be changed by the little crawling toy. For the train crossing the prairie in the early dusk was the one which brought the girl home to the square farmhouse behind the cottonwoods.

CHAPTER IV

THE LOCKED DRAWER

O N Saturday morning the girl in the south bedroom of
the old farmhouse woke with a start, not knowing
for a moment where she was. Then she remembered.
She was at home again. Any place where childhood has
been spent is home. Almost immediately she heard the
thump, thump of Aunt Biny's crutch on the bare kitchen
floor. It had been the first sound to greet her every morning when she was a little girl. Lying there in her bed she
lived over her home-coming and the joy that the old people
had shown. And to think that she had questioned their
attitude! She was glad she had come back. For two months
she would do all she could for their happiness, all she could
to make amends. For two months she would slip back into
her old environment and indulge in the half-lark of being
her old self.

She rose and went to the odd-shaped window in the south
end of her bedroom. Once in a wild burst of interest in
the interior of the house Uncle Jud had built on an addition
to the room which jutted out over the lower porch roof.
It was too small for a sun room and too large for a bay
window, but a queer arrangement of three large windows,
one of which looked to the east, one to the south and the
other to the west.

The girl looked out of it now to catch her first glimpse
of the old place by daylight. To the west was the long row
of cottonwoods that followed the lane to the main road.

36

To the south the grassy path led down to the gate with stiff cottonwoods standing like trained butlers on either side and the dusty road beyond. To the east lay the open country and the long low rolling hills, dotted now with pink pools of light from the first rays of the sun. In the northwest part of the yard were the outbuildings and a straw stack, with the orchard farther on and Tinkling Creek beyond. On the other side of the straw stack was the old cabin with its blistered paint. And Warner Field had been living out there for a week. It seemed incredible! She had known he was in Nebraska, but supposed it was Omaha. She wondered if he remembered seeing her. Most probably he did not. She would not enlighten him, of that she was sure. She jumped up and began dressing. Suddenly she threw back her head and laughed . . . high bubbling laughter. She went to the closet and got out an old blue calico dress and sun hat and put them on. She looked in the glass, tilting it up so that she could get the full length view of herself. Satisfied with her appearance, she slipped downstairs and went quietly out of the front door, crossing the lane road to the straw stack. Digging her bare feet into the sloping side of the stack she climbed to the top where she settled herself and peered down the steeper side. Torn between her desire to try the long descent and a cautious fear of the consequences, she hesitated for a moment. Then her love of excitement winning over any wariness she may have felt, she threw out both arms, stiffened herself and moved downward. According to laws immutable, the tendency of all falling bodies is to accelerate in speed. That nature plays no favorites was apparent to the girl as she shot down.

And so it happened that Warner Field, leaving the cabin at his usual time to go to Mattie's for breakfast, rounded the straw stack at the side of the lane road in time to see a young girl in a great whirlwind of swirling straw, calico dress, dust, bare legs and sun hat, roll down the stack almost to his feet.

He was so astonished that he only stood still and stared until the dust from the *mêlée* had died away. The girl's sun hat had fallen back and a shock of warm brown hair hung over her eyes. She sat up with a mischievous, breathless chuckle, tossed her hair out of her eyes and saw Warner. Apparently she felt a pain in her foot, for with a quick movement she pulled the hat over her face and, hand on her ankle, dropped back in a little huddled heap.

Warner stirred himself, stepped over to her, and slipping his arms around her, raised her up.

"Are you hurt?" If his question was inane it was anxious.

She opened her eyes at that and looked up at him. They were lovely eyes, big and brown and appealing.

"No, sir. I warn't hurt none." She spoke nasally.

It made him wince. She was so lovely that the miserable jargon she used seemed like the storybook toads from her mouth. In his arms she seemed dainty, too, in spite of the atrocious ill-shaped dress.

"Let me take you in to Mrs. Moore."

But the girl seemed alarmed at that. "Oh, no sir," she begged him, almost piteously he thought. "I was just playin' in here for a while. I never git no time to play and I snuck away for a bit. I'm all right now." She stood up, dropping her eyes and pulling the short calico skirt over her knees. Now that she was standing, he saw how slight she was. There was something boyish about the slim straight figure. A quick regret at her lack of education went through him. However did it happen? Girls as old as she . . . she must have been sixteen . . . didn't talk that way here in the mid-west. There were places where they did, mining communities, or out-of-the-way mountain towns, but here in this rich farming state everybody went to school.

"Do you live around here?"

"Down yander," she pointed vaguely across, Tinkling Creek. "Well, I gotta be a-goin'. My ankle's all right. Thanky, mister." She shot him a glance from her brown eyes, turned and went humming along through the orchard and down toward the creek bed. As she passed from his sight over the high bank of the stream she threw back her head and laughed . . . that gay bubbling laughter. "I guess you *don't* remember me, Mr. Field."

Warner thought of her all the way over to Mattie's. She looked so attractive that the terrible crudeness of her backwoodsy condition stood out in even greater prominence than if she had been physically different. He found himself wondering if he couldn't do something about instructing her.

At dinner he asked casually: "Who is a girl, sixteen perhaps, even seventeen, it was hard to tell, who lives down past Moore's on the other side of Tinkling Creek?" He decided not to speak of the straw stack part of the episode. He knew the description he gave of her was too vague but he felt a reticence in describing her further. And when he stopped to think about it how would he go about to describe the vague charm she seemed to possess? He had a feeling that if he made the attempt it would sound both foolish and far-fetched.

Mattie thought it must be Lena Denning. "Big and red-cheeked?" she wanted to know, "with light hair?"

"No, the girl's hair was brown," he was quite sure, "a warm brown, and she was small and slight."

"Jessie Seeger, Ma!" Walt guessed.

Mattie became voluble. "No, Jessie is little but nobody

but a color-blind person would call her geranium-colored hair brown."

Warner was sorry that he had started Mattie off. He turned the subject as quickly as he could. After all it didn't make much difference. But that awful language from a girl who looked like that! Advantages were not very evenly distributed in this world.

All day he worked hard over his writing . . . an earnest last attempt to construct something which seemed pleasing and sincere. By evening he admitted failure. Disheartened and restless he ran his car out in the hope of driving off some of his low spirits. He had scarcely turned into the main road until a tire went down. Caring as little about taking the trip as he did he merely ran the car with its flat tire back under the shed and returned to the cabin. To his surprise there was a light in it. The front door, he could plainly see, stood open. He walked quietly up to it and looked in. At the end of the room in front of the built-in cupboard stood the girl of the straw stack. She was wrapped in an old brown shawl, its dingy folds enveloping her head and slight body and the frayed wide fringe sweeping the floor. As he watched she leaned against the cupboard, a motionless, drooping figure, apparently overcome by some emotion.

The pitiful little figure made a silent appeal to Warner so that he opened the screen door and stepped in. But at the first creaking of the hinges the girl snatched the shawl from her shoulders and thrust it into the unlocked drawer. As Warner took his first step into the room she was banging the drawer shut, locking it, and turning hastily to him.

There was no mistake . . . it was the girl of the straw stack. But from the top of her warm brown hair to the toe of her daintily shod foot she was beautifully groomed. And she was erect, gay, smiling, in colorful contrast to the drooping little figure in the shawl he had just seen . . . a butterfly slipping out from a brown cocoon.

"Heavens! How you frightened me!" she said frankly. "I thought you had gone to town."

Warner stood stiff and unbending. The man does not live who enjoys being made a fool of. But evidently the unyielding attitude of the tenant did not particularly affect the interloper for she said immediately, "Forgive me for this morning." She threw him a frank, sparkling smile over white teeth and then broke into a laugh that was mischievous and merry. "It was pretty raw of me, but the way I was conducting myself . . . when I looked up and saw you, I just had to act the part. Under the circumstances I couldn't very easily say, 'How do you do? Mount Morris is my school. What's yours?' now, could I?"

Warner had to unbend at that. She was so frank and apparently so fun-loving that he could not carry the grudge, and he found himself swept by a sudden relief that she was not the uncouth gamin of her pretense.

"You've forgiven me, haven't you?" She put out her hand. "I'm Nancy Moore."

Nancy Moore!

As though a little information concerning her presence might not be out of order she added, "Uncle Jud and Aunt Biny left my things out here and when I thought you had gone away, I sneaked . . . I mean 'snuck' . . ." she grinned mischievously, "out to get some of them."

He was about to say, "And so *you're* Nancy Moore," when he realized that only through his spying in the cupboard did he have any knowledge of such a person. In a great sweep of contemptuous disgust for himself he was realizing that he had just read all her diaries . . . her innermost thoughts . . . and she must never know he had done so.

But she was explaining. "I've been away for four years. The last day I was home I started to slide down a straw stack for fun. But . . . something happened and I never did it. Now you see me coming back to take up my life for a few weeks where I left off. Well, I just naturally had to finish sliding down the straw stack, didn't I?" she asked naïvely, so that they both laughed.

Immediately she turned back to the cupboard and opened the door. "Do you want to be in on the opening of the tomb?" She had a gay little air of friendliness. "Mummies, centuries old . . . alabaster boxes . . . papyrus scrolls . . ." One by one she took the things down and looked them over: the doll, the dishes, some of the books. She handled them tenderly, making no apology for her silence. Against the light of the old kerosene lamp her profile, with its half-saucy look, was exquisite. Apparently she accepted Warner as part of the cabin's stage property. And Warner, who was doing nothing visible to the naked eye, was busy ordering his mind to jump through hoops. All because Nancy Moore was neither dead nor ancient but alive and twenty-two. Who then was the old picture? She would probably show it to him and explain. But when she picked it up she slipped it into the drawer and locked it.

Warner witheringly cursed his stars when the girl reached for one of the diaries. She read a few snatches here and there. Several times she laughed aloud and once he imagined she was winking back the tears. In a moment she turned to him again. "You're writing?"

He frowned at that. "Trying to," he answered shortly.

"It's odd to find some one here writing. Years ago when it was my playhouse I used to sit here and write. Wonderful stuff . . ." she shrugged her shoulder, "almost as good as the *Journal of Marie Bashkirtseff*. And you're from the East? How did you ever happen to come here?" Now

that she was certain that he did not remember her, she
would play the part too.

"East for many years . . . Omaha was my boyhood
home. I have known O. J. Rineland, president of the bank,
since I was a youngster."

"Alice's father? And what has become of Alice? Did
she live to grow up? She was too perfect . . . correct in
looks, speech, clothes, manners, actions."

In a voice that was an exact imitation of Alice's breathless, soft one, she went into a dramatic exaggeration:

> " 'And the stately lily stands
> Fair in the silvery light
> Like a saintly vestal, pale in prayer,
> Her pure breath sanctifies the air
> And her fragrance fills the night.' "

Warner was nothing if not loyal. So he said a little
stiffly, "Alice Rineland is a very fine girl and rather a good
friend of mine."

She laughed again, gayly, tolerantly. "Then she *has*
learned what friendship is? I'm glad of that. Me-aou . . .
me-aou! Catty . . . am I not? But then *I've* never had
any wings. Alice and I are made of different kinds of dust.
She's star-dust and I'm . . . straw-dust," she added mischievously. And they both laughed. "Could you, for instance, see Alice out of sheer exuberance of spirits putting
on that little stunt of mine this morning?"

"Good Lord, no," he said so quickly that once more they
both laughed. Which was not a bad thing for Warner
Field, who, an hour before, had no intention of ever laughing again.

The girl was leaving. It brought Warner to say, "If this
is your own particular cabin . . . I'm intruding. I was

leaving to-morrow afternoon but I could go at any time . . . to-night even.   My car is parked down by the corn-crib. And my possessions you see could be packed in a few minutes. . . ."

"Oh, no."   She seemed unconcerned whether he went or stayed.   "I'll take a few of the things over to the house with me.   I want to read some of these."   She reached up for a bunch of the books in account with Jonathan Fair. Warner winced and kicked himself for a cad.   "And Rosalind . . . poor youngster," she picked up the stiff china doll, "I'll take her, too.   What if you had done nothing for four years but sit and stare at a yellow pine door?"

"I can sympathize with her entirely.   For a year at least I've done nothing but sit and stare at a yellow pine door."

He watched the girl cross the lane road and the house yard until she disappeared behind the kitchen door.   Through it all he experienced a feeling that he had seen her somewhere before.   He could not throw off the idea that this was not the first time he had met her.   Perhaps after all the solution was no flesh and blood girl but a character in a book.   For she might have been Babbie who had come dancing through Caddam Wood and who was both gypsy and lady of high degree, mischievous, willful and tender.   But what was the thing that had happened to send her away? Something told him that he would not ask the Rinelands about her now nor even Miss Rilla.

For a long time Warner Field sat on the edge of the orchard and looked across Tinkling Creek to the rolling prairie land overhung by night and its thousand eyes.   Over the sleeping community the spirit of the prairie brooded, dim and deep and mysterious.   There were all the multitudinous sounds of the country about him, a tree toad, the low mooing of one of Jud Moore's cows, the whispered stir of birds in the maples.   In all this prosaic environment of the community into which he had been thrust by a turn of the wheel, was it possible that drama went on ceaselessly like the undulating motion of the seas of yellow wheat?

He looked at the white figures on his watch. It was nine-fifty. At that moment, over in Maple City, Alice Rineland came out on the balcony of the Italian Renaissance house built with Nebraska corn-fed-hog money and looked wistfully out toward the Jud Moore farm. Down on Main and Tenth Miss Ann and Miss Rilla sat on the east porch of the "Bee-House." Miss Rilla talked of the beauty of the night and Miss Ann scolded about the price of food. Twins! But as far apart as Mary and Martha, as far apart as the stars and pork chops. Inside the "Bee-House," Miss Gunn, a green shade over her eyes, read a treatise on mental culture and Marty Spencer read a joke book. The Kendalls blew hot and cold between denunciations and forgiveness. Ambrose Jones, the bore, sorted his neckties and brushed his neat, thinly worn suit. Mary Mae Gates sat at the old piano which the Judge had shipped out from Chicago in pioneer days, and sang "O Sole Mio," the vision of an enthralled opera audience before her. Helen Blakely did up her hair in sleep-destroying curlers . . . little pebbles with which to kill her Goliath in the form of Dr. Pearson. Major Slack dreamed over a box of pictures taken at Havana and San Juan. Essie Carlson, the waitress, breathless and anxious, hurried along home under the lacy elms. As she reached the porch of the little Carlson home by the creamery, Dr. Pearson, perspiring and tired, in a white operating gown, came out. "It's all right now, Essie. Another little brother."

A quarter of a mile away Mattie Thomas sat on the porch, trying to get a cool breath by whacking a stiff palm-leaf fan against her mountainous bosom. Walt came in from turning his heavy clumsy team into the pasture for the night. He walked hurriedly up to the porch where his mother was sitting and said breathlessly, a little thickly, "Ma, Nancy's come home."

In the box-shaped farmhouse near by, old Jud Moore finished reading his Omaha daily and threw it down on the floor beside his chair. Then he stood up, stretched his huge arms and said, "Well, I've always said a bed's a good invention," as he had done every night for years. Aunt Biny picked up the paper, folded it neatly and put it in the paper rack, as she had done every night for years. Nancy Moore laughed at them both, a gay little rippling laugh. It seemed that she had not been away at all . . . that things were just as they had been.

It was a cross-section of life. You may cut through the circumference of any community, anywhere, at any time of day or night, and find all the intergrown grainings of drama. It was as though, unseeing, Warner Field sensed all these details, could look into the homes. For a few moments he felt close to the people, sensitive to their desires and ambitions, sympathetic with their troubles and pleasures, a deep kinship with the community. The sensation almost lighted the blackened fagots of his talent. By the glow of its small flame, he seemed for a brief, breath-catching moment to be regaining the thing he had lost. Then like the tantalizing flickering of a match it vanished, and the old sense of dull disappointment and wretched failure enveloped him.

As he rose to go in he thought of the girl who had come home. Again that page, broken, blurred, erased, haunted him. "My mind is crowded with a thousand things to write but I shall never write in you again." What had happened to her? Why had she gone away? Why had she come back? And why did she want no one to see an old brown shawl?

CHAPTER V

SUNDAY

IT sprinkled at intervals all Saturday night.

On Sunday morning Walt Thomas was up and out early, mechanically doing his chores in the mist. He had not slept well. It was as though an old wound had been opened with Nancy Moore's unexpected arrival. He had been getting along fairly well the last year. For three years before that he had carried a dull ache around with him always. And now, just as he had been getting over it, she had come back. For a moment he hid his drawn face against the smooth coat of his best brood mare. Then his mother called him to breakfast and he straightened himself and went in.

Mattie, moving her enormous weight easily about the range, was taking up the breakfast. She had pancakes, sausage, baked eggs, fried potatoes, biscuits and coffee. She was hoping it was plenty for that nice Mr. Field.

Mattie Thomas had once had a husband. Where he was now she did not know and Mattie's greatest fear was that some day he would suddenly decide that he had misused her by departing unceremoniously to parts unknown and return to make reparations. As reparations, whether they be foreign or domestic, involve largely the elements of energy and activity, Mattie knew that they would never be carried out. For Hank Thomas had been one of those cheerful people to whom success lies always just over the brow of the hill. His pursuit of her had consisted of little short breathless runs which always ended in flat failure. One

47

of these brief journeys had consisted in peddling extracts and veterinary supplies and it might have ended in a vast fortune if the peddler, in a moment of daydreaming, had not sold horse medicine to a nearsighted country soul, who very nearly flavored her cake with it, and given a pint bottle of vanilla to a sick mule. The mule did not seem to care, but the fussy country woman did and, by a quick and judicious use of the telephone, destroyed his business. Once he had canvassed for a book. It was a bulky and gilt-edged volume on etiquette but when delivered was found to contain such out-of-date advice that if followed would have landed the perpetrator in a large brick building with bars at the windows. These books were now used largely in the Maple City neighborhood for doorstops or for the company's baby to perch upon while eating.

Hank Thomas's harness had been held together with cords, spikes, horse-blanket pins, ropes and chains. Pepper grass had killed his clover. Indigestion had killed his cow. Cholera had killed his hogs. The sight of work had killed his ambition. Walt's earliest and last recollection of his father was sitting on the parental lap while Hank sang a cheerful song both unenthusiastic and original:

> "Papa's got the shingles,
> And papa's got the na-ails,
> But papa hasn't pu-ut
> The shingles on the roof."

Mattie with grim endeavor had brought Walt up to work. If for one moment she detected a sign of loitering in him, she had gone after him rigorously. As a result Walt at twenty-three was industrious and hard-working. No one in the neighborhood could beat him in getting up early and into the field. He was all mother. His father was non-existent. He had just ceased to be.

Mr. Field had not come to breakfast. So the two sat down to eat.

"Anything more you want, Walt?"

"No, Ma, I got plenty."

When Warner Field woke that morning he heard the rain on the roof. His first thought was of the girl who had come home . . . Nancy Moore, who was not an ancient girl but a most modern one. His second thought was that he didn't care enough about one of Mattie's huge breakfasts to go through the rain for it. He dressed and sat down by the window that looked toward Tinkling Creek. The rain was not a hard one, rather a fine slow drizzle. The maples and elms drooped clammily but the cottonwoods shook off the drops from their gossamer-coated leaves. He had just started to read one of the books he had brought with him when there was a knock. He swung the door back to find the girl herself standing there. She had on an old battered hat and baggy, weather-stained coat of her uncle's and, dripping with rain, was apparently indifferent to her grotesque appearance.

With that characteristic merry laugh she held out a big basket. "I've brought you your breakfast. What big ears you have, grandmother."

"The better to hear you, my dear," Warner answered nimbly enough and they both laughed at their home-grown wit. Strange how she had the faculty of making him forget his troubles.

"Come in out of the rain," he scolded. "Good heavens, why did you do this for me?"

"Oh, don't give me the credit." She slipped in and shook off the water like the cottonwoods. "It was Aunt Biny. She had visions of finding your skeleton here on the floor by noon." She began taking out the dishes; baked apple, oatmeal, cream, toast and a pot of coffee. When she had finished she waved her hand invitingly: "Draw up. 'Better is a dry morsel and quietness therein than an house full of sacrifices and strife.' Aunt Biny made me learn that once up in my room after I had lost my temper and said a lot of saucy things to Uncle Jud."

"Yesterday morning," Warner said irrelevantly, "I was wondering if I couldn't find some way to teach you."

She laughed gayly and then grew suddenly sober. "Oh, there are things you could teach me, no doubt." In a few moments she had left as breezily as she had arrived. Warner had the feeling that a fresh moist wind had blown through the little cabin.

At noon he ate his last meal with Mattie and Walt. The boy was sober, noncommunicative, his somber eyes on his food. When Warner left, it was with a final word of praise for Mattie's cooking and a promise to come and see them again.

In the late afternoon he packed his things and went up to the farmhouse. Uncle Jud and Aunt Biny were there alone. The old man was complaining about the rain.

"There ain't been enough of it. Everything was dry and needed it bad. Ain't done nothin' but drizzle a little like it didn't know how. Ground won't be fit for winter wheat, you'll just see."

"Pa! Pa!" Aunt Biny chided him. "It all turns out all right. 'Twas a nice little rain and we'll get more."

"I'll believe it when I see it comin' down," he fussed.

Warner asked for Miss Moore, but she had gone to Walt's and Mattie's.

As he drove out of the lane and turned toward Maple City the roads were already nearly dry. A little sun and a little wind on a Nebraska road and it forgets it has ever been wet. When he came to the long row of Lombardy poplars at the edge of Walt's land he was still undetermined whether or not to drive in and see the girl. He decided it seemed a child's trick to follow her up to the neighbors. He would come out again in a few days. His foot, hitting the typewriter, reminded him that he had accomplished nothing. It brought back his dispirited mood. You cannot write because you have plenty of leisure or an appropriate place. Of that he was convinced for all time. His experience was like that of the man in Van Dyke's "Lost Word." He seemed able to do everything passably but the thing he wanted to do . . . get back again to his writing. He had lost the knack. As he passed the Rinelands' he could hear the exquisite notes of Godard's "Berçeuse" from Alice's piano.

At the "Bee-House" the usual monotony pervaded the lunch hour. Every one was in his place excepting the Kendalls and Dr. Pearson. The conversation was miscellaneous and disconnected. It had as little pattern as a hit-and-miss rag carpet, with each one harping on his own little complaint. Mary Mae Gates held the floor for a time. "I have to get in a practice with the choir before the service. I have to sing alone, too." She was hurried and drooping with fatigue. "At this late hour, even, I'm undecided whether to use an 'Ave Maria' or something from 'Stabat Mater.' So many people seem to like me in *both*."

The Kendalls, moving with Maple City's daring little group of Ishmaelites, had gone to a mah jongg lunch. They had to go in Oriental costume and George and Genevieve had had some words about it. "I hate the darn stuff and I feel like a fool in that heathen petticoat," he had said. What he had wanted to do was to take a walk out in the country after the rain. But Genevieve had set her foot, already encased in its red padded slipper, down on *that* crazy idea and they had gone to the lunch.

"Doctor is operating," Helen Blakely announced, unable to keep an inflection of pride out of her voice. She always pronounced the title "Doctor" as though it belonged exclusively to one man. "On the smallest Bornheimer boy for a lung drainage after pneumonia."

Miss Rilla's eyes filled with ready tears. "Poor Mrs. Bornheimer! She lost her husband so recently too."

"She ought to have known better than to let a child go out so soon after measles," was Miss Ann's acrid comment. "She's one of those people without a lick of sense."

Miss Gunn had been reading about the epoch of Chartism in Great Britain. "I couldn't remember the date of the insurrection of the common people against the Toll Roads," she explained apologetically. "For one thing I've been upset. My second-grade teacher has gone home ill and Dr. Minnish says she won't be able to come back. We'll have to have green normal-training students from high school for a few days until we can get some one permanently. It seems that life is just one thing after another."

Marty Spencer said he had seen a good one in the paper that afternoon. "A man asked a darky, 'Doesn't that mule ever kick you?' And the darky said, 'No, sah, he ain't yet but he frequently kicks de place where ah recently was.' Pretty good . . . what?"

Major Slack dropped a few weighty bricks of convictions into the conversational pool where they settled heavily and undisputably to the bottom.

Ambrose Jones darted his head foolishly here and there to catch what every one was saying. Warner answered a few questions. Yes, he had had a pleasant vacation. No, he hadn't found it too warm. He spoke pleasantly, perfunctorily, his mind preoccupied. *Good-by thrushes and lilacs and orchard and Tinkling Creek. Good-by my prairie! And most of all good-by Nancy Moore! Oh, Nancy Moore, I loved you! Good-by.*

CHAPTER VI

THE OLD GENERATION AND THE NEW

ON Monday morning out at the old square farmhouse Nancy Moore was dusting the sitting room. She ran the cloth tenderly over a brown plaster cast of Napoleon Bonaparte. "Bony," she addressed him confidentially, "I see you still have a chip off your nose and a crack behind your left ear from the time I threw you on the floor in a tantrum. I take this occasion to apologize. Inasmuch as I've had a chip taken out of my nose and a crack administered behind my ear, figuratively speaking, we'll consider all old scores settled."

As she stooped to dust the Hank Thomas book on etiquette that acted as doorstop, she told herself that not a thing in the house had been changed in the four years. Nothing was different but the dates on the First National Bank calendar and the Omaha newspapers. She rose and took an inventory of the old room.

The stout ingrain carpet with its familiar pattern was stretched taut over the floor. Nancy knew just what was underneath it . . . a layer of newspapers, a load of fresh oat straw, another layer of papers and then the carpet. She could see the old folks as they had put it down, Uncle Jud jawing and fussing and scolding as he stretched, and Aunt Biny, patient, mild, reproving him with her "Pa! Pa!" Uncle Jud had made and painted the bookcase. It had a red plush curtain run on a brass rod. The table with its fringed red and green cover held the newspapers and the Bible, the two pairs of glasses and the lamp. There was a tin thimble over the hole into which the pipe of the huge coal burner would be put in a few weeks. In one corner was the old piano and in another the lumpy, hollowed-out couch with the green denim cover on which Aunt Biny lay for many short periods in the day, her crutch by her side. There was Napoleon of the chipped nose and a bunch of silk sweet peas, long faded, colorless in a blue vase. There was a framed picture of the farm buildings themselves and an enlarged one of the little two-year-old daughter that had died, and whose place Nancy had taken. Three large portraits of past presidents looked tolerantly down from their vantage points almost to the ceiling. Lincoln, McKinley. Roosevelt, the ten commandments, Aunt Biny, Nebraska, and the Republican party . . . these were the pillars on which Uncle Jud's life was built . . . the things that were flawless, unchangeable and inviolate.

The room looked old and homely, but it had the look of a faithful friend, or a mother who welcomes her child to an ample lap. Nancy curled up in the big brown cretonne-covered chair. It was a homely cretonne with stiff bunches of cherries at stated intervals and with one of Aunt Biny's neat patches on it. But once Nancy had dreamed dreams in it and it seemed friendly. Some of those dreams had materialized. One of them she realized clearly was never to come true. She smiled ruefully. Oh, well, one's outlook on life changed. It made her think of the diaries upstairs. She wondered if she would enjoy putting down all her reactions to life now as she had done then. No . . . she would never write in them again.

And then Aunt Biny, rolling down her sleeves, came into the room. She had just finished her churning, eight pounds of butter for the Rinelands and the Baldwin girls' boarding house. She sat down now, near the bay window, her crutch by her side.

"Nancy, I've been alone with you so little, with Pa always around all day Saturday and yesterday. I've been wanting to talk to you alone. You're real sure you love this Mr. Farnsworth you're going to marry?"

For the flash of an eye Nancy caught her lip in her teeth and turned her head. Then she was poised and gay.

"Why, of course I do, Aunt Biny. At least I *will*. I'm just built that way. I'm just naturally crazy about everything that belongs to me . . . shoes, parasols, dogs, flowers, beads, husbands. . . ."

"That's flippant, Nancy."

"Flippant but true."

"Real love doesn't have a flippant attitude."

"Real love, Aunt Biny, belongs to another generation. It went out with rubber-tired buggies and castors for center pieces."

Aunt Biny flushed. "It better come back in then. It takes a lot of it to keep things going."

"It takes solid substantial silver sixpences to keep things going, dear one! Love is too fragile a star to hitch your little wagon to."

"It isn't fragile, Nancy. It's strong . . . the strongest thing on earth. It carries you through, somehow, clear to the end."

Nancy shrugged her shoulder. "You can't buy gasoline with it. Faith, hope and a bank account, and the greatest of these is a bank account."

"Don't say things you don't mean."

"But I mean them, Aunt Biny, every single word. I've been around. I'm not provincial any more. And it simply isn't done. People don't look any more for that high ecstatic love as you think of it. I may have dreamed dreams like that myself a few years ago. But I'm more practical now. It's nice to be here with you, Aunt Biny, for a little while. I'm foolish over the farm and getting back for a time. But I know little Nancy too well now to make myself believe I could give up the things I've been used to. They have become a vital part of my happiness and I'm wise enough to realize it."

"Love hasn't much to do with *things*."

"Which proves how weak-minded love is."

Two spots stood out on Aunt Biny's pale cheeks like the pinkest of her petunias. "Wait, Nancy, just wait until it comes. 'There be three things which are too wonderful for me, Yea four, which I know not. The way of an eagle in the air, the way of a serpent on a rock, the way of a ship in the midst of the sea, and the way of a man with a maid.'"

"Old stuff, Aunt Biny. Aviators have found out the way of the eagle. The serpents on the rocks turned out to be bathing beauties. Ships are as tractable as lambs and the maids are all wise to the ways of the men."

"That's sacrilegious, Nancy."

"Sacrilegious but *so*. It's the times, Aunt Biny. It's neither your fault nor mine that we're at such opposite points of thought. It's the times that have changed."

"Human nature hasn't changed."

"I think you're mistaken. You've been sheltered and hemmed in with your old-fashioned notions and they've grown to be your little household gods. You've worked terribly hard all your life to get the lower eighty paid for and now you're comfortably fixed. If I choose to begin at the other end with the money. . . ."

Aunt Biny looked down the petunia-bordered path. Her eyes misted a little.

"Yes, I've worked hard. When your Uncle Jud and I came we had a team and one hundred and eighty dollars. It took one hundred and sixty dollars to buy the upper eighty. A team, and some household goods, eighty acres of raw land . . . twenty dollars . . . the baby . . . Jud and I . . . and our love. . . ."

"I appreciate all that, Aunt Biny. I'm not hard-hearted, just level-headed. I think your coming here into the new country with the man you loved was wonderful. I think you were brave and courageous and I grant that you loved Uncle Jud dearly. But it would be perfectly witless for me to follow a poor man in the same way. I belong to the new generation and I'd die for the things I've been used to the last few years."

"*I* left nice things back in Indiana, too. Maybe you wouldn't call them so now. But in comparison with what I came to, they were very fine. But I went with the man I loved, just *for love*."

"It listens well, Aunt Biny. It sounds perfectly enticing. If I read it in a book I'd lap it up. If I saw it on the stage I'd be miserable until the play ended right. If it was on the screen my nose would be red when I came out into the light of day. But take note of this . . . the new generation comes out of the theater or lays down the book, all fired with romance . . . and trots right off and turns down romance for realism."

"I can't admit it, Nancy. I'm old and I'm a country woman. But real love hasn't lost its charm, I'm sure. When I look back and think of all of us young couples fifty years ago, coming across the new country in wagons, full of hope for new homes . . . and love the very warmth of those homes . . . I can't think the light of it died out."

"Maybe not, Aunt Biny. And it *was* really wonderful, that influx of young couples long ago. I was thinking about it yesterday when I came across the pasture from Mattie's. It was a wonderful and courageous thing to do, but there's nobody of that caliber any more. My whole point is that we're luxury-loving enough to prefer to warm ourselves at good old steam heat instead of the little will-o'-the-wisp light you followed."

At sight of the grieved expression on the gentle old woman's face, Nancy sprang up and ran over to her with impulsive caresses. "It worries you, doesn't it, Aunt Biny? I'm sorry. I guess I've given you nothing but worry. It's too bad you ever took me to raise. I'll be good. I'll try to idolize Mr. Farnsworth. He's getting a bit bald on the north mansard roof slope of his head and he's a little too short and a little too fat and a lot older than the hero ought to be. But I'll do my best to moon over him. . . ."

On Monday morning Warner went early to the bank. He went thoughtfully. As he turned out of the "Bee-House" yard into Main Street he was thinking that from this day he must apply himself with all his mind and energy to his present position. This was the day in which he was definitely making up his mind to stay by it, to work up in it, perhaps . . . who knew . . . to become eventually the head of the institution. It was his future. Walking along in the pleasant September morning, he reviewed the turn of the wheel that had brought him back to the mid-west in which he was born and from which he had made his escape years before. He had gone in a circle. His early days in Omaha . . . an eastern boys' school . . . college . . . a certain small success among the younger writers in the East . . . back to Omaha to attend his father's funeral and settle the estate . . . here in Maple City.

The Field family had been well known in Omaha. It had been forty years before that Matthew Field, Warner's father, had brought his bride to the young town that stood like an adolescent boy uncertain how large he is to grow or what he is to be. Omaha did not know then in which direction it was going to grow. It was not sure what type of city it was to become. There was a question concerning the trend of its chief industries. But it was busy. If it had little time for things artistic it was because of its constant labor.

Warner's father had been one of those men who seem to be essential to a city's social life but who never grow rich. His mother was one of those women who never become resigned to a change of abode. With her heart in Massachusetts, she spent all the days of her life in Omaha in a state of temporary residence, thinking that as soon as they had made money to retire on they would go back. She seemed always poised like a bird for flight. Every year she made the trip back East and returned discontentedly to the West.

She saw trees grow from saplings to huge living monuments of foliage. She saw cow pastures turned to trim residential grounds and virgin prairie to paved boulevards. She saw proud buildings rear their heads above the provincial hill streets. She saw the crude town grow into a sophisticated city, saw it develop in music and literature and art. And she never sensed the wonder and beauty of the growth.

Mr. Field had been entirely transplanted. His heart was in Omaha. He had watched it grow with deep rejoicing. If he could have had his way, his son and daughter would have gone to the public school, a great vigorous thing that constantly stretched and snapped its binding chains. But from much coaching of the son and daughter by their mother and eventual winning of her way, Warner and Eleanor, his sister, had gone away and stayed. Mrs. Field had the self-righteous feeling that she had saved them from some insidious influence.

On his way to the bank now Warner went over for the hundredth time the odd chance that had brought him to Maple City. After the war, he had become a member of the

Review staff, continuing in the meantime his free-lance fiction writing. Later had come his father's tragic death, with everything in an upheaval. Then had followed Warner's own and his mother's severe illness in the influenza epidemic, during which they had both nearly lost their lives. It was just at the close of his period of convalescence from pneumonia, that he had met his father's old friend, O. J. Rineland, on the streets of Omaha. They had gone up to the Commercial Club together, an organization in which Mr. Rineland held an out-of-town membership, and talked for a long time. Warner was just at the point of getting down to work again. His position on the *Review* filled, his father's tragic death a severe memory, a big debt hanging over him, Mr. Rineland's proposal came at the only time in his life when he would have given serious heed to it. The banker had come to Omaha for the express purpose of getting information from a banking bureau for the right young man to come into the Maple City institution. If Warner, now, had ever thought of taking up such a business, here was his chance. There was a small staff with more than an ordinary possibility of promotion. For some time they discussed it.

So, from this chance meeting with an old friend came the decisive hour. And so spider-fine are the threads that change the courses of our lives, that an Omaha policeman, halting traffic at the psychological moment on the corner of Sixteenth and Farnam Streets, had changed the direction of Warner's life.

For eight months then he had been in the Maple City bank. As for the old writing, to-day seemed to determine that he was putting it aside, perhaps permanently. One could not tell. He wondered if there was ever another writer anywhere who had experienced this same thing . . . apparently a complete loss of the faculty to execute. He could have written, of course, after a fashion. But his own critical sense would not accept anything he had done since his illness. He could almost hear the comments: "Poor Field . . . he's certainly flattened out into nothing." Better not write at all than subject himself to that sort of criticism.

The past week had been a test . . . the only time since his illness in which he had held himself down definitely for hours to the work of composition. And with all his endeavors, the knack of it simply would not return. Perhaps there was left some definite effect of his illness that touched the delicate portion of the brain which had done constructive work. Almost immediately he was scoffing at the idea. He felt too well again, too fit. Such a trouble would have left its trace on his general health. No, it was just a slumping of ability. No excuse existed. The fault was his own. Perhaps if he kept on fumbling at it he might some day strike the lost . . . why, it was like the old song of the lost chord. Perhaps, then, by constant fumbling, he would some day hear that "grand Amen." He grinned at the thought. Thank heaven, he hadn't entirely mislaid his sense of humor if he had lost his power to construct.

He went through the heavy swinging doors of the old bank now. Strange how the trim, newly decorated room with its tasteful polished desks seemed so jail-like. He set his lips in severity. He said in self-chastisement that he was lucky to get in with Mr. Rineland at all. Mentally he took himself by the collar and shook the dissatisfied creature he was and told him to take cognizance of the fact that from henceforth he was in the banking business.

In a few moments Marty Spencer breezed in, with, "Good morning, Merry Sunshine." Marty always affected that surfacelike gayety. Mr. Rineland, neat, dapper, dignified, every gray hair in place, came in. The other boys took their places. The first school bell rang. The town clock pointed to eight-thirty. A little old lady came timidly in for a dollar in change and one of the grocerymen deposited his Saturday night's receipts. The day's grind had begun.

In the late forenoon Alice Rineland came into the bank. Warner looked up to see her standing by her father's desk, soft-eyed, pale and pretty in a blue dress. Outside he could see her sedan, spotless and shining, standing at the curb. Alice talked to her father for a few moments and then walked over to Warner. Marty Spencer winked at the paying teller. "Better keep in Field's good graces. Your future boss, mayhap."

Alice greeted Warner with that warm flooding of her gray-blue eyes. "You spent a whole week in the country?"

"Yes, summer-resorting on the board walk of Tinkling Creek." He made light of it.

"However could you? When I go away from Maple City, it's to get right into the heart of things . . . theaters, operas, a big hotel. Maple City itself is countrified enough for me. Mama and I are going to New York in the winter."

"That's fine. You'll look up Mother and Eleanor, won't you? Oh, I enjoyed the country, tramping around. You know 'to him who in the love of nature' etc. And Jud Moore proved to be a very interesting man."

Alice opened her gray-blue eyes. "That old man with his pioneer yarns? Why he says 'have went' and 'that there.'"

Warner laughed. "Yes, I guess he does that all right."

When Alice went out Warner was wondering if she knew that Nancy Moore was back.

From that, the thought of Nancy Moore persistently intruded between the files on which he was working. He told himself there was something aloof and tantalizing about her. Part of her was away. One knew that all of Alice Rineland was definitely before one. But—something warm

and personal about Nancy Moore was gone. Something cool
and teasing remained . . . as though she only talked to you
from far away. He caught himself up. At least he would
make no comparisons between the two. And Alice Rineland
was a nice girl. He found himself defending her. "Did
she live to grow up? She was too perfect." He heard
Nancy's laugh, far away, gay, mocking.

CHAPTER VII

NANCY COMES TO A DECISION

O N Wednesday morning Warner knew the moment he awoke that he was going to drive out to the Moore farm before night. It was the courteous thing to do. There were swift heavy showers all morning but cars were running again by late afternoon. After dinner he ran his car out from the turreted old Baldwin barn. As he did so, Miss Rilla stepped out on the back porch to hang up some rinsed tea towels. He called to her, "Get your hat, Miss Rilla, and drive out in the country with me."

Miss Rilla flushed with pleasure. She was fifty-four by the acknowledged statement of her twin sister but in her heart she was twenty. She came down the steps in a remarkably short time, a plump, motherly figure . . . she who was no mother.

Everything in the country seemed fresh after the rain of the previous night. Nature had scrubbed all her decorations. The sumac showed its pink tips instead of the tawny dust-covered leaves of the days previous. The orchards were heavy with apples. It had been a good year for them and the multi-colored fruit weighted the trees. Already the Farmers Union storage house was being filled with yellow-green Golden Glows and shining red Jonathans. The goldenrod waved gay clean plumage at the roadside. A flock of blackbirds circled and winged and wheeled themselves in aeronautic formation.

They drove into Mattie's and Walt's side yard, a bare place with a big pile of wood near the porch. Miss Rilla knew both of them. Mattie, it seemed, had come into town once to help them out with their cooking when Miss Ann was sick. Walt brought them their cobs every fall and sometimes sausage and spare ribs. Mattie, voluble and hospitable, carried her huge bulk out to the car. She wanted them to get out and come in and eat something. It took quite an effort to persuade her that food was unnecessary to them at that time. Walt stood back a little, quiet and sober. Warner had learned to like him. He drew him out to talk about the farm work.

The sun was down at the horizon when they turned into the Moore yard behind the cottonwoods. Warner saw the white of the girl's dress before they were out of the lane. She was crossing the barnyard with a basket of eggs which she waved gayly if perilously. As she came up to the car, Warner acknowledged to himself that the curve of her throat and the contour of her face were lovelier than he had remembered.

Miss Rilla got out of the car with prim heavy slowness and kissed her. As per her usual custom she nearly shed tears. "I've never seen you since the night you graduated, Nancy. You looked so pretty and girlish standing there with your diploma. I said to sister afterward: 'Well, maybe Alice Rineland had the finest dress there but Nancy Moore looked the prettiest.'"

Nancy laughed. "And I'll wager Miss Ann said, 'Don't ever tell her so. It would turn her head.'"

"I expect she did. Sister means well. She just never lets herself say all the nice things she thinks."

A little of the girl's gayety vanished. "Aunt Biny had a bad spell this afternoon. That makes the second in less than two weeks."

Together the three walked to the house. Uncle Jud had just finished his chores and was standing by the side door telling Ma he had a notion not to plow the little piece of rye ground by the creek. "Believe I'll let that little passel go till spring. If the creek runs over, like it did last year, the plowin' is wasted. Don't feel like doin' any work any more that ain't necessary. Gettin' as lazy as Hank Thomas used to be." Aunt Biny had noticed several references lately to a lack of energy on Uncle Jud's part.

Miss Rilla and Nancy went into the house but Warner stopped on the porch to talk to the old man.

"Dandy weather, Mr. Moore." Warner knew that the weather topic never failed to appeal.

For the average city dweller, weather is fairly inconsequential, a thing to be enjoyed, endured, or ignored. To country people it is the big thing . . . the god of the farm . . . the arbiter of destiny. Fortune responds to its smile. Disaster follows its frown.

"Pretty good . . . *yes,* sir. Not like some I've seen. Wind! that's the worst. Seen the wind blow here in Nebraska like old Nick himself. Biggest dust storm we ever had was in April . . . eighty-two, I believe. Ain't right sure about that. Ma!" He stepped to the screen door. "Which year'd old man Denning die in . . . eighty-one or two?"

"I don't just recollect, Pa," Aunt Biny said weakly from her chair. "I got it in my scrap book, though."

"Anyway, remember 'twas when the old man died. Blew three days steady from the southwest. Everybody had plowed. You wouldn't believe it, but it blew the plowed dirt right out o' the field. That's God A'mighty's truth. Blew it in great sheets, where it piled up agin' trees 'n hedges. Got a place in my pasture can show you to this day where it made windrows of the dirt, piled it in long swells like waves. Rain come at the end of three days and packed it. Made that pasture hummocky ever since. Old

man Denning died first of the three days. Buried him on
the last. Had him in a spring wagon. Six pallbearers had
to walk alongside and hold him down. Thought it'd blow
his body into kingdom-come alongside o' his soul. Don't
blow that hard much any more. Wind hits it up pretty
fair once in a while but it's been years since I've seen the
land raise right up and Nebraska pretty near blow off the
map. Funny how a country changes. Settlin' it all up, I
s'pose. Vegetation or somethin'. Or mebbe too many real
estate men like Major Slack talkin' for wind to run any
competition." He slapped his knee and roared, loud enormous laughter.

" 'N snow," he went on, "that's a horse of another
stripe . . . had lots of blizzards but when they say 'the
blizzard' put it in your pipe that it means *The* Blizzard.
That was in eighty-eight. Ain't no trouble to remember that
date . . . twelfth of January . . . eighty-eight. Day was
mild 'n ordinary, even warm . . . no indication of what
was to come. I rec'lect Nick Denning come down to see
me about some fences . . . wanted I should go in with him
for a fence on the south half of the upper eighty. Set
talkin' in the front room of the old house out there. He'd
tied his horse to a post right near where that there straw
stack is. Clouds come up in the northwest . . . rolled
up like slate-colored smoke." Unconsciously dramatic, he
pointed out everything with his long powerful arms . . .
the old house, the post, the clouds in the west.

"Rumbled! Like wagons comin' up the road. Snow
started. Just fell in big clammy bunches at first. I mind
how Nick looked out 'n said, 'My horse's broke loose 'n gone
on home. I'll have to walk.' Broke loose, nothin'! Was
standin' there all the time but we couldn't see him. 'Twas
just before four o'clock 'n people began goin' after their
youngsters at school. Got lost 'n went around in circles.

Run into each other in pastures 'n off the road. Some children was froze tryin' to get to shelter. We didn't have no children to go after . . . had buried our little girl afore that. Name was Emmy. Beats all . . . remember how Ma said to me when the blizzard got so bad, 'Well, Emmy's safe, anyway.' Always remember her lookin' out the window into the solid, peltin', tearin' snow 'n sayin' that in a kind-a pleased way, 'Well, Emmy's safe anyway.' " As though ashamed of his bit of emotion, he started up bluffly, "Well, it kept her up, wind fairly boilin' the snow, blowin' fifty miles an hour. The 'mometer thirty and more below. Lasted three days and blamed if another one didn't start soon's it died down. When it was over sun come out as pretty as a picture . . . the sky smilin' as innocent as a lamb, as though a hundred folks hadn't froze, and more stock than you could count."

As the old man stood there on the porch in the afterglow of the sun, telling the simple tale of the weather which had been both friend and enemy to him, Warner felt an admiration for him. The big head with its shaggy graying locks, the swinging arms that had held scythes and plow handles, that had planted and husked, seemed suddenly to belong to the patriarch of a people. He appeared for the moment to Warner as the victor of a vanquished race, as the conqueror of a new world . . . an aged John the Baptist who had prepared the way in the wilderness for a new civilization.

Warner went on into the house to speak to Aunt Biny who sat in the big chintz-covered chair by the window, pale, a little shaken yet.

"We mustn't stay longer," Miss Rilla was saying. "We'll tire her too much just now."

"Come out again, then," Nancy said, "Sunday . . . to supper, both of you. Will that be all right, Aunt Biny?"

"I'd like it."

"I don't suppose I can," Miss Rilla's eyes watered at the invitation. "It's my turn to have charge of the table next Sunday, but I'll send Mr. Field."

On Thursday morning Warner drew a circle around the Sunday date of the bank desk calendar. All day at his desk he saw it shining like a beacon light across the monotony of the week.

Nancy slipped back easily into helping with the household tasks. And they are legion in every farmhouse. Chickens, canning, baking, cleaning, churning, mending, soap-making. It seemed that Aunt Biny finished one task only to begin another.

"How can you be so satisfied with it, Aunt Biny?" Nancy was helping in the kitchen on Saturday morning. "The monotony of it would drive me to drown myself in Tinkling Creek."

"It's my home and my work," Aunt Biny said simply. "And there's always been a satisfaction to me to know a thing was well done . . . a nice sweet pound of butter, a box of flaky white soap, a flock of plump chickens . . . you feel as though you had done your little bit well."

"Believe *me*, it doesn't sound enticing to me."

"Probably not." Aunt Biny was finding that she must be very patient with this new Nancy. "And I don't say that any other woman is called on to do my same kind of work. But I do say that no woman in the world will ever find happiness for herself if she *doesn't* work, at something."

"But why work if it isn't necessary?"

"Because it's part of the scheme of things." Aunt Biny's philosophy was simple but it would admit of no modification.

And then Uncle Jud was bringing in split wood for the range, a last armful before leaving for Walt's to help him put in his winter wheat. And only a few minutes later some one came up the grassy path that led between Aunt Biny's petunias. Nancy stopped by the window to see who it was. It proved to be Mr. Rineland, president of the First National Bank. How dapper and immaculate he looked, she was thinking. Whoever would believe that he had been a farm hand when he first came to Nebraska? And what did he want? Uncle Jud, of course, and he had just gone.

But it was Nancy that Mr. Rineland had come to see. He was pleasant and cordial. "Well, Nancy, you've grown into a very lovely young woman."

"Surely you've not taken to flattery, Mr. Rineland?"

"Truth is never flattery, they say."

"How are Mrs. Rineland and Alice?"

"Both well, Alice is at home with us now. She finished her music course at the University. She talked some of wanting to go to Boston for more study, but recently she has given up the idea." Nancy would have laughed her mocking laugh if she had known why she had given it up. "You must come to see us, Nancy. Of all the little girls who used to play with Alice you were always my favorite."

"Thank you! And you've a beautiful new home?" Nancy fancied it better not to commit herself about the visit.

"Yes, Mama and Alice wanted it. As for me . . . my wants become fewer every year of my life. I'm almost down now to old Omar's 'book and loaf.'" He had a pleasant, understanding smile that Nancy had always liked. "But it was about you, Nancy, that I came to talk. I'm president of the school board and we find ourselves without a second-grade teacher in the Whittier School. I wondered if you would take the room?"

"I? Why . . . it's funny you thought of *me*. It wouldn't be possible . . . I'm sorry. I have to. . . ." Nancy was floundering a little. "I only intended to stay a few weeks, you know. . . ." Some perverse thing in her kept her from telling the reason. "And I never taught."

"Of course, I don't know your plans. But I thought it would be nice for you. You could stay at the 'Bee-House' during the week. Miss Ann and Miss Rilla are still running it and they would take good care of you. You could come out home every Friday night. The old folks have missed you, Nancy. I was sorry you went away."

A quick flash of tears swept across Nancy's brown eyes and she had to wink them back.

"It seems to me you'd better consider it . . . the frail way your Aunt Biny is . . . and your Uncle Jud losing his grip . . . I've noticed it a great deal the last few months."

"He does look different." There was a quick little catch in her voice. "He seemed a giant for strength when I went away. He's an old man now."

"Of course the teacher part, from our standpoint . . . we can get some one. It isn't impossible, just a little hard as everything has opened up. But it was of you I was thinking . . . how it would keep you here with the old folks until May. And I'm not afraid of your ability. Miss Gunn is willing to help you all she can and is favorable to your coming."

"Oh, you meant stay *the whole school year?*"

"Why, yes."

Nancy looked out of the old sitting-room window toward the gate with the horseshoe swinging on a chain. The cotton-wood leaves danced and shimmered in the morning sun-shine. The road beyond ran like a brown ribbon garlanded with yellow bunches of plumed goldenrod. As she looked, the morning train from the West crossed the stretch of prairie, its smoke standing thickly back in the stillness of the blue. The next time she would go away on it, it would be to leave the old life behind forever. And after all, it would not be long. Eight months more of her own . . . nearly a year of freedom . . . nearly a year to be the old Nancy Moore. One squanders Time lightly when one is young.

Mr. Rineland named the salary. "That isn't as much as we pay the others here but of course you're without experience."

"Oh, yes, there's a salary." But it had not been of the money she was thinking. To take up her life where she had left it . . . go on as though nothing had happened!

"It tempts me! I have a half notion to do it." Suddenly Nancy threw up her head. "I believe I'll do it."

When Mr. Rineland had gone she went up to her old room. Nancy's old writing desk was in the queer bay window addition and she sat down to it now. She wrote a letter to Mr. Farnsworth, who was a "little too fat and a little too old to be the hero." In point of fact she wrote several but none of them pleased her. The last one, which had consumed a half dozen pages, she read and tore up. "Methinks the lady doth protest too much," she said aloud, and wrote a briefer, more definite epistle.

And so that evening at dinner in the "Bee-House," Miss Gunn was feeling more cheerful. "Well, I hope my troubles are temporarily suspended," she said brightly. "We've a teacher for the second grade and that means a new boarder for the 'Bee-House.' I'm sure I don't know what she'll do. She's had plenty of schooling but not definite training. She was bright enough when she went to school to me . . . too bright, in fact, for she kept thinking up mischievous things to do. I'll have to help her, I suppose. You never can tell how they'll turn out. Some are born teachers. Some achieve it through much training and some have it thrust upon them. Nancy has had hers thrust upon her. You remember her, Miss Rilla . . . Nancy Moore?"

Miss Rilla's eyes performed their moist duty. "Nancy Moore? So little Nancy Moore is going to teach school with you? She'll do well."

Miss Ann did not see it so optimistically. "She was a tom-boy," she said curtly.

"There's nothing else any more." Major Slack threw his statement into the ring. "They're all tom-boys now."

"Here's a good one." Marty Spencer chuckled at his own forthcoming wit. But he did not get a chance to tell the story, for Dr. Pearson was wanting to know if the girl was pretty, and George Kendall was informing him that she was a pippin for looks. At which Genevieve looked sharply at her liege lord. She didn't get along any too well with him but she intended to see that no one else did.

Essie Carlson, bringing in the creamed peas, flushed at the conversation and put Miss Gunn's dish on the wrong side, so that the carbohydrates of the peas were very nearly side by side with the proteids of the toasted cheese. So Nancy Moore was going to stay in Maple City! Then Essie's little dream of Walt Thomas would vanish into the place from whence it had come. Oh, well, nothing ever came her way. She might as well get used to expecting nothing and she would never be disappointed.

"I wonder if she can sing?" Mary Mae Gates asked anxiously.

"Let's pray she can't," Miss Ann answered tartly.

Only Ambrose Jones, the bore, and Warner Field were silent on the subject of the new teacher. The bore could think of nothing to say. And Warner Field thought of too much.

CHAPTER VIII

THE PRAIRIE MAKES ITS APPEAL

ON Sunday afternoon Warner told himself that he ought to go to the Rinelands'. He had not been there all week and probably they had noticed it. So in the late afternoon, on his way to supper at the Moore farm, he turned his car into the sloping asphalt drive.

Mr. Rineland met him at the door. "It's you, Warner . . . come in. I'm glad you came. I want you always to feel free to drop in. Your father was my friend . . . I want his boy to feel at home here." He was cordial and hospitable. Warner felt his sincerity. "I'm all alone. Alice and Mama are out in the car. They've gone to see a little girl out in the country . . . Nancy Moore. She isn't really a little girl, of course, but after all it seems only a few years ago that she used to come sometimes to play with Alice. She's just come home now and she's going to stay and teach in the schools. I talked with her about it yesterday. And I told Mama and Alice they must go out and see her. Of all the little girls who used to play with Alice I fancied her most."

Mr. Rineland had a different manner in his home than in the bank. There he was all business, everything rotated about the affairs of the Old First National. He was not exactly stern, but at least silent and slightly austere. Here he was pleasant, talkative. Warner had come to think of him as two men—the banker and the man at home. To

his surprise he had found him a deep reader. Just now he
felt a vague relief that Mrs. Rineland and Alice were not
there.

Mr. Rineland took Warner into a small room lined with
books. It contained a library table, two big chairs, a man-
sized desk. "It's the only room that's my own, Warner.
When we built, I told Mama and Alice I was like Eugene
Field when he said all he wanted was 'an orange and a few
kind words.' All I wanted in the whole house was a corner
for my books and the desk with some old keepsakes in.
Alice wanted it for some kind of a little den but I said,
'No, as long as you've got a papa, you've got to let him
have a corner of his own.'" He was having Warner sit
down; was childishly pleased to have him there.

Warner picked up a small leather copy of *Macbeth*
from the table. "I see you're reading one of the new six
sellers."

"Well, sir, I've been reading the plays all over. There's
so little time for these things in the grind, and yet I like
to think of them up there waiting for me." He motioned
toward the cases. "I have a sense of pleasure in thinking
that Mr. Pickwick and Becky Sharp and a dozen other
old friends are up there ready to come at my bidding."

They talked a little of some of the modern things, agree-
ing comfortably at times, arguing mildly at others, expressing themselves freely. "Warner," the older man
summed it up, "you can't please a lot of us with a grue-
some episode in life or a salacious experience. I'm tired
of a lot of the stuff. It's neither helpful nor entertaining.
I've seen some raw things in my life and I've had some
deep griefs. My first wife died when my little boy was
eight . . . a great grief to me! It left me completely
wrapped up in my boy. You don't remember, maybe, but
when he was twenty they brought him home to me from

college . . . killed in a train wreck on the way home.
All the hopes I had held for him! . . . Deep, deep grief!"
He waited a moment and went on, "No, if you've lived
life deeply . . . touched bottom as it were . . . it takes
away any inclination to sit and wade through pages of
sex stuff or even wearily follow somebody's ponderous
mental reactions. They call it all real life. At least if it's
a sordid thing they say it's real life. If it's decent, it's
bunk. Are indecency and slime all that constitute real life?
Here's Maple City . . . nobody is rich as riches are
counted now, and yet everybody is rich as compared with
the old pioneer days. Nobody is highly successful as the
world counts it. There's nothing here out of the ordinary.
Yet, there's drama here. There's deep grief here . . . the
quiet kind of grief that doesn't rant openly nor accept its
trouble stoically either one, but goes on taking up its daily
life as cheerfully as it can. There's service here. There's
great joy here. There's deep love here. Most of the marriages are built on high hopes and old Doc Minnish will
tell you that there are more children welcomed than those
that are not."

Warner enjoyed him. He asked a question or two to lead
him on.

"A great wrath rises in me when I read the stuff from
onlookers telling their opinions of my mid-west from the
housetops. It makes me angry all through." He spoke
with genuine feeling. "And yet it ought not, I suppose,"
he added parenthetically, "for the highest type of tolerance
is that which is tolerant of intolerance. There was one of
those articles in an old *Review* that I picked up the other
day. It had that old time-worn theme: the grasping and
the sordidness of the middle west, the country without ideals,
the country destitute of artistry, the stolid old stigma that
it existed without any sense of the finer things of life."

He fussed around on the big table until he found and handed it to Warner. Warner read the ironical unsigned article through, but it was not new to him. He had written it. Moreover he had been sincere when he had done so, as honest in his convictions as he had been scathing in his criticism. He had written it with the complacent knowledge that he knew the mid-west.

"Poor fool," Mr. Rineland went on, "to see it that way. I don't suppose there's anything that touches me more than a denunciation like that. A hurt to my family couldn't sink deeper than those things about my mid-west. For it *is* my mid-west, Warner. I helped to make it. I came here a stripling boy. I had no money then to put into the development of it. But I put in what was more to me . . . my youth and my energy and my love. I curried Judge Baldwin's horses when he was spoken of as a 'rising young lawyer.' I worked here and there and everywhere to get a start . . . farm hand, husking jobs, one summer with a gang putting through the first railroad in this county. And, all the time I was working, I had the feeling that I wasn't doing it just for myself . . . that I was putting into the new country all the youthful energy I could muster. I've raised my head from laying ties and looked across the prairie to imagine mighty trains sweeping across it. And I've lived to see all that and more accomplished. So everything that strikes at it hurts me. It is a part of me. It is *myself.* We all feel that way, the old settlers around here who planted the trees and turned the first sod. It's our mid-west and she's like our mother. You wouldn't, of course, expect that writer . . ." he motioned toward the article, "to admire our old mother. That's the way she looks to the critic . . . old and wrinkled and bent. But we know what she has meant to us . . . our prairie mother."

Warner sat unspeaking. He could see that Mr. Rineland was deeply touched. He was saying things that no doubt seldom crossed his lips. "And here's another." He reached for a magazine. " 'How can a poet come out of Kansas?' We're not Kansas but we're close enough to know that we are slapped on the wrist too. Answer it, Field. Lord, if I could handle a pencil like you! The thoughts tear around in me but if I'd sit down to corral them, they'd be off. 'How can a poet come out of Kansas?' Well, how could Howells and Mark Twain and Grant and Garfield come out of the little towns? How could Lincoln come out of Springfield? And how could any good come out of Nazareth, for that matter?"

It touched Warner, the deep feeling which the little, dapper, elderly man had been showing. He remembered his father speaking in the same way . . . expressing a sort of brooding love for Omaha and for the prairie and the prairie towns. He left, half reluctantly, with a feeling of having looked upon something very intimate if not sacred.

As he stepped out of the formal entrance, Mrs. Rineland and Alice got out of the sedan and came up to the steps. Mrs. Rineland was as slim and willowy as Alice. When their backs were turned no one could pick mother from daughter. But in her face Mrs. Rineland looked very old. All the manipulating and face lifting and massaging could not bring a line of youth to her. She had been a widow in her late thirties when she married Mr. Rineland. In all these years she had fought Time like a tiger. But for a decade Time had been using his own claws. With her beadlike eyes and a birdlike curve to her nose, she gave one the impression of a hawk . . . something watching covertly. She usually overdressed, a thing of which no one could accuse Alice, whose taste was perfect. This afternoon the mother had on too much of everything, including rouge, powder and jewelry. Warner felt a vague dislike for her, of which his genuine liking for Alice and her father made him ashamed.

"Come back in," Alice put out a soft white hand, "and have some lunch."

"Thank you . . . you're always kind. But I've an engagement for lunch."

Little green points penciled themselves in Alice's gray-blue eyes so that a faint touch of jade shadowed them. But she was poised. "For dinner to-morrow night, then?"

"Why, yes, I could, thank you."

Warner drove directly to the Moores'. When he turned in behind the cottonwoods there was no one in sight. But Nancy met him at the door of the shabby old farmhouse with mock awe. "Alice and her mother have been to call on me," she announced immediately. She clasped her hands dramatically and rolled her merry eyes. "We were sweeter than honey in the honeycomb to each other. Lovely, gracious things dripped out of our lips. . . ." She pirouetted about on an agile toe and kissed her finger tips to the air. Then she added mournfully, "And froze in long icy stalactites." And her suppressed laughter bubbled forth infectiously.

"Nancy! Nancy!" Aunt Biny reprimanded gently.

Uncle Jud scolded her outright. "You ought to be ashamed of yourself. You ought not to talk that way . . . a great big girl like you. Making fun . . . nice rich folks to take the trouble to come out here. You ought to be paddled."

Nancy laughed at him. "Uncle Jud has threatened to paddle me ever since I was two," she told Warner, "and he has never touched me yet."

"I will yet, young lady. You go to talking about folks that way and no tellin' what I'll do."

"Pa! Pa!" Aunt Biny remonstrated. She was afraid that Warner would not understand Pa's sputtering, which was as common to her as the chirping of the English sparrows.

Warner found that Walt and Mattie were invited to supper, too. They came in a little while, Mattie, huge, warm, voluble, carrying her bulk along in that light-footed way which was a marvel to Warner. Walt, clean and quiet and brown as a hazelnut, effaced himself. He seldom looked directly at Nancy, but when he did Warner could see that his heart was in his doglike eyes.

They all sat on the porch in the green painted rockers until Aunt Biny and Nancy told them to come in. The dining-room end of the kitchen was the same clean plain place, with its yellow painted walls and its mopped floor with rag rugs on it. The dishes were the same, brightly decorated, a little heavy. But the girl had done something to the meal. It might have been the way the table was set or the great mass of purple and lavender asters banked in the center. And the girl herself! Warner, watching her pour tea, noticed again what grace there was in every movement. She was gay and talkative and unembarrassed at Uncle Jud's clumsiness. She chided Aunt Biny for drinking too much tea. "You'll have tea in your veins instead of blood, Aunt Biny." She drew Walt into the conversation when he was too long silent, with that gift of the natural-born hostess who makes congenial parties from guests with little in common.

After lunch they all talked again out on the porch, Uncle Jud on his favorite topic . . . pioneer days. "When we got ready to build the first house after livin' in the sod one," he pointed to the two-roomed cabin in which Warner had stayed, "we had to haul the lumber from down Nehawka way. They had the first sawmill there. Mr. Isaac Pollard run it. We'd come across yonder. . . ." He pointed again with a huge stubby forefinger. "Wa'nt no roads, just take a bee-line across the prairie. Used to take us as long to get that load o' lumber from down there as it takes now to drive across the state in an auto. Had its advantages though . . . goin' slow did. Drive like the devil now . . . don't see much of nothin' on the way but trees and telephone poles slippin' by. Went so slow then . . . could see wild flowers and take notice o' coveys o' prairie chickens and quail and the way the white clouds slipped acrost the sky. Folks have had to pay the price o' livin' close to roadside things when they traded in the oxen and horses for gasoline." He dwelt on the subject, revealing that same brooding love for the country that Mr. Rineland in his more cultured way had disclosed to Warner earlier in the afternoon.

And then the old man and Walt were discussing the corn crop. "It's going to be just opposite that of the wheat," Walt predicted. "The whole corn belt will have a bumper crop. It's going to be bigger even than our first estimate."

"I've noticed that's always the way," the old man philosophized. "Of late years we get a good corn crop and the wheat's low, and vicy versy. I been down through my lower field yesterday and it's goin' to be 'way over last year."

"Mr. Rineland is advising carrying stock through to grass. Now that the corn is going to be available, they'll not have to go this fall at a sacrifice." Lately Warner had found himself unconsciously beginning to take an interest in the business. And if he had learned one thing more than another it was that a small-town bank is a farmers' bank, that the country banking business is not only related to farming, it *is* the farming business. There was a little more conversation relative to the situation and then Walt said he must be getting back to the chores. So he and Mattie left, Mattie walking sideways down the steps lightly, buoyantly, like the inflated balloon of which she always reminded Warner.

When they had gone Nancy turned to Warner. "Let's walk . . ." she invited frankly. "Up the road to the end of the Denning hill where we can see over the country."

They went down through the grassy path with the lavender petunias bordering it and out through the gate with the clanking horseshoe on its chain. The road was gray and dusty from much Sunday travel. As they walked at the side they scattered dust from the shepherd's-purse and rag-weed.

"Stop here a minute," the girl commanded. "Look back through the cottonwoods that line the road. Isn't that as lovely as anything abroad?"

"You've seen Europe?"

"Some of it . . . but nothing that I've liked any better than this. I grew up under the cottonwoods and I love them. They're the happiest, merriest trees in the world. When everything else is still and doleful and pessimistic, they dance and laugh and twinkle. I think sometimes we don't appreciate the things we're used to . . . don't see our commonest things as they really are."

For the fraction of a moment Warner's mind flashed to that little marked volume in the old cupboard:

"That which I see not teach Thou me."

But he would not have been human if his mind had not been more upon the girl than upon her philosophy. "Tell me about yourself," he demanded. "What you've been doing since you lived here before."

She darted a swift look up at him. "There's little to tell. I lived with Uncle Jud and Aunt Biny until I was eighteen and then I went away. I've been in college since, spending my vacations with friends. And now that I've marched up the hill, why, here I am all marched down again to the place where I started. About the teaching. . . . I don't know how it will turn out. Sometimes a person does idiotic things. I know I've done a lot of them. . . ." She stopped abruptly. "But I didn't bring you out here to discuss me. I brought you out to talk about *you*." She dropped her light bantering tone and a sincerity crept into her voice. "I haven't, up to this moment, been exactly honest with you. It would be much more fair if I should tell you that I know all about you. At least," she added lightly again, "I know who you are and where you came from and what you used to do and that's a lot more than most folks in this community know."

He knew it would come some day. And this was the day. And because he was taken off his guard he said evasively, "You're a bit uncanny. Do you by any chance operate a clairvoyant studio somewhere?"

"Oh, not that bad," she laughed. "I just happen to know some people who know you. Which in turn makes me know that if you're Warner Field out here, it's a deep-dyed, villainous alias, for you're really Jeffrey Warner Field of the *Review* and other publications. I think I've read everything you ever wrote but your private letters."

He made light of the discovery. He was not, of course, in hiding. That would have been ridiculous. But he had felt a sensitiveness about falling into such a slump over his writing. He had taken his work seriously, had cherished some ideals concerning it, and because he had failed in it he carried a vague soreness, a heartsickness, about with him and wanted little said about it.

"And why . . ." the girl was asking, "do I find Jeffrey Warner Field of the *Review*-and-other-publications in a small bank in the middle west?"

"A bank is a perfectly good place to be," he returned lightly. "There are even people so benighted as to consider the banker the big man of the town. I'm not *the* banker, but did you ever hear of a bank president that hadn't at some time in his early career oiled the adding-machine and taken the monthly mouse out of its trap? At sixty I'll be president of the institution and have a gray-lined limousine and a crabbed disposition and no waist line."

Quite suddenly she visioned his jesting words as a possibility. And equally as suddenly the connection with Alice flashed through her mind . . . Alice, who that afternoon had referred to him frequently in her soft, clinging voice. Nancy grinned to herself. So *that* was it, was it?

"And who are the friends that we possess in common?" Warner was asking.

"I'm going to ask you not to go into that just now. I'll tell you some day but just now I prefer not to." If she was to be free to live her old life out here this year she wanted to feel so in every way.

As Warner was more interested in the girl herself than in any vague mutual acquaintance, he dropped it quite definitely.

They were at the top of the long ascent of the Denning hill. So gradual was the slope that they scarcely realized the height to which they had climbed and the extent of the panorama that was now spread out before them.

"It's the highest point in the county. 'There lies sweet Auburn, loveliest village of the plain.'" Nancy turned to him, "Now . . . isn't it lovely? What could be more so?"

West of them, Maple City lay almost concealed in its mass of trees. Only a few roofs and the church spires showed above the interlacing of elms and maples and cottonwoods . . . a huge *boutonnière* on the breast of the prairie. To the east and south two other towns nestled in their green foliage. All about them the long, rolling hills lay like waves of the sea molded into solidity. There was the vivid green of alfalfa, the yellow of wheat stubble, the tawny brown of corn, the black of fall plowing and a half dozen shades in the pastures. From the northeast, Tinkling Creek wound through a dip in the hills across the lowest part of the country, easily traced by the fringe of willow and cottonwood and wild plum along its course.

"I've been gone four years and I've never been quite able to forget it," Nancy said after a moment. "It seems to be born in the blood . . . the love of the prairie country. The mountains hem me in. I don't like them. They're grand and awe-inspiring but I have mental asthma when I'm chucked down among them. The sea fascinates me, but I'm afraid of it. But this . . ." she threw out her hand to take in the landscape in its soft September haze, "there's nothing like it anywhere. Its very odors are different . . . the loam and the soil . . . and the orchards. Why, a breath of wind from off an alfalfa field in blossom nearly anæsthetizes me. If I could write like you can, wouldn't I get after the elusive something that's in the atmosphere and catch it and imprison it in black and white for people who are away from it to read and hold and enjoy for themselves?"

Three times he had heard it in the same day . . . the beauty of the prairie-mother. And he who was prairie-born had fled from her.

"Of course there will be rough winds over it," she went on, "tearing the very dirt from the fields and there will be frightful blizzards and deluging rains, but it seems to me that between these times it's like a jewel burnished to its great beauty by the very ferocity and roughness of these elements."

She turned to him and threw out her hands in a little characteristic gesture. "Not that I've been true to it by any means! Here's a confession. All my life I listened to Uncle Jud and Aunt Biny tell about their pioneer days and I used to be bored to distraction. I've always been ashamed of coming from a farm in the mid-west, ashamed of knowing anything about corn and cattle, wheat and hogs and alfalfa. I used to laugh and half apologize when I'd tell the new eastern girls where I was from. Isn't that small and snobbish and cowardly? And I'm promising myself that I'll never do it again. Oh, why haven't we the common decency to stand up for our own?" she asked suddenly. "Why can't we be honest and say we *like* the *prairie* and the *cottonwoods* and the *low rolling hills?* Why can't we be loyal enough to say that our mid-west people are developing some of the arts? What makes us ape and imitate and follow after everybody else when we might be evolving something of our own? What made Alice Rineland and her mother stick an Italian house out here on the prairie when we've a wide-porched, hospitable kind of architecture of our own? We haven't any of us the vision and courage of the old pioneers themselves. Aunt Biny was talking to me last night about their coming on from the East . . . and it was really a wonderful thing, wasn't it . . . women like Aunt Biny, delicate and gentle and refined, coming here in wagons, and men like Uncle Jud . . . courageous and energetic and strong? Of course there was the riff-raff, but she says that most of the people who came into this section of Nebraska were high-spirited and brave."

Nancy turned to the west and flung her hand out toward the sun slipping over the edge of the world. "Think of it! Right here where we stand! No roads, just wild prairie grass blowing in the wind. Tinkling Creek over there with a few cottonwoods and wild plums along its banks. The sky like a blue bowl turned over to meet the green bowl all around the rim of the prairie. Just a wagon here on the hill where we are . . . with a lone man and woman and a few tools and household goods. No one to aid them but themselves. Just their hands to do it all . . . to dig and plow and plant and harvest. Two pygmy people to conquer the brown earth and wrest a living from it and make a home!"

Warner caught the spirit of the picture. "You and I wouldn't do it, though," he said definitely. "We're too smug and sophisticated. But how they must have loved adventure!"

"And how they must have loved each other," Nancy returned.

"Well, one is about as passé as the other," Warner added dryly, "courage like that and love like that."

They made no further comments. For a few moments they stood together looking at the country as it lay stretched in the lush mellow warmth of the late summer with that vague suggestion of fall in the air. Warner was human enough to be conscious of the girl's loveliness, but his mind was on the things she had been saying. He had not been impervious to the beauty about him nor the achievements of the pioneers. Through his father, he had been steeped in the traditions of that section of the country. But the very commonness of the subject had been too apparent to take much of his interest. Now as the girl talked in her enthusiasm, a bit of the vision of the early days and a trace of wonder over that which had been accomplished were revived if not actually born in him.

The two walked back to the farm where the old folks sat reading on either side of the red-covered drop-leaf table.

Warner took his leave. When he drove past the Rinelands', Alice, who had been watching all the passing cars from the little upper balcony, went back into the house.

That night Warner did not go to sleep readily. The seed of suggestion which the girl had thrown down all unaware of the trial through which he had passed, was germinating. He could not throw off the consciousness that there had been a romance of the prairie. It was his last waking thought. When he dropped into sleep the idea did not relax its hold upon him but stayed in his subconscious mind. All through his sleep a wagon crawled slowly over the prairie and another and another. There were brawny men in them like Uncle Jud, who shaded their eyes and looked hopefully to the west. There were soft-spoken women like Aunt Biny, who shaded their eyes and looked wistfully back to the east. From one of the wagons a girl slipped out and stood on the brow of the hill . . . a long, low, rolling hill . . . and laughed gayly as she pointed toward a creek where a few cotton-woods and wild plums grew. She had warm brown hair and merry brown eyes. The curve of her throat and chin was a lovely thing to see. She was like a candle in the dusk . . . a flame in the dark! He hurried to join her, fearful that she might go on without him. As he neared the top of the hill she threw him a laughing, tender look over her shoulder and the flame of her vanished into the west and mingled with the sunset. He wakened and lay wrapped in the vividness of the dream, so shadowy and elusive and yet so real that he was shaken with the memory of it.

CHAPTER IX

ALICE RINELAND

ON Monday morning Warner went to the bank still conscious of the thing. A certain exhilaration was upon him. He could not put his finger upon the cause, but all during the walk down Main Street there persisted the feeling that something new had come into his life, something of great interest and great charm.

At the bank, Marty Spencer followed him in with, "And so we have with us to-day the ever-popular Mr. Field! . . ."

Mr. Rineland came in, dapper, neat, every gray hair in place. The other boys took their places. The school bell rang. A groceryman came in to deposit his Saturday night receipts. An old man came in to get some change. It was his little grandson's birthday and he was going to give him a dollar. The day's grind had begun.

Down at the Whittier School, Nancy Moore in a leaf-green linen dress was going up the same walk she had trod when she was a little girl and the steps that were worn with the tramp of a thousand feet. The building was old. She could see a few straggling cracks in the bricks like the faint tracings of woodbine. She put her hand on the latch. Even that was familiar with its huge iron thumb-piece. Inside, the old hall seemed welcoming her home. The long stairway that turned in three directions up to the four higher grades was just as she had pictured it. For a few moments she stood and let the recollection of the years sweep her like a tidal wave. She could see herself climbing those stairs,

her brown hair in a braid, and wearing the ill-fitting dress
of blue serge with a red-and-blue plaid yoke into which
Aunt Biny had put so many delicate stitches with such
clumsy results. How sensitive she had been about those
clothes, her heart aching for things like Alice Rineland's!
That had been only nine years ago. And the places she
had been since and the clothes she had worn! The little
girl who was before her now in fancy seemed for a few
moments to have no more connection with herself than a
strange child. A sudden swift flash of tears swept her eyes
as she involuntarily looked up to the vision of the clumsily
dressed girl from the country with her books and her dinner
basket mounting the stairs. But almost immediately she
was brought back to the present, for Gus Carlson was coming forward to greet her as though he were the host. The
average small-town schoolhouse janitor is not a mere tender
of fires and a sweeper of dirt. He is a sort of Lord High
Chancellor of the building. And Miss Gunn was stepping
out from her office, too, and meeting her. Other teachers
came up . . . the grade teachers . . . and the kinder-
gartner, a Miss Hays, with that sprightly, cheerful, affected
tone that a few (and only a few, thank heaven) kinder-
garten teachers think they have to assume. They seemed
pleasant, all of them. Miss Gunn, dignified, calm and
slow-moving, asked Nancy to come into her office for a
short talk.

"I'll help you all I can, Miss Moore," she said. "I'm
going to call you that right from the start. You may be
'Nancy' to me at the 'Bee-House' but here you're 'Miss
Moore.' It would take away from your dignity a little,
you know, for the children to hear."

Miss Gunn's talk hit the target as it were. "You're handi-
capped at the start without the definite training that the
other teachers possess. But I remember you well enough

to know how quick you are at everything. I had rather trust you to pick up what you'll need to know than some girls with training. There are stupid people in every walk of life and whatever you may lack, you're not stupid, Nancy . . . Miss Moore." Nancy grinned, but Miss Gunn, humorless and earnest, did not. "Every night after school for a time I'll assist you with your work. I think you will get along well. Remember this: children are not empty buckets that you have to fill with something. You can't pour knowledge into them. Initiative is everything. They must do what they're told . . . yes, not with just blind obedience but with an intelligent obedience that understands why they do it. Get every brain to thinking for itself and every hand to doing for itself and you won't be driving the children at all. They will all be living, as Kipling says, 'Each for the joy of the working.' " It summed up quite neatly many a three-year normal-training course.

There were a few more specific directions for the day and then Nancy went into the room where she herself had gone to school. How tiny the desks seemed! They had been quite huge in her day. The windows looked practically the same and the woodwork. The walls above and below the blackboards, white in her time, were now a pale apple green. Miss Addison had been her teacher, a large soft-spoken woman. Nancy wondered what had become of her since she married some elderly man and moved away. That was the way with most of them, to teach for a time and then marry. All excepting women like Miss Gunn, with no emotional side, all intellectual.

Standing just inside the bare, clean room, incidents long dormant in her mind came back like yellowed pictures torn from the leaves of an old scrap book: Uncle Jud bringing her into town every morning behind the old fat team; the day she was coming down with the measles and, feeling sick, was still too timid to tell Miss Addison so; Aunt Biny coming in to attend a special program, wearing a funny old-fashioned hat and cape, her crutch making hard sounds on the schoolroom floor; the Christmas tree and the dazzling thing it had seemed to her. Now that she was really going to teach she would have a Christmas tree for the children . . . a big one to bring the dazzle to other eyes. How queer life was! Realizing that the thought was not original and would in no way assist her in the morning's work she took off her hat, gave her hair a pat into place and took an inventory of the material in the cupboard.

Miss Gunn came in, went over the books with her and gave her an outline for the day. "To-night we'll go over the work together so that your view of the entire fall program will be comprehensive." How patient and unruffled Miss Gunn was!

The children began coming in. Roxy Swanson arrived first, blowing in gustily with a sort of "Well, here I am" air. Jakie Cohn came with the nose-marks of his race upon him. Johnny Bornheimer came, clean and patched and darned. Two of Gus Carlson's big flock came. Thirty-one pupils were enrolled.

The room was rather in chaos, the first teacher having barely made a good start. The previous week had been a succession of girls from high school. Miss Gunn had not been able to give them all the help she would have liked.

The last bell rang. Nancy faced the battery of sixty-one eyes, Jakie Cohn, because of too great curiosity over a firecracker, being the possessor of a glass eye which he would remove for the edification and entertainment of any one who paid him a cent.

To Warner Field that new interest in life persisted all morning. His mind seemed to be divided quite definitely into two compartments. In one he did his mechanical work correctly. In the other, shadowy, vague, but definitely existing, those prairie people moved on their journey, drew together, confided their plans, drifted apart. He had the sensation that they were going about their work on the prairie, building their sod houses, breaking the wild ground, setting out trees, stepping lightly, speaking softly, that they might not disturb him. He had a queer whimsical notion that he would like to have them wait for him. "Wait until I can join you," he seemed to be thinking. "Wait until my task is finished and I'll go on with you."

At noon, as he left the bank, they were waiting for him. They came trooping to him when he started home. On his way up Main Street they accompanied him, strong virile men and wholesome women. And all the time a slim girl, laughing at hardships, taking gayly whatever the toilsome journey brought forth, danced like a will-o'-the-wisp ahead of the others and beckoned to him to come and see the beauty that lay on the rim of the prairie. She had on a coarse blue calico dress, but now that he had arrived at the "Bee-House" he decided that she looked very much like the girl who was coming into the dining room in cool leaf-green linen with a boyish white collar turned back from her merry face. For Nancy Moore looked as lovely as a narcissus, even though the day was hot and sultry.

The new place laid for her was up at the far end of the table, but across from Warner, where he could see her. She had stopped near his chair and was speaking to Essie Carlson, the waitress. "Why, Essie, how are you? I didn't know you helped Miss Ann."

Essie colored to the roots of her moist light hair. "How are you, Miss Moore?"

Nancy took both of the girl's hands. "Essie Carlson, don't you dare 'Miss Moore' me." She turned to Warner in explanation. "We were all in the same high-school class

. . . Walt and Essie and Alice Rineland and I. There are quite a lot of us here now." She had turned back to the girl. "We must have a class reunion."

"Oh, I don't think we'd better try," Essie gave a little short laugh. "Alice Rineland don't even know me these days."

There was something about the lunch that was gayer than usual. An atmosphere of fun pervaded it, a sense of exhilaration was upon every one. Nancy Moore seemed in some inexplicable way to be responsible for it. There was something infectious about her approval of life. She and Major Slack immediately crossed swords verbally, the girl holding her own in a defiant little way that tickled every one immensely. It was as good as a vaudeville act.

Nancy's afternoon proved not to go as smoothly as the morning. It was extremely hot and a little of the novelty of appearing noble before the new teacher having worn off, the children became a restless, squirming, perspiring bunch. Roxy Swanson, as a self-appointed critic, took it upon herself to tell Nancy at short intervals in what particular way she taught school differently from the old teacher. Johnny Bornheimer cried softly at his desk and would not tell her why he cried. Herman Guggenmeier got on a stubborn streak and sat with his under lip hanging down. What under the sun did one do with a boy like that, wondered Nancy. Lessons she could manage. Seat work . . . she had a dozen nice ideas for it. But a boy who merely sat and did nothing with a lip hanging out like a chute from the back of a coal wagon . . . what did one do with a youngster like that? And quite suddenly Nancy, who had had dealings with many masculine creatures in her short life, with wonderful insight, decided that she would treat him just as she would treat a mature one . . . by ignoring him altogether. It had a most happy result, for finding that he created neither excitement nor even interest on the part of Miss Moore, he hauled up the coal chute, as it were, and became an active, progressive citizen.

As three-thirty arrived, Roxy Swanson with her deep knowledge of "Who's who" in the schoolroom and "What's what" arose and informed Nancy with considerable *éclat* that just before they went home every afternoon they sang the bally-fiction. As Nancy had already perceived, after a brief day's association with her, that Roxy was a juvenile Mrs. Malaprop she decided with nimbleness that she meant benediction. So they stood by their seats and bowed their heads, Jewish and Gentile, Catholic and Protestant, Fundamentalist and Modernist, and sang in at least four keys but with a great seriousness:

"Now the day is ended, night is drawing nigh . . . .
Guide us in Thy mercy . . . hear Thy children's cry . . . ."

For some unaccountable reason it touched Nancy. It was always to touch her a little, no matter how trying the day had been, that final gathering together before some vague unknown Throne and casting of their little burdens upon it. Well, she would be a good teacher to them. For the first time, she sensed a responsibility in the thing she had done. Hitherto she had thought only of herself and the half-lark she was indulging in, given heed only to her own viewpoint. Why, there was another side to it! Swiftly she visioned the children's standpoint, saw, not what freedom the year would give her, but what she might do for the children. What would they get out of life in the years to come because of her association with them? Quite suddenly, Nancy, who was not very orthodox, cast herself upon the same childish unknown Throne and made a little promise. "I'll do my best for them if You'll help me." And humble as it was, it must have reached the ears of the Head Teacher, for Nancy was to do a great deal for these little folks of the poorest ward in Maple City.

Miss Gunn, as patient as though it were only eight in the morning, went over the work with her after school. When they had finished, Nancy, with a little of that divine impulse still upon her which had come while the children were chanting the prayer, said, "Miss Gunn, I've something I want to tell you. It isn't very important maybe, and I don't know that I can just put it into words, but I took this position with little more than an impulse of pleasing myself . . . I'm pretty selfish when everything's simmered down . . . but I want you to know that this afternoon when the children were leaving, something happened to me." She laughed a little sheepishly. "For all at once I felt a great inclination to do something for them . . . every child in here . . . give every one the very best that is in me . . . make them interested in everything fine and big in life. . . ." She broke off. "That's pretty hazy and indefinite, isn't it? I guess you'll not quite understand just what I mean."

Miss Gunn stood looking at the great patches of bare ground surrounding the teeter-boards. For a moment she did not answer. Then she turned. She looked tired. Miss Gunn had taught many years. "When I was a young girl like you, Nancy," she did not even remember the "Miss Moore." . . . "I made a vow to carry the living flame of knowledge to boys and girls. I shall die some day after school has closed and they will lay me away. But something of mine can never die. There will be no more remembrance of me after a short time, but the thing I have done . . . the torches I have lighted from mine . . . do you see? . . . they will never go out with my own."

Nancy was touched as she always was touched with a

beautiful thought. Why, what a good woman Miss Gunn was! She was humorless and she was a little boresome at times. But she was fine and big and good.

In her new-found zeal, the second-grade teacher stayed until ten minutes of six. She planned her work for Tuesday, put white ruffled curtains up to the bare windows, scrubbed two imitation cut-glass vases, wrote a memory verse on the blackboard and stenciled a border of goldenrod in the front of the room.

With her hat on, she paused in the doorway and looked back. She was extremely tired from her unwonted tasks and experienced a sudden let-down of her enthusiasm. "Why did I ever decide to do it?" she asked herself. *Oh, Nancy, why did you?*

Gus Carlson came to the door and noisily deposited a mop, two brooms and a dustpan. She had a gay word for him so that he told Jen, his wife, that night, that Nancy Moore was going to be just as jolly and easy to get along with as when she was a little girl, not like that Miss Hays, who bossed him around like she was Mrs. Vanderastor and he was the butler.

As Nancy walked down the front steps, worn by the soles of a thousand shoes, she carried with her two readers, a music book, "Outlines and Suggestions For Teachers," and a load of responsibility like Bunyan's Pilgrim. As she turned up the street, a smart shining sedan drove past her. Ahead of her a little way it drew up to the curb. When she came up she saw that Alice Rineland was at the wheel waiting for her. Alice had on a clinging gown of blue with a girdle of silver. Her small hat was a Frenchy affair of blue cornflowers. She looked elaborately polished, cool and poised, and Nancy, from much reaching of high windows and much erasing of smeary blackboards, was not exactly a model of well-grooming.

"A lift, Nancy? I'll take you around or up or over or down."

"To the 'Bee-House,' James . . . providing always you can ride with as rumpled a person as I."

Alice gave her an appraising glance. "And you always like to look so pretty, too, don't you, Nancy?" she said sympathetically.

Nancy shot her a swift glance. Did these things that Alice was always perpetrating upon her intentionally have stings, or was she merely built on tactless lines? Was she cruel or merely blundering? But Alice was looking sweet and composed, and she was saying, "So you're going to teach down here in the Whittier?"

"Yes, I'm back where I started."

"However can you? I'd be so helpless and hopeless too, I suppose."

"Oh, it will be no dinner dance," Nancy admitted, "but pleasant enough I dare say."

"I don't know what I'd do if I had to get out and work."

Nancy gasped at the inference. For the flash of a moment she had a heathenish desire to tell the smug, self-satisfied girl at her side the news of her unannounced betrothal. It would be worth a good deal to see the surprised look that would come into the cool complacent face at Mr. Farnsworth's name. No, on the whole it would be more fun to keep it to herself . . . to laugh in her sleeve all year at Alice's condescension, to allow all of Alice's snobbish ways and smug statements to accumulate like a pile of dried leaves and then blow them away in the spring with one little nonchalant announcement. Nancy nearly laughed aloud at the humor of it . . . the picture of herself humbly swallowing Alice's condescension all year and then springing her news just before she left Maple City. It tickled her so much that she grinned impishly at a telephone pole. "Pity the poor working goil," she remarked with assumed pathos.

Alice sighed, "I guess I was just cut out to be a home girl."

"You do the part lovely, Alice," was Nancy's dry comment.

As they drew up to the "Bee-House," Alice darted a glance from the corners of her soft gray-blue eyes. "You're having to do without your Mr. Field to-night. I'm waiting to take him home to dinner."

It irritated Nancy. But then Alice Rineland had always possessed the faculty of rubbing her the wrong way. Tired from her unusual labors she said tartly: "Oh, save your sympathy, Alice. The Lord will let us worry through the meal somehow."

"Well, Nancy," she said to herself, as she went up the "Bee-House" walk, "you could hardly say of the short drive that a good time was had by all." As she mounted the steps, Ambrose Jones, twisting his hat in embarrassment, bowing and scraping and smiling foolishly, arose from a porch seat and plastered himself against the wall to let her pass by, so that Nancy was smiling again on her way up the wide winding stairs. On the landing she met Warner Field coming down. She waved her hand toward the big front door. "Yonder your carriage waits, m'lord . . . pumpkin, rats and the *fairy godmother*." She was laughing at him. As he looked back at her up the stairway, she was looking over the banister, still laughing gayly, her brown eyes twinkling mischievously. She had that vague, far-off, elusive manner . . . like Babbie! Babbie, who danced devilishly and wantonly through Caddam Wood! He wanted to turn around and go up after her, catch her and shake her and make her tell what she was laughing at. When he went down the front steps of the "Bee-House" one could not truthfully say that his under lip stuck out like a coal chute, but in a perfectly refined and mature way he felt like Herman Guggenmeier.

In her room Nancy paused a moment to think. What was Alice doing across Tinkling Creek in the creamery ward, so much out of place in her shining car? Had Alice deliberately waited to see her come out and to bring her home so that she might know Warner Field was going to the Rinelands' for dinner? Oh, well . . . she was capable of it. The Ethiopian hadn't changed his skin, she imagined, in four years. Then she put the thought aside for Essie was tapping at the door. She had a special delivery letter from Mr. Farnsworth and a box of roses . . . a mass of silvery-rose Caroline Testouts with cherry-red hearts. Yes, she would always be well looked after, would always be deluged with things. "Love hasn't much to do with *things*," she heard Aunt Biny's voice, patient, gentle.

Nancy divided the roses. She put some in a jar for her room and took the rest down to the dining-room table.

"And did you find it possible to instil anything in your young hopefuls' heads, Miss Moore, may I *awsk?*" Marty Spencer greeted her with his surfacelike gayety.

"A great many things, Mr. Spencer, most probably not found in the narrow confines of your knowledge," Nancy retorted. "For instance a lesson on the grasshopper." In exact imitation of Miss Hays' high childish voice she gave forth: "The mother grasshopper does not have a pretty nest as the birds do. She puts the egg in a hole in the ground and leaves it there. The little egg lies all snug and cozy all winter but when the warm days of spring come it begins to feel alive and out comes a funny little thing. He eats very much and grows very fast. And then he does a funny thing. He crawls right out of his coat and has a nice new one under it. Then wings begin to grow.

Day by day he begins to look more like his father and mother. He is very happy and very hoppy. Day by day in every way he gets *happier* and *hoppier*."

Everybody laughed for it was quite evident that Nancy was going to handle Mr. Martin Spencer as ably as she had handled Major Slack.

Up in the Italian house on the hill Alice was playing for Warner, the lovely melody of Siegmund's Love Song from *Die Walküre*. She played beautifully. She looked delicately lovely under the soft rose light of the piano lamp.

The last chord melted away. She dropped her hands in her lap. "A penny for your thoughts, Warner!" If Eve did not say it to Adam, at least Sheba's queen was guilty of it. Alice's voice was soft, caressing.

Warner rose to leave. He gave her a light evasive answer. He had been wondering what Nancy Moore was laughing at on the stairs.

CHAPTER X

THE BEE-HOUSE

WHEN Warner Field went home from the Rinelands' he involuntarily glanced up to the third floor of the corner of the "Bee-House," the tower corner that looked like a silo. A window screen swung outward and a dark head followed it. "Hst! I'm Bishop Hatto in the mouse-tower," she called down to him.

Warner, stopping on the front walk, observed that the porch was surprisingly free from its usual quota of boarders. "Come on down," he called back, "it's too nice an evening to be incarcerated at Bingen-on-the-Rhine."

So Nancy came down and the two sat on the edge of the porch under the old porte-cochère which no one in town had ever had the temerity to pronounce.

"How did the Columbuslike venture of teaching turn out on its first day?"

Nancy laughed. "Well, it has all the Ringling and Barnum shows beaten for swift activity. There are thirty-one youngsters and we have thirty-two dispositions. They do the funniest things. Roxy Swanson can mispronounce more words than she has in her vocabulary. We had a story with a Russian Cossack in it and she said she wished I'd read more about the Russian Cow-stack. This afternoon I told Jakie Cohn to sit on the front seat for the present and at recess he told me he 'set there a long time and never git no present.'"

It made Warner smile. Nancy liked to make him smile.

She liked the way his mouth relaxed its sternness and drew up at the corners and the way his eyes lost their sober, depressed look and crinkled humorously. "I think I'm going to like teaching, though, and I *love* the 'Bee-House.' It's the queerest thing to me to be living here, for I always thought this was the grandest house that it was possible for mankind to build. I used to drive past with Uncle Jud when I was a little girl. I'd be up on a load of shelled corn or maybe in the hayrack and the place had the most wonderful fascination for me. I used to feast my eyes on it as long as I could see it and wonder where in the world there was anything else so rich looking. I used to wish I could faint away out in front or fall off the lumber wagon and break some little thing like my neck and be carried in."

"And you were never in it until now?"

"Oh, yes, I was, once. Miss Ann phoned Aunt Biny one eventful day to see if she could get a setting of eggs and Aunt Biny had me come in on a load of cobs with Uncle Jud and hold the basket in my lap so nothing would happen to them. I remember it turned cold and Aunt Biny pinned a big brown shawl over my cloak. I went up to the front door with the shawl trailing along behind me like a court train. When I rang the bell old Mrs. Baldwin in her black silk and her cameo pin as big as a waffle iron came to the door. I guess she didn't know about the eggs. Anyway she said, 'What do you want?' kind of crabbed. I had been frightened stiff enough as it was just to go to the door and so when she said, 'What do you want?' I said, in a little scared voice, 'Nothing!' 'Well then, run away,' she said. And I sure would have . . . I'd have run to San Francisco, eggs and all, if Miss Ann hadn't jumped out ahead of her mother just then and ordered me fiercely to go round to the back door. She met me back there and told me snappishly to wipe my feet and come in. She set a chair for me just

inside the kitchen door, but Miss Rilla came out and asked
me if I wouldn't like to go into the library and see the
stuffed birds. The glass chandeliers and the beveled mir-
rors and the thick carpets looked like fairyland to me.
When we were standing in front of the case of old stuffed
owls and parrots, Miss Rilla suddenly put her arms around
me and drew me up to her and kissed me and cried. I
thought she was sorry for me because I didn't live in a
house like she did, but I know now, of course, that she
would cry if she looked at an oyster." Nancy grinned her
boyish grin.

"When did the old people die?"

"The Judge, when I was a little girl. I can remember him,
as pompous as a blowfish. He used to swing a wicked gold-
headed cane when he walked along the streets. And to see
him go downtown was like seeing a Cunard liner leave
port. I think one son and one daughter died before I was
born, but the old lady died just since I've been away. She
was as proud as a peacock, too, with her cap and her lace
collar and her smelling-salts. It must have galled her terribly to have the girls keep boarders. Miss Ann and Miss
Rilla used to handle her as if she were a piece of cloisonné.
She had watersacks under her eyes and her head shook like
this. . . ." Almost immediately, Nancy, in the moonlight,
had shriveled up into an old lady with tremulous shaking
head.

Warner laughed aloud. Nancy had that same degree of
satisfaction she always felt in having created a little interest
for him, temporarily broken up his graveness.

And Nancy made Warner and all the others laugh again
on the day that followed. After dinner she dropped down
on the bench of the old grand piano which Judge Baldwin
had shipped out from Chicago when Miss Ann and Miss
Rilla were small. It was past its prime, scuffed and marred,

but holding up its head proudly. Like Miss Ann! Every one stopped in the faded grandeur of the parlor while the old Judge scowled down on the usurpers. Miss Gunn was there, a little fearful that she was taking too much time from her work. Major Slack, bombastic and decisive, was there. And Dr. Pearson and Helen Blakely, gravitating together, sat down on the built-in seat by the stairway. Marty Spencer, with his superficial gayety, was there and the Kendalls in a temporary state of congeniality not warranted to last for any length of time. Ambrose Jones, the bore, stood a little to one side to let the ladies pass by . . . watching . . . watching . . . his pale eyes alight with pleasure.

"And so you sing?" Mary Mae Gates asked Nancy, her voice holding both awe and respect.

"Like Galli-Curci," the irrepressible Nancy announced. She jumped up and went back to the dining room for one of the roses which she stuck over her ear and coming back to the piano she trilled, "Non . . . non . . . non . . . non . . . non . . ." in an exaggerated operatic manner.

Mary Mae Gates was visibly horrified. It was as though one had been flippant before Euterpe. At the other boarders' applause she curtsied and then said, "And also Schumann-Heink." In some weird manner her slim boyish body seemed to swell into matronly proportions. She puffed her cheeks and the heavy notes of:

> "Morgens send' ich dir die Veilchen,
> Die ich früh im Wald gefunden. . . ."

rolled out.

Essie, laughing, stopped in the doorway with the bread-plates in her hand. Miss Rilla wiped her ever-moist eyes. "Isn't she happy and jolly?" she said to Miss Ann in the dining room.

"Isn't she noisy and forward?" was that amiable lady's retort.

To Warner she seemed a fresh breeze blowing across the monotonous desert of the "Bee-House."

By the next night Nancy's head, pedagogically speaking, was bloody but unbowed. "I thought teaching would be easy," she confided to Warner after dinner on the seat by the stairway in the big hall. "I have more problems to decide than the umpire at a world's series. And I *wish* I could remember all the funny things they say. I know Jakie Cohn asked me to-day what Hiawatha smelled. I couldn't think what he meant and then I discovered that he had reference to Hiawatha's Melody. He thought it was 'Hiawatha Smell a dee.' It made me think of myself when I was a youngster. I thought the song 'Jesus Loves Even Me,' was 'Jesus Loves Eve 'n Me,' that Adam's wife and I had a sort of monopoly on Jesus."

It made Warner laugh. From that time on Nancy found herself saving all the funny little happenings at school to tell him in order to see that humorous look that came into his sober eyes. They were fine eyes, clean and sincere looking. Something worried him and it worried Nancy to think he was worrying. It must have been something to do with his writing. Over and over she pondered on the fact that he was in a bank evidently doing nothing with his talent. She wished she could help him. But not being able to help him she did the next best thing . . . she began amusing him. Quite often the two are synonymous.

CHAPTER XI

UNCLE JUD AND AUNT BINY

UNCLE JUD MOORE was the last farmer left in the community to own no auto. Whenever he took Aunt Biny to town he still hitched up a plodding team to a two-seated surrey. If he went alone he used a rattling buckboard. It irritated him, that constant tooting of horns at his left, and the drawing over to the right of the road to let his neighbors go by. But half in stubbornness, half because he felt shy about learning to drive one of the little "pesky things" as he called them, he refrained from investing. Some of the neighbors put a great deal of money into their cars. Nick Denning, for instance, on the north, had a monstrous shining affair that would have done credit to a multi-millionaire. To be sure, they were something of an incongruous sight in it, Nick at the wheel, with his unshaven face and his wide straw hat, Mrs. Nick thin and tall and angular, with her hair screwed up in a high hard knob on top of her head, sitting stiffly in the fine upholstery of the back seat.

Nick Denning was one of the "best-fixed" farmers in the country. Some day some one may be able to arise and tell the world the reason for the financial difference in the results of the farming of two men who live side by side, whose land seems of the same degree of fertility and upon which the same sun shines and the same rain falls.

The Denning land joined Uncle Jud Moore's on the north and east. Old Nick Denning had purchased his first eighty

from the railroad company for the same cash price which
Uncle Jud had paid for his. By the time Old Nick died
he left behind him double that amount of land together with
other excess baggage which he did not need on his long
journey. Young Nick, having caught his father's falling
mantle, as it were, proceeded to hold his own in poor years
and make more money than any of his neighbors in good
years. As a result the Dennings had the finest farm buildings
on the road east of Maple City. The house was modern if
not unduly artistic, possessing a private lighting plant, steam
heat, and two bathtubs, although Nick, as a matter of fact,
did not expose himself to the slippery perils of either one
very often.

Nick owned four hundred and eighty highly improved
acres, all of the section excepting Uncle Jud's farm, much
stock, and had some money out at interest. Uncle Jud's
assets were one hundred and sixty acres with a smaller
amount of stock and twenty-five hundred dollars in time
certificates in the First National Bank.

Nick Denning had worked early and late and so had
Uncle Jud. Mrs. Denning was not extravagant. Aunt Biny
was less so if that were possible. Answer the problem!
Something in the management had made the difference,
some head work of Nick's that Uncle Jud had not exercised.
It is "X," the unknown quantity, whose identity can never
be named and after which no one can write a Q.E.D.

On this Friday afternoon in September Uncle Jud had
come in from putting in his winter wheat.

"Tireder than a dog after a skunk hunt," he complained
to Aunt Biny. "What in tunkit makes me feel so lazy?"
He dropped down in a kitchen chair, his long limbs stretched
out to another one.

Aunt Biny limped over to him and put an old Omaha
daily under his feet on the painted chair. "Maybe you need

some medicine, Pa. Like's not you've got some little ailment.
Maybe you better see Doc Minnish."

"Lord, no!" Jud Moore had never had a doctor for himself. Old Doc Minnish was one of his best friends but he
had no notion of placing himself unqualifiedly in his
hands.

"Ain't I got a bottle o' medicine around some'eres?
Bought one from a medicine man after Seeger's auction
sale. Paid a dollar for it, too. Ain't I got a lot o' that
left?" It was as though he was proud of his economy.

Ma limped into the "buttery," as she called her pantry,
and laboriously climbing a chair and pulling her lame leg
after her, went over the contents of the upper shelf. Liniment, a bag of dried catnip tea, sassafras, some outlandishly
odorous asafetida . . . the bottle of patent medicine. She
climbed painfully down and brought out the bottle.

"I ain't real sure you ought to take it without just knowing
what's the matter with you." Aunt Biny believed in dis-
playing a little caution.

The old man read the elaborate and promising label.
"Well, it's a cinch it's *one* of them things that ails me.
I'm goin' to take some. It can't hardly miss it for it's good
for everything from boils to epilepsy." He slapped his knee
and roared his enormous laughter. "Ma, j'ever hear about
the doctor that didn't know what ailed a patient 'n he
decided to give him somethin' to throw him into fits . . .
and then he could cure the fits?"

Yes, Ma had heard it. She had, in point of fact, heard it
at stated intervals for more than forty years. But she did
not let on that she had. Of such is the kingdom of happy
marriages.

After many preparatory rites in the way of getting water
ready and measuring the medicine in two different sized
spoons, Uncle Jud courageously took a dose of the con-

coction and was compelled to finish the ceremony by eating a crust of bread to take the taste out of his mouth, which he described vividly to Aunt Biny as an apparent mixture of parsnips, rotten eggs and wintergreen.

He had scarcely recovered from his unusual adventure into the realm of pharmaceutics when some one drove into the lane road. It was Major Slack, carrying his rotundity like a pouter pigeon.

"What in tunkit's a real estate man tacklin' me for?" Old Jud flung out crossly as he went out of the kitchen to meet the Major. "Keepin' me here gassin'. Got to go into town after Nancy."

The Major, florid, a little pompous, threw his challenge into the ring: "What kind of a price will you make on your farm, Mr. Moore?"

Uncle Jud spat adroitly at a chip. He felt anger rising like a tidal wave from somewhere within his huge interior. The feeling of rancor was as strong within him as the taste of quinine which lingered over his salivary glands. "Why didn't Nick Denning come to see me himself?"

The Major tapped a pair of gloves across a plump hand. "This has nothing to do with Mr. Denning or any one else. I'd merely like to have a price on it so I can list it. You're getting on in years and I have an idea you will want to be retiring soon and coming into town."

Uncle Jud straightened himself. "No, sir! No, *sir!* I've got a dozen years of farming left in me yet. I'm healthy as an ox. I'm stronger than most of the young fry." He held out enormous arms. "You can come back again, Slack, 'n ask me the price of this farm after I've put ten crops in that there barn over there."

The Major, knowing the old man meant every word, smoothed him down a little and left.

Uncle Jud went back to the house. For nearly a half

century he had turned in every pleasure and in every trouble
to one person . . . Aunt Biny, his wayside shrine. Old
Jud Moore never talked directly to God. He would have
said he did not have to. He had Aunt Biny.

Miraculously his anger left him on the way to the
house. His statement concerning his strength was mere
braggadocio. No one knew it better than he. But he did
not want to give up. He did not want to sell the old place
to Nick Denning. That was all poppycock, he told himself . . . what the real estate man had said. It was Nick
who wanted it. Casting envious eyes at the old place every
time he came along the road! It would complete the section for him. But he couldn't have it. By gad, he couldn't
have it! His anger surged up again as he went into the
kitchen. Aunt Biny looked up from her mending basket.

"Why, Pa, you worse?"

"No," he snapped, "I'm too mad to be sick."

"Why, what happened?" There was no anxiety in Aunt
Biny's voice, nor did she stop mending. Pa was a little boy
in many ways, she would have said, and only needed
handling as such to calm him.

"That fat drum major Slack was out here as swelled up
as a poisoned pup. He wanted I should put a price on the
place."

"Well," Aunt Biny's voice was gentle, unruffled, "that's
a natural thing for him to do. That's his business."

"I ain't goin' to sell the place," he growled. "They
might's well know that on the start."

"Well . . . nobody's going to make you. Now you just
cool off and go hitch up and get Nancy."

The old man left, muttering a little, like the small boy
Aunt Biny knew him to be. In the doorway he stopped. "I
got to take the lumber wagon 'n get some new two-by-fours
for the chicken-house."

"Pa . . . you ain't going to get Nancy in the lumber wagon?"

"*You've* rode on lumber more'n once. What's good enough for you's good enough for her," he scolded.

Aunt Biny sighed. It was his anger that was making him obstinate. He didn't have to get those two-by-fours to-day. He would drive up in front of the "Bee-House" for Nancy, and young people were so sensitive. It might make her angry too. She and Pa had had more than one scene in their lives. Nancy was happy and jolly, but she was tempery.

But it turned out that Nancy was not angry. And by the time the lumber wagon drew up creakingly in front of the "Bee-House" Uncle Jud was good-natured too. "What'n tunkit did I bring this lumber wagon for?" he said apologetically to Nancy, as though he had just discovered he was riding in one.

Nancy laughed, high bubbling laughter. "Now, Uncle Jud, look me in the eyes. Didn't you say to yourself, when you hitched up, that if a lumber wagon was good enough for you it was good enough for me?"

The old man grinned. "Well, now't you mention it, seems like I did notice at the time that I was hitchin' onto the wagon."

They started rumbling down the paved street through the business part of town. Marty Spencer and Warner were leaving the bank as the wagon passed. Nancy waved to them gayly from her perilously wobbling perch on the noisy vehicle. Warner found himself resenting it. He wished she would not do such a conspicuous thing on Main Street. Alice Rineland would not. . . . He caught himself up. Surely it was no business of his that Nancy Moore chose to go home that way. He had not been appointed her guardian yet, he told himself with fine sarcasm.

On Sunday afternoon, with no previous engagement to do

so he drove out to the farm to bring her back to town.
The old man unconsciously made Warner's unannounced
arrival easier, "Glad you come, Field. Saves me hitchin' up
the surrey. Gettin' lazy. Tireder'n a old plow horse
to-day."

Nancy accepted his appearance cheerfully. If it was a
trial to her, she concealed it admirably. On the way into
town she conceived the happy notion of driving into the
cemetery. So they went in under the arched iron gateway,
left the car on one of the graveled drives and walked among
the old graves. There were flowering bushes by some of
the graves and thistles by others. Nancy showed Warner
the grave of Uncle Jud's and Aunt Biny's little girl who
had slept there for forty summers. There was a group of
graves on one side of the hill that Nancy pointed out.

"It's nice, isn't it, to think they're all here together?
All these folks in this section of the yard came into
Nebraska in their wagons about the same time," she told
him. "They were a sort of clan . . . the Rays and the
Sterns and the Dennings. . . . Uncle Jud's and Aunt Biny's
old friends and neighbors. They broke the prairie and
planted the trees and lived near each other. And now they
are all neighbors yet in their little houses on the sloping
side of the hill. Isn't life queer?"

One old tombstone said: "He died an old man and
full . . ." and when they had laughed about it and pulled
the weeds away they found the sentence finished, "of
years."

Walking there in the old graveyard that afternoon with
Nancy, a gentle Nancy, who was neither mischievous nor
aloof and yet strangely alluring, Warner felt a peculiar
sense of contentment. It even seemed to suggest an end to
restlessness.

CHAPTER XII

PATRONS

O N Monday night Nancy started in to call at the homes of the children. She went first to the Bornheimers'. The house was tiny with a frail little sloping porch in front, a cardboard sort of house which the wind could have crumpled. Nancy, in front of the cheap thin door, had a feeling that she must not knock on it too hard. A young, half-frightened looking woman came to the door. Life had buffeted Mrs. Bornheimer about a good deal. Her young husband had been killed. There was some effort to get compensation from the creamery company but it went awry. She did not have a case they told her. It had been his own fault. She had been a newcomer to Maple City just before her husband's death, so Nancy had not known her. Nancy introduced herself and was invited in.

The house was clean. But there was a pinched look about everything. Nothing was plentiful. The curtains were skimpy, the rug too small. Nancy wondered if the children had enough food.

Johnny was pleased to see his teacher come in. His brown eyes lighted up as one turns on the light in bulbs. Freddy was sitting in a big chair with a quilt made from irregular patch pieces behind him. He was pale from his long illness. Nancy was a little embarrassed. With her own exuberant health she did not know for a minute just how to fit in. Above all things she wanted to show only friendliness, with no condescension in her attitude. She talked to Freddy and to Mrs. Bornheimer about him.

114

"He's getting better fast now, is he?"

"Yes . . . he's going to do just fine now, ain't you, Freddy?" The mother's voice had the assumption of cheerfulness. Nancy felt vaguely that she did not feel as optimistic as she talked.

"Doctor Pearson's taken such good care of him. He couldn't have acted more interested in a boy of his own. He's been so kind about his pay, too. He's having me make some operating gowns to help pay." She went over to the sewing machine and brought back one of the white baglike garments to show the teacher.

Nancy started to say, "Would you be glad to get some more sewing?" and changed it to, "Would you be able to take on a little more sewing . . . making some work shirts for my uncle?" Nancy gave the order on the spur of the moment. Aunt Biny had made every work shirt that Uncle Jud had ever worn, but that was no reason she always should.

Yes, indeed she would do so. She had been hemming a table cloth for Mrs. Rineland. It was a beautiful thing . . . something they bought in Omaha last summer. She went to a cheap-looking sideboard, opened the bottom drawer and took out the cloth to show Nancy.

"I wish I knew what to charge her. Mrs. Rineland says it's not worth much, just straight work like that, but I find it takes a lot of time, such tiny stitches all over and over. So I hardly know what to do."

Nancy felt a hot resentment toward the small-souled woman. "I'd certainly charge all you felt you ought to get, Mrs. Bornheimer."

The woman fondled the cloth. "I've learned to love it . . . working with it this way. It's beautiful, isn't it . . . the faint satiny wild-roses all spilled over it that way? It's for Miss Alice's hope chest I gathered from their conversation. Folks say she'll marry that nice-looking man in the bank . . . that Mr. Field."

"Is that so?" Nancy bent over the cloth to examine it. She found herself resenting *that* statement a little too.

"Johnny's doing all right in school?" the mother was asking.

"Yes, indeed," Nancy flashed her quick smile toward the boy, "he's one of my right-hand men . . . sits in the front seat and helps me a lot . . . takes care of the supplementary readers and cleans the erasers." And Johnny, succumbing no less to that smile than a few other masculine creatures had done, made high resolve to do something heroic for Miss Moore, carry her out of the burning schoolhouse maybe, or earn a quarter to buy peanuts for her.

When Nancy left, the young mother followed her out on the rickety porch. The boards gave forth little creaky sounds under their combined weight. "You go back, Johnny, and stay with brother," she ordered the teacher's gallant escort. "I wanted to tell you," she lowered her voice, "Mrs. Rineland tells me I ought to put the children in the state home for dependents. She says I'm not doing by them as well as they'd be taken care of there. But I won't do it. You don't think there's any way they could be taken without my consent, is there . . . if I work hard and take good care of them?"

"No, of course not."

"Well, I couldn't stand it. I've stood a lot and I can stand a lot more . . . but not *that* . . . not having them taken away. Mrs. Rineland said they'd have better food than I can get and that there's lots of good things about the Home. But they wouldn't have their mother's love and it seems to me that *love* is just as important as *things*."

Nancy looked up half startled. When had she heard something like that before? But the mother went on, "She

said all this before Johnny, too . . . it was one day last
week and it worried him so . . . he cried about it a lot."

That was what he had been crying about at school, Nancy
thought, when he would not tell her why he cried. Why,
how necessary it was for a teacher to know about a child's
home. How it would interpret for her his school life! And
how much the little family needed help. She wanted to
leave some money but she was not sure she ought to offer
it. There was a pride about the young woman, an inde-
pendence which kept her from making the gift. Instead she
promised the sewing with the frantic prayer that Aunt
Biny could be wheedled into giving up the annual job.

When she left she was thinking, "This is my family.
Johnny is mine. I must do something for him more than
merely assign his lessons. A real teacher is a real friend
to her pupils."

From the Bornheimers' she went down by the creamery
to the Carlsons', the janitor's home. The house was larger
than the other and more substantial, a wing-and-upright
affair set back behind a picket fence. The yard was as neat
as a pin, all the leaves raked up and the tree trunks white-
washed. When Nancy knocked, Gus himself came to the
door, a pipe in his hand. Smoking was prohibited in the
school buildings and he was embarrassed when he saw it was
one of the teachers, so he hastily slipped the offending ad-
junct into the sewing-machine drawer at the risk of a con-
flagration. The house was as tidy as the yard. It did not
have that usual jumbled look where many children live.
It was nearly supper time now and there was an odor of
cooking meat and cabbage.

"I'll call Jen, Miss Moore. Set down, set down." Gus
surreptitiously retrieved his pipe which had burned only
a few ravelings.

Nancy sat down in a rocker in the room into which she

had just stepped. It opened directly into the kitchen and she could see the table set for supper. A clothes basket was resting on two chairs near the stove and she knew the baby was in it for she could plainly hear little queer sucking sounds coming from it. The baby was only two weeks old and Jen Carlson was already thinking of starting back to the "Bee-House" for cleaning work.

In a hurried sweep of the sitting room Nancy's eye caught glimpses of the art work that the children had done at school . . . goldenrod, a green tree on a hillside, a map of the state. Suddenly she felt that she knew what school meant to these children, why the teachers of Whittier complained about them arriving before the first bell rang. And then Mrs. Carlson came in and little Emil and May and Lily were not far behind. Mrs. Carlson did not know just what attitude to take with Nancy, the familiarity of old times or deference to the children's school-teacher. She wiped her hands.

"I declare I don't know w'at to call you . . . Miss Moore or Nancy."

"Well, I know what to call you, Ma Carlson," Nancy laughed. "I remember how you mothered me when Essie and I came home from a school picnic and I was caught here in a storm and had to stay all night."

"And I was dat *ashamed* I had to put you in de same bed wid Essie and Elsa."

"Anyway, I never slept better."

"I'm dat rumpled up. You must excuse me. I been chasin' de Swansons' chickens. Their old Rhode Island Reds pester my late tomatoes, eat de insides right out and leave de skins holler. Our own Plymouth Rocks never act dat way I'm tellin' you. . . ."

"How many children are there now, Mrs. Carlson, with the new baby?"

"Eight. Ain't dat a pile? And de new one's de nicest one yet." She displayed him with many cluckings and much pride. As he reminded Nancy of nothing so much as a new little Duroc Jersey pig, it required both courage and finesse to say the approved thing.

When she had been there a little while another member of the family arrived: Elsa, younger than Essie and much better looking, home from the store where she was clerking. She was dressed simply, in excellent taste. In the way she had of getting under other people's skins, Nancy sensed that Elsa was ashamed of the house. If she could have spoken she would have said: "Oh, Nancy, this house hurts me so with its red and green rug and its oak rockers." Nancy, remembering the sensitive way she had once felt about Aunt Biny's rooms, was sorry for her. She felt a keen pity for the feelings of the young girl and an equally keen pity for the hard-working, child-bearing mother.

"How do you like your job, Elsa?"

"Like arsenic, Nancy."

"You do? Why do you stay in it?"

Elsa shrugged her shoulder. "Why do I eat?"

"What would you like to do?"

"Design costumes."

"You would?"

"Morning, noon *and* night." She jumped up and went into a bedroom, coming out again with a bunch of little watercolors.

Nancy saw at a glance that they were artistic and original. "Would you like to have me help you get into a costuming shop where you can work up?"

"I'd be dead and gone to Heaven!"

"I think I can . . . next May when I leave here. We'll talk it over later."

There was only time to make one more call. She went

in to the Swansons', next door. Like the Bornheimers they, too, had arrived since Nancy went away.

The yard was as untidy looking as the Carlsons' had been neat. A little of everything littered it, a tin can or two, a wagon wheel and some scraps of gingham. A broken ladder rested dejectedly against the front porch and a rusty corn-popper stood upright near the door.

Mrs. Swanson came to the door. She looked as rusty as the corn-popper, as dejected as the broken ladder. She was not exactly fat but she ran all together in a blurred figureless sort of way.

"Oh, it's the teacher, come in." She was unenthusiastic about it.

Inside there was the effect of a huge egg-beater having whipped up the contents of the house.

"Have a chair," the hostess invited, spiritlessly.

Nancy would have had one if any had been available, but wishing neither to sit upon a roll of dirty clothes, a pile of child's playing blocks nor a Maltese cat, she stood, hesitating.

Mrs. Swanson, eventually seeing the situation, languidly poked the cat off, the cat being one unit and not requiring the exertion needed to pick up the component parts of the dirty clothes or blocks.

Nancy, with the mental resolve to brush, clean and air her dress as soon as she got home, sat down.

The children came in, Roxy at the head of the cavalcade with the same air of leadership she possessed in school. Looking at the alert child as with new eyes, Nancy felt that it was inconceivable that she belonged to the phlegmatic, slovenly woman apparently dragging so aimlessly through life.

Mr. Swanson followed the children in. He was small and wiry looking and somewhat greasy. His stolid helpmate affected an offhand and laconic introduction by saying, "Miss Moore, this is Jim."

Nancy had an uncontrollable desire to laugh. It was all she could do to keep from saying, "Hello there, Jim." Already she was picturing to herself the joy of impersonating this interview to Warner Field. She could hardly wait to tell him about it and see the corners of his mouth relax and then curve up.

The family was almost a replica of the Carlson family. It was funny the way there was child for child in age.

Mrs. Swanson began nasally on her troubles. "Well, I suppose you seen Jen Carlson out chasin' my Rhode Island Reds. Such mean neighbors! They make everything out so big . . . such a fuss over nothings. They act like Plymouth Rocks know better how to behave . . . always talkin' like they learned them manners. I guess a Plymouth Rock's as ornery as a Rhode Island Red any day."

"Jim" agreed amiably, "That's right . . . what Myrt says. Gus and Jen set up nights tryin' to think of some way to do us dirt."

Heavens! Was this what Roxy had for her environment? If she amounted to anything it would not be through guidance or advice. Nancy looked at the child with her pretty face, her keen eyes and her young maturity. Whatever did the future have in store for her? It made her feel like warning her, protecting her, putting into the year all she could that would be a foundation for her, laid as it were on the quicksands.

Nancy made the call as short as she could consistently do. Immaculate and dainty, she had a feeling of pulling herself away from an atmosphere that was thick and sticky.

She started home. The three calls were all she could make this time. "They are my people," she thought again. She must keep in touch with the children, must know more about their dreams and visions and desires. Whatever one did, one ought to have a love of humanity with it, a watchfulness and care for the people about one. As she climbed the long slope of the hill toward Main Street she was thinking of the good a person could do by the simple process of being kind to the people with whom he worked. The churches with their ponderous creeds and their eternal questioning of beliefs . . . did they make the whole thing more weighty and complicated than it really was? After all, wasn't it merely that kindness should leaven the daily life? When Aunt Biny put the little yeast cake into the flour and potato water to make her bread it permeated the whole pan, went into every portion of the mixture and became a part of it. Wasn't that all there was to any religion . . . the whole thing that men made so ponderous and huge? If kindness just permeated your every act when you taught school or dug ditches or sold groceries or doctored a sick family . . . wasn't that all there was to it?

She was nearly late for dinner. As she went up the steps of the "Bee-House," Ambrose Jones, who had been sitting on a porch seat, rose and with elaborate bowing and scraping and smirking, plastered himself against the wall to let her pass in. "Good evening, Miss Moore." His little short foolish bows nearly convulsed her. "Do you not think it will rain before night?" It was all she could do to hold herself in.

To Helen Blakely, hurrying down the stairs to the dining room, Nancy said, "Did you ever see such an old wooden jumping-jack as that Ambrose Jones? Some day I am going to lose my head and say right out, 'Oh, no doubt, you old fossil, and some day it may even snow.'"

She hurried upstairs, got into a rose-colored dress and fastened a silver bandeau in her brown hair. She was as gay as her gown at the dinner table. Afterwards when the crowd lingered in the old reception hall with its inlaid floor and the faded grandeur of its rugs and draperies, she gave Warner Field a thrilling account of her "pastoral calls" as she called them.

"And now to sum up the points I've made in the lecture," she finished, "the three salient items are that the Bornheimers need money, the Carlsons need encouragement and the Swansons need baths."

And Warner laughed, his sober mouth and serious eyes breaking up into mirth, just as Nancy wanted them to.

CHAPTER XIII

THE DIARIES CAST THEIR SHADOW

BREAKFAST at the "Bee-House" was not the social meal of the evening dinner. It was served at any time a boarder came down. Miss Ann specified a law that was like unto the Persian . . . no one was to be served after eight-thirty. As every one but Genevieve Kendall had to be at work by that time it was no hardship. To be sure Nancy Moore, with one brown eye on the clock, sometimes breezed in as one coming under the ropes at the last moment. But on Tuesday morning almost every one was at the table. Major Slack was there in pleased and pompous contemplation of a stack of griddle cakes. Mary Mae Gates was there, brain-weary already at the thought of the long day before her in which she was to further the music of the spheres. George Kendall, cross from having played bridge so late, was in his place, but Genevieve was still upstairs, getting her beauty sleep. Miss Gunn was there, breakfasting slowly, eating so-many carbohydrates and so-many proteids, chewing so-many times on this bite and so-many times on that. Helen Blakely was there, her thoughts serving two masters at one time, an outline for her English class and Dr. Pearson across the table. Ambrose Jones darted his head foolishly around that he might not miss what any one was saying. But his gyrations were quite useless for no one was saying anything. At least not until Nancy arrived gay and breathless in a brown dress and a chic little hat over her brown hair.

124

By a mere chance of circumstance Nancy and Warner came into the long dining room at the same time. "Here come the Grave Digger and the Sassy One," Marty Spencer remarked, sotto voce, to the others.

Nancy heard him but she did not let on. The quiet around the table disappeared before her chatter. Every one warmed up. She had that faculty always. The moment she descended upon them, the ice crackled a little and then broke. She had spent the evening before writing some invitations for a class reunion picnic out at the farm, she told them all.

"They're quite clever," she assured them blithely; "by a stretch of imagination one could almost think that Marty Spencer might have written them."

Every one laughed at the turn of the table. Nancy passed the invitations around. They read:

"Backward, turn backward, Oh Time, in your flight,
Make me a Senior again just for to-night."

The verses ended quite touchingly with:

"Rock me to sleep, mother,
Rock me to sleep.

(Bring a rock with you)."

Essie, plain and neat as usual, came in with Nancy's toast. "A little billie-doo, Essie!" Nancy handed the girl her envelope.

Essie looked at the invitation and her face lighted up, then it clouded. "I don't suppose I can go," she whispered, "at dinner time that way."

"Oh, yes, you can, I'll talk to Miss Ann about it."

Essie carried her invitation in her waist all day where it clung like a little memory come to life.

After the noon lunch she took it out and read it again in the kitchen. Then she started in on the long dishwashing job. Miss Rilla always helped with the breakfast dishes but Essie did the lunch ones all alone while Miss Rilla lay down for a while. Miss Ann did not lie down. She considered it a weakness. Nothing about Miss Ann ever relaxed, her body, her mind, her thoughts, her vigilance.

The great mass of sticky dishes was piled around Essie now. They surrounded her whole life. She would never be able to climb over them into the outside world. As she cleaned and stacked them she was wondering why it took so many to feed a few people. Who was the lunkhead that had invented bread and butter plates? And why did one person have to use more than one spoon? They went into the same mouth, didn't they?

As she started washing the glasses from the big pan in the sink, she could feel the little invitation against her breast. That was nice of Nancy to get up the reunion. But she couldn't go. She scarcely had the nerve to ask Miss Ann to get off and would rather not ask at all than be let off grudgingly.

It made her fall to thinking about Nancy Moore. What she really wanted to do was to hate Nancy. But try as she would, she couldn't even dislike a girl who was so nice to her. She had been sorry beyond words when she had heard that Nancy had come back to Maple City and then to live at the "Bee-House," for she had thought she was gone for good. And now Nancy was here and already she was liking her again, just as everybody liked her. As Walt Thomas liked her! Essie fell into a daydreaming which certain efficient specialists say is a form of dementia. Ah, then, how demented most of us are!

She was on the silver now, washing away mechanically and summoning Walt Thomas into her mind in a way that made him seem almost real. It was the high-school class picnic four years before that pictured itself in her thoughts. The class had gone over to the woods beyond Postville and right after supper she had wandered off to pick some flowers and had turned back in the wrong direction. While she was trying to decide which way to go somebody had hallooed and it was Walt Thomas looking for her.

"Well, Essie, what you trying to do . . . give us the slip and elope with somebody?" She could remember every word. He had taken her arm and helped her up the bluff. There had never been another moment like it in her life.

And Walt loved Nancy. She had always known it. Every one in high school had known it. And now that Nancy was back, he would be with her some more. Mr. Field was paying a lot of attention to Nancy too. He had limbered up since she had come, had sort of come to life. How pretty Nancy was! Why couldn't everybody be like her? Her hands still in the steaming suds, Essie turned and looked across at herself in the kitchen glass. She had two eyes and hair and a mouth too, just as Nancy had. But what a difference! Her eyes . . . how pale blue they looked . . . and Nancy's were big and brown and full of something like bright lights that came and went. Her mouth . . . how straight and big it was . . . and Nancy's had a butterfly curve to it over pretty teeth. Her hair . . . taffy-colored and stringy . . . and Nancy's was soft and brown and fluffy. How disgusting she looked in the glass with her face moist from the heat. Her hands . . . she pulled them up from the water. Red as flame and swollen.

What made such a difference between two girls anyway? Besides her good looks Nancy had gone away to school and knew lots more now than she. High school had been the end for her. She had stayed home a year to do the work and then Miss Rilla had come down to see if she would help for a week or two. That was three years ago and she had been here ever since. She was good for nothing but housework. Something told her there was nothing else in the world she could do well.

Why was life made up of things one had to do? Why couldn't duty and desire lie in the same direction? Always duty went one way and desire pulled another. What if some magic wand could be waved and give her a wish! She glanced furtively around. Miss Ann and Miss Rilla were in the front of the house. Mrs. Carlson was upstairs cleaning. It made her feel less ashamed of her dream because she was alone. This was it: To marry Walt Thomas and live with him. Every day. To do dishes just for herself and Walt . . . to cook for him . . . and raise chickens . . . and have a flower garden. *And a baby*. It was wicked to think like that. But she didn't care. Nobody could enter into that inner place in her brain where the dream lay. And nobody would ever know it. She and Walt and a baby . . . that was her wish, right out plain in her mind. Miss Ann opened the kitchen door and Walt and the baby hastily vanished into the land from whence they had come . . . the land that was only desire.

All afternoon Essie went about her tasks, hope of anything different drowned in a sea of boarding-house dishwater. All afternoon she took orders.

"Essie," Miss Ann would say, "get the things ready for the potato salad as soon as you are through. And don't forget that Miss Gunn doesn't want any and we'll have to have something else for her. There are carbohydrates in the potato salad. My soul . . . you'd think they were some kind of crawling bugs, to hear her."

"Essie," Miss Rilla would say, "will you please ice my cake? You do it just as well as I do now." Miss Ann gave commands. Miss Rilla made requests.

At four-thirty o'clock, Miss Ann opened the door from the old butler's pantry and put out her head.

"Essie, there's Walt Thomas driving in with the load of cobs. I happened to hear the crunching on the drive. Go out and tell him to push all the old ones to the far end of the shed first."

Essie, half frightened at the news, as though her thoughts might have called Walt out bodily from that country of the heart, wiped her hands and gave her hair a swift pushing into shape. She went down the back steps and out past the fancy old barn. There he was swinging down easily from the high lumber wagon. He looked very big and fine and strong.

"H'lo, Essie," Walt spoke good-naturedly in that disinterested way that she had long since schooled herself to expect.

"H'lo, Walt. Miss Ann sent me to tell you to please push the old cobs back to the far end first." Miss Ann had not said "please" but every translator reserves some privileges.

Walt threw back his head and laughed. "As though I wouldn't have had the gumption to. That old lady ought to have been a section boss."

Essie laughed too. It seemed a relief to hear some one criticize Miss Ann herself, the way she picked at other people.

"Did you get an invitation to the doings?" Walt asked.

Her heart leaped against her throat. "Yes."

"Is Nancy home from school yet?"

Essie's heart settled back. "I think so."

"Ask her if she'll run out here a minute, will you?"

So Essie called Nancy, who had just come in, and went on with her dinner work, a plodder with nothing but dreams for hyacinths upon which to feed her soul. Nancy ran out to the cob shed with, "Hello there, Walter, led-by-the-halter," an old phrase from their childhood.

Walt wanted to take Nancy to the class reunion.

"But Essie and I are going to put up our lunch together," she said frankly.

Walt grinned. "Then you mean I've got to ask Essie too?"

"Yes, I do. United we stand, divided we fall . . . short of eatables."

So when Walt was through with his work he tied the team to the cobhouse door and went up to the back porch. "Essie, I'd like to take you and Nancy to the picnic," he told her, "unless you've a date for it."

Walt might have known she had no date. She flushed so that it left her wistful face half pretty. Of course she knew it was all Nancy's doings, but she was too kind-hearted to embarrass him by saying so. "Why, thank you, Walt," she said, "I'd like to go."

Upstairs Nancy was dressing to make another call. She was going up to the Rinelands' to return Alice's and her mother's visit at the farm. She dressed carefully, with many backward thoughts to the time when her clothes had been so neatly and so clumsily made by Aunt Biny. Satisfied with results, she left the "Bee-House" and went up the hill to the Italian Renaissance house.

The grounds were well platted with shrubbery but it was small yet and the newness of the place accentuated by it.

Nancy stepped up to the formal entrance and lifted the gondola-shaped knocker. "It's a wonder they didn't dig a canal in front and build an imitation Bridge of Sighs across it," she thought.

No one came. Nancy knocked again. Then she slipped some cards in the door and left. She could not know that Mrs. Rineland had peeked cautiously out from behind the rose and lace draperies and when she saw who it was had decided not to go to the door. Alice was not at home. She was glad of that for she was not anxious to have Alice "get thick" with the girl.

The class reunion with its picnic supper was to be on Wednesday. Miss Ann growled a little when Essie broached the subject to her. Miss Rilla came to the rescue with tears in her eyes. "I'll do as much of her work as I can, sister, if you will let her go."

But it was Nancy who walked up to the stiff Miss Ann and slipped supple arms around the hard unyielding waist. "Miss Ann, you know down in your heart you wouldn't have Essie the only one to miss this for the world, now, would you?"

Miss Ann's face relaxed a little but she held herself stiffly and gave forth, "Well, I know *somebody's* got to be working in this world all the time. And it seems like it has to be *me*."

Walt came for the girls with his cheap car all clean and shining. And Walt, too, was clean and shining even though he was as brown as the corn-tassels in the late September fields. When he saw the girls with their basket in the old reception hall he was not sorry he had been inveigled into asking Essie too. Essie was a nice girl. She wasn't lovely like Nancy but she was neat and he sort of liked her. She was so quiet and didn't worry a fellow. Nancy now could make him feel pretty cheap sometimes when she talked off on a tangent over some fool thing so that he didn't more than half get her. But Essie was easy to understand.

Warner Field came up the front walk just as they were leaving. "Don't you wish you had graduated from the Maple City High School four years ago?" Nancy smiled at him as they passed.

"Don't I, though?" Warner smiled too. It was easy to

smile with Nancy Moore. Her gayety seemed infectious.
Up in his room he told himself that he had better watch his
step. He had known her a scant three weeks and already
was thinking too much about her. She was saucy but she
had a certain charm for him. At times she was flippant but
she fascinated him. She was really not the type that he
admired at all. To be quite specific Alice Rineland was the
type he admired . . . gentle, womanly; soft-spoken. And
he had never been able to shake off the knowledge that
Nancy had left her uncle's home under some sort of a
cloud. Granted that he should never have known it, the
fact remained that he did know. Conceded that he had been
all kinds of a cad to have read those diaries, the fact remained that he had done so. In his room he went over
and over the memory of the diaries again. Those last pages
he knew by heart. She had been happy and contented and
then something had happened. No small thing either, for
it had driven her away from a good home, and she had not
been back until now. "Something has happened . . . something dreadful. My mind is crowded with a thousand
things to write. But I shall never write in you again. Good-
by, little diaries. Good-by, thrushes and lilacs and orchard and Tinkling Creek! Good-by, my prairie! And
most of all, good-by, Nancy Moore! Oh, Nancy Moore, I
loved you. Good-by."

He stood by the window, looking down in the "Bee-
House" yard, unseeing. What was it? What had happened?
He had reason to believe Walt Thomas knew. The only
thing he could think of was . . . damnable. He whirled on
his heel as though to walk away from the sickening picture
which his mind had conjured. No, she had been sweet and
lovely. All through the girlish diaries she had been like
a fragrant breeze. And she was, now . . . sweet and
lovely . . . and like a fragrant breeze. With his hands in

his pockets he walked about the room restlessly thinking
it over. If he himself had kept decent it was because of
a certain self-respect and not because he hadn't seen rotten
things on all sides of him. They happened . . . everywhere. But not to Nancy. He was clenching his fists . . .
not to Nancy Moore! He brought himself up with a jerk.
Why should he *care?* He would stop thinking about it . . .
one way or the other. It was her own secret, whatever it
was. He had troubles enough of his own without adding
to them a by-gone incident in the life of a girl he had
known three weeks and who was not laboring under any
weight of trouble herself. He had control of himself again,
was grinning at the idea of Nancy Moore, the light-hearted,
crushed under any burden of woe. This was the last time
he would ever give a thought to it. If he was going to stew
around like an old woman, he had his own financial worries
to think about. He had four hundred dollars saved toward
the debt. A heck of a lot, wasn't it, he said to himself
sarcastically. At this rate he'd be in his dotage by the time
it was canceled. Yes, he had lots of reason to give any
thought to a girl, he said dryly. After which decision he
proceeded to lie awake that night until he had heard
Nancy's high bubbling laughter down on the porch.

At the breakfast table Warner asked the little waitress
girl, "Did you have a nice time last night, Essie?"

"I should say . . . the best time!" Essie broke into a
happy girlish smile. "But we wouldn't if it hadn't been
for Nancy. She stirred everybody up. She made us all
feel like we were kids again. She gave every one some work
to do. She sent Walt Thomas and me after dead branches
to make the fire, and she got Alice Rineland to dish up the
lemonade and pass it around to us." Essie giggled as though
a great event had been consummated. She glanced around.
It was early and there was no one in sight but Major Slack,

in fond and silent contemplation of his cakes. She said it almost savagely, "Nancy Moore is the loveliest person I ever knew."

Warner Field wondered whether he was in any state of mind to argue the point with her.

CHAPTER XIV

THE PRAIRIE PEOPLE LIVE

OCTOBER in the mid-west, when she lives up to tradition, is a beautiful thing. Great splashes of brilliant maples, shining bronze-leaved oaks, elms as tawny as a lion's mane! Scarlet-flamed sumac, walnuts bursting their green leathery cases, pears clinging to sepia-colored branches. The winter wheat, looking out of place as though it had come at the wrong time, is faintly green in patches against the brown of the newly plowed earth and the tan of the cornfields. There is a haze on the hills, a soft blue far-away haze, that is dissipated as one rides into it. It seems to cling between the hills but when one descends into the valley it is not there. It is a mysterious thing . . . to disappear . . . and then to be seen in the distance again . . . ghostly smoke from the Indian campfires of long ago.

It is the month when the winds cease. There is a quietness upon the earth as though nature had set aside the month for prayer. The evenings are cool, the nights frosty, the mornings balmy, the afternoons warm as summer, only to slip again into the cool of evenings and the frostiness of nights. And over all hovers that brooding calm, that hush in the temple of God.

It always intrigued Aunt Biny. Long moments she would stand on the back porch and look to the rim of the prairie. The hills swelled and dipped, black with their newly turned earth, yellow with their wheat stubbles, tawny brown with their corn, green with the first faint promise of winter

135

wheat. The picture satisfied her very soul . . . the fulfillment of the miracle of spring. She thought many beautiful
things standing there leaning on her crutch. She found
voice for them in words that rose to her lips from the
depths of a thankful heart. "I will lift up mine eyes unto
the hills . . . from whence cometh my help. . . ." Aunt
Biny's schooling had been limited, and her experiences circumscribed; her days had been filled with pain, and her
life held its sorrow; but the words of her mouth and the
meditations of her heart were acceptable in His sight.

Uncle Jud had none of her definite expression of thankfulness. He only knew that he liked his farm, that there
was no place else on earth he would live. He had that one-
ness with the land which the faithful have, a feeling that he
was as rooted there as the things which grew and thrived
and bore for him. To have a neighbor find fault and move
away to another state was to rile Uncle Jud into a wrath beyond understanding. For months he talked of nothing else.
"Must think he's goin' to paradise," he would say crossly.
"What more's he want than good old Nebraska?"

Nebraska was a person to him, a living personality. He
spoke of it as "she" and extolled her virtues as one would
compliment a woman. "How'd they get along without her
wheat 'n corn 'n meat 'n butter 'n eggs 'n potatoes 'n apples, you tell *me*, will you?" He would argue one-sidedly
with people who had not even contradicted him. He would
have been as loyal, of course, toward any other state in
which he had located. Faithfulness, loyalty, they were part
of him. He had fought prairie fires. He had seen grasshoppers take the last green bit of his crops. He had seen the
wind in its madness lay them low. He had watched the hail
strip his corn as clean as the grasshoppers had done and in
far less time. He had seen drought hang over the land like a
huge spirit of malediction. But he did not blame Nebraska.

She was like a woman to him, ill, in trouble, and sad. He was more sorry for her than for himself who had to stand by and watch the consequences of her illness. He would no more have thought of reviling and leaving her than of reviling and leaving Aunt Biny when she had one of her bad spells.

Nick Denning on the north particularly irritated Uncle Jud at times. "What d' we get out of it all?" he would say to Uncle Jud. "Work from morning till night, take cheap hogs to market and bring home high-priced sugar and coffee. Take cheap cream in and bring home sky-high shoe leather and the middlemen getting the profits with the farmer at the bottom of the heap."

"Doggone it, Nick," Uncle Jud would snap back . . . "You're always wantin' to know what you get out of it. You get a darn good home. Your children get the finest kind of an education. You get a plenty to eat. You ride in a big car like John D.'s and nobody tells you 'this is the day you gotta do so-'n-so'; 'n you get the feelin' that you're livin' in the best state in the union. That's what you get out of it."

On the first Sunday afternoon in October Nancy came into the sitting room where the two old folks sat. The big coal burner stood now in its place, its huge blackness as shiny as an Ethiopian, its nickel trimmings burnished to a mirrorlike surface. There was no fire in it. Its isinglass gave forth only hollow depths of gray. Uncle Jud with the help of Walt Thomas had devoted a half day on Saturday to the task of getting the bulky thing into place. It was a ceremony that he performed every fall on the first Saturday in October regardless of weather conditions. "You never can tell," he would opine. "I ain't goin' to be caught in a cold snap with me in the house 'n the stove in the barn."

The two old folks were having a little argument about it now.

"Ought to a-built a fire in it the minute it was set," Uncle Jud was complaining. "Chilly in here right now."

"Why, Pa! No!" Aunt Biny contradicted gently. "It's so warm and mild everywhere to-day."

"No 'tain't . . . not in here. I just's soon be plum cold 'n be done with it . . . as that kind-a-chilly way with little waves of it up 'n down your backbone."

Nancy stood looking fondly at the two. She had a maternal feeling toward them. They had taken her when she was tiny and cared tenderly for her, and she had grieved them sorely. She was making up for it this year, was trying to think of all the things she could do for them to make amends. Just now, hearing the argument, she said suddenly, "Folks, why don't you sell the place and go to California? It would be just fine for you . . . so mild and nice and you could be out so much all winter. Why, it's just the thing. Why haven't we talked about it before?" She was waxing enthusiastic as she always did over any subject.

Uncle Jud flew up immediately. "Sell nothin'. What's the matter with folks! That's what I hear on all sides lately. Nobody's been talkin' to me about anything but sellin'."

"Pa, Pa!" Aunt Biny cautioned him. "Not a soul beside Nancy has said a thing to you but Major Slack."

"Well, that's enough, ain't it?"

"Now, why don't you, Uncle Jud?" Nancy came and sat down on a stool near him. "What's the place worth, one hundred and seventy-five dollars an acre?"

"A hundred seventy-five, nothin'! Two hundred if it's worth a cent."

"Well, so much the better. That's thirty-two thousand

dollars. Why, that's fine! And what else have you, Uncle Jud . . . in the bank?"

"Twenty-five hundred dollars on time."

"Good . . . and the corn this year and some of last . . . and the stock and machinery. How much more would that bring?"

"Oh, maybe two thousand more."

"All right . . . say thirty-six thousand and out at interest would bring you . . . let's see . . . five times six . . . eighteen hundred dollars a year. That's only a hundred and fifty dollars a month. I wonder if you could live on a hundred and fifty a month?"

"My, the fifty would be plenty," Aunt Biny contributed, "for just Pa and me."

Nancy laughed. "You blessed old Aunt Biny . . . how far do you think fifty dollars would go if you got away from home? About as far as that little candle throws its beams, and 'the good deed shines in a naughty world.' You folks don't realize what you've had on the farm . . . milk, cream, butter, meat, chickens, eggs, soap. When you start to buy these things, Aunt Biny, you'll think you had a big income here. And anyway you wouldn't have to live on the hundred and fifty. Get into the principal of your money for at least a thousand dollars or more a year. It's yours, and who else is entitled to spend it? I'd like to see you use every cent for yourselves, and not leave it for relatives to scrap over. You folks must do this now . . . plan to sell right away. When I leave in May you go back to Indiana and then to California in the fall."

"Well, I ain't goin' to quit farmin' for a while and that's all there is to it," Uncle Jud finished crossly.

But by the time Warner Field drove into the yard in the early evening Uncle Jud's crossness had left him. A casual reference of Warner's to the splendid corn crop had set him off, taken him back to that old pioneer past of which he was so fond.

" 'Tain't much like eighteen seventy-four, Field. That's the year the grasshoppers come. 'Twas in July. Crops was all doin' well. Corn was knee high 'n better. Gardens was full of tomatoes 'n radishes 'n potatoes 'n onions. Was early afternoon and the' come up what looked like a big cloud from the west 'n covered the sun. 'Twan't no cloud a-tall. 'Twas them pesky grasshoppers. First we knew here 'n there a grasshopper kept droppin' on the ground. All at once they just come down . . . rained down . . . poured down . . . the sons-of-guns! They covered everything . . . a crunchy, wiggly, crawlin' mass of 'em.

"They started to eat their supper . . . and doggone it . . . it was some supper. First time I'd see Ma cry since we come West. Set down with her apron over her head and cried. Couldn't look at her garden she'd worked so hard on, bein' et up. One of the first things they et was onion tops. Wasn't stylish grasshoppers a-tall. Liked 'em fine. Et 'em clean off to the ground so's you'd never know was onions there. Ma 'n me saw the' was no savin' the corn so we come a trick on 'em. Next night they got sluggish 'long supper time. 'N we went out to the garden and drove 'em off into the cornfield. Took brooms 'n swept 'em 'n drove 'em. Had a well, you know, with bucket 'n rope. Had to keep the bucket covered tight 'n the well too. Or we'd pump 'em up."

"How long did they stay?"

"Stay? Lord, they wa'n't sensitive. They stayed all summer. Wore their welcome out 'n stayed on. Et up everything and laid their eggs for the next year. Et? Lord, Field, they et the handles off the pitchforks and that ain't a joke either. It's the A'mighty's truth. Bored in 'n et the soft wood handles off the pitchforks. Darn near et my coat off my back. Went up to old man Denning's . . . Nick's father . . . 'n when I got there had a hole as big as a saucer in the back of my coat."

"How did you live? What did you eat?"

"Well, we lived some on potatoes and some on charity, I can tell you that. Folks from Iowa 'n Illinois sent carloads of grain out. Had some in the stores at Maple City 'n distributed it around. After the pesky things started hibernatin' Ma found a big beet under some boards 'n boxes that the things had missed. Had Dennings come down to dinner, 'twas such a treat."

"And yet . . . you stayed on." Warner's wonderment was genuine.

"Oh, lots of settlers was scared out. That was enough of Nebraska for them. But Ma, she kept tellin' me she knew the Lord wasn't goin' to pick on Nebraska long. If we'd stay 'n keep the commandments . . . " he winked at Warner, . . . " 'n say our prayers every night 'n plant some more crops, she reckoned the Lord would see us through. Well, I made a bargain with her," he said soberly. "I agreed to plant the crops all over the next year if she'd keep the commandments 'n do the prayin'." He slapped his knee with his huge hand and roared. "Worked fine. Good team work." He roared again. "Me workin' like a son-of-a-gun 'n Ma keepin' the commandments 'n prayin'."

"Pa! Pa!" Aunt Biny remonstrated. It worried her . . . to have Warner think that Pa was sacrilegious.

When Warner and Nancy drove away, Warner was still thinking about it . . . the hardihood, the faith, the courage of the people who stayed and saw the thing through. What a stupendous thing they had done for the country! He expressed these thoughts to Nancy. "It was war, wasn't it? The whole frontier was a battleline. They fought for civilization. The enemy was nature herself in all her primitiveness. The new furrows from the virgin soil were the trenches. They buried some who fell by the way. Others deserted. There was not even army discipline to keep them steadfast. Their own decision, their own courage bade them stay. Those who grew fainthearted could return East unrebuked. The more I see of your Uncle Jud Moore the more he seems a great personality . . . a man who had the faithfulness and the valor to fight for civilization. And your Aunt Biny, a gentle woman who would have been safer and more comfortable in the old eastern home, urged him to stay . . . a frail woman standing at his side as though to hand him the ammunition with which to conquer. And they *have* conquered, haven't they . . . your Uncle Jud and those others?" Warner threw out his hand to take in the picture. The country on either side of the two young people in the roadster lay bathed in the afternoon October sunshine. The road over which they were driving had once been an Indian trail but conforming to the compass of the surveyor now ran straight before them, hard packed as a pavement shining with the countless travel of huge cars. Great fields of cornstalks heavy with the golden ears of their bearing stood on every side awaiting the last two weeks of their maturing.

"Nebraska is conquered," Warner went on. "Like a huge giant it lies with man's foot on its supine body. Fields are fertile. Orchards are fruitful. Pastures yield their heavy gifts. There are cattle on a thousand hills. Great consolidated schools, substantial and comfortable, flags without and libraries within, center in many districts. And all in one man's lifetime! What a heritage your Uncle Jud and his coworkers have given to the new generations!" Nancy did not know whether he had finished . . . or paused, but she turned to him, her brown eyes glowing. "Write it . . ." she said.

That night Warner slept fitfully.   Around two o'clock he turned and tossed and half awoke.   He did not know whether he had been dreaming or whether, having pondered much on the subject, he was still merely thinking of it. Whether the thing lay in his conscious mind, was buried in the subconscious one or on the borderland between the two, he was not sure.   He only knew that he lay quietly, almost shaken with the reality of the vision.   The wagons crept slowly over the prairie . . . brawny men in them . . . and gentle women.   From one of them a girl slipped out and stood on the brow of the hill . . . a long low rolling hill and laughed gayly as she pointed toward a creek with its fringe of cottonwoods and wild plums.   She had warm brown eyes and brown hair and the curve of her chin and throat was a lovely thing to see.   She was like a candle in the dusk . . . a flame in the dark.   So vivid was the picture that he lay still, almost fearful that the thing would vanish like a mirage.   He had the dual sensation of looking on and being one of the men.   He saw himself hasten to the top of the low hill to join the girl, fearful that she might go on without him.   As he neared the top of the hill she threw him a laughing, tender glance over her shoulder and the flame of her vanished into the west and mingled with the sunset.

His pulses were throbbing.   His mind, too, seemed pulsing with its effort to catch and hold the half-dream.   Suddenly he rose, threw on his bathrobe and sat down at his desk.   He wrote quickly, enthusiastically, warmed by the fire of his emotions.   The pages he cast hurriedly to one side so that they made an untidy mass around him.   He merely outlined, touched rapidly the high points of the story.   Like a sculptor he was shaping the first big crude form from clay.   Later would come the real writing.   Tonight he was only catching the idea that, like the dream it was, might be gone in the morning. He wrote feverishly. Clay in the hand of the potter! What matter that other people had written it? What matter that it was only one more approach to the romantic history of the building of the mid-west? No one had written *his* story. Each one sees life differently. No one had felt the same sympathy with the adventure of the man in the prairie-schooner who was to wrestle with the land and in time to put his foot on the supine body of the giant. No one had seen the elusive charm of the brown-eyed girl standing on the brow of a hill and pointing to the rim of the prairie. And no one had felt the sweeping love that the man bore for the girl who was like a candle in the dusk . . . a flame in the dark.

Not in all those weary months since his father's affair and his illness had his mind gathered together its forces as it was doing now. He felt for the first time the old thrill in constructing, an excitement in working, a pleased expectancy for the result. He had the old sensation of hot blood coursing through his veins, of being unable to write fast enough, a tingling and tenseness of nerves. It was the old fire. When he went to bed it was nearly dawn. Tired from expending so much emotional energy he still had that strange exultation over catching and caging the flying evading thing he had sought. With a great feeling of thankfulness he lay down. The lost word . . . was it coming back to him? The terrible cloud of worry which had hung over him . . . was it to be dispelled?

After breakfast he hurried to the bank with a new elation upon him. Rather it was a renewed elation for he had felt it many times before, that pleasure in catching a fleeting vision and holding it. He begrudged the mechanical hours before him at his work. A few weeks ago he had said he would forget his writing and give his entire time to enlarging his knowledge of the business. Already he had a feeling of disloyalty to Mr. Rineland, knowing that the months were numbered in which he would want to sacrifice so much precious time.

He went into the bank. The school bells were ringing. A groceryman came in to deposit his Saturday night receipts. Jim Swanson came in to see if he could borrow two dollars and fifty cents. Once more the day's grind had begun.

CHAPTER XV

THE FRIENDSHIP PROGRESSES

ON that first Monday night in October the boarders lingered about in the old reception hall, listlessly, a little aimlessly. No one seemed to know just what to do. It had taken Nancy to start things and keep them going and Nancy was not there.

Warner Field did not even stop in the hall but sprang up the long curving stairs boyishly. His evening's work was before him. He went to it in a pleased frame of mind, hopefully, and with keen interest. When he closed the door of his room it was as though he shut it upon the boarders and the mechanical work of the bank and closeted himself with the prairie people.

One by one the boarders drifted to their rooms, all but Dr. Pearson, who had a date with a patient, and Marty Spencer, who had a date with a girl.

Nancy was in the kitchen. "I came out to wipe the dishes," she had announced to Essie, when she breezed in. The kind act brought the tears to Miss Rilla's eyes.

"I guess Essie can do it herself," Miss Ann said a little snappishly. She had been around town paying the bills of the past month and it made her cross to think the boarders had consumed so much provender.

"I wish I could feed them on oatmeal and kippered herring a whole month until I got ahead," she had said savagely to Miss Rilla.

But Nancy wiped the dishes. It took more than Miss

Ann's growling to phase Nancy Moore. When she had finished, she said, frankly, "Now, Miss Ann . . . all I ask for pay is that you'll let me make a batch of candy."

Miss Ann was amazed. No boarder had ever had the temerity to come into the kitchen, to say nothing of dipping into the food supplies. She protested crossly, "Everything will be sticky and what will you have to show for it?"

"Nothing will be sticky . . ." Nancy coaxed, "and I'll have the best tasting stuff you ever let melt in your mouth to show for it."

To Essie it was nothing short of miraculous to hear Miss Ann's grudging, "Well, go ahead, and leave things clean."

When the candies were finished the maker and finisher of them went to the various doors on the second and third floors with her "burnt offerings" as she called them. She knocked first at Warner Field's. When he answered her knock she asked, "Fudge or taffy?" and added pertly, " 'Better fifty years of Fudge than a cycle of Taffay.' "

She took the opportunity to dart a glance in Warner's room. She could see papers everywhere around his desk. And the typewriter stood open with a paper in it. He was working at his writing again. For some reason she was unaccountably glad.

She tapped at Ambrose Jones's door. He opened it a few inches so that only one eye showed. Nancy could scarcely keep her face straight. When he saw who it was he slipped out from the smallest possible opening and closed it tightly behind him. Nancy grinned to herself to see him so fearful and so disturbed. Outside he scraped and smiled and bowed over and over against the tightly closed door of his room.

She went to the Kendalls'. She could hear them talking. They were not very discriminating in the choice of tones with which they were addressing each other. She could hear

George, "Fat chance I have of getting anything ahead."
Genevieve's voice rose pettishly, "You wouldn't care if I
went around looking like a gypsy." Nancy stood her ground.
She was not going to run away. When Genevieve came to
the door her voice changed, "How lovely, Nancy!" Nancy's
lip curled. What a marriage!

She went to Major Slack's door. The Major swung the
door open wide. He was pompous, and pleased. Behind
him Nancy could see the tray of a trunk across two chairs.
He waved his hand toward it. "My pictures and diaries of
the Spanish-American War," he explained concisely. "I've
been looking at the one and reading the other. This is the
date on which we received orders from Major General Lee,
ordering the Seventh Army Corps to make arrangements to
proceed to Savannah in preparation to embarking for Cuba.
General Lee had been in Washington and the order came
from there." He would have gone on indefinitely if Nancy
had not started away. He munched his candy with superior satisfaction. The Major liked to eat. "He should
have married Mattie Thomas," Nancy thought as she left.
"It would have been an ideal combination."

She tapped at Miss Gunn's door. Miss Gunn had on a
green eye shade. She held her finger in a closed book of
portentous size. "I was reading about our ancestors, the
monkeys. When you came I was so far in the past I could
scarcely bring myself into the present to think who you
were."

Nancy's high mirthful laughter bubbled forth infectiously.
"Miss Gunn cracked a joke and didn't know it," she told
Helen Blakely.

All evening and far into the night Warner wrote. The
story was unfolding rapidly. Nancy Moore seemed to be
in it . . . not this modern Nancy but a pioneer girl of the
same gay spirits braving the hardships of the new country.

She was part of the prairie . . . the breath of it. She came out of the sunrise and rode into the sunset.

Miss Ann and Miss Rilla in their own room on the second floor, spent the evening in discussing their finances. They sat there together, similarity in their looks, their navy blue dresses with white lace fichus made just alike. But Miss Ann was discouraged, Miss Rilla was optimistic.

"It's no use," Miss Ann decided, "it's making no money. For all the work I hardly break even." She assumed all the responsibility.

Miss Rilla's eyes moistened with the happiness of her thought. "It was a hard month, sister. Things were unusually high and we had to replace some table linen and get those dishes. This month may not be so much better but I'm just sure that next month you'll come through with flying colors."

"Next month," Miss Ann's voice was bitter, "will be Thanksgiving and the next one Christmas, and in January we'll burn up all our profits and in February we'll eat them up and in March come the taxes. I declare a person might better be dead and free from worry."

"Oh, I'm *glad* I'm alive." Miss Rilla held on to her happiness as a child clutches a plaything.

"Oh, *you!*" Miss Ann's worries made her acrid. "Your middle name is Little Sunshine!"

They went to bed. Miss Rilla humbly asked the Lord to help them. Miss Ann's attitude toward her Maker was that she guessed she had the gumption to manage things yet awhile herself.

At two o'clock Miss Rilla got up to shut a banging bathroom door. There was a light under Warner Field's door and it worried her so that she tapped to see if anything was the matter. She had grown enormously fond of this grave, courteous young man.

"No, I'm all right, Miss Rilla, thank you. I'm sorry about the light. I'll stop now." There were papers all over his desk and his typewriter stood open.

"There's nothing wrong," she told Miss Ann when she came back to bed. "He's been writing."

"Nothing wrong but the crack in his brain," was Miss Ann's pleasant rejoinder. Considering the boarders usurpers as she did, she held a warlike attitude toward their very existence. And this one, who was burning electricity at fifteen cents per kilowatt, particularly irritated her.

School was going fairly well now for Nancy. She bungled some. But Miss Gunn was helpful and patient. "I never half appreciated her," Nancy told Warner the next evening in the seat by the stairs. "Now, you'd think she was uninteresting, wouldn't you, she's so full of her old statistics and culture and mental improvement. But she's the most patient woman I ever saw. She's quiet and she's dignified, and there isn't a mean kid down in that district but what will kowtow to her. She never loses her temper with them. She's just even and calm but as firm as Gibraltar. I've seen those big eighth-grade boys act like the old Nick but let Miss Gunn come casually upon the scene and they flatten out like melted butter. She doesn't punish them. Once in a great while she gives somebody an old-fashioned punishment, but they are few and far apart. Most of the time she just looks at the youngsters and they shrivel up and blow away."

"And how are your families down there?" Warner wanted to know. He enjoyed watching her when she talked, the way her brown eyes lighted, the curve of her mobile mouth, the lovely contour of her face. Just now her eyes twinkled and her mouth melted into delicious laughter.

"You've no idea how attached one gets to them," she confessed. "Take the Carlsons. I've grown so wrapped up in them that I feel just like one of them. It worries me trying to think of some way that we can paper the sitting room this fall and wondering whether it would be better to set out lilacs or syringas between us and the Swansons. The Swanson next-to-the-littlest baby eats everything, indoors and out, so we don't know whether he'd let the bushes grow or masticate them into a pulp. And then the Rhode Island Reds . . . we get so mad at them that we're going to kill them some day and hang their old red heads on the fence between us."

Warner grinned. Naturally quiet and uncommunicative, he never talked much when he was with Nancy. He never had to. He sat back and let her ramble on and enjoyed her.

"On the other hand," she said soberly, "I am equally at home with the Swansons now. We don't think our Rhode Island Reds pester them half as much as they try to make out . . . the stubborn things! They've got Plymouth Rocks themselves and once we found one of their old hens pecking at our soap we had hardening outside in a tub. And did we make any fuss? We did *not*. All in the world we said was we hoped it would clog her old gizzard and kill her."

Warner's laugh was ample reward.

"Life is certainly queer," Nancy was suddenly sober and sincere. It was one of her charms, Warner thought, her quick changes from humor to sympathy. "Friends of mine . . . in college . . . and others . . . if they give people like the Carlsons a thought at all . . . and it's precious little they do . . . it's just with a sort of contempt for them. I wish I could make them understand. I'd like to go back and tell them. But what would be the use? People with preconceived notions don't want to have them changed. The Carlsons . . . why are they to be held so in disdain or pitied? They are decent and law-abiding. They all work. The children are healthy and normal. The girls are clean and neat with good wholesome ideas. And there's one thing they have, a happy outlook on life in just as great measure as most of the people I know. They're not entitled to any disdain and they don't *want* any pity. I can't just express it but it's something like this: If you are an outsider and look *into* the house, you pity a family like that. But if you are a member of it and look *out* of the house, you don't pity yourself. You are busy and full of hope for better things. I wish I could make . . . some people understand it."

"I'm afraid you'd not make a typical social uplifter."

"I suppose not. But isn't life queer?"

"Quite queer!" Warner repeated it ironically.

"Now there's this marriage question." She tackled it earnestly. "Mrs. Bornheimer's husband is dead and she's grieving all the time about it. Mattie Thomas's is gone, and she's tickled to death over it. And here are George and Genevieve Kendall hanging on and worrying each other into shreds. Did you ever think that if they would just say funny things to each other once in a while how much better they would get along? They're so solemn about everything. They take themselves so horribly seriously. If Genevieve would just laugh back at him when he rakes her over the coals about her old bridge parties and if she'd just *once* in a while give up her way to him, but she gets all 'het up' over everything. A sense of humor ought to be cultivated like cauliflowers."

But Genevieve Kendall had no sense of humor, nor in fact a sense of many of the important issues of life. It was only the next day that Mrs. Carlson, cleaning at the "Bee-House," saw Lily bringing the baby upstairs where she was. The baby was hungry and Lily told her mother she thought it was better to bring him up than to let him get too hungry and overeat and have colic. Lily was only eleven and already she knew more about baby tending than many young matrons in town. So Mrs. Carlson, apologizing to Miss Ann for the time it took, nursed the baby and then put it in George and Genevieve Kendall's room because the sun was shining across the bed and he could lie and watch it until he went off to sleep. She took the pad out of his cab and put him on it with the pillows in front so he wouldn't fall off. It got to be noon before Mrs. Carlson was aware of it, and the Kendalls came in. And the first thing they saw was the baby. When they went over to him he was kicking his feet and waving his arms about in jerky objectless gestures. They were both astonished to find him there. George put out his hand and the baby bit with little soft toothless gums onto his finger. It melted George into a substance resembling putty. He laughed and was more amused than he had been for months.

"Look, Genevieve," he said, "just look what he did. Held right on to my hand, strong as a little ox. Bit too, the little nut! Isn't he cute? And see . . ."

Genevieve was starting to the door. But already Mrs. Carlson was running down the hall. When she saw Genevieve's face she apologized:

"I'm sorry if he boddered you, Mrs. Kendall. I left him in dere w'ile I did de rest of de work."

Genevieve, without words for the effrontery of the working woman, merely stood indifferently by while the mother got her baby. George wanted to smooth it over. "He's a dandy, Mrs. Carlson. Sturdiest little kid I've seen in a long time. Give you a month's salary for him any time you say the word."

Mrs. Carlson smiled at him. All the way down the hall she hugged her husky little son to her breast and kissed him. "S'e didn't like you, darlin'. It's a good t'ing you belong to me instead of her."

In the room Genevieve turned to the glass of the dresser to powder for lunch. George went into the bathroom to wash and with infinite pains slammed the door.

CHAPTER XVI

MR. RINELAND DREAMS

ON Friday afternoon of that same week O. J. Rineland sat in his private office with two customers: Major Slack and Nick Denning. The Major was pompous, well groomed. Nick Denning was neither. He was slouchy, unshaven. His hat was on his head. And where else should it have been, Nick would have asked, if pressed.

Mr. Rineland's office was small, simply furnished with one large desk and a smaller one for the typewriter, some chairs, and a filing case. A shelf of books completed the plain appointments.

No one is capable of measuring the influence on a community of a man like Mr. Rineland. Placed as he is with, his hand on the financial pulse of the people, his position is one of physician to their various businesses. He is also a combination of teacher, preacher, lawyer. There are those who look upon the small-town banker as a hard man, grasping, extorting, squeezing blood from turnips. It is a favorite indoor sport of fiction writers to picture him as a Shylock, whetting his knife behind the grated window. The country banker is a high-type man, calm, level-headed, just. Where one goes wrong, a hundred stay right. When the money market is stringent, his nerves are taut from steering his bark safely through the troubled waters. When money is plentiful and his customers go off their heads with the alluring beckoning of wild-cat schemes, his nerves are still taut from making of himself the stabilizer in their financial aeronautics.

In war time when the Maple City farmers were flushed with the big money from their crop returns, Mr. Rineland, in his back office, had talked and explained to them, even pleaded with them to play safe. Some took his advice. Some pretended to and went out and secretly purchased a little blue sky. Some openly told him to watch them get rich. And it is proof of his sterling character that when they came back to him, beaten and chagrined, he looked upon them in sorrow rather than scorn, a little like a father who pitied his children.

Nick Denning had taken Mr. Rineland's advice. And now Nick had money when some of his neighbors had gilt-edged chromos lithographed in pretty colors. Nick was a good business man. As far as cleanliness was concerned he may not have been very close to godliness, but he was hard-headed, and a hard head maketh a merry income. Just now he was doing the talking.

"You use your influence with the old man, Mr. Rineland," he was saying. "My boy Carl wants to get married in the spring and we want him on the Moore place. Old Jud thinks your advice is mighty good. He'll pay attention to what you say."

"I'll talk to him," Mr. Rineland agreed, "but I can't do any coercing. It's his and he'll do as he thinks best. Personally, I think it time for them to come into town and rest. They've been hard workers and Jud's breaking. Any one can see it. I'll do what I can." Mr. Rineland moved his desk chair a little as though the interview were over, but the men lingered. Nick Denning settled back in his own chair and went all over the situation again. Mr. Rineland listened attentively to the tiresome reiteration. It is another characteristic of a country banker . . . patience.

A city banker may handle a thing snappily. But there is no snap in the conversation of the average farmer customer. If country bankers charged for their time they would be wealthy beyond their pleasantest dreams.

So it was late in the afternoon when Warner Field tapped at the door and opened it. "Mrs. Rineland and Alice have asked me to call you, Mr. Rineland. They're here with the car and want to know how soon you will be ready to go."

The men rose. Nick Denning may have been as thick-skinned as he was hard-headed, but the Major knew the amenities.

Alice and Mrs. Rineland were standing in the lobby of the bank. Alice looked pretty and polished to the nth degree. Mrs. Rineland looked like a painted old scarecrow, but to her husband, always loyal to his own, she was "Mama," and that was enough.

Every one was leaving . . . Marty Spencer and the cashier and the paying teller.

"We'll take you up, Warner," Alice's voice was soft, clinging.

Marty Spencer dug his elbow suggestively and painfully into the paying teller's none-too-cushioned ribs. "Cleopatra beckons her Antony," he whispered through closed teeth.

"Let's all drive out to the Moore farm," Mr. Rineland suggested. "I want to see Jud Moore, and there's plenty of time before dinner."

Warner hesitated. He had planned to go right to his story the minute he got home and he begrudged the time for the drive. And he could not seem to get up any enthusiasm over driving to the Moores' with Alice.

Little green lights penciled themselves in Alice's lowered eyes. But when she raised them, they were gray-blue and guileless. "Will you, Warner?"

"Why, yes, I can." After all, the Rinelands were the best friends he had in Maple City.

Out in front Alice took the wheel and made room for him beside her. On the bank steps Marty Spencer chuckled to the paying teller: "Nice little family party. But I'm betting *now* on the little sassy eye-knocker at the 'Bee-House.'"

So the Rinelands and Warner drove in the shining sedan down Main Street, out across the railroad tracks, past the creamery, past the Carlson and Swanson houses and out on the road east of town between the cottonwoods and the Lombardys. Alice drove well. She handled her car as dexterously as she handled her baby-grand.

Mr. Rineland enjoyed the drive. He was contented. Mama and Alice and Warner! He liked to have Warner with Alice. Warner was clean and courteous and sincere. And he liked the country. *How* he liked the country this October afternoon! "Look at the corn, folks! Doesn't that satisfy the eye, though? They'll be going into the field next week. I tell you, you'd appreciate it if you had seen it like I have in the old days, stripped to the stalk, standing like so many skeletons on both sides of the road. Everybody discouraged. No money in sight. All of us in the same boat, bankers as scared and discouraged as the farmers."

Alice did not like the inference. "Oh, Papa!" She smiled at him over her shoulder. "I guess *you* weren't as bad off as all that."

"Wasn't I, though? Indeed I was, my dear, with the crops for security and crops failing on all sides." Mr. Rineland talked on reminiscently. But Mrs. Rineland did not say much. She never did. She had a little smile that usually rested on the elaborate make-up of her thin face. It was somewhat superior and somewhat knowing, as though

she were secreting many things that were best not told. It
was what gave Warner an intuitive dislike for her and for
which thought he often reviled himself.

"Are we going this fall to the County Bankers' Convention, Papa?" Alice was wanting to know.

"Why, yes, I have to be there. Sure, we'll all go. That
will make a fine drive too . . . down south through the
hills to Postville. I haven't taken that drive for years. We
can all go. You, too, Warner. We'll have an early lunch
and start at twelve-thirty or one o'clock, so we can be
there by the time the afternoon program begins. That will
be a nice drive. That's Columbus Day, the twelfth. It's
next Tuesday, with the bank closed."

"You'll go, Warner?" Alice's blue eyes plead.

He did not want to make the promise. He wanted the
day at his desk. Already he was so wrapped in his story
that he seemed to be living it constantly.

"Of course Warner will go," Mr. Rineland put in. "It's
essential to meet the other bankers of the county. We're
not any of us independent, you know. And that question
of interest is coming up. It will be a good thing for you to
hear the speeches and I'd like to have you take part in
the informal discussion of it."

There was nothing to do, of course, but acquiesce. He
was an employee and as such obeyed orders like any good
hired man. But he was disappointed.

As they passed the Thomas farm they could see white
wood smoke pouring out of the kitchen chimney. Warner
knew that Mattie was starting the fire, preparatory to cooking a huge supper. At the Lombardy poplars the car came
up to and passed a rattling buckboard. Old Jud Moore,
taking Nancy home at the week's end, turned out to the
right with, "Gol durn it! If they'd all go by at once
instead o' one every few rods."

The sedan drove into the lane road behind the cotton-woods. "Old Mrs. Moore has been our butter woman for years," Alice told Warner. People outside of Alice's set were not personalities to her. They were "the butter woman," "the wash woman," "the seamstress," not flesh and blood creatures, but machines that did their work automatically.

The "butter woman," on her crutch, came out of the old square farmhouse now, the late afternoon sun shining on her placid face and her soft white hair. She was hospitable. She wanted Alice and her mother to get out and come in. But they said no, it was Papa who was there for a short time on business.

The rattling buckboard came into the lane road and Nancy hopped out. Uncle Jud unfolded his long camel-like legs and got out, too, a little painfully.

Mr. Rineland went up to the porch with the old folks to talk to them. The others stayed by the big car. Nancy had that old sensation she had always felt in the presence of Alice and her mother, the knowledge of a condescension from them that she had sensed ever since she was little. It exasperated her but she could not combat it. They were always cool and poised, and Nancy, hot tempered and emotional, could never rid herself of the feeling that she would like to fly at them, and break through that hard snobbish exterior.

She did her best now with the conversation. Warner seemed to be helping her and she was grateful to him but it was not a startling success.

"Do you like your teaching?" It was as though Alice, from her heights of leisure, had asked, "Do you like bi-chloride of mercury?"

"Why, yes . . . it's work, of course, but it's very enjoyable."

"You were lucky to get in here without experience." Mrs. Rineland's beadlike eyes darted from Nancy to Alice.

Nancy shrugged one lithe shoulder.

"I guess I was just born that way . . . *lucky*." She had that same wild desire to tell them at once of her unannounced engagement to Mr. Farnsworth, whose wealth and position were known even to Maple City, so that she might see their surprise and chagrin. She hated herself for the feeling, but wealth was the only weapon that could penetrate their particular kind of skin. With that same sense of unholy glee she knew that if she kept the news of it to herself, until she was leaving in the spring, she would be repaid tenfold. All year to swallow the condescending remarks, to take all their little snobbish airs meekly and then to experience that high moment of mirthprovoking laughter in which she was to spring her engagement. It gave her back her own poise, that knowledge of the upper hand she was to hold in the spring. It made her gay again and careless of what she said so that Warner, grave and serious, watching her, saw that same mood come upon her which he had learned to know . . . as though she were Babbie dancing wantonly through Caddam Wood . . . Babbie, who was both gypsy and lady of high degree.

Mr. Rineland was talking to Uncle Jud and Aunt Biny about the farm. "You'd better consider it, Jud. I think you owe it to yourself now and to your wife. It's a good chance to sell."

"It's Denning, ain't it, that wants it?"

"Yes, it's Denning." Mr. Rineland did not like dissemination.

"No, I ain't goin' to sell," old Jud Moore finished the interview stubbornly.

"That's all right. I told Major Slack I'd talk it over with you. But you know best." Mr. Rineland had not dealt with old Jud Moore for nearly a half century without gaining definite insight into his character.

After the Rinelands had gone, Jud Moore, like a rubber band snapping back after being drawn taut, began taking the other side of the question in his own mind. And, as he could not carry anything long in his thoughts without sharing it with Aunt Biny, he voiced it to her after supper.

"Might consider sellin' and goin' to Californy if you warn't so set ag'in' it."

Aunt Biny smiled surreptitiously at Nancy, who grinned back knowingly.

"Well, you do as you think best, Pa."

The first of the next week Jud Moore went into the field. In the mid-west the expression, "going into the field," has specific reference to the great events on a farm, the spring planting, the summer wheat harvesting and the husking. Old Jud rode into his cornfields in the early morning. The dried and brittle stalks rubbed noisily against the wagon. The huge ears fell with dull thud in the high box . . . but slowly, more slowly than in other years. More slowly than those which Walt Thomas, a quarter of a mile away, threw into the high box of his wagon. Walt worked quickly and steadily, brown, alert, a perfect figure of healthy young manhood . . . Apollo in a cornfield. As he worked he was thinking many things, how pretty the clouds were in that long white row like sheep going over a blue hill. How far away they seemed . . . like so many things one wanted and could not have. It made him depressed . . . that old longing for Nancy. But by noon, when he went to the house and had eaten his mother's good dinner, he experienced a boyish lightness of heart. After all life was good. And who knew, maybe there was a girl somewhere to take Nancy's place.

And over in town the boarders, too, had just finished

their lunch and were out on the wide porch of the old "Bee-House" in the summer warmth of the October noon.

Nancy was there, perched on the edge of the railing like a gay little linnet. Warner, grave and serious, and Marty Spencer, light-hearted and debonair, were standing near her. Major Slack was there, stuffed to a state of torpidity. Mary Mae Gates was there, discussing a musical date she had at one-thirty. "My interpretation of 'The Willow Song' is somewhat different from Madam Alda's," she was saying.

"Oh, is that *so?*" Nancy remarked in a pleasant aside to Warner and Marty. "No doubt Verdi sent word back to Mary Mae how he wanted her to do it."

The Kendalls were there but their domestic temperatures had dropped again, and so far as Genevieve was concerned, her mercurial affection hovered around the degree that is named indifference. Dr. Pearson and Helen Blakely sat close together on the steps, where the word "Baldwin" was picked out in colored stones.

Miss Gunn was on one of the porch seats, methodically taking her noon rest, eyeing her wrist watch to see that she ceased resting at the exact moment of her allotted time.

The "bore" stood with his back against the red brick of the wall, smiling and scraping foolishly and darting his head around to catch what every one was saying.

Miss Rilla had followed the boarders out on the wide porch. She enjoyed the chatter and the bits of news. Miss Ann had no such childish moments. Life was real and life was earnest to Miss Ann, and so far as she was concerned the grave was not such a bad goal.

Marty Spencer nudged Nancy now with his elbow and received a frigid look for his ill-timed gesture. It did not phase Marty. "Looky," he pointed one wiggling thumb toward the two ensconced together on the top step and another toward the Kendalls. "Before taking," he whis-

pered, "and *after*. Not for Marty, then . . . the gay
wedding march and the dread hangman's noose."

The Rinelands, starting for the county bankers' convention at Postville, drew up in front for Warner. The sedan
was shining and spotless. Alice was at the wheel.

When Warner had gone down to the car, Marty nudged
Nancy again with an active elbow and went unrebuked.
"There's the shadow of the next hangman's noose! But not
so *bad* . . . *not* so bad . . . the only child . . . the only
heir . . . the First National Bank . . . some farm land
. . . the Wop-house on the hill . . . *and* a beautiful old
mother-in-law." He went off into a spasm of laughter.
Nancy did not join him. It was not so excruciatingly funny
that a man like Warner Field was eventually to tie himself
down to a small-souled, humorless creature like Alice Rineland.

Nancy joined Miss Gunn and together they walked down
to the Whittier. A great discontent was upon her. She
was angry with herself that she had taken the position
. . . by far the silliest thing she had ever done. The warm
October afternoon was not meant to be spent in a stuffy
schoolroom with the Swansons and the Carlsons and the
Bornheimers. It was meant to be spent . . . in a sedan
out on a country road. She went up the front walk worn
with the soles of a thousand feet, at complete variance with
the whole world.

The Rinelands and Warner spent the afternoon and evening at the convention where the county bankers discussed
a few little pleasing topics as the income tax law, excessive
interest, the crop outlook, the guarantee fund and a county
clearing house. There was an evening banquet of home
cooking served by the Postville ladies in the American
Legion hall and afterward the choice of a movie show or
dancing with the bankers' wives and daughters. From

which statement one may deduct what a gay, wild fellow the mid-west banker is when he is off on his semi-annual convention spree.

Warner and Alice danced. Alice danced as well as she did everything else. Yes, Alice Rineland was almost perfect.

It was midnight when the sedan turned into the asphalt drive toward its garage. Mr. Rineland did not feel sleepy after a coffee indulgence, so he went into his library and sat down in the big chair. Suddenly he got up and went over to his desk, unlocked a small drawer and, with hands that trembled a little, took from it two of his most cherished possessions: the picture of his first wife and his son. For a moment he looked at the old-fashioned picture of the woman and then placed it gently back. The young man's picture he took with him over to the big chair and sat looking at it a long time. Only twenty, and the fresh young life had gone out in a flash! Full of life and vigor with a splendid career before him! A split rail . . . and there was no more vigor and no more life. The enormity of the grief overwhelmed the father again, as it so often did. He shook with the passion of it. He had no son . . . he had no son!

For a time he sat there until the poignancy of the memory had passed. Well, one must make the best of life. And life had been good to him. It had given him Mama and Alice, he told himself loyally. He hoped that Alice would marry well . . . some one he, himself, liked, too. Warner Field, for instance. Warner was clean and courteous and sincere. Everybody respected him. Yes, he hoped it would be Warner. He put his head back in the big chair and thought of the possibilities of it. He saw himself older . . . retiring from active work . . . out of the bank . . . free from the monotony of the day's grind there but still keeping his eye on the business, advising and assisting. He could keep his old office and go to it whenever he wished. The young folks could live right at home with him and Mama . . . the house was big enough. Warner would work up easily to the head of the old bank . . . he was dependable in every way. And he, himself, would be free to drive away any day into the country among the farms . . . to fish a little and hunt sometimes . . . to go back to the things he loved . . . the prairie and the hills . . . the orchards and the cottonwoods . . . the smell of the loam and the alfalfa fields. . . .

He pulled himself up suddenly. What had he been doing? Indulging in fancies over the realities of which he had no control. After all, young people had to work out their own destinies. But an old man . . . who had no son . . . an old man could dream dreams, couldn't he?

CHAPTER XVII

THE SINISTER THING STALKS

BY November everybody in the "Bee-House" was calling everybody else by his first name. At least the younger people were doing so. One would as soon have thought of calling the Queen of England by her first name as addressing Miss Gunn as "Sarah."

The first half of the month was warm and cold, dry and rainy, uncertain in temperament. "A little of everything," Nancy said to Warner, who was taking her out home, "like the lessons in my second grade. Since I've started to teach we've studied Hiawatha, the carpenter, goldenrod, corn, milkweed, ants, Longfellow, spiders, Columbus, the squirrel, Thorwaldsen and the stars . . . everything, in fact, but bridge whist, child labor laws and evolution. The inside of the youngsters' minds must look like a pawn shop or a junk pile."

Warner laughed. It was as easy as ever to laugh with Nancy. She never palled . . . never failed to hold his interest. The Friday was cold and sunless. When the two turned down the lane road at the farm, behind the cottonwoods, Aunt Biny already had the swinging lamp lighted in the kitchen. There was a savory smell of cooking and it took real courage for Warner to refuse Aunt Biny's invitation to stay.

"It's no use, Aunt Biny," Nancy informed her, "the First National Bank can't locate seventeen cents and they've all got to work this evening and find it."

167

After Warner had gone back to town, Nancy ran out to the old harness shed where she could see Uncle Jud fussing around. He was getting down the muskrat traps, dragging their clanking chains noisily from the wall.

"Goin' to set 'em to-night. Season opens to-morrow, but I reckon settin' 'em a few hours early won't hurt if I post a notice up for the rats not to pay no attention to 'em until after midnight."

"I'll go with you, Uncle Jud. It's been ages since I did it. The crowd I chase around with doesn't set muskrat traps, you know."

The little family of three ate supper together under the hanging lamp and immediately afterward Uncle Jud and Nancy set out with the traps. Nancy wore a long coat, a wool cap pulled down over her brown hair and a pair of Aunt Biny's homemade woolen gloves. It was cold and frosty. Uncle Jud carried over his shoulder a gunny-sack filled with traps and in the other hand the lantern that made a circling light in the dark of the orchard. Nancy chatted as she swung along beside the old man. It reminded him of when she was little. The years had turned back for him and she was not a mature young woman, but a little brown-headed thing chattering along by his side on the way to other muskrat expeditions.

He wanted to tell her this, to let her know how glad he was that she was back; how sorry he was that she had left them; how he had missed her; how lonely were the creek and the orchard without her. But it would not come. Always when he opened his mouth to approach it, he became stupid and inarticulate. That's the way he always was, he told himself . . . talked like a blue streak when there was nothing to say and was tongue-tied when he ought to be talking.

As cold as it seemed in the November evening, Tinkling

Creek was not frozen. As they walked along its bank, they saw a long V-shaped rippling of the water slip downstream. In a moment they came upon them, the slides in the bank worn smooth by the tobogganing of the colony. Just under the water at the bottom of each, they set the evil-looking traps. Nancy set a few, herself, opening their iron jaws with her foot and staking them to the bank.

When they had finished the task and returned to the house, the light and the warmth of the old sitting room enveloped their chilliness like a garment. Uncle Jud sat down with the Omaha paper in whose political policies he held implicit faith.

Aunt Biny was setting the bread. Nancy curled up in the chintz-covered chair to watch her. She liked the definite way Aunt Biny's hands worked with the material. There was a certain fascination in watching her. When the bread was set in its pan and wrapped up in a patchwork quilt to keep it warm, Aunt Biny washed her hands and came limping over to a chair near the girl's.

"Nancy, I've been trying to get the courage to talk to you about something. You're grown up and are your own boss, but some way . . . I can't see you get so friendly with Warner Field when you're a betrothed woman, without warning you about it. Somebody is certainly going to be hurt."

Nancy flushed a little. "Just *who* is going to be hurt, Aunt Biny?"

She meant it for slight sarcasm, but sarcasm had not been included in life's curriculum for Aunt Biny. "That's hard to tell, Nancy. Maybe Mr. Field. Maybe you. Most certainly the man you're engaged to."

Nancy grinned. "It would take a whole lot more than either a friendship or a flirtation, Aunt Biny, to hurt the man I'm engaged to. Warner Field is no doubt going to marry 'the lily maid of Astelot,' named Alice Rineland, and *me* . . . *I'm* immune, I assure you."

Aunt Biny ran her hand nervously up and down the shining smoothness of the old crutch. It was hard to talk to Nancy. She was so glib and so modern. The things she said confused the older woman. "No . . . you ain't, Nancy . . . you ain't immune, as you call it. You've never yet told me you love this Mr. Farnsworth and you'd be glad and proud to tell me if you did. And if you've never known what real love is yet . . . you're . . . you're going to be hurt some day. And you owe it to the man not to have so much to do with Warner Field."

Nancy laughed outright. "If that isn't provincial, Aunt Biny. Now, I'll tell you something I never told you before. Mr. Farnsworth is one of Warner Field's friends and Warner doesn't even know that I know him. His son, Rod, and Warner were classmates in college and Warner has visited in their home many times in years gone by."

"His *son*, Nancy! Is he that old?"

"Yes . . . he's *that* old. You see, he's the father of Fay Farnsworth, one of my best girl friends. I told you he was a lot older than the hero ought to be, but he has money to buy the pyramids. And I don't want you to say anything about it to Warner. It's my little joke and some day I'll tell him all about it. I even saw Warner once in their house . . . the last time he was ever there . . . and he doesn't know *that* either. I was on the landing of the stairs with Fay Farnsworth and I looked down over the banisters and saw Warner just as he was leaving. He looked up and saw me leaning over the banisters, but he seemed serious and troubled and didn't pay any more attention to me looking down at him than if I had been one of the spindles. I've always wanted to tell him about our friends in common and about seeing him that time, but I can't do it without dragging in my engagement and I don't want to do that."

"Why not?"

If Nancy was a bit confused at the direct question she covered it with her elaborate explanation.

"Well . . . you see, if you are going to be married, it is something like stepping off the dock in the dark . . . pretty vague and uncertain just how deep the water is . . . and I thought I'd sort of like to play around on the wharf a bit first. You'd rather I'd do that, wouldn't you, than do like most of them . . . climb up the piling and play around just the same way afterwards?"

"Oh, my *dear!*"

"Poor Aunt Biny! The world and the flesh and the devil . . . you do try to make yourself believe they don't exist."

Aunt Biny ignored the pointed observation and again went straight to the thing on her mind: "You ought to tell Warner Field, now. It isn't right to see so much of him. You're doing a lot of people a wrong . . . Alice Rineland for one, if you think he wants to marry her."

"I don't think he *wants* to but I think he's *going* to. It's the best thing for him, you'll have to admit . . . with Mr. Rineland's property."

"You're not looking at these things right, Nancy. You're . . . I don't know how to express it . . . only touching the surface of things. Real love is both proud and humble. It asks nothing and gives all. It's like a growing thing . . . with roots. Deep, deep roots that draw their sustenance from our very beings."

"Roots? All right, Aunt Biny, for the first time this evening, we agree heartily. 'Roots,' as the dictionary so ably states, 'constitute a food reservoir or support for the growing plant.' That's what I've been trying to tell you all the time. . . . 'A food reservoir or support' . . . the more money a man has the more food you get and the more support." She went off into high bubbling laughter at Aunt Biny and finished it with a little demonstrative hug to take off the sting.

So Aunt Biny's loving counsel ended where so much loving counsel ends, in the place it started, with no one affected by it but herself.

Nancy went to bed trying to be both blithe and unconcerned with apparently nothing more important on her mind than the fact that Uncle Jud was to call her very early. "For I'm to be queen of the traps, Uncle. I'm to be queen of the traps," had been her parting word to him. But she did not go to sleep. There were many things which disturbed her.

It seemed in the middle of the night that Uncle Jud was rapping on the stovepipe below and calling her. It was frightfully early and dark. For a few moments she lay in the warm bed, regretting her promise. The thought of some of her friends seeing her crawl out at that uncanny hour and into her cold clothes tickled her so that she jumped out and lighted the hand lamp. But she picked up her clothes and carried them downstairs to dress behind the huge base-burner as she had done when she was little.

Aunt Biny was already dressed and starting breakfast. When Uncle Jud and Nancy started out with the lantern, its eerie shadows swinging around them, the cold of the morning seemed almost bitter. The old man did not walk nearly so fast or so springily, Nancy noticed, as he had in other years. He trudged along heavily like a machine that was wearing.

The first two traps they visited were empty. At the third one little bubbles of water formed the center of a circle of ripples so that they knew the trap held something. Uncle Jud pulled out a big struggling muskrat, dripping with

water, its wet fur giving no promise of the softness it would
have when dried. He held the trap on the ground and hit
the animal over the head with the blunt club that he
carried.

Nancy gave the elegy: "Poor little Musky! You'll make
some rich saleslady a mink coat or a sable neck-piece."

The iron jaws yielded nine pelts. Uncle Jud put them
into the gunny-sack after he had reset the traps. "There's
something tragic about it, Uncle Jud. Life for just a
summer or two. Life and freedom and animal happiness
and in the end a clout over the head."

"Guess it amounts to the same with us," the old man
said, simply. "Life and freedom and happiness for a few
summers and in the end a clout over the head."

It grew light. Great splashes of color were drawn across
the east. In layers like a huge staff of music the harmoni-
ous shades lay piled one above the other. God's tubes
were neither twisted nor dried that morning.

The old man called Nancy's attention to it. "Never saw
it two times alike, and I've seen it every mornin' since we
come to the state. Nature ain't ever monotonous."

Uncle Jud seldom spoke in generalities. Life was a con-
crete thing to him: wheat, weather, corn, taxes. They were
tangible. But freedom, happiness, beauty . . . they were
too vague and shadowy for him to discuss. Now that he
had inadvertently fallen into a generality, Nancy took advantage of it.

"If you had your life to live over, what is there about
it that you would change?"

They were going toward home now, had reached the edge
of the orchard. Uncle Jud shifted his gunny-sack to the
other shoulder.

"Don't know's I think of much. Onct I had a chance to
buy the east eighty of Mattie's whilst was cheap. Believe

I'd do that now. Mebbe I'd build the barn on the northeast side o' the house 'stead o' the northwest."

Nancy smiled at the simplicity of his thoughts. "I mean big things, Uncle Jud . . . to make your whole life different. Would you be something besides a farmer? Do something entirely different with your life? Live some other place than Nebraska? Marry some other woman besides Aunt Biny?"

Even the importance of the first questions were overwhelmed by the enormity of the last.

He almost stopped in his tracks. "Lord A'mighty . . . your Aunt Biny was the only girl I ever . . . liked." "Loved" was too big a mouthful. "Farmin' is the only thing in the world I'd do. Nebraska's the best state in the whole kit 'n bilin' of 'em."

Nancy laughed. The only state, the only occupation, the only woman! Well, why wasn't life as simple as that for every one? When you got old like Uncle Jud you could look back at your life as from a hilltop. But when you were young you went blindly as through dense thickets. She fell into silence for the rest of the way home. A moodiness and vague uncertainty annoyed and depressed her. Uncle Jud's commonplace remarks were as something afar off. But when she opened the kitchen door, the odors of sausage, coffee and cakes were too humanly attractive to allow her momentary moodiness a chance to exist.

The month slipped away. Life seemed to amuse Nancy. She laughed at every one and everything. She laughed at Miss Gunn's dearth of humor and her abundance of statistics, at her partiality for proteids and her abhorrence of carbohydrates. She laughed at Ambrose Jones rising and bowing and scraping foolishly when the ladies passed by. She laughed at Major Slack with his pomposity and his bombasity and the ridiculously heavy statements with which he settled all the great world problems. She laughed at Mary Mae Gates throatily practicing "Knowest Thou the Land?" on the old cracked and scuffed piano. She laughed at Marty Spencer's immature idea of wit, at Miss Rilla's emotional tears and at Miss Ann's crabbedness. She laughed at the seriousness with which Helen Blakely and Dr. Pearson took their love affair and the seriousness with which the Kendalls took their *un*loved one. But she did not laugh at Warner Field. She laughed with him a great deal but not at him. Occasionally she slipped into a thoughtful mood in which she admitted that she ought to tell him about everything. Maybe she ought not to let him come out after her on Sundays. Maybe she ought not to see so much of him. Maybe . . . but it ended in nothing but a half-formed resolution that faded off into nothing. Because she liked to be with him, they continued to drift together as naturally as the tides to the moon. Nancy Moore was a little too careless to face life as it should be faced. On the whole she felt very happy and free. Life was a pleasant thing . . . with youth and laughter and friends.

And life to Warner Field had picked up. The monotonous months when he first came to Maple City seemed ages before. The days were not long enough for all that he wished to accomplish. Always there was the story with him, a living vital thing being created. All day long in the bank his mind seemed to be divided into those two compartments. In the one he did his bank work correctly. In the other he was conscious that his characters assembled, talked to each other, lived their lives, waited for him. He could scarcely wait to get back to the "Bee-House" to write. The moment he got home in the afternoon he was at work. He muffled his machine with a thick pad, kept his door closed and worked constantly. When he would pick up his scattered pages to read and revise the tale, it sounded fresh and good. Saturday nights he never went to bed until toward dawn. Miss Ann complained more often about the amount of light he burned. "If he's writing a book, as you seem to think you know from the pages on his desk," she said sourly to Miss Rilla, "he can just pay me back for all this electricity if he ever sells it . . . not that those one-horse writers ever get enough to pay for electricity."

And then quite suddenly it was Thanksgiving time before any one was aware. School was out on Wednesday for the two days' vacation.

All the afternoon Warner's roadster was parked by the bank, for he intended to take Nancy out home. Several things detained him so that it was late when he came out to get the car. Alice and her mother alighted from their sedan at the same moment so that the three stood together on the curb. And then Nancy Moore came by.

They all spoke. In one of those swift childish moods of mischievousness, from which Nancy had never freed herself, she paused. At the sight of Alice, standing there by her shining car, so complacent, so perfect and so smug, Nancy, in the perversity of her nature, asked, "Has any one here seen Walt Thomas? . . . because I'm going to ride out home with him on a load of hogs."

Warner frowned. Why did Nancy say those things? And before Alice and her mother, who were such sticklers for the conventions. He wished she wouldn't. Try as he would, he could not help but know that he was beginning to feel responsible for Nancy's actions.

"I'm going to take you out," he said, still frowning a little.

"Oh, no, you're not." Nancy was airily cool. "I was brought up with pigs. I don't mind them at all." She smiled artlessly over at Alice, correct and aloof.

Warner opened his car door. "I'm going to take you out," he repeated.

"No, thank you."

"Get in this car," he ordered sternly.

Nancy impishly threw Alice a languishing look that said many things, and with an exaggeration of mock fear fell into the seat.

In the car she said, "Heavens, we sounded like George and Genevieve Kendall. Why did you do it?"

Warner's frown relaxed its hold. "I don't know, do you?"

"No." And they both laughed.

"Well . . . you saw for yourself?" Alice turned to her mother when they were back in the sedan. "What have I been telling you?" There were little green points in her eyes and her expression was neither sweet nor gentle.

Mrs. Rineland's small face with its elaborate make-up wrinkled to the extent of its possibilities into an odd little smile. There was shrewdness in it, a touch of cunning.

"I could settle *that* young lady with Warner Field," she announced. "The type of man he is . . . from the kind of family he is . . . with that streak of pride in it. It's in him, too, you know . . . whether he thinks so or not . . . a pride that came from generations of Massachusetts people with years of English pride behind that. I've kept it from you, Alice, but . . . if she is really making a difference with Warner's attitude to you, as you say . . . it's your right now to have the information. She was your classmate . . . and I've always tried to shield you . . . to keep you from these things . . . but it's yours now to use. You must be careful how you use it . . . not in any superior way, just a suggestion. Men are contrary creatures at times . . . you mustn't antagonize him. . . ."

So on the way up Main Street, up the sloping asphalt

drive, she was telling her daughter a subtle stinging thing.
And like many another intriguer, she told only a half-truth,
half-truths quite often being more dangerous than whole
lies.

Uncle Jud, Aunt Biny and Nancy ate a noon Thanksgiving dinner with Mattie and Walt. Mattie's table looked
like the food exhibit table at the State Fair. Everything
was very informal, both service and conversation. Aunt
Biny half-bashfully read some verses that she "made up."
They were a little faulty as to meter and a little trite as to
rhyme, but they came from the depths of a thankful heart.
Uncle Jud, with much detail and much roaring laughter,
recalled other Thanksgivings. Mattie bounced springily
from kitchen to dining room with one savory dish after
another. Nancy was Nancy, which is synonymous with
merry chatter and bubbling laughter. Walt drank in her
beauty as one quaffs water.

Warner ate a six o'clock dinner at the Rinelands'. There
were a half dozen other guests, new friends of Mrs. Rineland and Alice. Mr. Rineland was happy to have them all
there. He enjoyed having people in his home. He wished
Mama and Alice had company in more often. There were
a lot of people he would like to have for a meal and a long
pleasant evening afterward in which they could talk over
the early days . . . some of the old settlers around in the
community . . . but Mama didn't seem to have time. It
made him think of the old days now . . . the contrast
between the beautifully appointed table and those other
ones. He spoke of it to them all.

"My first Thanksgiving dinner here was eaten with Gus
Carlson's father's family in a one-roomed house right where
the creamery stands. I had been working for Judge Baldwin
some then for a few months, taking care of his horses and
husking for the settlers around. I earned seven dollars in

cash that fall and had to take the rest of my pay in good wishes and corn."

Then he saw a little look on Alice's face that made him stop suddenly. He had forgotten for the moment that Mama and Alice did not enjoy references like that. He could not quite understand it. What was there about one's early hard days to embarrass one's family? It hurt him a little, but then he should not be critical. If he could not quite comprehend their attitude toward his early years of labor in the new country, he ought to be fair about it and remember not to speak that way when they had guests.

After dinner the little company all went into the living room and Alice played for them: Thöne's "Simple Aveu" and Chopin's "Nocturne." When she had finished she went over and sat down on the mulberry davenport where her pale prettiness stood out cameolike. To Warner she looked sweet and womanly, even a little melancholy and wistful. He walked over and sat down beside her.

"You play beautifully, Alice."

"I'm glad *you* think so, Warner."

He was going to say something more about it when one of the guests, in a voice that included them all, asked if every one had heard of the recent arrest for a burglary crime of a young boy from Maple City's one outstanding trashy family across the creek. There was a little discussion of the local happening.

Warner said, quietly, "Well, blood isn't *everything*, perhaps, but it's apparently very essential that children should be rightly born."

The green light came into Alice's eyes. She had not dreamed that luck would play into her hands so quickly and so easily. She was breathing fast and trembling a little. She touched Warner's arm gently and dropped her eyes. "You ask . . ." she steadied herself. Then she raised her eyes slowly to Warner and they were soft and blue. "You ask Nancy . . ." she was smiling lightly, " . . . sometime . . . just ask Nancy Moore what *she* thinks about that . . . and where she keeps the brown shawl?"

It seemed to Warner that he could not look away from Alice. She knew something about Nancy, then . . . the sinister thing that had stalked along beside his friendship for her . . . the thing in the diaries that he had so brazenly read!

CHAPTER XVIII

NANCY WEAVES A TAPESTRY

DECEMBER came in with no winterlike mien. It was mild, cloudy and damp . . . uninteresting weather. The elms and maples, gaunt and unlovely, unless one loved their huge bare strength as Nancy did, stood in the old "Bee-House" yard like men stripped for the Olympics.

No sooner had the month arrived than Nancy plunged deep into preparation for Christmas down at the Whittier. She almost swam through a sea of fat Santa Clauses and skinny reindeer. In the second grade, balsam and fir boughs lined the upper part of the boards, shadow cuttings of the wise men on stork-legged camels strode along one side of the room, and the star of Bethlehem hung a little tipsily from the ceiling. Nancy talked a great deal about the coming event at the "Bee-House" table. One evening at dinner it brought on a discussion concerning the ethics of the Santa Claus myth. Major Slack hurled the definite statement into the air:

"It is children's first lesson in untruth."

"I've often observed," Nancy remarked pointedly, "that people who are careless of facts in every other particular, quite suddenly develop a deep sense of righteousness over that special question."

With moist eyes Miss Rilla said, "I know of no sight so beautiful as children at Christmas time."

With a well-bred snort Miss Ann contributed, "I know of no sight so foolish as the emotion displayed during the holidays."

Miss Gunn came in with her statistical contribution, "More money is spent for holiday gifts than on educational matters."

Marty Spencer told a story about a kid waiting up for Santa Claus. "Pretty good . . . what?"

Mary Mae Gates said, with husky, fatigued voice, "Between my music lessons and getting the church music ready, I'm nearly beside myself. The choir is putting on a cantata. I have so many solo parts, the whole thing seems to hinge on me."

The "bore," smiling foolishly, turned his head hurriedly this way and that to catch every word that was said.

Genevieve and George Kendall did not enter into the conversation. They had had words in their room. George's mother had written, asking them to spend Christmas with her. George wanted to go but Genevieve had said she guessed not when they were invited to the Rinelands' for a six o'clock Christmas dinner. It wasn't everybody in town that got so special an invitation to the Rineland home and she guessed his mother could get along once without them. "But mother's old and she's not well and she's expecting us," he had argued with her.

"She'll be a year older next year and she's thought she was an invalid ever since I knew her, and the Rinelands are expecting us," Genevieve had announced complacently.

George had ground his teeth. She was so lazy and so stubborn and so susceptible to the unimportance of the two-by-four society of Maple City.

Essie, serving the dessert, well knew what Christmas would bring to her: two extra courses of dishes, for there would be some of the boarders staying on at the "Bee-House." Christmas would be something of a farce for Essie unless she could go down home for the day.

But Nancy was saying in her breezy way: "I have a plan. It just sprang out of my forehead full-fledged like Diana or Minerva or one of those dames . . . wouldn't all of you that are to stay here at the 'Bee-House' like to come out to the farm for dinner? I mean you, too, Miss Ann and Miss Rilla. Close up shop for a day and come out to our house? Dr. Pearson is going out to Helen Blakely's if Grandma Carlson's heart doesn't get to jazzing or the Swanson baby doesn't swallow a door knob or the mouth organ. Marty, here, has been invited by all of his girls to visit them. George and Genevieve are moving with the super-élite at the Rinelands'. But here's Major Slack, and Miss Gunn and Mr. Jones and Miss Ann and Miss Rilla and Essie and Warner Field, who could come out. Mattie Thomas and Aunt Biny will get the dinner together and what Mattie won't think of to cook just isn't in the eleven cook books that she possesses. And Aunt Biny has peach pickles and cucumber pickles and tomato pickles and apple pickles and watermelon pickles. . . . She pickles everything but gourds and acorns."

"I think it would be fine." The tears welled into Miss Rilla's eyes. How she clutched at happiness! It was so fleeting, so transient! To Miss Ann there was not even fleeting happiness . . . only duty and stern realities. "The rest of you can go. There are a few little essential things like looking after fires in winter that always tie *some* member of the family down."

After dinner Warner came up to Nancy in the big hall. "That was thoughtful and kind of you, Nancy." Whatever Nancy's secret . . . whatever had happened when she was eighteen . . . she was everything that was charming and lovable now. Alice's innuendo had worried him not a little. There was no mistaking its suggestion. But when he was with Nancy, it faded into the background, a mere nothing that Nancy could blow away with one bubbling laugh.

"Warner, do you know things aren't divided right in this world? All the jolly ones . . . the ones that always have a good time . . . have some place to go for Christmas. The others haven't. I guess Aunt Biny is right when she says 'To him that hath shall be given.' I'm asking you early before Alice clutches upon you for there simply has to be somebody there besides the antiques."

"They have already asked me . . . but it was Mr. Rineland. I'm pretty sorry, Nancy."

It did not disconcert her. "Dinner at night, of course, you mean?"

"Yes."

"Oh, that's easy," she laughed. "You ought to know by this time that dinner at our house is when the sun is at the meridian. You can eat on our plain painted table at noon and then at night you can dine from an Italian Renaissance table and sit in a golden chair and gaze at the beautiful daughter with tresses of comet's hair." There was no envy in her voice, nothing but banter.

With all her bustling preparations for Christmas, Nancy still took time to make the round of calls again among her pupils.

At the Bornheimers' she found a condition not to her liking. The thin little house looked more frail than ever. The fire was small. Not one of them looked comfortably dressed. Freddy gained too slowly. She must talk to Dr. Pearson about him, she told herself.

"Does he have plenty of fresh eggs and milk?" she wanted to know.

Mrs. Bornheimer's expression made Nancy angry at herself for her bluntness.

"I'm going to see that he gets more, Mrs. Bornheimer. You'll let me, I know. We'll bring him in some from Uncle Jud's every Sunday afternoon. Maybe we can find a way to get extra milk from out there again in the middle of the week. Walt Thomas would bring it in or Mr. Field at the 'Bee-House' would get it, if I asked him."

"I thought he was Alice Rineland's beau."

Nancy laughed. "I guess he is . . . but he's my friend, and you know a friend is sometimes more useful than a 'beau.' "

She talked to the boys about the Christmas tree she was planning at the schoolhouse. "Freddy must be well enough to come too, by that time. I'll have somebody get him . . . Dr. Pearson, maybe . . . or Mr. Field . . . unless you think we have to get permission from Alice Rineland," she laughed.

At the Swansons' the general scrap heap appearance of the house on her former visits was augmented now by the presence of the stove, around which there were divers chunks of coal and ashes, feathery wisps of dust, burned matches, dirty dishes and spools of thread. The next-to-the-smallest baby was eating the pink wax coating of an ancient looking birthday candle.

Mrs. Swanson, extremely healthy as to body, but with an air that one might look for her expiration at any moment, let the teacher in. With her usual vivacity Nancy turned her conversation toward the coming Christmas and the good time she hoped the children would have. There was no answering spark of mental fire from the lethargic woman. Yes, she knew Christmas was coming. Her tone implied that the end of the world was also on its way, and there was as little use of getting up any excitement over the one as the other. Mrs. Swanson's mind, it seemed, while declining to exert itself unduly, clung as tenaciously to the subject of the Carlsons as one of her own Rhode Island Reds clung on occasion to its roost.

"Well, they're at it again," she said nasally to Nancy. "Chasin' 'em back home mornin', noon and night." With no explanatory subject and a nameless object in the sentence, Nancy knew neighborhood gossip well enough by this time to supply the missing ideas. "Nothin' in the garden anywheres to hurt . . . not a leaf over there to eat . . . and them a-chasin' and shooin' like my Rhode Island Reds was rep-*tiles*."

Jim Swanson slipped in from the kitchen, as though his cue had been called. "Myrt's right. You can hear that 'shoo . . . shoo' most any time you want to listen. Some folks does like to make a molehill out of a mountain."

Nancy's nostrils quivered at the inverted metaphor, but she kept her face straight.

"Well, all come to the Christmas tree!" She was leaving as quickly as possible.

"If I ain't there," Mrs. Swanson emitted languidly, "it will be because I got so much put on me to do."

"If you ain't there," Nancy said to herself, as she went down the muddy steps, "it will be because you need new cylinders and a spark plug."

It was a relief to run into the Carlsons', where things were fresh and clean and wholesome.

"It tries my patience t'rough and t'rough," Mrs. Carlson told Nancy. "Their chickens muddy'n up the walks and porch. I tell Gus if we had any spunk we'd get de law on 'em."

It was late and Nancy's call was brief.

"Well, all come to the Christmas tree!"

"Oh, I wouldn't miss it for anyt'ing. Every kid I got will

be dere. I tell Gus dey're just young once and when dey
get big, I want 'em to remember dey had a lot o' fun too,
even if dey did have to work . . . and den de work ain't
hurtin' 'em.''

When Nancy returned to the "Bee-House," dinner was
nearly ready. The warmth and an appetizing odor greeted
her cheerfully. How pleasant the "Bee-House" was and how
thrilling it was to be young and healthy and enthusiastic.

The "bore" stood by the table which contained the afternoon's mail, but when Nancy came up he stepped aside and,
backing against the wall, bowed and scraped and smiled
foolishly.

"I think it may sleet a little before night. Do you not
think so too?"

"It's quite, quite possible," she agreed dramatically, and
picked out her mail . . . a large envelope, directed in a
businesslike hand.

In her room, she threw her wraps aside and opened the
letter. As one's eyes go immediately to important things,
she took in the text of it at a glance:

. . . "so I think I can arrange to run out for about three
days . . . Christmas . . . two days after . . . isn't convenient for your Uncle and Aunt . . . at the hotel. . . ."

Oh, no . . . *no* . . . not *that!* Not *here* . . . not in
Maple City . . . nor out at the farm! Not to spoil her
plans for Christmas. *Spoil* them? What was she saying?
She stopped in amazement, appalled at the chaotic jumble
of her thoughts. Mechanically she walked over to the
window seat in the tower corner of the room and sat down,
the disturbing message falling into her lap. Something must
be done to stop his coming. He wouldn't enjoy himself. He
wouldn't mix with Uncle Jud and Aunt Biny and the
plain old farmhouse any more than oil and water mix. They
lived in two worlds. When school was finished she would

go back to that other world where everything was gay and pleasure loving. She fitted in there easily, as easily as she fitted in here, but they just didn't *mix*. She took the letter in her hand again. Why, her months of freedom were scarcely half over. She didn't want him to come *now* . . . not *yet*. . . .

"Why not?" She could hear Aunt Biny's voice, clear and honest.

She looked away from the letter, down at the old trees in the "Bee-House" yard, the elms and the maples, stripped and gaunt. They looked stupid and uncaring. A quick flash of tears swept her eyes. She felt small and childish. She wanted to take her disappointment to some one as a child does. Warner Field, big and clean-cut and substantial, was coming up the "Bee-House" walk and looking up toward the tower room. Suddenly she wished she could tell Warner Field about it. Warner would understand. When he saw her he waved his hat boyishly. Nancy smiled through her tears and waved her hand . . . the hand with the disconcerting letter in it.

Christmas was to be on Saturday. Contrary to usual custom, school was closing on Friday for only one week. All the school programs were on Friday afternoon, all but the Whittier, which was to be in the evening. "It's Nancy Moore's doings," Miss Gunn said. "I think I've let her wind me around her finger. She said it would be nicer at night and the fathers could come too, as well as the mothers. She thought the fathers needed to come as much as anybody. I'm sure I'd rather have the commotion in the afternoon and get it over." Enthusiasm varies inversely with the number of years one has taught.

Nancy, herself, was less enthusiastic about the coming event than formerly. It made such an incongruous picture, Mr. Farnsworth being entertained on Christmas Eve by the

various Swansons and Carlsons, and eating Christmas dinner
with Uncle Jud and Aunt Biny, Mattie and Walt and the
tag-ends of the boarders. There was something wrong in the
scheme of things. Over and over she assured herself that
it was because she was in a different environment; that
when she went back everything would be all right.

And then, quite suddenly, before she had told any one
but Aunt Biny that he was coming, Nancy heard from him
that he could not come at all. She had the sensation of one
who is being pulled hard with a rope and is suddenly let
down. She was ashamed at her feeling of relief and took
infinite pains to conceal it from Aunt Biny.

On the morning before Christmas there was something in-
describable in the air. At breakfast Warner could see it in
other people but he, himself, could not feel it. As he
walked to the bank he was thinking how queer it was that
you couldn't respond to the Christmas thrill when you got
older. He had been as crazy about it as any one when he
was a kid. The swift vision of their pleasant home in
Omaha reeled itself into his mind like a moving picture.
Father, knobby with bundles, trying to slip in unnoticed,
Mother interested and enthusiastic, putting the last touches to
the table. Eleanor, although much older, as full of girlish
excitement as he. There was the smell of food, the stolen
glimpses of the tree . . . stockings . . . fun . . . excitement. It had been long ago . . . all of it. Times were
different now. The entire world had slumped some way.
Life seemed one long grief with only flashes of the old
spirit. He thought of his book. Having worked too hard on
it, he was having a period of depression about it. Born in
enthusiasm, it was dragging a little. He wondered if it
was as good as he had thought at first. If his publishers did
not like it, he was through.

His mind wandered to world conditions. There was seething unrest in the labor unions. The farmers had not altogether pulled out of their state of depression. Business, while more confident, was just getting on its feet after a staggering blow. There were foreign troubles. Crime was rampant . . . immorality common. Christmas! After all it seemed a travesty to go through with it. Gifts . . . candles . . . the babe-in-the-manger-story . . . the mockery of "peace on earth"! Why didn't humanity ditch the whole thing and not go through with the dishonest farce?

He opened the heavy swinging door of the bank and went in. Marty Spencer looked up. "Well," he said jauntily, " 'Twas the day before Christmas and all through the bank, not a creature was stirring, not even the crank." He was light-hearted, debonair. He put a wreath in each window, stuck a sprig of holly in his buttonhole, another in the penholder and made a facetious crack about hanging mistletoe over the paying-window before the teachers came in with their salary checks.

There were a hundred routine duties. A constant stream of the community folk flowed in and out of the big revolving doors. Warner was uniformly courteous, habitually pleasant. It was one of his assets. So he spoke blithely about Christmas to each customer although there was not much genuine Christmas feeling in his heart: "Expecting your son home to-night, Mrs. Miller?" or, "By George, Mr. Denning, I'd retire and come to town if I'd sold seven turkeys like you have." But that inner feeling of generosity . . . peace . . . the thrill . . . would not come. He was as callous and unfeeling toward the holiday spirit as the adding-machine.

By noon there were a few snowflakes, fat, feathery, lazy. Nancy blew in to the "Bee-House" lunch with her eyes sparkling. "I ordered the snow," she announced. "I've prayed every day: 'Lord, make me pure in heart and bless the heathen and give us snow for Christmas, but if you can't do it all, don't mind me or the heathen!' "

She scarcely had time to eat. "I wish you'd all come to-night," she addressed the boarders *en masse.* "We're having one grand spree. It's early, at seven, so that the kinder-garteners won't fall asleep and tumble off their chairs. We've enough candy and peanuts for all the parents and all of you. Dr. Pearson would be a handy man to have around with his medicine-case. There's a grand tree that touches the ceiling and everybody has a 'piece.' To be sure, Roxy Swanson speaks one that needs an interpreter. In reality it is 'Let us in,' they clamored, 'let us in' they say. But it sounds like 'Lattuce-in-the-clabbord-lattuce-in-the-say.' "

By afternoon the rush at the bank was greater . . . mer-chants' deposits, cream checks . . . farmers' wives in for their shopping . . . Christmas bundles on the desks . . . small youngsters with their parents. School was out. It was snowing in a more businesslike way now. Crowds of children flocked past the bank windows, laughing, jumping up for the flakes.

At dinner time the table was in holiday spirits. There were several vacant places. Helen Blakely and Dr. Pearson were not there and George Kendall had gone home on the six-fifteen to spend Christmas with his mother. Genevieve had not known what attitude to take, that of hurt martyr or to let on that it had been their plan all the time. Pride got the best of her now and she was saying, "George couldn't bear to miss Christmas with his old mother, but as we had accepted the Rineland invitation before we knew he could get away, I'm staying here to keep the first dinner engage-ment."

Nancy appeared at the table in a creamy lace dress with pink rosebuds in her belt and a band of little satin ones in her hair.

"My word, Nancy," Marty Spencer put his hand over his face. "You'll knock an eye out of your youngsters."

"I may," she admitted coolly, "but just so it isn't Jakie Cohn's, he having none to spare."

Most of the boarders went down to the school. The idea did not appeal to Genevieve Kendall. Neither did Miss Ann go. "Everybody in this world can't take time to go galavanting around to things," she remarked acridly at the table. But Miss Rilla went, in a soft black silk dress with a spotless white lace collar. The Major, stolid and pompous, went, and Marty Spencer, who kept them all laughing, and Ambrose Jones, excited to the point of childishness. Warner took Nancy in his car. They were loaded with packages, and a crowd of pupils, like Arab beggars, surrounded and took possession of them on the walk in front of the schoolhouse. In the hall, when Nancy took off her coat, Johnny Bornheimer came up and touched her dress softly. "Miss Moore," he whispered, "you look like ice cream."

Walt and Mattie came, bringing Uncle Jud and Aunt Biny in Walt's car, Aunt Biny being able to sit in the back seat with Mattie only because she and her crutch were providentially of one and the same thickness.

Miss Gunn, dignified and calm, managed things. The parents from the district seemed to hold her in awe and respect! Some of the mothers who came had shawls over their heads. Some were plumed and decked in cheap jewelry. Some were dressed modestly and in good taste.

The tree in the old assembly room was a glittering thing. Electric lights in rainbow colors and all the variety of tinsel and ornaments that the town afforded were on it. Miss Gunn had scolded Nancy for spending so much. Mrs. Carlson was there with the three-months-old baby. It cried in a high thin piping voice. Gus took it part of the time and walked about the hall, jiggling it deftly, like an old hand at the business. Mrs. Carlson had started to get the children all ready at five o'clock. "A few months ago I'd have said, 'What's a woman want to take a baby anywhere for?'" Nancy told Miss Hays. "Now I have more sympathy for her."

The Swansons were there . . . Jim and Myrt and the children. Myrt, in a weird combination of slovenly wrapper and flashy fur-trimmed coat, sat and looked upon the spectacle with sluggish interest.

The program was on in full blast. Roxy Swanson spoke "Lattuce-in-the-clabbord-lattuce-in-the-say," with the boarders from the "Bee-House" politely avoiding each other's eyes.

Nancy's room had some tableaux. There were Joseph and Mary and the Babe in them. Joseph, in a blue table spread and turkish towel, stood first on one foot and then on the other, pressing his pasty beard onto his chin, and grinning sheepishly at his big brother sitting in the audience. But the little Mary knelt and looked into the painted, staring eyes of the doll in the manger with a great light and wonderment in her own. Potential motherhood, she was, with the first sweet gleam of the love of a mother in her eyes. Every one sat watching the children but Warner Field looked only at the little slim lace-gowned body of Nancy Moore, slipping in and out of the rows of pupils.

And then the entire school, with the lovely notes of the old song filling the assembly room, was singing:

"O little town of Bethlehem, how still we see thee lie."

As he looked at the earnest singers, their eyes shining with the unquenchable light of childhood, it came suddenly to Warner that the world was not in chaos to the children, any more than it had been to him when he was a child. Here was a new generation in all its freshness and its eagerness with high hopes and ideals. To the children it was still a most beautiful world, generous, forgiving, peaceful. Why in the name of humanity, as they grew to maturity, couldn't they keep it so?

It was after the song, and in the confusion of the children getting back to their places, that Nancy beckoned Warner into the hall. "Be Santa Claus for us, Warner, won't you? Gus Carlson thinks he ought to be banking the fires."

"Good heavens, Nancy. No."

"Please. For me! It's time to dress."

It was a little thing to do for her. So, feeling foolish, he put on the suit and the false face and distributed the gifts. From seeing the upturned faces of the children, something got into Warner's heart that had not been there in the morning. Not the old thrill, far from it, but something that served as well; a sense of pleasure in the small service . . . a warmth of feeling toward childhood.

"O little town of Bethlehem, how still we see thee lie."

The shrill voices rose and swelled again for the last time. Then they all went home. Johnny Bornheimer and Freddy and the young mother who had taken courage in seeing the happiness of her two boys. The Carlsons . . . Gus carefully carrying the new and eighth baby, asleep now, warm and dimpled and healthy.

"Maybe he'll be the smartest one yet, Gus."

"I bet he will, Jen."

The Swansons . . . Mrs. Swanson, phlegmatic and uninspired . . . Roxy, with the happy plan to become an actress and speak "Lattuce-in-the-clabbord," on a theatrical stage . . . the baby, having eaten all the candy that had been given him, starting now on the paper sack.

Warner took Nancy out to the farm. She wanted to be there early in the morning to help. The car slipped around some in the new snow. Warner would not come in. He had a package for her though. It was only a book he said.

So it came about that when Nancy went up the narrow built-in stairs to her room, she carried two unopened packages. She opened Mr. Farnsworth's first and exclaimed aloud from the sheer delight of seeing the creamy pink luster of the matched pearls that lay on the velvet cushion of their box. She took them out and held them across the firm young flesh of her arm, reveling in their sheen. Then she laid them back in the box and opened the book. It was one she had said she wanted to read. And Warner had remembered it. She turned the leaves. She wished she and Warner could read it together. But there was little chance. They were so seldom alone. Some one was always around, the boarders, or Uncle Jud or Aunt Biny. She wished she could see more of Warner. A swift rush of thoughts like warp wove themselves across the woof of her mind, forming a mental tapestry: a fireplace . . . a burning log . . . two deep chairs . . . candle light . . . the book . . . and Warner. For a long time she stood by the dresser in her old room and looked in bewilderment upon the wondrous results of her weaving. *Nancy, Nancy, did no one ever tell you that some tapestries are priceless?*

CHAPTER XIX

CHRISTMAS

O little town of Bethlehem!
How still we see thee lie.

WARNER at first thought he had been dreaming the melody of the Bethlehem song, but as it rose clearer, he could hear it plainly down below. It was Mary Mae Gates with the Congregational choir out in front of the "Bee-House." They had been around town singing the carols in the various neighborhoods. It was frightfully early and it must have been cold. Somebody else, then, was doing something that would give pleasure to others.

All night the snow had fallen. It rarely happens in the mid-west that there is a snowy Christmas any more. Even the Decembers are becoming sophisticated. Winter scarcely ever gets under way until after the holidays. So the snow was welcomed.

Out at the farm Uncle Jud and Aunt Biny and Nancy were all astir early. Nancy's room was cold and the snow was piled up against the east window. When she was dressing, she stopped to take the pearls out of their case again and enjoy their creamy rose luster. But she did not tarry with them long for the morning was to be full of tasks. When she went downstairs the three had their little tree and gifts together. After breakfast Nancy began to ask Uncle Jud to get out the old bobsled preparatory to going into town for the company. Uncle Jud protested vehemently.

"What in tunkit you want to do that fool thing for? Cars'll come right through this snow. Walt'll get part of 'em and Field'll run his car too."

"No," Nancy teased him. "It'll just start the day right to have the bobsled."

He fussed and fretted and fumed. And all the time he was arguing he was sitting by the range and oiling the harness, getting ready to give in to her. Nancy laughed at him. "When I was a little girl, I'd have lost my temper and stamped my foot and said things to you. And you'd have jawed me back. And we'd have ended in a regular tong war. But you can't make me get angry at you now. I know you too well. Your jawing and scolding is every bit of it on the outside of you, like the prickles on a thistle. Inside where your heart is, you're soft and silky and kind and nice and accommodating."

Uncle Jud laughed foolishly. An hour later he drove up to the door in the old bobsled, the bells jingling cheerily. Nancy brought down the robes from the attic . . . two old fur ones and a gaudy plush one, all smelling of moth balls.

Over at the Bornheimers' the snow sifted under the door of the cardboard house, but the tiny living room was warm. Miss Moore's old Uncle Jud had brought a load of wood the day before and piled it by the back door. There was a branch of a pine tree set up on a little stand and under it the Christmas packages from school and warm overcoats for Johnny and Freddy from Miss Moore. Mrs. Bornheimer cried a little over the coats when the boys were not looking.

Down at the Carlsons' the celebration was an hilarious one. Not a great deal of money but a great deal of energy had been put into it. "The' ain't no mudder livin' but what's got a duty to have de biggest and best Christmas for her kids she can get up," Mrs. Carlson had said to Gus, while she singed the pin-feathers from two of the well-mannered Plymouth Rock roosters. All the children were home but Essie. Mrs. Carlson couldn't understand what possessed Essie to be so crazy to go out in the country. "She said she'd be home for Christmas supper and all evenin', but no persuasion could get her to give up goin' out dere at noon."

And at the Swansons', the dynamic Roxy was engineering a noisy program of activities, in lieu of any energies on the part of her mother. She had wanted a Rhode Island Red rooster for dinner, but had been told that round steak wasn't so much work to get ready. "And anyway," Mrs. Swanson emitted nasally, "I ain't goin' to kill a single chicken . . . it'd tickle them Carlsons too much."

At the big house on the hill the gifts were very elaborate. Mr. Rineland gave Alice and Mama each ten shares of stock in the old First National and Alice and Mama gave Papa some Italian hand-carved candleholders they had long wanted. Warner sent a big box of roses. It was Alice who opened them. When she saw the accompanying card, she frowned and little green lights came into her eyes. Then she surreptitiously removed the card before any one could see it. Innocently enough it had said, "A Merry Christmas to the Rineland family."

Down at the "Bee-House," Miss Ann sat in her own room and observed Christmas in a very luxury of quiet. She did not comb her usually neat hair nor get out of a loose house wrapper. She read a little and dozed some and when the telephone rang, she said to herself, "It's likely to be some inspired fool wanting to say 'Merry Christmas' to me," and did not answer it.

It was eleven-thirty when Uncle Jud got out to the farm

with the boarders . . . Miss Rilla, Major Slack, Essie,
Warner, Ambrose Jones and Miss Gunn. Miss Ann sent
her regrets without explanation to Nancy. "No, you don't
need to make any excuses. I'm not going to tell her the
real reason and I haven't come to the point where I can lie
glibly," she had told Rilla. Walt and Mattie came together,
Mattie in her old black fur coat, stepping lightly in that
uncumbersome way, looking like a huge bear walking on
its hind legs.

The table was pulled out to its full length. Mr. Farnsworth had sent Nancy a big box of crimson roses and they
were everywhere in the old rooms. A mass of them she had
arranged for the table in a milk crock and banked smilax
around it. The dinner was a thing to be remembered. Miss
Gunn, in a wild orgy of celebration, mixed carbohydrates
and proteids with alarming disregard of consequences.

Major Slack, torn between his desire to settle conclusively
all the topics of conversation and to do justice to the mouth-
melting food, compromised somewhat disastrously by
attempting them both simultaneously.

Her eyes swimming in moisture, Miss Rilla, in the absence of Miss Ann's dampening influence, fairly oozed happiness.

The "bore," after his preliminary weather observations
had nothing more to say, but with a foolishly exaggerated
look of interest, bobbed his head this way and that to catch
every word emitted by the others.

Nancy had seated Walt by Essie. "Where you can
reminisce about the days when you and I were young,
Maggie," she had told them. Essie had to pinch herself at
intervals, with, "This is you, Essie Carlson, and this is
Walt Thomas helping you to food on Christmas day."

When the big dinner was over Essie went immediately into
the kitchen to help with the dishes. "No," Mattie said to her

with amazing insight, "you ain't goin' to touch a single dish for *one* day in your life," and sent her back to the others.

They all went into the shabby old sitting room and gathered about the huge coal burner, under the watchful eyes of the deceased Republican presidents. Warner sat back in the shadow of the room, watching Nancy's slim boyish figure slipping in and out of the crowd.

When they were settled, Nancy got Miss Rilla a box of old photos to look at. Miss Rilla wiped her eyes every time she picked up a new one. "And here's Lulu Whitney. My! My! It seems like yesterday that she was a little girl and used to run away. She was always anywhere but home. They lived in that old house back in the trees on Main between 6th and 7th. They had a parrot. Her mother would come to the door and call, 'Lu-*lu*-u-u.' All day we'd hear that and half the time it was the parrot calling her 'Lu-*lu*-u-u.' You couldn't tell the parrot from Mrs. Whitney. And here's Bertha Dean. Poor thing . . . she wanted to marry Ossy Smith and her father wouldn't let her . . . said Ossy wouldn't ever earn his salt and what do you suppose he is now? A way-up man for the Union Pacific, riding in a private car. Here's an old one of Dan Stevenson in his band suit. He played the fife in the fife-and-drum corps. Such a monkey . . . always up to tricks. When I was a young girl once he sent Sammy Platt, a foolish boy, to the door with a note for me asking me to go buggy riding. It was signed with Sammy's name and Dan had cautioned Sammy to do nothing but hand it in to me. But Sammy was only half-witted and had to spoil Dan's joke by saying, 'Dan Stevenson sent this to you.' " Miss Rilla wiped her eyes, moist with memory. It was a long time since Miss Rilla had enjoyed herself so much.

Nancy miraculously found out that Ambrose Jones could sing and persuaded him to demonstrate. She played the

old piano for him while he perpetrated in a guttural voice
but with an intense enjoyment: "Out on the Deep when the
Sun is Low." One gained the impression that the water
was very, very deep indeed.

And then Uncle Jud got started. He leaned back in his
big armchair and opened up. It was about an Indian scare.
"They sent word the Injuns was comin' down Tinklin'
Creek and Ma and me got ready to go with the crowd.
We aimed to get together and get into Postville. Ma
gathered up a lot o' stuff and we put it in the wagon as
quick as we could 'n made tracks toward Postville where
others was leggin' it. Awfulest scared bunch of folks you
ever see. And do you know, the thing I recollect plainest
about that there scare? Well, sir, 'twa'n't the scarey part
a-tall. 'Twas Lucindy Ray . . . she's long dead now . . .
'twas Lucindy Ray openin' up her wild strawberry jam just
'fore the wagons started, and spreadin' it two, three, inches
deep on slices o' bread for her children. 'I swear to Goshen,'
Lucindy says, 'there ain't no heathen papooses goin' to eat
this jam when we're gone.'" Uncle Jud slapped his knee
and roared. His huge gaunt frame shook with mirth. "Do
you know, nothin' come o' that scare. 'Twas a false alarm,
as luck would have it, and the Injuns rode off in another
direction and the wagons all went back. 'N what do you
suppose Lucindy Ray talked about all the time afterwards?
That there jam she'd went and opened. Jawed about wastin'
it, continually. Harped on it fer a year." More laughter
rolled out of Uncle Jud's hairy throat. "Don't it beat you?
Might'a' lost her scalp and instid o' being thankful the
whole scare went into nothin', just kep' complainin' over 'n
over about wastin' that jam."

It was after five when the company left. When Mattie
realized they were talking of going, she insisted on putting
on "a little snack" first. The "little snack" consisted of

cold turkey, potatoes, gravy, two kinds of salad, cake, raisin bread, pie, pudding, fruit, rolls and jelly. She hoped they would all get back to town through the cold ride without getting hungry. She suggested that each one take a piece of cake or something to eat later in the evening in his room.

Warner did not sit down to the lunch. "He's going to Rinelands' to their dinner, so please don't punish him by insisting on a lunch, Mattie," Nancy told her.

So Nancy and Warner had a few moments alone in the old sitting room. They stood together by the geraniums in the bay window.

"You've given them all a happy time, Nancy."

"I enjoyed it. It's funny how a little unselfish service reacts on a person. Sometimes I wonder if it's the biggest thing in the world . . . service."

"No, the biggest thing in the world is money."

Nancy looked up. Warner's tone was bitter. The mood was a strange one in him, and she did not like to see it. So she said, quickly:

"Thank you for the book, Warner. I'm going to enjoy it."

"I thought perhaps we could read it together." His tone was natural again. "I'm going to be very busy this coming week . . ." he was writing diligently every day . . . "but I'd like to come out next Friday if you've no other plans . . . and watch the old year out with you."

Nancy stood looking into the glowing coals of the old base-burner. Common Sense cautioned her. Desire beckoned her. Common Sense argued volubly and practically. But Desire sat down at a loom of dreams and wove a tapestry out of red firelight . . . a candle . . . two deep chairs . . . a book . . . and Warner. Nancy raised her eyes from the loom: "And I'd like to have you, Warner."

The morning after Christmas, Uncle Jud was cleaning the stalls of the cow stable. He did not feel good, was having one of those spells he had experienced several times recently . . . a lassitude so intense that it was with the greatest will power he kept on with his task. He told himself that it was all foolishness to tremble; that a big strong man like he was shouldn't be so babyish; that after he had finished the stable, he would clean the chicken house. He was beginning to be a regular Hank Thomas about the work; guessed if he paid no attention to feeling tired, he'd forget it.

Several times he leaned against the stall to steady himself. It was during one of these temporary resting periods, that Nick Denning and Major Slack appeared in the doorway. Because he was feeling such physical exhaustion, he felt a mental one also when he saw the two. He did not want to sell, but quite suddenly it seemed impossible to combat their combined robust wills. So he sat down on a box and listened with unaccustomed patience to their inducements. When the interview ended he committed himself to the extent of saying he would talk it over with Ma. But when he went into the house he felt too cross and tired to open up the subject.

On Friday night Warner was to come out. Before his arrival, Nancy put a few little finishing touches to the appearance of the old sitting room . . . straightening a picture or two, turning the chairs. What a homely old room! And what a quiet way to spend New Year's Eve! And yet if she were to be truthful she wondered which of the last four gay ones she would exchange for this.

Warner came through the snow. Soon after Uncle Jud threw his paper on the floor and stretched his huge arms with "I've always said a bed's a good invention." Then he wound the clock noisily, put a final bucket of coal in the huge burner and went to his room. Aunt Biny, too, slipped away after a while.

Warner and Nancy read and talked. Once when Warner made a special reference to something that happened during his senior year at college, Nancy realized that she ought to say, "Warner, I've never told you that your old friends, the Farnsworths, are my friends, too, and that when school is out I am going back East to marry Mr. Farnsworth."

It would have been the easiest thing in the world to say and the most natural one. She said it over to herself. But it seemed the hardest thing in the world and the most unreal. She put it off again. For a long time they sat in front of the red glow of the stove.

The hands of the Seth Thomas clock on the shelf pointed to the midnight hour. Then, a little wheezily, because of its half hundred years, it struck. Warner stood up and came toward Nancy's chair. Nancy stood up, too, hastily, a little frightened. But Warner stopped suddenly by her chair, thrust his hands deep into his coat pockets, and held them there. All he said was, "Happy New Year, Nancy."

"Happy New Year, Warner."

Now! Tell him now, Nancy!

So scarcely realizing that she was beginning, she said quickly, "Warner, there's something I want to tell you . . . that I *ought* to have told you long ago."

Warner thought he knew what she meant. The diaries . . . something that had happened when she was eighteen . . . something that had to do with the old brown shawl in the cabin. He did not care now what it was, so he only said, "There's something I want to tell you, too, Nancy, but not just yet."

So it went into nothing. Warner went away and Nancy had not told.

Aunt Biny, rousing up, thought that Nancy had gone

upstairs and left the light burning. So she got slowly out of bed and without her crutch worked her way from bed to chairs out to the sitting-room door. But Nancy had not gone upstairs. She was standing motionless by the outside door, with a look on her face Aunt Biny had never seen. Aunt Biny crept back to the bed and got down painfully on her knees.

CHAPTER XX

TRAGEDY AT THE BEE-HOUSE

AFTER New Year's winter got down to business. Day after day seemed very much alike. Snow . . . wind . . . sunlight on snow . . . blinding sparkles of it . . . dark gray days . . . low fleeting clouds . . . more snow . . . wind . . . long rows of stark poplars . . . black maples . . . dingy gray elms . . . English sparrows . . . crows . . . an occasional redbird against the white snow to make glad the heart of a poet . . . a poet like Aunt Biny with beautiful thoughts that she could never get down on paper.

Down at the Whittier the children were studying Eskimo life. "Miss Gunn says everything must be seasonal and correlate," Nancy remarked to Miss Hays. "But I don't see why it wouldn't be pleasanter to study Fourth of July things now and Eskimo life when the warm days come."

On the second-grade table was a miniature representation of life in the arctic. There were shoe-box igloos covered with cotton snow and parts of a broken mirror from the Carlsons' made a satisfactory if overly reflective icy sea. Pieces of rock salt playing the part of icebergs stood jauntily on the mirror. A papier-mâché seal which Roxy Swanson had brought from home, apologizing because the omnivorous baby had bitten off a piece of its tail, added a sporting touch. Woodpeckers, owls, jays, chickadees, doves and hawks entered largely into the daily conversation of the children.

Warner was working on the story every moment he could get. He felt now that it was good. His own sense of the value of things, his dramatic instinct, told him so. The old knack of expressing himself had come back and with it a deeper understanding of humanity. Many of the anecdotes which Uncle Jud and Aunt Biny told, some of the reminiscences of Mr. Rineland, his own childish memories and the tales of his father he wove into the pattern of the story.

Life at the "Bee-House" took on something of an uneventful routine. In the midst of the unexciting days Roxy Swanson took a hand and relieved the even tenor of things by breaking out with smallpox as thoroughly as she did everything else. She "didn't feel good," she said, and Nancy, remembering the day she had been afraid to tell the same thing to Miss Addison, had taken Roxy into her lap and held her for a while, a motherly but unpedagogical proceeding. That night Dr. Pearson called Nancy aside before dinner and told her the result of his trip to the Swansons'.

Many of the children were vaccinated. Dr. Pearson did some of the work deftly in his immaculate office. Old Doc Minnish, in his dusty office, with his dog nosing familiarly about, did the rest. He dropped the vaccine points on the floor and felt around in the dust for them, but apparently nobody was any the worse for it.

A few days later, Nancy, coming in late to dinner at the "Bee-House" and passing the dining-room door unobserved, took in the fact that there was no conversation although every one was in his place. A dull air of monotony pervaded the table. She stole swiftly up to her room, emerging some time later to take her place among them with unaccustomed quiet.

Miss Gunn was the first to speak. In an awed voice she asked: "Why, Nancy Moore, what is the matter with you?" Mary Mae Gates jumped up from her chair with a nervous half-stifled scream. Warner Field's heart leaped to his throat. Nancy's face was a mass of little red spots.

But Dr. Pearson rose leisurely and sauntered over to Nancy, took her by the arm and turned her about with: "Little girls who eat here are required to wash their faces before coming to the table." It had been one of Nancy's foolish tricks to paint her face with water colors and throw a little excitement into the dullness of the day. Yes, Nancy was the Peter Pan of the "Bee-House."

Out at Uncle Jud's the farmhouse seemed to sit drearily waiting in the wind until Friday night when Nancy, gay and snowy, would blow in like the breeze that came with her. Aunt Biny limped about all day doing the hundred tasks that awaited her. Uncle Jud was not doing anything more than the chores these days. He fussed and fretted a great deal to Aunt Biny about the cold. Never had known it to be so penetrating. He had a half notion to take Nick Denning's offer and move to Californy. Maybe he could get warm once he was out there. Aunt Biny, listening patiently, thought that it was all talk, that nothing could pry him away from the furrows he had first turned out of virgin soil.

In the third week of the month Alice Rineland and her mother left for New York City. They were to have two or three weeks of shopping, sightseeing, music and the theater and another week with Warner's mother and his sister Eleanor at the latter's home. Mr. Rineland and Warner saw them off on the night train with the baggage man, the agent, the fat mail boy and the hangers-on assisting at the ceremony. Warner sent messages to his people. When the train was coming in noisily, Alice put out both hands and raised blue eyes to him, "Four weeks is a long time, Warner."

It irritated and worried him. Her tone was unmistakable. Since Thanksgiving he had half suspected it and to-night he felt sure that she was misinterpreting his friendship for the family. So he had to add this knowledge to his other troubles, did he? All the way back to the "Bee-House" he was thinking it over and wondering if by any chance Mr. Rineland was misinterpreting it too. It was Nancy he loved. And Nancy? He could not be sure of her, of course. She seemed never to settle down to one mood. Does the butterfly settle down or the swallow? But in whatever mood he found her, she was infinitely dear and alluring. He looked up at the tower-corner bedroom. Things must drift along as they were until after the decision of the publishers. He was glad Alice was to be gone during these weeks. By the time her trip was over, he would probably know where he stood with the publishers . . . and Nancy. Whether he would stay in the bank was a question he evaded. For the time his mind must be on the work in hand . . . finishing the story.

He sprang up the stairs to his room and went straight to work on the manuscript, polishing, turning, cutting, inserting, retyping, putting all the little deft touches upon it which a sculptor puts on stone. He knew he was not treating himself well physically. This getting only a little sleep was wearing. But a few weeks more would finish the whole thing.

The next morning he arose, took a cold plunge to get himself fully awakened after the short night and went to the dining room. Dr. Pearson and Miss Gunn were the only two at the table. Strangely enough Nancy blew in next, looking as fresh as the cold morning itself. They joked her about the early hour. Scarcely had they dropped their banter when Miss Rilla, in extreme agitation, called from the stairway:

"Dr. Pearson . . . all of you . . . come."

The doctor was at her side in a moment. The others had risen, too, and followed him out.

"It's Ambrose Jones," she told them. "He's dead, I think."

It was so. When they got to the second floor room, he lay in a crumpled heap by the dresser, flattened up against it as though he had stepped aside to let the ladies pass by. His boyish blue tie was still in his hand. Miss Rilla explained many times, that she had been in the hallway, had heard a sudden choking sound and then some one falling. Dr. Pearson made a hurried examination. The "bore" was gone.

But even death itself could not keep the boarders' eyes from the little old lady who sat in the big chair at the far end of the room. Miss Rilla was crying in her tender-hearted, emotional way. "She's daffy," she told them. "Has no mind at all . . . is just a child."

The little old mother of Ambrose Jones in a neat dark dress and white cap sat folding pieces of bright-colored ribbon-ends and placing them in piles. She paid no attention to Dr. Pearson or Warner Field as they put the still figure on the bed. She went on smiling and humming and folding little gaudy-colored pieces of ribbon-ends that her oldest boy had brought to her from the store where he worked.

"He never wanted us to tell any one about his mother," Miss Rilla was telling them. "He couldn't bear to put her away in an institution. They've lived here almost two years and I don't believe anybody knows it but Sister Ann and Mrs. Carlson and I. He's always kept his door closed. They came one evening after dark. He has taken all the care of her . . . dressed her every morning and combed her hair. We've cooked her food but he always fed her himself. He told us she'd been that way for years . . . so gentle and harmless, poor dear. And poor Mr. Jones . . . poor boy . . . . I guess he never had a good time in his life with young people. He always acted hungry to see and hear them."

Nancy and Miss Gunn heard it from the doorway. Warner stood by and listened dully. The "bore"! He had cut him off short, had started off when he saw him coming. And the fellow had been hungry for companionship, had given the best of his life to protect his mother from prying eyes, as he himself had shielded his own mother from his father's disgrace. And now the "bore" lay still on the bed no longer able to stand between her and the curious. *That which I see not teach Thou me.*

Warner walked downstairs with Nancy, who was shaken. "I guess there's something in every one's life, Warner," she said suddenly. "How thoughtless we are of each other. I remember how he slipped outside his door and closed it quickly one night when I was taking candy around to everybody. I laughed at him because I thought he was embarrassed. I've made so much fun of him just to make you people laugh. Sometimes I think I'll never say a funny thing again."

But of course she did. She could no more have abandoned that gay little way of hers than she could have changed the color of her eyes.

Everything at the "Bee-House" was quiet and subdued for several days. They took the little old lady away, smiling, with her package of bright-colored ribbons in her hand. And they took the "bore" out beyond Tinkling Creek where the snow was thick on the cedars. It plunged them all into a realization of the great dark things of life. Especially to Nancy was life beginning to seem complex. There were so many more raw things about it: her own half-acknowledged troubles; the Kendalls all worked up over real or fancied wrongs; the "bore's" death; the Bornheimers barely existing; Uncle Jud's slipping health.

But is was not long until every one was gay. In a few days there began to be the same stir and small pleasantries at meals. Mary Mae Gates came in one night and dropped languidly into her chair. She was so fatigued she told the table. "I've been getting music ready for the Community Bazaar. I don't know why it always has to be *me*. Surely there are other people in this town who could take charge. But I'm shouldering it as usual. They are having twelve booths, one for each month and everything in it . . . just *everything*, appropriate to the month. Even the music, you know. In the May room I'm planning to have the duet: 'Oh, that we two were Maying.' That will be pretty and artistic. But appropriate music for some of the other months is going to be hard to get."

"That's easy," Nancy shrugged a lithe shoulder. "Just change the words of the same song. In the July room, you know, you could sing: 'Oh, that we two were *haying.'*"

In the midst of the general laugh Dr. Pearson added, "Sure, and in January: 'Oh, that we two were sleighing.'"

The others took it up noisily, "Oh, that we two were braying . . ." "neighing" . . . "laying" . . .

And the dinner went into one of those noisy jolly affairs to which the house had been accustomed before the "bore's" death. Life always closes over the vacancy and goes on.

CHAPTER XXI

"I LOVE YOU!"

FEBRUARY came in mild and sunshiny. On the second
the all-powerful groundhog saw his shadow and with
one whisk of his tail turned the whole tide of weather
affairs back to winter. On the surface of things the month
seemed to come in uneventfully. But months are never uneventful to a community. Some one has a deep trouble, a
great joy, a cruel disappointment, a thrill of anticipation.
To Warner came the pleasure and fear of calling his work
finished. In a small way he had the sensation of the Creator,
who, looking upon his handiwork, beheld "that it was good."
As he went over it for the last time he felt confident that
he had caught in it the spirit of the pioneers . . . the long
dip and swell of the prairie grass . . . the song of the
robins in the cottonwoods . . . the sunlight across the low
rolling hills . . . the rush of the high violent winds that
sweep the country . . . the hush of the low whispering ones
that die away as the dawn comes in. With all his writing
of sophisticated things he had been dissatisfied, but now
he had indited a goodly thing . . . the simple story of the
land that is neither east nor west. Warner not only felt
this but he understood fully what flame had relighted the
low burning embers of his talent.

And so the first part of February saw Warner and Nancy
seeking each other as naturally as the flower and the sun,
or the lark and the sky. It saw Nancy plunged into deep
groveling depths of depression for long moments, to emerge

213

as gay and nonchalant and unconcerned as though life were simple. It saw Uncle Jud sitting by the range, never quite warm enough, looking questioningly at his hands stretched out before the fire, watching them tremble, wondering what had become of the strength in those huge palms that had turned the prairie and built a home. It saw Aunt Biny limping about her homely tasks, stopping to look out of the window to watch the sunlight on the snow of the rolling hills. It saw Miss Ann troubled about many things; interest, grocery bills, insurance. It saw Miss Rilla anointing all the little troubles and joys of the town with the ointment of her tears. It saw George and Genevieve Kendall in a state of anger and resentment, straining at the chains that bound them. It saw Walt Thomas mending fences, cleaning the stables, getting all the odd jobs done before the avalanche of spring work came upon him, questioning the reason for Essie Carlson's plain little face seeming to haunt him. It saw Miss Gunn patiently adhering to her duties, looking forward to the day when she could begin to have some fun; Marty Spencer, light, frothy, touching at the tips of the blossoms of pleasure; Major Slack, pompous, bombastic, settling all the questions of the universe. It saw Mary Mae Gates practicing her scales and dreaming of concert halls and thundering applause; Dr. Pearson, scientific and immaculate, saving lives; old Doc Minnish, dirty, axle grease on his hands, oats in his pockets, saving others. It saw Essie, washing hordes of dishes, wistful, wondering why the Great Sculptor formed some girls lovely and gave them charm and vivacity and made others common looking and uninteresting. Tangled roots!

At the Whittier, the second-grade schoolroom took on the festive air of many birthdays. Among those prominent people whose natal days were scheduled for celebration were Washington, Lincoln, Longfellow, Jakie Cohn and the

Carlson twins. Every one lived in the thrilling anticipation of patriotism, cherries, hatchets and valentines.

And at the farm on the second Thursday of the month, Uncle Jud and Aunt Biny prepared to go to town. Uncle Jud got into a clean shirt laboriously. Strangely enough he was not fussing about it . . . that it had "too much starch in the blamed thing." He was very meek and very quiet. Aunt Biny, too, limped about the rooms, touching her crutch lightly to the floor, as she assembled her wraps for the journey. It was as though they were stepping softly in rooms where the dead lie sleeping. This was "The Day." Earthquakes have shaken mountains with no less sweeping effect. Revolutions have swept empires leaving no greater radical change. *They were selling the place.* He who flits lightly as a bird from shelter to shelter may not understand. He who changes abode easily does not know the love of such as these for the rafters that have stood the battering of the storm, the sheltering walls that have heard the roar of rains and the chimney from which has gone up the altar smoke of a home.

This place was home; and here were hearts made glad
With simple things, bread, laughter, wind and sun,
Red dawn, gray dusk, and rest when day was done.

And now it was to belong to some one else . . . to go to the Dennings. They had decided it definitely the day before and the Dennings wanted to see it through at once. Nick and Mrs. Denning came for them in the big car. They drove in the lane road and turned around before stopping. Uncle Jud and Aunt Biny were ready. Uncle Jud helped Aunt Biny into the back seat with Mrs. Denning and then climbed in the front with Nick. Nick had cleaned up for the event. Mrs. Denning, tall and angular, was clean, too, but she had spoiled the looks of one of the highest priced suits and hats in Maple City.

All the way into town Uncle Jud did not say much. Aunt Biny, too, left the conversation largely to the neighbor woman.

They went immediately to the bank where Mr. Rineland took them into his private office. The contract was drawn up. Uncle Jud signed it. Aunt Biny signed it. Warner Field witnessed it. Mr. Rineland, as notary, acknowledged the execution of their voluntary deed. Mr. Denning paid down a thousand dollars cash. The date of possession was given as March fifteenth. Ten thousand dollars cash was to be paid on that date and the balance with a note secured by a first mortgage on the land. All business transactions. All dry data. All in the day's work of the bank. Just a sale of "one hundred and sixty acres with all buildings thereon." But nothing of the sale of the wood thrush that sang at evening, the phlox that grew on the way to the well, or the light that lay on the rim of the prairie. In the transaction nothing included the transfer of a half century's hopes and fears, or the title to love and service and memories.

When the deal was over, Mr. Rineland told Jud he was glad he had done it. "You can rest now and take things easy."

Old Jud Moore nodded his huge gray head in affirmation.

On the way home Nick was loquacious. He felt good that the deal was over. "You'll see some changes when you come back from Indiany or Californy visitin' us," he chuckled. "Carl and I got a lot o' plans to fix it up. Your old orchard for one thing. 'Tain't been my business heretofore . . . that that ain't been profitable. But now 'tis. Carl 'n I plan to cut the trees 'n grub out the stumps. Turnin' that ground into popcorn will pay better than those few old apples you're gettin' now. We're goin' to cut the cottonwoods too. Never could bear that white fuzz blowin' around."

There were other changes to be made. The row of osage oranges in front of the corn was to come out, he explained. "They sap out the life of several rods of good corn land. Likewise part of the maple windbreak, soon as we can get the choppers. Whole thing's too shady, Jud."

Uncle Jud helped Aunt Biny out with no word. The Dennings drove away. Aunt Biny limped into the house and Uncle Jud went out to the barn. He did not stop there but walked on past it down the lane road and toward the orchard . . . walked along in his Sunday suit, his best overcoat and muffler and thick winter cap, dressed as though he had come from a funeral. The snow crunched under his buckled overshoes. In the orchard he stopped and looked around him, dazed. He put a huge calloused hand out on one of the trees, touching its moist gray bark gently. He went on until he came to Tinkling Creek, tramping along its bank and thrusting aside the wet frozen branches in his path. He came then in time to the edge of the cornfields and the wheat land and the pasture and looked long at them lying under their quilts of snow. He made the entire rounds of the place in the chill of the late afternoon, coming back to the house lot past the maple windbreak and the cottonwoods. Under the maples he stood for some time and looked up into their gaunt towering branches. A hundred empty nests swung idly in the wind . . . houses from which the soul had gone. Then old Jud Moore turned and went slowly up the back path to the kitchen door.

On the third Saturday of the month Warner heard from the publishers. As he picked the letter from the mail he had a nervousness, half fearful, half pleasurable, about opening it. The letter was brief. The story was the best thing he had done. They wanted him to come on East for a conference. He laid the letter down on his desk and sat quietly, humbly before it. He had no boyish joy over the acceptance. The feeling lay deeper. He had worried and worked and anguished too much the past year, to spring into any expression of pleasure. Only a deep thankfulness, a welcome relief was within him. As soon as he could catch Mr. Rineland alone, he went to him with the letter and asked how he felt about the trip. He would make it as quickly as possible, he explained. A day down in New York, one day out with his mother and sister, a few hours in Chicago to attend to some business and he would be back before that busiest time of all country bankers . . . March first. Mr. Rineland, kind and accommodating as always, readily assented to the plan. Mr. Rineland had received an important letter too, he said. "Alice and Mama will be home Sunday night. They've had a nice trip. I'm afraid Maple City will seem a little monotonous to them."

Warner immediately set Sunday night as the time of his departure. He was anxious to have everything cleared up, a whole series of unsettled things . . . payment for the serial, a partial cancellation of the debt, his feeling for Nancy put into words, his friendship for Alice back in the place it belonged, a decision made on his future work. He did not like uncertainties.

Sunday night at the "Bee-House" supper table, the conversation was largely about Warner's leaving for New York. For one of their number to be going to the big town was an event. There was a good deal of talk about the whole boarding house going down to the station to see him off.

"It's too late," Major Slack settled the question. "Eleven-five is too late for anybody to sit up."

In the evening Warner went dutifully up to the Rinelands' to see the travelers, first-hand knowledge of his mother and sister his only reason for going. He excused himself early and somewhat incoherently for one of his usual straight-forwardness. Alice cried a little when he had gone. And she felt a certain resentment toward Mama. It was the first time she had ever wanted anything that Mama did not get her at once.

It turned out that three of the boarders did go down to the train with Warner . . . Nancy, Dr. Pearson and Helen Blakely.

When Helen and the doctor stopped at the weighing machine inside the stuffy waiting room, Warner and Nancy went outdoors and sauntered down past the baggage room. There were empty milk cans piled high a little way beyond. They walked on past them and past chicken crates from which came a rustling feathery sound. With that sixth sense that lies buried somewhere in the region of things intuitional, Nancy felt a vague uneasiness. So she covered it with small chatter. "These same chickens were here five months ago when I came."

At the end of the freight shed Warner broke into the monologue. "I wanted to tell you alone the reason for this trip, Nancy. It's to see my publishers. When you came last fall I was in a blue funk over my writing. I think you're responsible for helping pull me out of the slump into which I had fallen. I've just completed and sold a book-length story."

Far off the incoming train whistled for the grade. "I suspected it, Warner." Common sense waved frantic signals to her, but to save herself she could not help what crept into her voice. "But I wanted you to *want* to tell me."

The long screech for the first town crossing sounded shrilly. "I *want* to tell you many things, Nancy, but I'm waiting until I come back." Suddenly he caught her to him. "No . . . I'm not waiting either." He held her close, and kissed her. "The first thing . . . and the last one . . . is *I love you*." The train was sweeping in. "All the others in between, I'll tell you when I get back."

Nancy forgot everything in the world, excepting that he was Warner, and clung to him. Then all the love that was in her face was swept out on a tide of remembering. The train was snorting like an angry animal with snow on its back. Warner was hurrying her by the side of it and she was gazing stupidly at him swinging up the steps of his sleeper. Then she was with Dr. Pearson and Helen walking toward the doctor's car. She stumbled a little when she stepped in.

"Cheer up, Nancy . . . it's only for a week," the doctor joked her.

And Nancy, the saucy, had no answer for him.

At the "Bee-House" she slipped up the two flights of stairs and into her room. But she did not turn on the light. Just inside the door she stood with taut nerves and tense body. She must think the thing out immediately, plan what to do. She should have told Warner the circumstances months before, but it was futile now to waste time in regrets. The thing was to decide what to do with the present situation. But she could not think clearly for remembering those last moments at the station. She closed her eyes under the memory of them. In all her joy of living she had not dreamed that life could give so rare a thing. Love then was the high ecstatic thing at which she had scoffed. It was all Aunt Biny had said it was . . . deep and very precious. It was not fragile. It was strong. And it had nothing to do with *things*. How right Aunt Biny had been! Aunt Biny, who was neither educated nor sophisticated . . . how wise she was!

She had a sudden great desire to see Aunt Biny, to tell her everything, to ask her what to do. She wanted to go out

home and sit at her knee and ask her help. She went over to
the window seat and looked out, with some wild thought of
attempting to make the trip. But it was dark and slushy
and almost midnight. She dropped down on the floor and
buried her face in the pillows of the window seat in an
attempt to make some plans. But she could do nothing
much but fight the memory of Warner; and while she was
doing so, old Judge Baldwin's clock on the stairway struck
midnight and one and two. It was cold. The wind blew
around the room in the tower. Once she got up and put
on a warm bathrobe over her dress. Down on Main Street
the electric light on the corner made an eerie circle of shadows in the street. Always her thoughts came around in as
circuitous a track as the shadow in the street . . . Warner
. . . Mr. Farnsworth . . . her position . . . the contract
with the board . . . Uncle Jud and Aunt Biny . . . and
then Warner again. Life was no longer merely "queer" to
Nancy. It was tragic.

Nancy was not the only one awake in the stillness of the
cold night. Warner Field, in the small quarters of his
berth, lay with his hands under his head and thought of
many things in his life; when he was a little boy in Omaha,
his years in preparatory school, his college days, his first
accepted writings, the careless free-handed way in which
he had spent his income, the thing his father had done, his
debt, his own and his mother's illness in the epidemic, the
turn of the wheel that had sent him to Maple City, the new
story . . . Nancy! Everything in his life seemed leading to
her. Even his troubles had been necessary for the
meeting with her. Was it possible that things worked out
that way, that griefs and anxieties were necessary threads to
be woven into the cloth of happiness? And lying there with
his eyes on the swaying curtain, he lived over that last moment at the station with Nancy. How lovely she was!

Every feature was full of youth and vitality. He tried . . . and without success . . . to decide what was the most exquisite thing about her . . . her wide brown eyes, tender and merry . . . her soft laughing mouth or that lovely line of her throat.

And Jud Moore was awake. He was too cold to sleep. Even the extra comforter that he had pulled up cautiously made no difference. And he kept thinking of queer things . . . seeds that rotted in the earth and never came up . . . empty birds' nests that swung all winter in the wind and never saw spring . . . snow that drifted and drifted and never melted. . . ! Moving slowly and stopping every few moments to see if he was waking Ma, he got out of bed and made his way to the kitchen. Shutting the door so that she might not hear, he lighted the lamp. Then he built a fire in the range and heated water, putting his feet in a pail of it to see if he could warm himself. This was Sunday night he was thinking. Nancy wouldn't be home until next Friday night. He must have a talk with her . . . wouldn't put it off again. That was the trouble with him . . . doggone it . . . always talked a lot when there was no need of it and was tongue-tied when he ought to be talking. He wished he felt good. February and March were bad months. He'd be all right again in April. He'd be ready to go into the field by the time the frost was out of the ground. God A'mighty . . . *he had no field*. The slow, painful tears of an old man slipped down his hairy cheeks.

A quarter of a mile away Walt Thomas was awake. He was having one of those restless spells again. He wished he could get that queer new problem settled in his mind: If a person had loved once, could he love again?

Over in town Johnny Bornheimer was awake. He was hungry and he cried softly to himself so that his mother might not hear. At the "Bee-House" Genevieve Kendall was awake. She had been in to the bank that day to ask Mr. Rineland what lawyer was the best one for her to retain for divorce proceedings. Mr. Rineland had made her angry, had tried to tell her that George was all right, said that everybody had something to put up with. She guessed she knew George a lot better than Mr. Rineland did. Miss Ann was awake. The spring taxes would be due in a few weeks. Manage as she would this winter, the income from the boarders only seemed to set the table again and pay Essie and Mrs. Carlson. She thought of the pride that her father and mother had taken in the big house and the pride that was keeping it in the Baldwin name. Pride! It had been the Baldwins' Nemesis. Out on a country road Dr. Pearson was awake. He had to grit his teeth to keep the numbness of sleep from creeping over him as he drove in from a country call. Several times he jerked himself up on the verge of letting the enemy overtake him. A moment of succumbing and the steering wheel would turn traitor and snuff out his life. Helen Blakely was awake. She had heard Dr. Pearson's car go out and he was not back. It made her think of anxious women everywhere . . . fishermen's wives standing on wind-swept shores, miners' wives at the yawning mouths of pits, aviators' wives looking up at tiny specks in the sky. For a few moments all over the community many people roused and thought of the things which lay close to their hearts and turned and could not sleep.

But Miss Gunn slept. She had reviewed the causes, remote and immediate, of the French Revolution and her mind was easy because of the important thing it had accomplished. And Miss Rilla slept, comfortable and wholesome. Marty Spencer slept, his mind as unruffled as a boy's. The Major slept, snoring as spasmodically as the guns at San Juan, sunk in oblivion as deep as the battleship in the waters of Havana. And Mary Mae Gates slept and dreamed of a curtain that raised and raised, before which she bowed and bowed. In the Italian Renaissance house up on three terraces, Alice Rineland slept. She and her mother had perfected a plan in the evening after Warner left and because she felt a sense of certainty that things were to come her way, she had fallen into a contented sleep. Across the creek the Swansons and the Carlsons slept, healthy and crowded, three in a bed. And out beyond the arched iron gate under the bending cedars, Ambrose Jones, the "bore," slept most quietly of all.

CHAPTER XXII

ALICE RINELAND PERFECTS A PLAN

ON Monday it turned warmer so that the snow began to slush and slop under foot and the culverts to run water. Nancy went to school, weary and troubled. Her head ached from worry and loss of sleep. School did not go well. Herman Guggenmeier had a stubborn streak and sat idle with his under lip hanging out. Nancy was too impatient with him to employ her usual tact and shook him briskly so that he went from a comparative state of stubbornness into a superlative one. Roxy Swanson irritated her beyond measure with her mature didactic way of suggesting various improvements in Nancy's mode of teaching. With supreme sarcasm she said, "Roxy, do you want to change places with me and do the teaching?" a suggestion which delighted instead of abashed Miss Swanson. In the middle of the forenoon the fire gong sounded. It was only drill, but Nancy's stripped nerves jumped to meet it. The Superintendent took this auspicious morning to arrive on an inspection trip. Because there was slushy snow in front of the building he drove up to the side, so that Nancy did not see him until he opened the door of her room. To Miss Hays, at recess, she accused him of sneaking up on them like an Indian.

At lunch Marty Spencer greeted her with an inane, "Feeling like a grass widow, Nancy?" and was silenced by Nancy's unspoken speech. Essie, bringing creamed salmon, which Nancy detested with a hate as deep as the waters in which it was speared, whispered as she passed her chair, "He forgot to take a bunch of clean collars he had laid out on his dresser."

How they all connected her with Warner! The friendship had drifted into its present state by such infinitesimal progress, too. And she must summon all her courage and be ready to meet Warner with the truth when he came back. She had decided to stick it out. For a time she had thought of precipitate flight. It was the easier way and the cowardly one. But her contract with the board was not a trifling matter. No, she would face Warner and tell him what she should have told him long before. There was no one to blame but herself. As she was finishing lunch, Essie called her to the 'phone. Even then her first thought was of Warner. Nothing had happened to him, had it? Then she was reviling herself for thinking of him first, when Aunt Biny might be ill. But nothing had happened at all. It was Alice Rineland wanting her to come to dinner that evening. She would come for Nancy in the car at six she said. Why this sudden burst of friendship, Nancy wondered listlessly as she accepted? At least if she went to the Rinelands' she would be spared the insipid jokes of the boarders concerning Warner's absence.

The afternoon in the second grade at the Whittier was typically miserable. Nothing big occurred, just a swarm of irritating things that would not have seemed so if she had not been in a constant state of worry. When the books were put away and the thirty-one heads were bowed, that: "Now the day is ended, night is drawing nigh," was as welcome as the lighthouse to a tired mariner.

Nancy dressed carefully for the Rinelands, remembering those other days when she had felt sensitive about her clumsy clothes by the side of Alice's dainty ones.

At six Alice came in the sedan, the water splashing the

running-board as she drove up in front of the "Bee-House." Essie was putting on the table the dishes of radishes which Miss Ann was begrudging. "They expect them, though, this time of year, so what are you going to do about it?" she had growled. Essie looked out. "My! Nancy, you're climbing up in the world," she called from the dining room as Nancy came down the stairs. "My goodness," she added, "you look like a million dollars."

Nancy went down to the old granite carriage block from which Miss Ann and Miss Rilla had once stepped into their pony cart.

"You shouldn't have brought out your shining car for me, Alice."

"Oh, we keep a man to clean it, you know." Most people could have stated it as a matter of fact. In Alice's voice it sounded smug, complacent.

At the Rineland home the two girls went into the big living room with the mulberry davenport and the overstuffed chairs, the silk-shaded lamps and the grand piano. Straight as a needle to a magnet, Nancy's eyes went to a big picture of Warner on the fireplace mantel. Out of a room rather overfurnished with *objets d'art* the picture caught her the moment she stepped inside.

Mr. Rineland was there, his clothes immaculate, every gray hair in place. He was pleasant and hospitable, was glad Mama and Alice had asked Nancy to dinner. He shook her hand cordially. "It's nice to have you here, Nancy. Of all the little girls that Alice knew, I used to enjoy your coming the most."

Nancy smiled at him. Dear Mr. Rineland! He said that same thing every time she saw him.

"Well, your Uncle Jud has sold his farm, Nancy."

"Yes, I'm glad. In one way I hate to see the old place go, but it's best for them."

"He's a great character . . . Jud Moore is . . . loyal and honest . . . the salt of the earth."

Mrs. Rineland came in. She was overdressed. She had on a rose-colored dress cut on sixteen-year-old lines and long seed-pearl earrings. Her small peaked face seemed squeezed between the two dangling appendages. She was feeling a sense of elation over the fact that Nancy was no doubt overwhelmed at the grandeur of the house. It was the greatest pleasure she had in Maple City, to be able to catch a look of wonder and admiration on the faces of her local callers when they were ushered in. If she had known how little it was awing Nancy, the evening would have been spoiled for her.

Dinner was served. It began pleasantly enough. It may have been more elaborate than the occasion warranted.

"I haven't had a chance to ask you about your trip, Alice."

"It was very nice. Mama and I enjoyed it. We spent a week, you know, with Warner's people." She spoke quietly and gently. Nancy was uncomfortable. She could feel the blood mounting to her face.

"Fine people," Mr. Rineland expressed himself. "Fine family. I have known them since the days when they first came to Omaha. Matthew Field was a rare man, college-bred, from an eastern family of splendid lineage. The mother was a real lady out here in the young West, when the word meant something more definite than it does now. Mr. Field's untimely death shocked every one. Warner is a great deal like him, courteous, clean-cut and sincere. Everybody respects Warner. There is something extremely likeable about him."

Nancy could have cried from the way she was shaken. She was afraid they could hear the pounding in her ears.

"We're looking for Mrs. Field and Eleanor to come out in the summer," Mrs. Rineland said. "They will visit in

Omaha first and then come to us here. Aren't those the
plans, Alice?" She shot a sharp hawklike glance from Alice
to Nancy. Alice's gray-blue eyes were soft, guileless.

"The present plans," she smiled. Nancy felt horrid and
vexed. She had an instinctive sensation of being caught in
a trap and politely tortured. Mr. Rineland was sincere.
The women sounded as though they were giving a well re-
hearsed dialogue. She changed the topic of conversation
herself. And then after a time dinner was over.

Mr. Rineland went to his library to smoke. Mrs. Rineland, too, excused herself rather incoherently. The two
girls went into the living room again. Nancy curled up in
a big chair near the piano. "Play, Alice," she urged. "It
will be nice to hear real music, again. I amuse myself with
it at the 'Bee-House' and Mary Mae Gates amuses *herself*
but she's no Ponselle and I'm no Rachmaninoff."

Alice chose something at hand, not too discriminatingly.
When she had finished, the final chord ending rather
abruptly, she slipped over to the davenport. Her soft pale
prettiness stood out cameolike. "Let's just talk now, Nancy.
There's something I've been wanting to discuss with you
for a long time."

So there *was* a reason for the invitation! Unaccountably
Nancy's heart stood still and then raced headlong.

"It's a delicate subject," Alice had the air of one shrink-
ing from an ordeal. "I want you to take it all right." She
was hesitating. There was something sweet and diffident
about her approach to the subject. "It's about Warner."
She looked up, her gentle face bland and free from any
malice. "Nancy . . . Warner . . . is seeing too much of
you for his good. You needn't think I don't know it. I want
to be fair with you though. I don't think you consciously
mean to . . . but you just naturally get men to like you. It
was that way even in high school you know. Walt Thomas

and the other boys . . . all seemed to like you." For a moment she evaded Nancy's brown eyes which, wide as full moons, were gazing disconcertingly at her. Then she met them again with soft blue ones.

"Nancy," her voice broke a little, "before you came things were just at a crisis with Warner and me. Everything was all right. He was happy and contented . . . and then you came. Remember, Nancy, I say again just what I said before . . . I want to be fair . . . I don't think you *consciously* did anything wrong. If it hadn't been for the 'Bee-House' and your being thrown in there so constantly with him, this little confession wouldn't be necessary. But we have to accept men as they are, and . . . there's so much in *propinquity. . . !*"

Nancy's lip curled a little.

"It isn't a fair advantage you have had," the smooth melting voice went on, "to be able to see him every day that way. . . ."

Involuntarily Nancy looked over at Warner on the mantel. How substantial he was and strong and decent and *sincere!* A quick flash of tears swept her eyes.

"I wanted to come straight to you and lay the facts before you," Alice explained gently, "instead of doing anything underhanded. That's not *my* way. I thought maybe . . . if you understood . . . you'd do what was right. I've always thought of you as one of my best friends and it seemed to me the honest thing to do was to throw myself on your mercy . . . as humiliating as it is . . . for it *isn't* easy, you know, to discuss this with an outsider . . . and tell you that before you came we were practically engaged . . . there was a tacit understanding even if we had no formal engagement." She was very careful to put it honestly. "I can't think for a moment you did me an intentional wrong . . . but being there with him every day . . ." She brushed tears from her

gentle eyes with the daintiest of handkerchiefs. Nancy sat
tense, unmoving.

"It *was* humiliating, Nancy . . . back at Warner's home
. . . in all the questions from his mother and Eleanor . . .
to have to evade anything about your growing friendliness to
him and your being with him so much." By those little surreptitious touches of which she was past mistress, she was
deftly crediting all the activity of the friendship to Nancy.
"And all the time that tacit understanding between us and
between the families. Papa, you know, worships the ground
Warner walks on. You heard him to-night. He has
planned so much on . . . on *us*. And he'll do so much
for Warner. You can see for yourself how he is training
him in the business. He talks everything over with him
. . . loans and notes . . . grooming him for his own
place when he retires." She explained the fact gently to
Nancy, as to a child. "It will all be his . . . some day . . .
Nancy . . . the bank, the farm, the house. Leaving myself
out of it, rising above my *own* feelings, Nancy, merely to
look at Warner's best interests . . . *his* future life and success . . . it seems too bad that he should . . . should risk
his future for a little mild boarding-house-table flirtation.
Now doesn't it . . . *honestly* . . . dear?"

She paused and when there was no answer from the slim,
brown-eyed girl, curled up in the big chair, she took courage
and went on, "I'll put my pride in my pocket, Nancy, and
admit there's something about you that must be fascinating
to him. He's even made that clear to me . . . that when
you're with him you're more or less physically attractive
to him. . . ."

Nancy's lithe body sprang into tenseness. Her eyes
flashed. Her hands clenched into hard fists. A fury seized
her that she was compelled to listen to this insult. She had
not felt that temper in years. It seized her now, rolled over

her in red throbbing waves of anger. All the little soft veiled thrusts, all the mean gently-given innuendoes of all the years flew to her mind like the return of a thousand buzzing stinging insects. They infuriated her. She wanted to injure the soft white girl sitting there and saying those things. Her fury shook her, carried her to her feet. She bent before it like the wheat of her prairie before an onslaught of the southwest burning wind. It unloosed her tongue. "You're lying, Alice! Warner Field has never discussed me with you that way . . . not at all . . . *not ever* . . . at any time. You're just suggesting it . . . like you always do . . . suggesting little soft slippery lies that one can't refute. I had rather see a person *sin* frankly and regret *nobly*, than go through life small and underhanded, pricking people with their little needle thrusts. This time I'll not take them like I was a weakling. I used to take them all . . . all the little mean underhanded things you used to say . . . and swallow them . . . I thought I had to. . . . I was afraid of you even as a child . . . because you were rich and we weren't . . . because you had lovely things and I didn't. But I'm not afraid of you any more. This is the last time you'll ever say things like that to me . . . I won't take them any more. You're not telling the truth and you know it. . . . Warner hasn't *ever* humiliated me in his conversation to you . . . not *ever* . . . you *lie* . . . do you hear? . . ."

"*Nancy!*" She heard it as plainly as though it had been spoken in reality. If it lay in the realms of the subconscious it did its work just as effectively. Her body still tense, her face livid, her hands clenched, she whirled toward the picture on the mantel. The steady, severe eyes of Warner Field called to her. "Nancy!" they said, "be quiet." She stood for a moment gazing in wonder at the picture. Then all her anger left her, like a garment dropping away. She sank back in her chair, quiet, contrite, humiliated. Her temper!

She thought she had conquered it long ago and now it had
risen to confront her, a stark, strong, mean, unlovely thing
of which she was ashamed.

Alice, whose handkerchief had covered her face during the
tirade, stole a surreptitious glance through her fingers. She
had gone too far. Very well, she had one card left, the sur-
prising thing that her mother had told her last fall. "Don't
use it," her mother had said, when they planned this conversation, "unless it becomes necessary." It seemed necessary. Her hands fell away from her face and little flecks
of green covered the blue of her eyes. Her mouth was a
hard straight line. She looked like her mother. "Maybe
you don't believe it, Nancy," her voice was soft and low.
She spoke without anger as though showing Nancy how a
lady would act in a trying scene. "Maybe it *is* hard for you
to believe that any man could like another girl when *you*
are around. But if that's hard for you to believe, it isn't
going to be at all hard for Warner Field to believe what I
shall tell him about *you* . . . why you left your home hurriedly four years ago. Did you take it with you . . . East,
to college . . . the *brown shawl*, Nancy? Why don't you
show it to Warner . . . and tell him all about it?"

The color dropped away from Nancy's face. She sat
staring at the girl on the davenport. "I didn't know any
one knew, Alice," she said quietly.

Just outside the living-room door draperies, Mrs. Rineland slipped away as softly as the shadow of a hawk moves
over the prairie at dusk.

For a few moments there was no sound in the room.
Alice, examining the lace of her handkerchief, looked up
through her lashes. Nancy sat unmoving with no words.
Then she stood up and threw out her hands in a helpless
sort of gesture. "Well, I'll go . . ." she said, but it was as
though she spoke to Warner on the mantel instead of Alice.

"I haven't had the courage to face it. But now . . . I'll go."

She turned back to Alice. "I'm sorry for my temper," she said quietly. "I thought I was over such childishness. It was unforgivable after your hospitality. I shall suffer for it all the days to come, far more than you. I'm going . . . right away . . . before Warner gets back . . . to-morrow, I think. But I want you to know, Alice, that neither thing you have told me is the reason for my going." She spoke without emotion, not angrily, but as one giving ordinary facts. "It's not fair to myself to leave, letting you think that you have accomplished this by bringing me here and telling me what you have. I'm not unselfish enough to go without telling you that I can see through you like tissue paper. I'm not going to give you that satisfaction for I'm not that quixotic. I've bungled things dreadfully . . . and I'll go. But what you've said to-night about your 'tacit understanding' and what you say about the shawl and my leaving home hurriedly . . . neither of those reasons would have the weight of a feather if things were different. It would be for Warner to say about the 'understanding' and no one would be more fair and kind and just about the other than he. I'm going . . . but neither cause you've given is the reason."

This was the time, now, to tell Alice about Mr. Farnsworth. This was the moment to spring her news . . . the high laughter-provoking moment in which to crow over Alice. But she had no heart for it. In some inexplicable way Alice seemed to have won. In some manner, not readily to be grasped, it was Nancy who seemed to have met defeat.

Alice rose too. "I want you to do what you think is best, Nancy." Seeing that the thing was working out well, coming her way, she was gracious. It never paid to be anything other than courteous. "I've just laid the facts before you.

I'm sorry you fail to believe me." Her eyes were soft, dove-like, blue. "But it's lovely of you to settle it this way. I've always said that at heart you were good and noble."

Nancy sighed and shrugged her shoulders. "Never mind the noble stuff," she said dryly.

"Just one thing more I'm asking before you go . . . and it means a lot to me . . ." Alice threw herself again on Nancy's mercy, "that neither Warner nor Papa need know of this talk. You can imagine how humiliating it would be to have either one know."

"You needn't worry," Nancy's head was high. "I'll not tell your father and I'll not . . ." if she drooped a bit it was only momentarily, "I'll not even see Warner."

CHAPTER XXIII

NANCY LEAVES MAPLE CITY

ON Tuesday morning Nancy made an early appointment to see Mr. Rineland in his office. All the way downtown from the "Bee-House" she was dreading to tell him about breaking her contract. But the interview proved to be short and Mr. Rineland very kind. "I'm sorry, Nancy, to have you leave this way." He followed her out into the bank lobby as though there were more he wanted to say. "And I hope you will be very happy. Any young man who holds your love is fortunate." Nancy did not tell him that the man was not young and held only her respect. But when she was starting away again and he told her confidentially, "Of all the little girls who used to come to see Alice, I liked you best," she could even smile a little at that.

There was a great deal for Nancy to do, so many things, in fact, that she was too busy to think much about her own mental reactions. She telephoned Aunt Biny next, so that her leaving would not be too abrupt. While the first bell was ringing, she slipped into Miss Gunn's office and told her. Miss Gunn stood by her west window and looked silently out at the sodden day. Stiffly she put an arm unused to caresses around Nancy's slim boyish shoulders. "Nancy, *I* had a lover once," she said, simply. "He died . . . and after that I gave my boys and girls my whole life."

Nancy looked up at Miss Gunn; plain, middle-aged, intellectual. And Miss Gunn once had been young and eager and loved a man. "Anyway," Nancy said a little bitterly, "if he's dead, he *belongs* to you."

236

Yes, she could teach all day, she told Miss Gunn. The children wouldn't need to know anything about it. It would be better that way. She was sorry to upset the room again. But did Miss Gunn understand that because she was to go she wanted to do it quickly while she could? Quite surprisingly, Miss Gunn, who put school before everything else, understood.

Nancy taught hard. She tried to crowd into those few hours all the things she would like to have done for the children. She loved them all . . . the plain, the pretty, the dull, the vivacious. Every little face was like the face of a child to its mother. She looked hard at each one so that she might never forget it. And she brooded over them during the swiftly moving day as a mother broods over her children during the swiftly moving years. Every real teacher experiences the sensation no matter how troublesome her charges have been.

The same little problems confronted her, but now she wished she might stay to solve them. Johnny Bornheimer cried at his desk and would not tell her why he cried. At noon she took time to run into his home. Mrs. Bornheimer was sewing. "Aren't you having lunch?" Nancy asked. Mrs. Bornheimer looked over at Johnny. "Not this noon. But to-night we're going to have a fine supper, aren't we, son?"

Nancy wrote her a check for half a month's salary. "I don't need it at all, really I don't," was her answer to the woman's protestations. "I'm going away. Oh . . . I tell you, Mrs. Bornheimer . . . there's an awful lot of unhappiness in the world. If it isn't death it's something else."

At lunch the boarders discussed a colonial party for Washington's Birthday. They asked Nancy for suggestions, and because she wanted to slip away without any fuss she entered into it as though she were to be there.

The afternoon at school passed quickly. Never had the hands of the round walnut-cased clock on the schoolroom wall gone so fast. It seemed no time at all until three-thirty had arrived. All the books and working material were put in the desks. Roxy Swanson with mature fore-sight informed Miss Moore that she thought they ought to begin reading "Robinson Crusoe" to-morrow. She did not know there would be no to-morrow there for Miss Moore. Nancy opened the hall door where the rows of rubbers stood, wet and muddy, and the little coats hung. The children stood up by their desks. Nancy bowed her head. The chil-dren bowed theirs.

"Now the day is ended [they sang, earnest, a little off-key].
    Night is drawing nigh.
  Hear us in Thy mercy.
  Hear Thy children's cry."

She had to bite her lip and make herself say it steadily: "Good night, children."

"Good night, Miss Moore."

She slipped out soon after the children. There was so little time before the six-fifteen. At the "Bee-House" she finished the packing she had begun at noon and 'phoned for the baggage man and a car to take her out home. She said good-by to Essie and Miss Ann and Miss Rilla. Before she left, Helen Blakely came from school, so that she saw her for a few moments, too. Miss Rilla was completely upset. She shed sincere, if ready tears. Miss Ann looked at it more practically. "Rilla, there'll be somebody else along soon to take that plate at table. I've always found it so. When one leaves, another one turns up to fill the place."

"No," said Miss Rilla with unaccountable firmness. "There'll never be anybody along to take Nancy's place." Poor Miss Rilla! Life had been full of inhibitions for her and Nancy had seemed all the lovely things which she had dreamed and missed.

As soon as Nancy got home she sat down on the old couch in the sitting room beside Aunt Biny. Uncle Jud stood over by the big coal burner. He shivered a little while Nancy talked. "I'm going right away to-night . . . on the six-fifteen if I can make it," she told them. "You mustn't feel badly about it. It's better all around for me to go now. Even if I stayed, you would be leaving by the fifteenth of March you know. And I'll come back to see you before you go to California. That will give you a nice long visit with the Indiana relatives . . . from March to September. When you get back here you go right to the 'Bee-House' and stay there until you're ready to start West."

"Mattie wanted we should come there," Aunt Biny said.

"Maybe you *would* like that better."

"When will you be married now?"

Nancy did not know. Quite soon she supposed. They would probably go abroad.

No one said anything more. The homely old room suddenly grew quite still and desolate. The silence and the loneliness seemed a tangible thing, cold and very cruel. Nancy put it into words. It is the young who can talk.

"That's a long way apart for us to be, isn't it . . . you in California and I in Europe, and the old home . . . missing us . . . in between? Well," she stood up and threw out her hand in that little characteristic gesture, "there's very little time . . . and I want to write a note."

Uncle Jud put on two coats and a muffler and went out and sat in the doorway of the harness shed. Near him there were old walnut shucks piled high around a stump in which the hatchet was sticking. Water stood in pools in the dirty snow of the barnyard. Over in the chicken yard the flock crowded against the gate waiting for supper. After a while he got up slowly and went after the cows in the upper lot. It seemed a long way up there. Maybe he'd better keep the stock in the barnyard until the sale.

Nancy slipped up the narrow built-in stairway to her room, went to her desk and wrote hurriedly to Warner. There was no time to make a nice choice of words or weigh their meaning. Once or twice, only half-seeing, she stopped to stare out of the queer window that looked three ways. To the west the old straw stack where she had first seen him was sodden, snow-spotted. The maples stood stark and unlovely unless one loved, as Nancy did, the gaunt strength of the half-human things. To the south the road beyond the cottonwoods looked streaked and soiled like a dirty ribbon. To the east the low rolling hills lay bare and sullen and uncaring.

When she had finished and taken her bag downstairs, she found Aunt Biny still sitting on the edge of the lumpy couch, her crutch by her side. At the sound of the stair door opening, Aunt Biny roused herself as from a stupor. "You'll want something to eat. I'll go get it right away," she got up stiffly and went out to the kitchen, her crutch pounding on the wooden floor.

There was no time to linger. Nancy sped down through the dirty snow to the old cabin and put her letter in the empty cupboard where the diaries had been. "That's sentimental," she told herself, "like children playing post-office." But she wanted to think of Warner reading it there in the little house rather than with his mail in town. She took a moment to look into the drawer under the cupboard, locking it again hurriedly as one shutting away an undesirable thing.

Walt came for her in the car. The wheels had skidded some when he came over, so he decided to put on the chains. Nancy said good-by to Aunt Biny. Tears came to her eyes, but she would not let them flow. She had a feeling that if she allowed them to start, they would turn her into an uncontrollable Niobe. So she patted the old woman's cheek and said lightly, "Be real gay and giddy with your money, Aunt Biny. Buy some new clothes and have a good time. You deserve it."

"I hope you'll be very happy, Nancy. *Every* girl deserves that."

Nancy forced a smile through the unshed tears. "I'll be happy, Aunt Biny."

Uncle Jud was still down by the barn. In moments of great emotion he always sought the outdoors. So Nancy sped down there.

"Well, Uncle Jud, you're not angry this time?"

He shook his head. He wanted to tell her how much he thought of her, that he loved her even when he was crossest, what a comfort it had been to have her there again, how he hoped she would be happy all her life, how he wished she'd take care of Aunt Biny if anything ever happened to him. But he only stood stupid, inarticulate, miserable. It is hard for an old man to say what is in his heart.

Walt and Nancy turned out of the lane road. Beyond the long row of Lombardy poplars, they stopped at Walt's for Nancy to say good-by to Mattie. Mattie came out of the kitchen door, almost unhumanly huge, but walking lightly, springily down to the car. She had a package of food for Nancy. Walt reddened a little. "Ma, Nancy won't eat out of a box. She goes in a diner."

At the sight of Mattie's crestfallen expression, Nancy leaned out of the car and kissed her big fat cheek, so cushionlike that it seemed pneumatically blownup. "Yes, I will. Thank you so much, Mattie." She was leaving enough hurt feelings in her wake without adding Mattie's to the list.

They went on into town, both thinking of that other time she had gone away. His eyes on the road, Walt drove carefully through the slush, while Nancy told him about Mr. Farnsworth.

"Not *the* Farnsworth?"

"Yes."

"Gee! You'll fly high." In a moment he added casually, "I kind of thought it was going to be Field. Did he know about this?"

"No. I just wanted to be free, Walt, a little longer . . . and so I never told any one but Aunt Biny."

"You ought to have told Field, Nancy."

"Oh, Walt, I know it now. I've written it all to him in a letter down in the cabin."

"If I couldn't have you, I'd rather have it be Field than any one I know. This will hurt him, Nancy."

Nancy looked out over the gray, soggy country. "Warner isn't the only one that it will hurt." During the few minutes' wait at the station, Nancy said: "Essie works awfully hard, Walt. She's such a *good* girl. Go to see her sometimes this spring and give her a few little pleasures."

Walt reddened a little, and said that he would.

The train was on time. Nancy had scarcely settled herself when she was skirting Tinkling Creek and then passing opposite Uncle Jud's place. She could see the stark cottonwoods and maples, the outbuildings, the straw stack, the house. For just a moment the gray of the sullen clouds in the west lifted and a soft tint of light lay in rose pools on the low hills and the prairie.

As the train curved to change its direction, she looked back toward town. The last thing she saw, silhouetted against the pink light, was the Italian Renaissance house sitting up on three terraces, like a lady with her skirts pulled up from the street.

CHAPTER XXIV

THE MEETING

WARNER was passing through the city of Chicago
but not stopping now. That was to be on his return. If all went well, he would be back the first
of the week to stop for a few hours and with some definite
thing to tell the friend to whom he owed the debt. His debt!
That old man of the sea! For the first time he would be
able to shake it off. At last he could face Mr. Farnsworth
and look him in the eye. It was not nice business, this feeling cowardly and obligated. He would feel decent again and
confident. All the way East on the fast train he had that
feeling of elation, that life was very full once more. His
writing and Nancy! Life was a fine old thing after all.

In New York he went almost immediately to his publishers. It was pleasant to come back. "Come back!" It had
a double meaning.

Sidney Thompson, one of the associate editors, gave an
hour to him. J. R. McClough, the illustrator, came into the
office. Mr. Rankin himself talked with him in the late
forenoon. They all congratulated him on his best work. It
had a vein running through it which his earlier work had
not, they told him . . . a sympathy, a human understanding
which made it stand out. They thought it would live. They
discussed some changes, a redivisioning of the work, and
talked over the payment.

Warner left the office with his check. He was ready to
turn it over, to feed the huge monster of debt that, for over
a year, had yawned and lashed its tail and before which he

had cowered. Best of all, confidence in himself had returned . . . that confidence which like blood from his veins had oozed forth the last year. And it was Nancy who had helped him, not consciously but just by being Nancy.

Thinking of Nancy, a deep regret seized him for a time that he could not keep the money for himself, but he soon put the thought aside. Not after those deep distressing months of vain endeavor to write something creditable, would he spend any moments in regret.

He spent two days with his mother and sister, Eleanor, out at the latter's suburban home. He had to explain many times to his mother how imperative it was that the trip be short. He had not been there long until he told them he had found the girl for him in Maple City. They were pleased about that. They would always be very proud of Alice, they said almost together.

He laughed at that. "But it isn't Alice," he told them. They couldn't understand it. They had gained the impression from Alice . . . ! And she had laughingly carried off Eleanor's picture of him. . . ! They were frankly sorry, a little dubious about the whole thing. They had to know all about the girl and only half concealed their doubts at her suitability when Warner tried to tell them about Uncle Jud and Aunt Biny. Sensing their inability to understand his rather boyish description of the old folks, he drew back into his grave, taciturn self.

Before he left, his mother called him into her room and talked to him. It was hard for her to speak about it, but she wanted Warner to tell her if he was living up to the ideals his father had set for him, whether he was everything his father had been. She had his father's picture in a silver frame on her dresser. Warner was glad he had protected her, had left her ideals to her.

It was late Monday afternoon when he got into Chicago.

He telephoned at once to the Hyde Park house. It had been like home to him in his college days when he had been a classmate of Rod Farnsworth's. Rod was married now to an Emily Somebody . . . and they lived in the old home with Mr. Farnsworth and Fay. It was odd to think of Rod married. Fay, the sister, had not married, at least not that he had heard. She might have done so during the past year, for he had not communicated with the family at all. Only once had he written . . . the time he mailed his interest on the note from Omaha. So long as he was under that deep obligation to Mr. Farnsworth with no immediate likelihood of paying the debt, he had felt like staying away and keeping silent. When the time came that he could begin to cancel the obligation, then he would resume his friendship with them. And the time had come. He felt a deep thankfulness that he had hold of himself again.

When he 'phoned the house, Mr. Farnsworth himself answered, said he was delighted to know Warner was in town, told him to come right out. His tone was welcoming and cordial. It gave Warner a pleasurable feeling to think of the renewal of the old friendship with the Farnsworths. In a world of work and worry it was nice to know old friends were interested in you, that old ties could hold.

Unlike the Rineland residence in Maple City with its ostentatiously new appearance all the furnishings in the Hyde Park mansion had a mellowed look. Its rugs and tapestries and rich carvings had been picked up from time to time in the countries which produced them. Money, to the Farnsworths, was not a new experience. It had been their background for three generations.

Warner had a renewed sense of that mellowed luxury and the old-world atmosphere of the place as he was admitted to the reception hall, with its massive dark wood stairs leading to a balcony. There was no further time to gratify his senses with a renewal of the appearance of the delightful surroundings, for almost immediately he was being warmly welcomed by Mr. Farnsworth.

John Farnsworth was in his early fifties, heavy, well cared for, the prosperous man of the world. Just now he was grasping Warner's hand with both of his own, apparently deeply pleased at seeing him.

"Why did you drop us so unceremoniously, Warner? You've not been writing us."

"I couldn't, Mr. Farnsworth. Not until I was ready to take up my obligations to you."

"The last we heard of you, you and your mother were ill in the influenza epidemic."

"Yes, everything seemed to drop on us at once. We both had pneumonia following the flu . . . and I topped it off with an abscessed lung."

"You're well again?"

"Thoroughly."

"And your mother never learned the truth of your father's affair?"

"No, and she never will now. That's what makes me most grateful to you."

In the interest of the meeting again both seemed to have forgotten to move on. They were still standing.

"I was glad to do it for you, Warner. From the first time you ever came here with Rod, you seemed like one of us. It isn't entirely unselfish to do a thing like that. I felt good doing it for you . . . you were so thoroughly miserable over it. And besides, don't discredit my intelligence. I knew what I was doing. It was a business proposition, and I was fully aware of your ability to handle it."

"I don't know, Mr. Farnsworth. I'm afraid you didn't realize the risk. The thing struck me like a bolt of lightning. I fell into something of a slump for a while. But from now I can go on. I've just made a very satisfactory sale and that's what brings me here." As though anxious to get it over, he took out his check, immediately endorsed it on the back of his bill-book . . . gave it to Mr. Farnsworth.

"If you feel that you can renew the note . . . send the new one on to me." A feeling of great relief swept him.

He put out his hand to the older man. He was not leaving. He was even staying until the next morning, but the business part of the visit over, he felt free from the oppression that had overwhelmed him and very grateful. "You know how I feel, Mr. Farnsworth. There's nothing in the world I wouldn't do for you, if it were in my power."

"I believe you, Warner, and thank you. It makes me feel as though I had a son . . ." he smiled wryly . . . "a little more dependable than my own. Not that Rod's bad. He's just the usual boy brought up the way he was . . . I only wish he were unusual."

"Oh, Rod's all right . . . just easy-going."

"Now that your own business is over, Warner, I want to tell you mine. I'm to be married right after Easter."

Warner was surprised and he was pleased. Mrs. Farnsworth had been dead for a half-dozen years. He was moved to put out his hand again. "Why, that's fine, Mr. Farnsworth . . . fine! I'm mighty glad."

Behind them the heavy dark wood street door was opening.

"There are the girls now."

Two young women stepped in. The first one was Fay Farnsworth, already running forward to greet him. The other . . . *No! It was not so! Nancy was in Maple City*.

"Warner, you're about to be presented at court. Nancy, I want Warner Field to meet you. Warner . . . my fiancée . . . Miss Moore."

For a moment Warner and Nancy stood carved into icy silence. The Confederate soldiers chiseled on the side of the rocky cliff are less inanimate and cold. Nancy was the first to move. A flood of pity surged over her that Warner was shocked and suffering. All the latent motherhood in her rushed to protect him. This was the way that he was finding out the thing she had kept from him. That she, too, was surprised at the meeting counted for nothing. She wanted to ease him from the impact, carry all the burden herself. She threw out her hands in a little characteristic gesture. With all her will power she made herself laugh . . . high bubbling laughter.

"Why, people . . ." she talked fast, naturally, enthusiastically. "Warner Field and I *know* each other . . . *well*. Hasn't he told you? He's been in Maple City, *too*. Isn't it *funny?* And introducing us . . . the world is certainly small."

Saving Warner from visible embarrassment, keeping the others from seeing any confusion of his, were her two great interests. She had bungled things and now she must make it as easy as possible for him. Talking against time, throwing out a perfect smoke screen of chatter to cover any feeling that Warner might show, she gave him her hand. It was trembling as it met his and without warmth.

Warner partially came to life then, too. He roused his stunned mentality to make it understand that it, too, had a part to play.

"I thought you had been in Omaha all this time, Warner." Mr. Farnsworth and Fay were saying it almost together.

"No," Warner told them gravely. "This last year in Maple City, fifty miles from Omaha."

"In the same town with Nancy and met her there?" Fay was repeating it to make certain. There was no little excitement and laughter about it. It was certainly odd.

Mr. Farnsworth went to the point: "Why didn't you write it, Nancy?"

Why not, indeed, Nancy!

"Well, you see," she threw out her hand in that little gesture. She had to think very fast. "It started with a joke. When I first met Warner I told him I knew some people who knew him. He asked me who they were and I said . . . for fun, you know . . . that I'd tell him some other time. And then I kept thinking he'd speak of it again, and I told myself . . . just for fun, you know . . . that I'd never mention it again until he did. And he never did. *Did* you, Warner?"

Warner stood, grave and silent, listening to the excruciatingly funny joke. "No, I think not."

And then Rod and Emily came in, and the smoke screen was a little thicker, for Nancy was explaining the joke all over rather volubly.

It was odd but not unduly so. The world was not large to the Farnsworths who had traveled into some of its far corners. Travel makes distances short, places common to all. They talked about it for only a short time. Everybody was glad Nancy knew Warner. It made it seem more like a little family party. It was nearly dinner time now. There were to be guests for dinner, two young couples, the Birches and the Townsends. The eight had been playing whist on Monday nights, they explained. Warner said he shouldn't have dropped in so unceremoniously. They laughed at him for that. It was too absurd to discuss when he had been so much at home there in his college days.

Every one went off to dress. The Birches and the Townsends came. There was just one moment before dinner in which Nancy found opportunity to speak to Warner alone. As they were ready to go into the dining room, she said hurriedly, "I *must* see you alone, Warner. I think I can arrange a way after dinner."

Grave and unbending, Warner inclined his head. Nancy had a feeling that the Warner she knew had gone to the end of the world and this was a strange man of whom she knew little and of whom she was afraid.

And then the ten people were at dinner in the fine old mahogany-paneled room. Nancy was gay, talkative, enthusiastic about nothing. Warner was grave, quiet, courteous. The Farnsworths saw no change in either.

Warner's was a sense of unbelief, a cold smothering numbness of unrealization, the feeling that soon now he would awaken. It seemed unbelievable. Nancy's first vague little reference back on the Denning hill, "Oh, I know some people who know you," was the key. Out of the world of acquaintances in common . . . the Farnsworths. And Nancy was to marry Mr. Farnsworth. Married to Rod's father . . . Nancy . . . married. . . . It throbbed hotly in Warner's brain and more loudly than the gay conversation. When he left the house, he would face it alone. At present there was nothing to do but act as naturally as possible, make himself talk and smile mechanically. No automaton was ever more wooden . . . no statue more devoid of feeling. The reserve which was natural to him, the graveness which was a part of him, now served him well. Wherever he looked, he could see Nancy up at the end of the table as in a maze. Sometimes she was pouring tea at Aunt Biny's plain painted table, passing the heavy dishes and joking with Uncle Jud. Sometimes she seemed at the "Bee-House" in her neat school suit, sitting up beyond Miss Gunn and arguing gayly with old Major Slack. And then his vision would clear and she was in a rose chiffon dinner gown at the Farnsworths' beautifully appointed table, just as gay and talkative, with that little nonchalant air of not caring for any one or anything. Something died within him.

Nancy's was a sense of the knife having fallen, the sword of Damocles under which she had sat so long before the feast. Through her mind ran the thought of the letter lying in the little cabin. How futile a document it was! She had pictured Warner reading it in the little house, away from other eyes, hearing the thing from the quiet pages of the note she had written. And he had heard it here before every one. Poor Warner! For the hundredth time she admitted that she should have told it all at first in Maple City. But she had wanted to feel free in her old environment, as free as the wind blowing over the prairie. And she had returned less free than she had gone.

The conversation was fairly general. Once Rod said, "How have you stood it out there, Warner? I can imagine Nancy getting a kick out of a desert island . . . but not you!"

"Just what do you mean, Rod?"

"Oh, the two-by-fourness, the smug-lotness of it. I was in a little jerkwater town myself once. Was marooned there for four days . . . ninety-six awful hours. Was at my great-aunt's, an old maid in a colonial house. She had a canary and a dog. The dog was the most interesting person I met there."

Warner smiled his slow, agreeable smile. "Nothing happened, I suppose, Rod, but the wind blowing and the clock ticking?"

"Yes, it did . . . one thing. They pulled off a fire for me. Most comical thing you ever saw. Got out the fire department and ran around to an old shack of a house. The old man that owned it was running around like a chicken with its head cut off. Everybody yelled at everybody else. It looked like a musical comedy. One chap

ran up a ladder and got the old fellow's seed corn out.
Great hero! They carried out a teakettle and turnips and
a little tin-horn phonograph and muskrat hides. I thought
I'd die with unholy laughter."

Every one laughed. It occurred to Warner that it was
the same kind of thing he used to write . . . the facetious
viewpoint of the superior onlooker. For a moment he
seemed to have a sudden composite view of the Maple
City community . . . Aunt Biny, her sweet face and her
crutch and the beautiful things she said were in her heart
but which she could never get down on paper . . . Uncle
Jud, wresting from the virgin prairie a garden spot of home
. . . Miss Ann and Miss Rilla, keeping up the old brick
house . . . the "bore" lying by the dresser, his necktie
in his hand . . . Doc Minnish fighting death with his old-
fashioned weapons and Doc Pearson fighting it with the
new . . . Walt Thomas, clean and decent and hard-working,
tilling his fields that the Rod Farnsworths might eat.

He looked over at Rod sitting there at ease, debonair,
sophisticated, a man who had never constructed a thing
in his life. He had added nothing to the progress of the
world, not a line to the world's literature, not a potato to
the food bins. He had not captured on canvas the beauty of
a sunset nor turned a screw in any mechanism. He was a
spender of other men's money . . . a critic of other men's
art . . . an onlooker at other men's labor.

And then quite soon the dinner was over. A little later
they were all back in the drawing-room and a maid was
bringing tables and cards. There was some discussion about
carrying on the regular game. Fay said they would play
something else so they could all have a hand.

"No," Nancy said decisively. "Warner Field and I are
not going to play with you. We're going off by ourselves
for at least an hour and have a talk. We know a lot

of folks that aren't intimate friends of yours at all . . .
the Swansons and the Bornheimers and the Guggenmeiers."

Everybody laughed. Clearly Nancy's manner was no
different among these people than toward the boarders in
Maple City. "Come on, Warner," she said carelessly over
her shoulder. "Let's go into the library and take them
all up in alphabetical order: Albrechts, Bornheimers, Carlsons, Dennings, Englekings, Flachenechers, Guggenmeiers . . ."

She threw back her head and grinned over her shoulder
at the crowd as it laughed. Warner followed her obediently
and silently into the library where she crossed the room to
a deep window seat. A great tapestry flanked the wall by
the seat. Strangely enough it was a knight taking the
ribbon from his lady as he went to the fray.

CHAPTER XXV

THE END OF THE STORY

THE moment they were out of sight of the others, Nancy whirled to Warner. Swiftly as the sun clouds over, her gayety was dropped. Her indolent manner became tense, every feature quickened. Her face was aflame with its emotion.

"Oh, Warner, I'm *so* sorry. I wouldn't have had it happen this way for anything. I've been frantic since you came. Not for *worlds* would I have had you hear about it like this. You didn't say a word about stopping here."

"I didn't know it was necessary," Warner answered without rancor, apparently without interest. It did not make any difference to him how the news had come . . . so long as it had to come. His arms were folded. He stood quietly, gravely, very courteously awaiting her explanation. It was as though there was no feeling in him, in sharp contrast to Nancy, who seemed all feeling.

"I blame myself *so* . . . for everything." Nancy's face was aquiver with sympathy. "Oh, *why* has everything I've ever done in my life seemed to go wrong? What is the *matter* with me?"

Warner did not offer any consolation. Unbending and uncompromising, he stood and waited. He seemed the personification of courtesy, the essence of indifference.

"Warner, I've written everything to you . . . it's in a letter down in the cupboard in the cabin. You'll find it there when you go back. I wrote it Tuesday before I

254

left." She spoke swiftly as though she would crowd into the short time a world of explanation. If she was moved to the depths, Warner was as stony as the carved Neptune out in the fountain of the grounds.

"Why didn't I tell you everything at first? I blame myself *so*." It was like Nancy, generous and courageous, to be severe in the denunciation of herself. "But because I didn't at first, Warner," . . . she threw out her hands in that old familiar gesture, "then I couldn't at all."

It would have moved almost any one, but it did not move Warner Field. He felt that nothing would ever touch him again. "I wanted to spend those months out there with Uncle Jud and Aunt Biny, feeling just like the old Nancy Moore I used to be . . . and so . . . to carry out the illusion . . . I didn't let my engagement enter into it. I see now where I was wrong, but I meant no harm, Warner." Her whole being begged for some sign of understanding from him, but he would not give it. One does not so easily forgive a sword thrust.

When he would not unbend, Nancy went on stumblingly with her explanation. "What I said to-night about it being a joke was really true, at first, too. I saw you . . . just once . . . here at the house, nearly two years ago and when I found you were in Maple City . . . with apparently no recollection of having seen me before . . . it seemed . . . sort of a joke, to keep it from you."

"Clever little joke, Nancy," Warner said dryly. "Nero played it on the early Christians."

A quick shadow of pain crossed her face.

"Don't, Warner! I deserve a lot . . . but not *too* much. There are other things," she steadied her voice, "I want to tell you too. Oh . . . if they'll just leave us alone for a little while . . . I can tell you all about everything . . . and why things are . . . as they are." She spoke quickly again. It was as though she must put into the short time a world of explanation. "I'll have to begin back with my birth, so you'll understand. Even that wasn't regular. I'm a waif . . . Warner . . . a doorstep baby. I'm no blood relation at all to Uncle Jud and Aunt Biny. I didn't have any gold locket on me. I didn't even have the specified strawberry mark on my right shoulder." Nancy would not have been Nancy if she had not referred to herself in that very way. "I don't know who I am and neither does any one else. I was just wrapped in a brown shawl and chucked on Uncle Jud's porch one summer night. I never knew it, though, until the day I was eighteen. No one knows how the world crashed around me when they told me."

Warner roused himself a little. The diaries, he thought. That was what happened the day she was eighteen. For the first time he felt a slight sensation in the place of that numb indifference which had held him as in a cast since his arrival, and the sensation was one of vague relief that the thing which had happened on Nancy's birthday was only that. But it did not make much difference anyway. Nothing made much difference now.

"To have consistently built up a structure of relatives from my babyhood," she went on with feeling, "and then to send it crumbling! No one knows the sensation. If I'd have been brought up in an orphan asylum I'd at least not have had that same anguished experience of the ground giving way under me when they told me." She had been bitter about it . . . was apparently still bitter.

She turned to him with sudden spirit. "I know one thing, Warner. Some day I'm going to adopt a little girl. I'm going to take her when she's tiny and bring her up to know that she's not my flesh and blood but that I love her dearly. For the jolt *I* had I'm going to do the right thing by some other child." That, too, was like Nancy.

Standing near the dark drapery of the window, her head thrown back, the curve of her chin and throat outlined against the dull blue of the tapestry, she brought to life suddenly in Warner the thing he thought she had killed. He had a wild moment of wanting her again at any price. It was folly to remember that now.

"I was terribly bitter about it. Right now it seems that I should have, *could* have borne it more philosophically. My bitterness now seems a little foolish, certainly supersensitive. But after all, I wasn't much more than a child four years ago, a provincial child, who had lived in a world of romance. But if they had only kept it to themselves, how much happier I would have been. Uncle Jud's niece was Nancy Moore and I always thought she was my mother. I had her picture and all her old playthings in the cupboard in the cabin and worshiped her memory for eighteen years." To Warner came the swift vision of the picture of the girl with flowers in her hair. "What difference would it have made to them or any one else to have continued to keep the secret? I should have been told at first or not at all. Aunt Biny and Uncle Jud had just come home from Nancy Moore's funeral back in Indiana on the evening they found me wrapped in the shawl by the door in the porch of the empty farmhouse. Whether the . . ." she hesitated, then changed the little word . . . "*my* people, abandoning me, *knew* it was empty . . . well, I'm glad I don't know that. I try to think they *knew* somebody would find me."

In a moment she went on quickly, "Well, it was Uncle Jud and Aunt Biny Moore who found me as they came home. They took me into the house and sent for Mattie. When Mattie came in the door she said, 'Oh, you brought your niece's baby home!' Aunt Biny told me that she and Uncle Jud gave each other a quick look and knew each other's thoughts. They just kept still and Mattie in her talkative way told it everywhere, and they accepted the decision that seemed easy. When I was a little girl, the people . . . whoever they were . . . sent some money by New York draft to Uncle Jud for me . . . conscience money, I suppose. Uncle Jud and Aunt Biny never touched it and of course it doubled in the years. It made a substantial sum. I tell you this, for it had its part in the quarrel Uncle Jud and I had. The day of my eighteenth birthday they told me. I'm sorry and ashamed when I remember how the day began and how it ended. I'm impulsive and hot-headed and Uncle Jud is, too, you know. When I'd get angry I'd just lose my head and say things I would be dreadfully sorry for afterward. I've been flattering myself I had outgrown it . . . but I haven't. I turned on Alice Rineland the other night like a wildcat." She shrugged her shoulder in disgust and then went on, "Aunt Biny is so sweet and gentle. I never quarreled with her. But Uncle Jud . . . you know him . . . with his fretting and saying things that make you provoked. Every once in a while he and I would have a scrap about something. We'd say mean horrid things and then we'd both be sorry. He never touched me in his life to punish me . . . would just jaw and scold in that fussy way and I'd say saucy things back to him. And then we'd both be sorry, although neither of us would admit it, and be the best of friends. I'd go fishing with him or trapping and stay around out-doors. Aunt Biny would never call me in to help her at those times. She seemed to want to have us forgive each other in that unspoken way." It seemed good 'o Nancy to tell all these things. She had concealed ther₁ so long from Warner that now she was profligate in the l .vishness of her explanations.

"The day I was eighteen I had a tea party of girls in the

afternoon . . . Essie and Alice and several others. After
they had gone, just for fun I went upstairs and put on an
old blue calico dress, took off my shoes and stockings and
started out to slide down a straw stack. It was a kiddish
trick of course and I told myself it was the last time in my
life I'd do it. When I came downstairs the folks were
sitting stiffly in the sitting room and Uncle Jud called me
in. I had a feeling that something was wrong . . . you
know how you will sense things . . . and Uncle Jud said
that he had something to tell me. And the thing . . . was
that. He said he thought he ought to tell me, that he
thought it was his duty, for beside my knowing the truth
because I was of age he felt that he didn't want to take any
credit for the money in the bank that was mine. For a
little bit I was too crushed to talk and then I lost my
head and turned on him. Poor Aunt Biny . . . she sat
there white and broken. I think she hadn't wanted to tell
me at all . . . that Uncle Jud had been headstrong about
the decision. I said things to him . . . that he'd lived a
horrible lie to bring me up that way. He called me ungrateful for that. I said I'd rather be ungrateful than
deceitful and all that sort of thing. All the time neither
one of us really meant the horrible ugly things we were
saying. He said that if they were so terrible maybe I'd
better get out. Aunt Biny just crumpled down in her chair
at that but Uncle Jud got angrier. All at once it came to
me that I was of age and that I had this money of my
own that I hadn't known about and so the thing was possible. I said I'd take him at his word. Aunt Biny tried
to talk to us, but Uncle Jud said, 'Let her go if that's all
the gratitude she's got. But she can't ever darken my door
again unless she asks our forgiveness . . . nor come into
this house again excepting down on her knees.' We were
really loving each other all the time. If I'd have laughed

at him or paid no attention to it, it would all have blown
over. But I felt too sore and crushed and angry. So the
day that began so happily ended . . . like *that*."

And Warner was back again in the cabin reading: "Good-
by, my prairie! And most of all good-by, Nancy Moore."

But Nancy had taken up her story again: "I went upstairs and packed a few things. When Aunt Biny saw that
I was in earnest . . . that for the first time in my impulsive life I wasn't going to give in, she got me to promise
that I'd go to an old friend of hers . . . a Miss Smith
. . . who taught at Mount Morris. She had visited us
twice at the farm and I was fond of her. Walt took me to
the station and I told him what the trouble was all about.
Walt thought he cared for me and wanted me to marry
him and live with him and Mattie. Poor Walt . . . and
he wasn't quite nineteen!" Nancy smiled at the recollection. "I kept my promise and arrived safely at Miss Smith's
in my best outfit that Aunt Biny had made for me. Miss
Smith took me under her wing and bought me some new
things and in spite of a list of applicants from wealthy
families, got me into the school with her. There I was
with my money. It seemed like a vast sum. It wasn't,
of course. I used no judgment. I was crazy for nice things
after wearing those clothes made from the pattern of Aunt
Biny's own girlhood. When I was smaller I was such a
tomboy that I didn't care about it but by high school I
knew the sensation of feeling antiquated. Alice had such
lovely things always. How I envied her! Even though
my graduating dress was of the nicest material it was funny
and different. So . . . with that craving and the money
that seemed endless but wasn't . . . I bought lots of nice
clothes. I had entered school in a bitter ashamed way
intending never to enjoy life again. But I wasn't cut out
for a martyr." Nancy smiled ruefully so that Warner

forgot the import of the interview and smiled too. She had a swift sensation that he had come back to her from some far-away place. "So it wasn't a week until I was making friends and having the time of my life." Yes, Nancy would do that.

"I did have spells of depression, of course, thinking about myself. Who was I? It made me bitter at them . . . my parents . . . whoever they were. Were they the covered wagon people who had been through the country that day? Presumably they were. Was I merely not wanted at all? Or shouldn't they have had me? Or were they too poor then to keep me? I've tried to think it all out but of course I get no satisfaction from going over it in my mind, so most of the time I proceed to forget it. But it had its effect on me. I've never felt *stable*, if you know what I mean. Oh, no," she added hopelessly, "*you* can't know, Warner, with your background of ancestors. You're the type of man you're supposed to be . . . like all the great-grandfathers behind you. But I . . . being *nobody* could be *anybody* . . . being *nothing* could be *anything*. It's almost as though I had several personalities, in any one of which I seemed to fit, but not one of which seemed durable or permanent. One of them was the girl who had been Uncle Jud's niece, looking at life wholesomely and clear-eyed. One of them was a luxury-loving person, not quite so wholesome and a little less clear-eyed, living for nothing much but her own entertainment. *That* Nancy Moore has skated on horribly thin ice, at times, has approved of things that the other wouldn't have countenanced, but something . . . the thought of her Uncle Jud and Aunt Biny . . . or her early training . . . or the memory of her orchard and prairie . . . or *something* . . . always kept her from going under."

Nancy did not say anything more for a moment. Out in

the next room a game had evidently ended for there were
exclamations and high nervous laughter. Reminded that
the time was short for her she returned quickly to her story.
"So many of the girls in school were wealthy. I went
home with them vacations. I had lots of invitations." Yes,
that would be true. She named two of the other homes she
had been in frequently. They were a well-known financier's
and a senator's. "I had chances to marry . . . a brother
or two and a guest or two at house parties. But I kept my
head level and watched for money." When she saw Warner
wince under the words she repeated them. "*Money*, Warner
. . . it was all I wanted. I knew that I'd never be happy
again without all the luxuries I'd had in the girls' homes.
It's better that you should know it. You'll not have any
illusions to carry back with you." She stopped, expecting
some comment, but when he made none she went on: "Fay
and I were particularly chummy the last two years."

The story was getting closer to Mr. Farnsworth. Warner
found himself bracing his shoulders as though he were to
encounter a physical object. "My money gave out as of
course it would the way I was using it. I had to go back
to Uncle Jud or else go to work. I was too lazy to work,
too fond of the life around at the girls' homes. All my
anger toward Uncle Jud and Aunt Biny had melted ages
before, but when I would think of the barnyard and my old
bedroom and the sitting room with the framed presidents
and Napoleon with the chip off the end of his nose . . .
and then *this*. . . ." She threw out her hand to take in
the lavish surroundings. "So I staged a little play," she
said deliberately. "I sensed how well Mr. Farnsworth had
always liked me here with Fay . . . like another daughter
I supposed." She seemed determined to hurt Warner, to
put it so grossly that it would finish his love for her. "So
I let him find me quite inadvertently here in the library,

crying as though my heart would break . . . and I cried
all over him and told him my financial troubles. . . ."
She looked up at Warner, standing there stern and stiff
. . . and waiting. "He felt sorry for me, as I had fully
intended he should . . . and told me not to worry . . .
that he was going to send me on through school with Fay
and finance me just as he did her." She could not quite
meet Warner's eyes, but when she did and saw the expression in them she said quickly, "Oh, *I've* been *wretched*
enough at times about it . . . accepting so much from him.
I should have been out taking care of myself, teaching a
country school, anything that was independent. Essie in
Miss Ann's kitchen is more honorable than I. He did as
he had said . . . and I accepted it all recklessly. Then
when I had finished, he told me he wanted to marry me.
Well?" She threw out her hands in that little questioning
gesture. "What was there to do *then?*"

To Warner, standing there grave and unbending, came
the question, "Was life nothing but debts and obligations?"
But he did not say anything. There seemed nothing to say.
After the silence, Nancy went on.

"He wanted to be married right away, but I . . . I
didn't. . . ." She dropped her eyes from Warner's stern
ones. "I wanted to go back first and spend a little time with
Uncle Jud and Aunt Biny. All the bitterness I felt had
died away long before and I saw only their kindness to me.
I knew I would never feel right until I had made some
sort of reparation to them. After all, they were the only
parents I had ever known. I finally got Mr. Farnsworth
to consent to it. So, without knowing what Uncle Jud's
attitude toward me would be, I went. I got in on the
evening train and walked out without any one I knew seeing me. I went up to the house and looked in at the window.
It seemed as though Uncle Jud was reading the same paper

and Aunt Biny mending the same stocking. The only difference was that they looked so *old*. I went up on the porch softly and curled myself up in as small a ball as I could right in the identical spot they had found me before. Then I reached up and knocked. When Uncle Jud came to the door I said in a high squeaky voice: 'Baby on your doorstep.' Uncle Jud slapped his knee and roared and laughed. Aunt Biny . . . oh, I'll never forget how glad Aunt Biny was to see me. It made me feel horrible and ungrateful . . . all the contemptible things in the world. It seemed nice and homelike and safe to be back. I didn't care whether Napoleon had *any* nose. . . ." Nancy smiled half tearfully. "The next morning I saw you by the straw stack." She sat down in the window seat. It seemed like the end of the story.

They were both silent for a moment, their silence loud with the unspoken thought that it was not the end of the story but the beginning.

CHAPTER XXVI

"GOOD-BY, NANCY"

IN a few moments Nancy spoke again: "I think that
Uncle Jud and Aunt Biny have been very happy to
have me there. I had intended to stay only a few weeks
but Mr. Rineland came out to see if I'd take the school.
It seemed a funny thing to do . . . sort of a lark. You
know how I act generally . . . on impulse. I thought of
it as my last free year. I'd see how it would be to work at
something. I wrote to Mr. Farnsworth that I was going to
stay until spring. I went at it just for fun. I felt superior
to everybody. I laughed at everyone and everything. I
used to laugh behind Alice's back whenever she talked in
that soft, lovely, large way about her gowns and things
. . . knowing what I could have. Noble character, am
I not? I planned to spring it on her sometime at the end
of the year . . . crow over her . . . make her feel foolish
over the things she had said." Nancy, on the window seat,
cupping her chin in her hand, looked up. "But when I
left, I didn't . . . feel like it."

Warner made no reply.

"Well," she threw out her hand, "it proved to be a happy
year. All of the nice things in life aren't the luxurious
ones. I've learned that. Mr. Farnsworth, with all his
money, can't buy a lovelier picture than the one you see
from the farmhouse when you look over the rolling hills.
And he can't hire a finer singer than the wood thrush that
sings along Tinkling Creek. And people . . . they're
no different. Their clothes and their surroundings and

265

their degrees of sophistication are . . . but vital things
. . . their joys and hopes and sorrows aren't, you know.
Rod and Emily won't think any more of their baby, when
it comes, than Gus and Jen Carlson do of theirs. And there
isn't a woman that I know anywhere with a keener intellect
or better judgment than Miss Gunn or one with a finer
sense of sympathy toward humanity than Miss Rilla. It
was a nice year." She repeated it wistfully. "After I took
the school I never dreamed of doing anything else but
staying it out. But the night after you left . . . it seemed
best not to."

For the first time, Warner spoke quietly: "You stayed
too long, Nancy."

She put up her hand to ward off something and then
dropped it as though there was no use in evading it. "Yes,
I know. . . ."

There was laughter again in the other room and a man's
voice rose and fell teasingly.

They did not speak for a few moments, Nancy on the
window seat, or Warner standing, straight and stern and
forbidding. Then the girl went on again. "I left on your
account. I thought it wouldn't be so very hard for me.
Even at the last I thought I was doing it more for your
sake . . . than mine. I kept telling myself on the train
that when I got back here where everything was easy and
pleasurable and lazy . . . I could forget a lot of things
. . . burn my bridges, you know. But," she averted her
head, "there are some bridges that won't burn, some things
one doesn't forget. . . ." She was at confessional before
the altar of truth. "And then to have you stop here!
Things are tangled . . . terribly, Warner, unless . . ."
she ventured it . . . "there's a way to unravel them?"

Warner had that same choking sensation that had overwhelmed him when he discovered his father's affair, a

feeling that the thing was beyond enduring. Love was like a presence, a living, breathing, vital presence. It stood near him, humble, expectant, awaiting the verdict. The brown of Nancy's eyes, the warmth of her hair, the curve of her mouth, that lovely line of her throat . . . all called to him.

"No," Warner said, "there isn't any way to unravel them." The presence near them drooped a little but it did not move. Love does not come and go at the snap of a finger.

"Maybe. . . ." The nearness of it, like a third personality, was making Nancy bold, "he has always been extremely kind to me . . . if I went to him and told him that you . . . that I . . ."

Warner was in a trench again, making himself prepare to go over the top. He had to summon every atom of courage that he possessed.

His voice sounded harsher than he meant it to be when he said, "No, he mustn't even know it." The statement hung heavily in the air, discordant, rough. Nancy looked up startled. To Warner she suddenly seemed very small and childish. He sat down on the seat beside her. "This is the reason, Nancy," he said gently. "A little over a year ago my father was found dead in his bedroom with his pistol by him. He had been cleaning it. The evidence was all there . . . some polish, some waste. It was very clear. He had been cleaning it and it had gone off. My mother was prostrated. She was wrapped up in him. He was in good health and had a fair law practice. There was nothing in the world to point to self-destruction. Over and over she told me how he had joked at the dinner table . . . some plan he had made for the next day. But I know. He took his life. He couldn't face what was before him in a month's time. He was guardian for a young fellow who would become of age in those few weeks. He had used the estate money. When I looked over his affairs, I knew. I was distracted. My mother's great love for my father and her complete faith in him . . . the complete faith in fact of the entire community was before me all the time. Every thought I had then, waking or sleeping, was what to do or where to turn. It seemed that I must do something to avert the crash. If I could replace the amount before the settlement, before any one knew . . . my mother most of all. I thought over and over the various men that my father knew, Omaha men . . . bankers . . . attorneys . . . merchants. There was just one man in the world I felt might help me. I came on to Chicago, had a talk with Rod's father . . . unburdened myself to him . . . asked him if he could possibly see his way clear to make me a loan. He questioned me about it, argued with me about the necessity of committing myself, tried to persuade me to let the bonding company pay the deficiency, talked over my future prospects with me and then made me the loan, with not much more to show for it than a piece of paper that was worth about what wall paper was worth. I took out insurance for the amount in his favor to cover it if I died. And if I lived, the work of my life was pledged to him until the debt was canceled. I was in such a hurry to get back to Omaha and fix the matter up that I was only here with him an hour or so."

"That was the time I saw you," Nancy said listlessly. "I was on the stair landing when you left."

"Following my return to Omaha my mother and I had those long illnesses. When I was up and out, try as I would, I couldn't get back to writing. Something hung over me constantly . . . the enormity of the debt . . . or rather the worry over the payment of it. With the payment of it depending on my brain work and the brain refusing to do its work . . . I got into an awful slump. It was just at that time that I ran across Mr. Rineland and decided to take up his offer to go into the bank. Then last fall I seemed to get hold of myself again. You're more or less responsible for getting me into the swing of the prairie story. They tell me it's my best stuff."

"You know how glad I am, Warner."

Neither said anything more for a moment. Then Warner spoke crisply, briefly. "To-day I turned over my first payment on the principal of the debt. Two hours ago I said to Mr. Farnsworth, 'There's nothing on earth I wouldn't do for you if it were in my power.'" It finished the matter. Warner stood up. Like a book that had closed with a snap, the story of Warner Field's and Nancy Moore's love was ended.

If Nancy's heart said, "What of *me?*" it made no loud outcry. But it seemed to shrivel and die. This was life then, she was thinking. Things like this had happened to other people and now they were happening to her. She, who loved life with every fiber of her being, was to find life a dried, tasteless thing robbed of its flavor like a squeezed skin.

"Say . . . you!" They turned quickly. Rod was in the doorway. "If you're down to Xerxes and Ypsilanti and von Zeppelin, come on and take a hand. The Birches are having to leave."

So they played whist, Warner and Nancy, whose lives were being dealt by a merciless hand that did not care who held the cards. Dramatic moments in real life do not end on the crest of the wave or on the highest point of the climax. They slip into troughs of the sea. They slump into commonplace activities. They asked inanely, "What was the trump?" and said thoughtfully, "If I had played low. . . ." Some of life's bitterest moments are also its most courteous.

They put the cards aside and talked for a while. At their questioning, Warner told them pleasantly of his new work. Nancy made herself relate a few foolish little incidents about school. Fay and Rod and Emily contributed occasionally to the general friendly conversation. Mr. Farnsworth said he was booking passage for their trip abroad weeks ahead on account of the heavy travel that was predicted. Nancy stared at him for a moment as though she were seeing him for the first time. Tangled roots!

Warner was leaving in the morning. He made no effort to see Nancy again. She was the fiancée of the best friend he ever had. That was sufficient. They ate breakfast together, all but Emily, who did not come down. There was an hour or more after that in the sun room and then it was time for Warner to go. He told them not to bother about him at all but they insisted on going to the station. Emily was not leaving the house but the others went . . . Mr. Farnsworth and Nancy and Rod and Fay. They talked of trivial, jolly things, a gay little family party seeing an old-time friend off. Once Rod turned to Nancy as though it had just occurred to him, "By George, that *was* sort of queer, you and Warner running across each other in a God-forsaken Nebraska town. It reads like a de luxe movie. Warner could pass for the hero all right. He fits the part. But you're no heroine, Nancy. You're too little and sassy."

Nancy shrugged her shoulder. "You're right for once, Rod. I'm no heroine."

The great train was ready to ride into the West. Warner said his farewells. He was pleasant and natural. "Good-by, Fay. If you'll come out to Maple City you can have your choice of our star boarders, young Marty Spencer or old Major Slack. Good-by, Nancy. We'll miss you at the 'Bee-House.' I know you will be very, very happy. Rod, let me know about Emily. Good-by, Mr. Farnsworth. You know how glad I am for you and how I feel about everything. Thank you again. Good-by, everybody, good-by."

Nancy, struggling for composure, fighting for poise, her teeth in her lip, saw him go in a mist.

CHAPTER XXVII

PAYING THE PRICE

HOW little we tell in the brief outlining of a man's life. Glibly we say, "In the nineties he did thus and so. In such and such a year he moved from There and Here." And when we have finished we announce, "That was his life." But it is only the skeleton. The flesh and blood are the high hopes laid low or the faith that did not falter, the shattered dreams of desire or the love that knew no waning.

Over and over on the train Warner lived the whole experience. Back to the odd circumstance that had taken him to the little cabin for the week, the childish trick of Nancy's by the straw stack, her offhand way of saying: "Oh, I know some people who know you." Nancy should have told him. But after all what difference would it have made? Is love to be chained like a captured thing? To the sound of the wheels in three states, his mind did not cease going over and over again every little item about her . . . foolish little things that were not foolish because they were Nancy. Above the dark depths of the depression into which the shock and disappointment had flung him, only one small light gleamed. His belief in himself was still left. One constant thing in life remained . . . a strange exaltation in his writing that Nancy, having taken his love, could not take. For long hours on the train he went over the various phases of his future plans. One decision came clearly and swiftly. He could not desert Mr. Rineland through the busy month of March. Temporarily, then, he would remain in the bank, sucked like a piece of rubber on to glass. He thought over the things with which he must now fill his life, and the predominating one was hard work.

Strangely enough he did not once think of Alice Rineland.

The "Bee-House" seemed strangely quiet and monotonous. Already Nancy's place was filled by a blond milliner who looked like a duchess ought to look and said, "So I seen by the paper."

The news of Warner's sale had leaked out, through Nancy herself before leaving. The effect of it was noticeable in the boarders' attitude toward him. A writer is a distinct species. One may sing, paint, model, lecture, or play upon many instruments, but let him put his thoughts down upon paper and he becomes a member of a queer genus.

The boarders' peculiar characteristics stuck out irritatingly like so many sore thumbs. Genevieve Kendall in a pretty new gown, her doll face made up in a way that made it completely expressionless, was going to one of her unending bridge evenings. George was not there. He had gone up to Omaha for a few days. "I've about come to the conclusion," Miss Gunn told the table, "that year after next I'm going to stop teaching and have some fun." Marty Spencer had an inane story about an organ-grinder. Mary Mae Gates was almost at the point of exhaustion. "If this town hasn't musical taste by the time I leave, it never *will* have," she predicted with tired pessimism. The Major shot his beliefs at the others as though at target practice. Dr. Pearson and Helen Blakely came into the dining room together, an odor of romance fairly saturating the atmosphere.

To Warner they seemed alien, people apart, little cars on narrow-gauge tracks, running around in circles, always ending at the places they started . . . themselves.

Only Essie seemed changed. Warner looked at her a second time. There was something vaguely and newly pretty in the expression of her thin wistful face.

In the hall after dinner, Miss Rilla, with moist eyes, told Warner how much she missed Nancy. Miss Ann, in passing, snorted audibly at the remark.

Trouble comes in many guises. Always it wears a mask and domino but they are of many colors and designs. To Warner, the unwelcome guest appeared behind the iridescent draperies of an unattainable love.

To old Jud Moore, it wore the somber garments of regret. Day and night it confronted him, a ghostly apparition that would not down. Morning and evening the sale of the farm preyed on his mind.

For the first time in his life he did not confide in Aunt Biny. And the secrecy caused a sort of mental festering. Once he said to her crossly, "Dog-goned if I'd care if I *never* saw Californy." He did not sleep well. In the hours after midnight he would waken with a start to face The Thing . . . the specter of regret. He would lie and stare into the blackness, harried with strange thoughts. They were not sensible, he told himself. But, even though he knew this to be true, he could not control them. Almost always they were about trees, queer fantastic forms of cottonwoods and maples and osage oranges. They seemed to be struggling all around him. They assembled into a strange intricate vision of a growing forest, whose roots on all sides twined and intertwined in the darkness. For long hours they seemed striving to exist, crowding, struggling, intertwining, writhing. When he would fall into an unnatural doze the nightmare would close in upon him, that queer, incongruous construction of twisting trees, branches, leaves, seeds and loam. And always, everywhere, roots that twined and intertwined and formed a network

over the room! When he would rise before sun-up the day
seemed no better than the night. In the night-time he faced
the abnormalities of dreams. But in the daytime he faced
the unnaturalness of realities. And the realities were harder
to bear than the dreams.

On the afternoon of the fifth of March, he was in the
harness shed trying to assemble the contents of the little
building into some sort of order for the sale. He pulled
down a few muskrat traps and then hung them back. Dog-
goned if he wanted to sell the traps . . . might want to
use them some time. He picked up a box of carpenter
tools. He wasn't going to sell *them.* He'd have to tinker
around a house no matter where they lived. He pulled a
popcorn sheller from a corner where it stood and then
suddenly pushed it back, deciding not to sell that either.
Half bewildered he looked around him. Well, what in
tunkit did he *want* to sell? Nothing. That was it. Not a
blamed thing. Least of all the land.

He went out and sat down in the doorway where the
walnut shucks were piled around the stump in which the
hatchet was sticking. He could see Ma crossing the lane
road and going into the old cabin. She had said at noon
time she was going over there to pack up Nancy's little
playthings. Ma was going right ahead getting everything
in shape for the sale next week. Beat all how he couldn't
seem to get his part of the articles ready.

Over and over he told himself that he had done the right
thing to sell. Mr. Rineland, whose judgment was unques-
tionable, had said it was best. Ma and he were old. They
had worked hard. They had a right to get out and enjoy
life. Well, what *was* enjoying life? Was it running around
the country like tramps who had no home? Was it moving
into town, chucked down between two other families whose
conversation you could hear and whose cooking you could

smell? Or was it plowing up the cool moist loam in the spring with the meadow larks calling to you from the fences? Was it planting and watching for the first glimpse of green in the fields? Or was it sitting on a bench and whittling in front of a grocery store in Maple City? Was it husking and harvesting? Or was it milling around the country with a lot of restless people a thousand miles from home? *This* was home. There would never be another. When his time came to die he wanted to be here.

It made him think of a dog they had owned years before, how it was shot over on the north road beyond Dennings' and how it crawled home on its belly, whining and whimpering. He wondered what made him recall old Sport to-day, crawling home over the pastures, over the fields and along fences, crawling home to die under the hop vines in the back yard. What if he'd get sick in Californy? He believed he'd crawl back too, whining, whimpering, over the desert and over the mountains, back to the prairie . . . ! Aching with the dull pain of the thoughts that assailed him, he got up and went into the kitchen.

It was at the same moment, over in town, that Warner Field started out to the Moore farm to get the letter Nancy had written him. Although he now knew all that she had told him in it, he still wanted it. His car slipped a little through the soft snow and the wind struck him stinging slaps on his face. The Lombardys and maples stood bleak against the white of the landscape, their north sides etched in snow, studies in black and gray and white. The farm-yard behind the cottonwoods looked desolate when he drove in. A few chickens were huddled together behind the wire of their fence. At first heavy coal smoke from the house chimney gave the only other evidence of life and then he saw some one across the lane road in the two-roomed cabin.

He left his engine going and crossed over to the cabin behind the gaunt, unfriendly cottonwoods.

When he opened the door he saw that it was Aunt Biny in an old black cloth coat with big sleeves. She had on a black knitted hood pushed far back on her head so that her white hair and the pink skin under the parting showed. She had been packing the things from the cupboard and her hands were red with the cold.

When she looked up and saw Warner she reached for her crutch and limped toward him quickly. "I'm glad to see you. It's awful lonesome around here and nothing seems right. You knew Nancy was gone, didn't you?"

Before Warner said more than a brief "Yes," she said, "Here's a letter she left here for you." Warner put it in his pocket . . . the most futile document in the world . . . and the most precious.

"I'm packing all her little stuff," Aunt Biny went on. "She said to put them in a box and keep it at Mattie's until she got it or sent for it. You don't happen to know anything about a key to this drawer, do you? I declare I've jiggled it and pulled at it, but it's locked for good. She told me to get everything and there's an old shawl in here she's always thought a lot of. But how can I get stuff out of a locked drawer and no key in sight?"

It seemed odd to Warner to see Aunt Biny so talkative. Usually reticent and soft spoken, she seemed changed, to be rambling on indefinitely. Warner could not know that the great thing that had happened to the old people had changed them both, had rendered Aunt Biny nervously loquacious and Uncle Jud painfully silent.

She had more to say, too.

"I'm worried about Pa. He don't seem like himself. He scarcely says anything all day long and he don't eat. This very noon I fixed baking powder biscuits in chicken gravy and he just minced at it. All his life he's liked that. Sometimes said he never yet had enough . . . and he just tasted it. I think it's selling the place. Seems like he was all right for a little while and then one day . . . come a couple of robins out by the back door . . . and he got his coat and cap and went out and walked all over the place and when he came in he says, 'There's a meadow lark singin' for all he's worth in the prairie pasture and a teal flew up out of Tinklin' Creek . . . I saw the green flash on his wings.' Right after that he got that blue acting way. So you see it's the selling. I think he's sorry he did. I declare I don't know but what I am too."

"Don't you think you'd better go over to the house now? It's too cold out here for you."

"I promised Nancy I'd do this."

"Nancy would want you to take better care of yourself."

"That's so, too. Maybe I had."

So Warner took Aunt Biny's arm and helped her through the soft snow and up to the house. On the way, limping, short of breath, she still kept on with her confidences. "All my life I've stood on the back porch and looked over to the rim of the prairie and wanted to go on beyond it, and the queer thing is, now I'm getting the chance to do it, I'm not anxious to. It seems too far away. I'd rather just stand and *look* over there and think about it than *go*. Seems to me I'd be happy, if I could know I was going to go right on same as usual. Three hens want to set already and I'd give anything just to set them as though nothing was different and start tomato seeds in a box and put in my sweet peas. . . . "

They were at the house now and stepping into the kitchen. On the table lay one of the bright pink sale bills with its list of household goods and farm machinery, its "Warner Field and Martin Spencer, Clerks," and the date only one

week away. Uncle Jud was in the sitting room beyond,
hugging the red coal-burner.

"Hello there, Field."

When Warner went in to him Uncle Jud began talking,
volubly, a little childishly. All day he had been silent
and now the thoughts rolled out like water gurgling from
a jug: "Ain't this cold for March? Seems like Marches
get colder every year. This is the last snow of the season,
maybe, but you never can tell. D'you believe it . . . we
had a big snow once in April . . . as late as the twentieth.
I remember the date because Nancy was eight months old
and had bronchial pneumonia. We thought she got it by
creepin' around on the cold floor. Doc Minnish come out
every day for five days. Peach blossoms was out and
dog-gone it, if they wasn't all crusted over with snow that
mornin'. Ma said she never saw such a pretty sight as the
pink blossoms showin' through the snow crust. 'N I said
I'd rather see a bushel of peaches any day than a pretty
picture. Doc Minnish said if Nancy wasn't better by the
next mornin' when he come he was afraid we couldn't save
her."

Warner winced at the words. But the old man rambled
on. "So me and Ma stayed up all night. Ma put com-
*press*es of hot onions on her little chest. I set here by the
range and baked onions all night in the oven . . . used
half a bushel I guess. I'd bake 'n Ma would put on a fresh
hot com*press* soon's the old one cooled off. When the first
light was comin' in across her crib we saw her breathin'
all at once easier and she had a little moist sweat on her
face, and kinda turned her head and went to sleep. What
do you s'pose Ma did? Set down 'n cried. Worked like
a windmill all night and then, when Nancy's better, set
down 'n cried. Women's funny, ain't they?"

And Nancy had been a waif . . . left on their porch!

Warner felt a deep tenderness toward the old folks for their love and care.

As soon as he could break in to the old man's talk he told them about seeing Nancy. They were as surprised and pleased about it as children. "I wish you'd tell me more about Mr. Farnsworth," Aunt Biny had taken off her things and sat down in the old chintz chair with her crutch by her side. "Nancy never seemed to tell me very much. When she first came, she told me that he was a wealthy man and would be good to her and that she would always be well looked after. But that's about all she ever had to say."

So Warner told them carefully and impartially about Mr. Farnsworth. He dwelt so scrupulously on his best points that Uncle Jud, sitting with his arms half around the red burner, said with pleased finality, "Well, Nancy is marryin' well. She'll be rich and have everything she wants."

"Yes, Nancy will be rich," Warner agreed.

Aunt Biny looked out at the wintery landscape. There was no sun and the yard looked desolate and unfriendly. "But that don't mean she'll have everything she wants," she said quietly.

CHAPTER XXVIII

UNCLE JUD FACES A CRISIS

WARNER had been back in Maple City four days and Alice had made no move as yet to see him. She had stayed sedately at home, womanly and gentle and quiet. She did not even go into the bank. She wanted to feel free from responsibility about Nancy's leaving and she had succeeded in feeling entirely so. In fact, she had worked herself into a mental state of genuine virtue by arguing that what little influence she had used had not turned Nancy's decision. Nancy herself had said that the confidential talk was not the reason for going. So there was absolutely no need for any feeling of accountability in the matter. As for Warner she would wait for him until Sunday. She would give him that length of time and, if he had not come of his own accord, she would tell her father to have him in for Sunday dinner.

But Warner came of his own accord. Alice smiled softly to herself when she saw him step into the big living room. And she smiled at Warner. There was nothing roguish nor mischievous in one of Alice's smiles. It was all soft and sweet and womanly.

It was on Saturday evening that Warner went up to the Rinelands'. One had to move about and do something, even if part of one had died. After all the Rinelands were old friends and they would notice his continued absence. As he went down the "Bee-House" steps, he passed Walt

281

Thomas turning on the walk that ran around to the back of the house. Walt's car was out of commission and he had walked in to town over the snow-crusted roads.

"Hello, Walt."

"Hello, Mr. Field."

They paused and stood a little uncertainly as though there were more they ought to say. But they did not say it.

"Cold night, Walt."

"You bet."

Up at the Rinelands' Warner found all three in the big living room before a leaping fire in the grate. Mr. Rineland, immaculate and dapper, was reading the paper. Alice was at the piano. Mrs. Rineland, in a beaded dress and beadlike earrings, was working on a beaded purse. She sparkled and jangled whenever she walked. Warner had a swift feeling of desire that with these old friends he might be able to find surcease for the soreness of heart that possessed him.

He had been there but a few moments when Alice remarked casually, "And Nancy has gone back to her friends again? To Chicago, Father said."

"Yes. I saw her for a few hours there on my way home."

Alice was as dismayed as she was surprised. She had to be very careful indeed in what she would say next. So she only asked courteously, "You did?"

"Yes, I found she knew the same family I had known well in college days . . . the Farnsworths. Rod Farnsworth was a classmate of mine and Fay Farnsworth was a classmate of Nancy's. She was there with Fay when I stopped. John R. Farnsworth, Rod's and Fay's father, has been a sort of adviser of Nancy's while she was East. He has been a widower for several years and now he and Nancy are to be married right after Easter."

There was no need of assumption now. Alice's amaze-

ment was genuine. "Mr. Farnsworth . . . the *big manu-
facturer?*"

"Yes."

"Why, Nancy was here all one evening, the night before
she left. We had the loveliest visit . . . like two chums
will . . . over everything." Alice's voice was melting.
"She told me she was going . . . but she never breathed
the reason . . . the little minx! She merely gave me to
understand she was tired of us all here. Father, it was to
be *married* that Nancy went away."

"Yes, she told me so the morning she left, but she asked
me not to say anything about it just then. And it's John
R. Farnsworth . . . that *is* a piece of news. Nancy is
doing well. I'm glad, I'm sure. Of all the little girls who
used to play with Alice, I liked Nancy best."

They had scarcely finished the subject when there was
some one at the door. Mrs. Rineland in her glistening,
jangling beads answered the knocking. To her surprise
and irritation old Jud Moore and his wife stood there asking
for Mr. Rineland. She was ushering them with half dis-
guised reluctance toward the library when Mr. Rineland
came.

"Well! Well! It's Uncle Jud and Aunt Biny. Come
in. Come in. I've always wanted to have you here in the
new home. . . ." He had their hands, was drawing them
into the living room. "Alice! Warner! Here are Uncle
Jud and Aunt Biny Moore!"

"Of all things!" Alice said in her low soft voice to
Warner. "The *butter woman!*"

"I'm glad you came to see us before you left." No one
could question Mr. Rineland's cordiality. "I've always felt
we didn't get together enough in a social way . . . we
old-timers. Remember how we used to go in lumber wagons
twenty miles and more to have a good time? We've lost

all that old spirit of getting together. Everything is business now . . . and even the old pioneer families have drifted apart."

"I guess it's business this time too, Mr. Rineland." Old Jud Moore faced him. "No," he shook his shaggy gray head. "We won't take off our things." Aunt Biny with her crutch sat down on the edge of an overstuffed chair, but the old man stood and nervously twisted his thick cap in his huge hands.

"I got to talk to you about the place." It burst from him as though catapulted by some great hidden force. "I can't stand it any longer. I got to keep the place. It's mine 'n I can't let it go. It's made me sick. I oughtn' to've sold it. I don't know what I was thinkin'. I must o' been crazy."

Alice turned to Warner and smiled. "Imagine! This time of day . . ." she said under her breath, "and at the front entrance."

But Warner stood watching the old man grapple with his deep emotion.

"I've thought about it day 'n night . . . givin' possession on the fifteenth . . . 'n I can't do it." Something made him unconscious of himself. The length of time his mind had dwelt upon it or the depth of his feeling was rendering him impervious to the surroundings. Usually reticent in the presence of people like the Rineland women, he was paying no attention to them.

"Why, I know every stick 'n stone on the place," he went on as though he and Mr. Rineland were alone. "I set out every single growin' thing there but my prairie pasture and the Lord Himself planted that. I can't part with it. I thought I could. But I can't. It don't seem fair to the place. Denning's goin' to cut down a lot o' the trees. I've thought about 'em day and night. He's goin'

to cut down the cottonwoods 'n the osage oranges 'n even
some o' the maples. It don't seem sensible that I should
care. 'What's a tree?' I've asked myself a lot o' times.
I'm willin' to go so far as to say it *ain't* sensible. But Ma
'n me put 'em in when they was little whips like your
finger, 'n watched 'em grow for half a century. When you
stop to think about it, Mr. Rineland, it just seems *awful*
. . . roots all twined everywhere under the ground, enormous 'n strong, 'n overhead shade for men 'n beasts 'n
homes of hundreds of birds . . . when they wa'n't no shade
here a-tall when we come. It just seems like undoin' the
work of a half-century. 'Tain't sensible I know . . . but,
God A'mighty . . . I got to stand by them trees."

He stood there in the overfurnished and overstuffed living
room, an alien figure in his coat and muffler and his buckled
overshoes, with his great shaggy gray head thrown back
against the silk hangings. No one moved. Even Mrs.
Rineland's and Alice's annoyance of expression faded a
little under the old man's emotion. Mr. Rineland stood
leaning against the fireplace mantel, half shading his face
with his hand. It came to Warner that it seemed like the
third act of a play in which some great old world-famous
artist was holding the boards with magnetic fascination for
his audience. But it was not acting. It was real life.

"And he's going to plow up that one piece of pasture
of mine that's real prairie," he went on. "I got one piece,
you know . . . it's only ten acres . . . but it's virgin
prairie. I been keepin' that all these years. Every year
the teachers bring the children in their classes out 'n show
'em. I'm the only one in the whole community, maybe
county as far as I know, that's kept any. It ought not to
be plowed up. The kids ought to see it . . . every generation of 'em ought to see the way it looked when the
world began. Denning don't care about that. He's all

for makin' more money. But there's things in the world besides money. 'N that piece o' virgin prairie ought to be let stay for the kids to see. I can't think of anything else durin' the night but me doin' that tom-fool thing of sellin'. I must o' been clean out o' my head. I belong there 'n I got to go into the field again. If you ever had anything prey on your mind like that you know how I been feelin'. I got to go into the field again when spring comes." He appealed to the silent figure by the mantel but the banker did not look up.

"So I been up to see Denning this late afternoon. It got so I couldn't stand it. I drove up just after supper and talked to him. He was sore about it . . . but I kept at him askin' what he'd take to destroy the contract 'n he says finally, 'Twenty-five hundred dollars.' He knew I had that exact amount on time . . . seems I said as much to him once. Well, I'm goin' to do it. It's stiff, but I've got to. I thought 'twas best to come and talk to you first so's I wouldn't get tangled in any legal procedure. That's legal, ain't it . . . if he agrees . . . 'n I pay him the twenty-five hundred 'n he destroys the contract? Nothin' ever could come up again, could it?"

"No," Mr. Rineland spoke from the shadow of his hand, "if you both agree to it."

"He's a close figurer 'n I suppose he thinks Carl can buy somewheres else near and make twenty-five hundred easy. It's stiff I know. I'm sorry it takes all that money. I suppose you think it ain't good business?"

Mr. Rineland drew his hand from his eyes. "No, it isn't. But *you had to do it.* Don't worry about it any more, Jud. I know how you feel. We'll fix it up Monday and call off the public sale. Nobody understands it better than I."

The old man brightened childishly. "With you and Ma understandin' about it, I don't care what anybody else thinks. That twenty-five hundred dollars was hard earned but even that don't count now beside the big mistake I made. That money seems just like a piece o' paper to me now. 'N I said to Ma, 'What's a piece o' paper beside our home with the maples 'n the cottonwoods that's been a half a century growin' . . . 'n the ten acres o' virgin prairie I'm savin' . . . for all the little kids to see? . . .''

Down at the "Bee-House" Walt and Essie sat in the kitchen. It was a big room built in the days when people baked whole hams, huge loaves of bread and big batches of doughnuts instead of stuffing a green pepper and opening a can of sardines in a kitchenette. Miss Rilla and Miss Ann sat in their father's library, where they had once perched on the arms of his chair and listened to his sonorous voice read "The Three Bears." He had imitated the high squeak of the little bear, the natural voice of the medium-sized bear and the guttural tones of the big bear so realistically that they had shivered with delight. And now Miss Rilla was saying, "Ann, it seems like we ought to tell Essie to take her young man into the parlor or the front hall."

"No, I'm not going to encourage her in this kind of doings. And I'm not going to have to see or hear any of their foolishness. I can't stand any lally-gagging around me. It's bad enough to have Dr. Pearson and Helen Blakely hanging around and talking low. It makes me sick."

Miss Rilla sighed. The realm of romance was a shadowy forest to Miss Rilla, very vague and far away. She had never walked in it, for her sister would never let her. But many times she had stood on the borders of its confines and looked in.

Walt and Essie talked about a few local happenings and the backwardness of spring. They were both conscious of the fact that they were saying things for which they cared little. Essie was crocheting lace for a dresser scarf. She looked plain and neat and pleasant. Walt said after a while, "I mustn't stay long enough to get the ogre after me. I'd just naturally turn and run if the fierce one stuck her head out here."

Essie smiled at Walt. It made her wistful face almost pretty. "Miss Ann isn't so fierce as people think. She's like old Jud Moore, all prickly on the outside."

Essie went to the door with Walt. They stood in the back entry where the big refrigerator was kept. There were glass jars turned upside down on top of it and a dish of salt mackerel was soaking for breakfast.

"Good night, Walt," Essie said cheerfully. "It was awful nice of you to come and see me. I miss Nancy a lot. When she was here I used to think all day when I was working how jolly it would be when she came blowing into the house in that excited way of hers. Mr. Field misses her too. I can see the look in his eyes. It makes me sorry for him. He couldn't help liking her . . . she was so likable. I wish I was gay and pretty and full of life like Nancy always was."

Walt stood counting the rows of jars. Suddenly he reached out and took Essie's hands. Milking cows is not conducive to cultivating a skin you love to touch and neither is dishwater a good hand lotion. "Essie, I wish I could tell you something . . . and have you understand me . . . without getting mad."

"Why, Walt, you can tell me anything and I wouldn't get mad."

"I believe it. Listen then. I used to think everything of Nancy. But that's all over. I'm going to put her clear out of my mind and forget that I ever did. But I'd rather be honest with you about it and start on the square. I guess you know who I mean when I say that there are other nice girls in the world . . . one of them, anyway. Just

this last winter . . . I've got to thinking a lot of you,
seeing more of you this way. I've got to work hard all
my life and I've got to always look after Ma too. I wouldn't
want you to not know that. But if you'll marry me . . .
Gee, I'd be glad and I'd give you the very nicest home I
could."

It did not seem true. Fairy tales were only in books.
Essie's honest heart was full to bursting. "Walt, I suppose
I ought'n to say it so bold but I'd . . . rather marry you
than do anything else in the world."

Warner left the Rinelands. The evening had not in any
way filled the void; it had in no way dulled the ache.
Alice's exquisite music after the departure of Uncle Jud
and .Aunt Biny had only served as a background against
which there persistently moved a slim little boyish figure,
fragrant and elusive.

On the way home he passed Walt.

"Hello, Walt."

"Hello, Mr. Field."

They both paused uncertainly as though there were more
they ought to say. But they did not say it.

"Getting colder, Walt."

"You know it."

Walt passed on in a state of humble elation. He thought
of Nancy who was so far above him. She was like something high and lovely and ideal but far away like the float-
ing dissolving clouds he watched while he cultivated the
corn . . . like the prairie lark that swung up from the
pasture. But Essie . . . Essie was a good pal, that's what
she was, pleasant and comfortable and easy to get along
with. She looked pretty to-night too in her blue dress
with a string of white beads at her neck. She fixed her
hair neat and nice and when she smiled she looked happy
and good-natured. They would build a bedroom on the

south. Walt's blood was warm within him. He'd buy two
more cows from Jud Moore. Jud said something seemed to
ail him. He didn't feel good. Well, *he* felt good. He'd
always feel good. Sickness was an alien thing . . . a thing
that happened to other people but never would to him. Poor
Field! He'd been scorched, too, near the flame of Nancy.
And Nancy was going to marry the president of the biggest
manufacturing concern in Chicago. He could even buy
the Rinelands out, bag and baggage, a dozen times. His
thoughts went back to Essie. It was funny he'd never paid
any attention to her in school, and there she had been all
the time . . . *his wife* . . . waiting for him. Wasn't there
an Essie somewhere for Mr. Field? Alice Rineland maybe.
He wouldn't want her though. Alice was good looking
and correct and she'd have all the Rineland property some
day, but he just didn't like her. Stuck-up! Always had
been that way through school. Walt tramped along in the
cold past the long row of stark Lombardy poplars.

At home he went to the barn to see if his brood mare was
all right. When he got back to the house he took off his
shoes and tiptoed past his mother's bedroom door. Then
he turned back, went in and sat down on the edge of the
bed.

"Ma," he shook her huge figure carefully at first so as
not to frighten her, "Ma, wake up. I want to tell you
something."

Mattie came out of a deep sleep. "The mare sick?"

"No. Listen! Essie's said she'd marry me."

Mattie was wide awake now. *"Essie?* After you grievin'
yourself about Nancy for four years?"

"Aw, forget it," Walt grinned. "Essie's a dandy girl."

"Well, I suppose it's got to be." Mattie had Spartan
blood in her. She met it, head on, as it were. "And thank
the Lord it's her. Essie'll be a good comfortable girl to have

around and she's got more work in her little finger than some girls has in their whole systems."

But she did not go to sleep again. For a long time she lay and thought what a little while ago it was that she was tucking Walt in his crib. Why did they grow up and slip away from your arms like that?

CHAPTER XXIX

FIVE-THIRTY O'CLOCK

EVEN though March had come in like a lamb, by Monday every one realized that it had grown a mane and tail. Winter was laboring doubly hard because of its laggard ways in the early weeks.

The First National Bank force was working like a traction engine. Almost one could hear the cogwheels and belts and pulleys of the business straining and squeaking. Country bankers' New Year's, like that of the Chinese, does not fall on January first. It is in March. There is not the slightest doubt but that one, Brutus, some little time ago, had country bankers in mind when he said, "Remember March . . . the Ides of March remember."

At noontime the little force of five drew its first long breath since the doors had opened at eight-thirty. Land deals, note renewals, settlements of various kinds . . . the whole morning had been rushed.

"Pretty busy," Mr. Rineland spoke crisply when he put on his coat.

"Things could be worse," the cashier admitted. "The examiner could arrive."

"A federal officer could drop in to check over the revenue stamps," Warner contributed.

Marty Spencer added cheerfully, "Or old Mr. Flachenecher could spend the afternoon with us and tell us how he and General Grant conducted the Civil War."

They were all back promptly at one. People began

coming in. The Millers and the Albrechts and the Guggenmeiers had a long and complicated interchange of land, checks, notes and liberty bonds. Other farms changed hands and several pieces of town property. Some of the parties to the procedures were so stupid that only the blood of many chivalrous ancestors kept Warner Field from slapping them. By three o'clock things were thickest. The air was stale. The force was beginning to feel the pressure. At four old Jud Moore and the Dennings came in. Mr. Rineland himself fixed up the deal. When it was finished Mr. Rineland said, "There, Jud, the farm is your own again."

Old Jud Moore nodded his shaggy gray head. "I had to do it," he said simply.

It was five-twenty when the force finally got into its various overcoats.

"Walk up with me, Warner." Mr. Rineland spoke to him in the lobby. "I want to talk to you a bit." On the way up Main Street he explained, "It's about your writing. I'm glad to learn that you've done something with it again. I'm especially pleased that apparently it hasn't affected your work at the bank. I'm wondering though if you've been using yourself well, staying up and all that. A man can't serve two masters, you know. I'm no old woman to gossip, but I've had a feeling that you weren't looking quite so well . . . not ill . . . but a little off . . . my imagination, maybe . . . but just not so fit."

"I'm all right, Mr. Rineland. I'm feeling as well as could be."

"Nothing on your mind? I'm not asking from idle curiosity, Warner. Don't tell if you'd rather not."

He was so sincere that it hurt Warner to say, "Oh, one has problems sometimes. Quite often they're not so serious as we think."

"You'll have some money coming from your writing. I'm wondering if you'd like to take a little stock in the old First National. It's not for sale. But your father and I were good friends and I'd like to let you have a little block of it."

He was cornered. After all, Mr. Rineland was his employer. He ought to know. So he said readily enough, "I had a debt . . . it's a source of regret to me. I have had to use my money for that."

"I see. That's all right." But it worried Mr. Rineland. He did not like the sound of it. A young fellow of Warner's age to be deeply in debt! The new generation did not know what it was to dig and delve and save.

Warner left him at the "Bee-House" corner. He knew that Mr. Rineland was disappointed in him. He himself was disappointed. A block of stock in a sound bank whose stock was not for sale! He went up the steps with a complete reaction of feeling concerning the part he had played. He should have allowed his father's disgrace to be known, and let the bonding company pay the loss. He had been a fool. Disgust with himself and a revulsion of feeling at his attitude in the affair were rampant as he entered the "Bee-House." And then he was back again with his mother clinging to him after his father's death. Wearily he admitted that he would do it all over again for her. As he went up the winding stairway he could hear low voices in the dining room.

The voices were those of Essie and Miss Rilla and Miss Ann. It was Essie who timidly approached the subject as she set the long table. "I thought I ought to tell you, Miss Ann . . . I'll not be here but a few months." She was plainly embarrassed. "I . . . I'm going to marry Walt Thomas."

Miss Rilla's eyes filled. "Why, Essie, how nice that is.

He's a good boy. They say he's so good to Mattie. He's turned out well when you think of the kind of father he had."

"Pst!" Miss Ann dished up her little dipper of cold water. "You can't get away from a father. He's got his father in him and if it's *in* I say it's bound sooner or later to come *out*."

Essie flushed. "Well, I guess I'm not afraid."

"No, of course not." Miss Ann's sarcasm was supreme. "They never are. They just go right on marrying and being fooled all over the world."

Essie stood her ground. Her love for Walt Thomas was too old and too strong to waver before the onslaught. "All right, maybe that's so, Miss Ann, but I'm ready to be fooled."

Her gray head high, her heavy body erect, Miss Ann walked out of the room. What could one do with an imbecile like Essie? And besides, whom else could she get to work so reasonably? In the kitchen she sat down heavily. From the front parlor came the sound of the old cracked piano and a throaty voice singing, "When you come to the end of a perfect day." Miss Rilla, with the vague idea of comforting her twin, came out to the kitchen.

"Are you ill, sister? Is there anything you want?"

"Yes," Miss Ann said crabbedly, "I wish you'd go in there and throw a dinner plate at that Mary Mae Gates's larynx."

While Miss Ann still sat weightily on the painted chair, Genevieve Kendall came into the kitchen. She looked out of place in her dinner dress and came stepping in gingerly, as one whose first-hand knowledge of kitchens was limited.

"I just thought I'd tell you, Miss Ann, that George won't be back at all. But I'm going to stay. We're through. I applied for my divorce to-day. It's just got so I can't stand things any more. I've had so much to put up with."

Miss Ann snorted politely. "I wish you'd go tell that to Essie Carlson," she said acridly.

In the room over their heads Major Slack had just finished reading an old newspaper clipping under the headline, "Youngest Volunteer Major In The Division." Then he walked over to his mirror and surveyed himself in a blue uniform with white stripes down the legs. The coat would not come together over the Major's pompous front, and the hard stiff-billed cap sat rakishly on his bald head. He passed his hand questioningly over his red puffy face. Where and when had youth slipped away?

At that same moment Miss Gunn came wearily up the hill from the Whittier. She had spent an hour with one of the Swanson boys over an arithmetic lesson. He was so dull, so phlegmatic and yet . . . perhaps some little seed sown in the hour would take root. Never would she shirk as long as there was strength within her. At the "Bee-House" steps Marty Spencer, light-hearted, irresponsible, joined her.

And down in the Carlsons' and Swansons' neighborhood, Gus Carlson scraped away the snow from a patch of ground in his back yard, made some parallel trenches and put in a few early radish and lettuce and pea seeds. "I suppose I'll have to sit on the fence with a shot-gun," he called loudly to Jen at the cob-house so that Jim and Myrt Swanson might hear and know he had specific reference to their Rhode Island Reds.

Myrt Swanson heard him from the cyclonically jumbled interior of her back porch and called to Jim, "Some folks ought to send their Plymouth Rocks to college . . . such smart polite chickens!"

Out on the highway east of town, Dr. Pearson was return-
ing from a country call. Helen Blakely was with him. The
doctor could have chosen no more unromantic moment nor
place than five-thirty of a dismal March afternoon on the
snowy highway near the Mattie Thomas farm to say practically: "I love you, Helen, and I want you to be my wife,
but it takes an awful lot of gall for a doctor to ask a woman
to marry him. It's like asking you to become a missionary
to Indo-China or the Belgian Congo. It means meals at
every hour but the one you'd expect me, to try your patience. It means keeping secrets from you that I couldn't
possibly tell you, to try your faith. It means a lot of
uncollected fees, to try your charity."

Quite surprisingly Helen Blakely used the same words
that Essie had just used to Miss Ann. "I guess I'm not
afraid."

Near the Lombardys at the Thomas farm they passed old
Jud Moore going toward home with the Dennings in their
big car. In front of the Thomas place they could see
Walt going into the kitchen door with an armful of wood.

When he went in, Walt found his mother, huge and
perspiring, stepping lightly about the stove. She had
pork steak, mashed potatoes, fried onions, creamed dried
corn, cake, coffee and jelly for supper. She was wondering
if she had plenty, whether she ought not open a can of
peaches, too. Walt put the wood in the box and started
out again. "Supper, Walt," Mattie called.

"All right, Ma . . . just a minute."

He went around the house, took a tape-line from his
pocket and measured a rectangle. It could be fourteen
by eighteen. It could have windows . . . a lot of them toward the south. Essie's rocking-chair and a little sewing
table could sit in the sun. After supper he was going
to look through all the different mail-order catalogues for

furniture . . . some of this light colored shiny kind with flowers painted on it.

When the Dennings let Uncle Jud out by the cottonwoods at five-thirty, he did not go directly into the house. He walked down the lane road past the harness shed and the barn toward the orchard. By the apple trees, he stopped and looked around him. He put out a huge hand, as gnarled as the tree trunk, and touched its moist gray bark gently. He went on until he came to Tinkling Creek, tramping along its slushy banks. A bluebird, like a wild gentian blown from its stalk, flew noiselessly across his path. He came then, in time, to the edge of the cornfield and the wheat land and the prairie pasture lying under the thin quilt of snow and gazed with supreme content upon them. He made the entire round of the place in the chill of the late afternoon, coming back to the house lot past the maple windbreak and the cottonwoods. Under the maples he stood for some time and gazed up into their gaunt twining branches. A hundred old nests swung idly in the wind, but as he looked a robin darted up to the limb on which hung one of these empty homes, and raising its rusty black head, flung out its soul in a welcome to spring. Old Jud Moore went up the back path to the kitchen door. "Ma," he called, " 'twon't be three weeks till I'll be goin' into the field."

At that same moment, just as Uncle Jud stepped into the kitchen, it was six-thirty back in Chicago. The city was dreary. In its own way it looked as stark and stripped of life as the country with the trees standing stiff and black in the snowy parks. The wind blew cold from the north whipping itself into a maudlin thing up and down the boulevards. But it was warm and gay and summerlike inside the big Hyde Park house.

Nancy opened the door of her own room and went in,

turning the lock as she did so. There was a prenuptial
dinner engagement and it was time to dress. For just
a minute she leaned against the door and closed her eyes.
In a whimsical moment she told herself that when she
opened them she would see the old plain bed and bureau
in her room at Aunt Biny's and through the queer old
window that looked three ways, Warner Field driving down
the lane road by the cottonwoods into the yard.

With childish disappointment she opened her eyes slowly
to the silk-canopied bed, the carved dressing table and the
lace-covered windows. Almost immediately they fell upon
a letter awaiting her. She tore it open hastily. It read:

Dearest Nancy: Warner has just left after telling me the
wonderful news. You were certainly stingy with it. Nancy,
dear, you would have saved me making myself so ridiculous
if you had just told me. I'm truly sorry I said what I
did about your friendship for Warner. You'll forgive me,
I know, and realize what depth of feeling on my part must
have called it forth. Warner gives me such wonderful
report of the wealth of the man you are to marry. We
are both so happy for you.

Please think of me less critically than you may be doing
because of my ill-fated remarks on our last night together.
Maybe I'm envying you a little living in Chicago. And
yet . . . who knows? . . . I can't quite think Maple City
will always hold me.

                    Your lifelong friend,
                        Alice M. Rineland.

Nancy, on the bench in front of the luxuriously appointed
table, bit her lip and tears of vexation welled in her eyes.
What could one do with a person like that . . . smooth,
suave, two-faced? For a half hour sheer jealousy clutched

at her and wrapped its stinging tail about her. Out of the long moments of heart travail, no other punishment for her stood forth more poignantly than the realization that Warner was headed straight into the rapids. It was inevitable. Warner, who was fine and big and sincere . . . who needed some one with humor and understanding! And Alice, who was smooth and small and selfish . . . absolutely humorless and wholly self-centered! When once she got him for her own she would bind him and hurt him and break him with those soft smooth slippery traits. Suddenly, it seemed that it must not go on, that Alice must not ruin Warner's life with her needle thrusts. She, herself, must *do* something about it. Impulsively she stood up as though to put her thoughts into some sort of action. But some one was tapping on the door and rattling the knob. Fay's voice called:

"Nancy, Dad wants to know what's become of you? Aren't you nearly ready?"

Nancy threw up her head. "Nearly ready," she called gayly.

CHAPTER XXX

BACK TO THE PRAIRIE

AUNT BINY thought it was sorrow over selling the
place and the reaction that followed getting it back.
Uncle Jud thought it was the result of the cold
ride in the open surrey the night he and Aunt Biny went
in to the Rinelands'. Old Doc Minnish would have known it
was neither one. All day Tuesday and Wednesday Uncle
Jud lay in bed for the first time during his maturity. Wasn't
sick, nothing ailed him, didn't want a doctor, just felt too
tired to dress.

Thursday was the day on which the farm would have
passed out of his hands had the deal held. Aunt Biny spoke
of it to the old man when she brought in his dinner on
a tray. But it was not necessary to remind him of the
thing that had burned into his brain. When she had taken
away the scarcely tasted food, he lay and thought of the
place, of the corn land and the wheat land and the pasture.
And thinking so, he determined to get up and dress. All
foolishness to stay there and imagine something he might
as well go out and see. Moving quietly, so as not to let
Ma hear, he got laboriously into his clothes. Planning
craftily he decided to go out of the front door and around
the east of the house which was opposite the kitchen side.
Ma had eyes in the back of her head. Glad that the washing
of the dinner dishes was holding her attention, he walked
cautiously through the sitting room and out on the porch.
Beat all how weak he was. That was what came from playing lazy and staying in bed when he ought to have been

working. The March sun was deceiving. Looked warm and was as cold as Greenland. At the corner of the house he stopped and steadied himself, one hand on the tin water-spout.

There it lay stretched out before him . . . his place. Every line of it was as familiar as the features of Ma's face. Looked pretty dull and somber just now. But, when the snow would go off and the warm days come, it would blossom forth again under his hand. The trees too . . . the cottonwoods and the maples and the gnarled old apple or-chard! He looked out toward the intertwined branches. They, too, would soon change. Queer how they drew their substance from the earth, how sap mounted up through their old roots and trunks, forming bud and blossom and leaf. How the leaves fell to the ground, turned to mold, sank into the earth, became part of it, were drawn up as sap, and again there were bud and blossom and leaf. Change and yet . . . no change. Like life! Babies and youths, mature men and old men. Like trees! Sap and bud, blossom and leaf. Leaves . . . falling off . . . mold . . . sap . . . bud . . . blossom . . . old men . . . falling off. No, not old men . . . *leaves!* He was getting mixed in his mind, becoming confused. Babies . . . youths . . . mature men . . . leaves . . . falling off. . . ! He was suddenly chilled and shaking. He felt cold, stricken, crumbling . . . like a shriveling leaf. He must get back to where it was warm . . . in bed . . . under the leaves. No, he meant *quilts.* Dod-goned if he could think straight.

He groped his way back to the bedroom and pulled off his shoes. Was too cold to take off anything more. Guessed he'd crawl right in that way, under the leaves . . . with the old men . . . fallen off. . . .

Aunt Biny in great fear sent for Doc Minnish. She blamed herself over and over for not hearing Pa go out-

doors in the cold. Aunt Biny could not know that in going
outdoors he had acquiesced in the Great Plan.

When Doc Minnish came and saw Uncle Jud, the old-
school doctor was no more helpless before the case than a
scientific man would have been. He followed Aunt Biny
out to the kitchen and told her that Uncle Jud had only
a few weeks left. Standing by the sink with the cistern
pump in it Aunt Biny went white and put her hand over
the treacherous heart. This was the day she had dreaded
for a half century. And now it was here. For a long
time she stood by the sink. *Two shall be grinding at the
mill . . . the one shall be taken and the other left.* Then
she turned and limped into the spare bedroom, her crutch
thumping over the threshold. She closed the door and from
a bottom drawer took out a black suit and a white shirt.
Her own gray silk dress lay folded in tissue paper in the
same drawer. Always she had wondered which would have
to be pressed first. And it was Pa's suit.

March stayed uniformly cold, monotonously snowy.
Every day old Doc Minnish drove his dirty car through
the packed single track that went east of town over the
railroad and across Tinkling Creek, still now in a gray
silence. Aunt Biny wanted his guiding counsel although
there was little for him to do.

Uncle Jud went down fast. It is often so. A half-invalid,
like Aunt Biny, drags along for three score years and
ten . . . and a strong man at the last crumples and goes
quickly. Walt and Mattie came and the Dennings on the
north. The countryside looks after its sick. Hearing how
his old customer was stricken, Mr. Rineland drove out in
the shining sedan. Alice sat in the car and worked on a blue
and silver bead bag while she waited for her father. Aunt
Biny limped out and asked her to come in but she said
no, she would just wait for Papa. It hurt Aunt Biny. She

would have liked Alice to come in. Gus Carlson caught a ride out with the mail carrier. Miss Rilla baked a huge fourteen egg angel-food cake and wrapped it in a snow-white tea towel.

"Good land, Rilla," Miss Ann was provoked at the extravagance, "that old lady couldn't eat that cake in a month of Sundays."

"I know it," Miss Rilla wiped her eyes. "But I just want to do *something* for her."

The heart of the whole countryside turned toward the white farmhouse at the edge of town. Tangled roots? Blind souls who can never find relief from their sordid surroundings? Poor thinkers! Not to see the shimmering growth that springs upward when the human emotions are touched.

Warner Field took Miss Rilla and the mammoth cake out to the farm, with Miss Rilla gingerly swinging the cake upward whenever the car struck a snow-filled rut in the road. Warner told Aunt Biny that he would not go into the bedroom. But Aunt Biny limped in and returned to say that Pa wanted him to come in. So Warner, feeling clumsy and noisy, went in. The old man held out his gaunt, calloused hand. He went straight to the thing on his mind: "Field . . . wish you'd write to Nancy. See if she couldn't come back for a few days. She's goin' to be married pretty soon. They're goin' on a long trip. Just can't bear to lay here and think of the ocean atween us without seein' her again. Got somethin' I want to tell her. Told me she'd come for a few days in September. But September . . . that's a long ways off when you're in bed. Might be I'll never have a September. A-body can't tell."

And Warner, back in town, remembering the pallor settling over Jud Moore's face as though Death were taking its first fitting, did not write. He telegraphed.

On Tuesday morning, the first day of April, Warner went
to the station to meet Nancy. Because March had been so
winterlike there was not now much more than the suggestion
of spring. Tulips were up but acting shy, their buds still
tight and green. White clouds were running across the
sky, hurrying somewhere as though on important business.
The sun was warm but when one stepped out of it the
cold penetrated. There had been pussy willows on the
"Bee-House" table. A few people were pruning trees.
There were many bonfires so that the air was scented
with the odor of burning rubbish. Such half-block pastures
as were scattered through town showed a faint flush. Only
the winter wheat stood out boldly to color the landscape.
Great emerald splashes of it seemed painted against the
brown earth.

At the station Warner walked up and down. His thoughts,
too, went up and down . . . up and down. . . . The twist
of the wheel that had sent Nancy back . . . the joy of
seeing her and the pain of losing her . . . of being with
her . . . and then trying to forget. Up and down . . .
up and down . . . past the baggage and the chicken crates,
the trunks and the waiting people. Love . . . hopes . . .
the fulfillment of dreams! Debts . . . obligations . . .
promises! Up and down . . . Old Jud Moore fighting
death until Nancy came. . . . He fighting life when Nancy
came. . . .

The train from the East was sweeping around the curve
and then Nancy was stepping down from it in that quick
alert way of hers and coming straight to him. It seemed
the most natural thing in the world to them both . . . like
a bird to its nest, the wanderer to his home.

"Is he living?"

"Yes. These sturdy old people . . . it's hard for them
to pass out."

Nancy put her thoughts into words as they were walking around to the car. "It's queer, but I've sometimes imagined how it would seem to be coming back this way . . . called back to see one of them go. It doesn't seem like a new experience. It doesn't even seem queer to have you the one to meet me, Warner."

"You knew they kept the farm?"

"Yes. Aunt Biny wrote me. I can't help but be glad they did."

They were in the car now. "How are the Farnsworths?" He could not evade the issue.

"All well. Emily has her baby. It's a boy. We're all terribly excited over it. Rod says to tell you he's built like a quarter back. He looks like Rod and he weighs nine pounds. He's a nice baby." She looked up at Warner mischievously. For the first time the old Nancy had returned. "I'll be his grandmother," she said with her impish grin.

They drove past the "Bee-House." Miss Ann had begun the semiannual orgy of house cleaning, which always had the effect of making her more bitter and cross. Nancy recognized the upstairs hall rugs on the line. The Rineland house looked down on them from its three terraces. "You've been seeing Alice?" She did her best with her voice but it did not obey her with any too much alacrity.

"Occasionally," Warner returned. They said nothing more until they had crossed the railroad track and were on the country road. Nancy sniffed the air. "Spring smells differently here than anywhere else." There was that same odor of burning, of newly turned loam, of air that was half warm, half cold. There was the green of winter wheat in great patches that stood out vividly on the huge checkerboard. There were the clouds that hurried on swift important business and the robins that flew across the road in short futile journeys. There was the spring wind that blew across the open sweep of the prairie . . . a wild, free, unhampered thing.

"I believe I could stand the thought of death more easily if winter were coming," Nancy said then. "But spring! With the orchards going to bloom . . . and . . . Uncle Jud liked spring!"

Warner honked the horn for a wagon ahead of them. An occasional kernel of shelled corn dribbled down from the box and two chickens hurried along after it pecking their omnivorous way down the road.

"It's Walt," Nancy said. "I must speak to him."

So Warner stopped and Nancy slipped out of the car and went over to the wheel. The horses backed and stepped around, huge, odorous things, their harness clanking. Walt swung himself down and took Nancy's outstretched hand.

"Aunt Biny wrote that you and Essie are going to be married. I'm *so* pleased, Walt."

Walt was red, visibly embarrassed. "Essie's a good girl," was all he could think of to say. He was as uneasy as the horses, shuffling about. It takes a certain degree of sophistication to get through a dramatic moment. And to Walt, who had loved Nancy, this was drama.

"Uncle Jud's going to die, Walt." For the first time the girl's voice caught and wavered.

Walt turned his head. "Yes, the old man's been going down the last few weeks. Seems like . . . after he sold the place."

When they drove into the farmyard, up through the familiar cottonwoods, there were several cars there. Nancy shrank from the ordeal. "Warner," she said, "I wish you didn't have to go away."

"I'll be right here when you want me," he told her.

Aunt Biny came into the bedroom to tell Uncle Jud

that Nancy had come. Uncle Jud opened his eyes even though it seemed like he was almost too tired to do it. He had been waiting for this. He was going somewhere after she got here. He couldn't think just where it was. Beat all how forgetful he was getting. But he could remember that he was going some place where Ma would come, too, after a while. That was queer . . . they had always gone together before . . . out to the State Fair or back to Indiany. Must think hard where he was going this time. Suddenly he remembered. It gave him a contented relief. *He was going into the field.* He wanted to see Nancy again before he went. Had something he wanted to tell her. And now here she was bending over him, and to save his soul he couldn't think what it was. That's the way he always was . . . dog-gone it . . . talked a blue streak when there was nothing to say and was tongue-tied when he ought to be talking. Nancy was a pretty girl. She was holding his hand and she was crying. Nancy ought not to do that. There was nothing to cry about. He'd try hard to think what that thing was. "Nancy . . . somethin' always wanted to tell you. Can't think to-night just what 'tis. Too tired . . . in the mornin'."

Something was closing Nancy's throat and choking her. "Never mind, Uncle Jud. Don't try."

"Say, maybe 'twas about a playhouse." He brightened. "Fixin' you up the old cabin . . . so's you can keep your dolls and play out there. . . "

For a while they sat so, Nancy's wet cheek to his hand. Then, "Field come with you?" he asked. And a moment later, "Can't he come in?"

So Warner, too, came in and, grave and troubled, stood beside the bed.

"Always liked you, Field. Feel safe about Nancy with you." Uncle Jud's failing old mind was mixed. He was thinking it was Warner that Nancy was to marry. And it was not Warner. They would have to ignore an old man's vagaries. "You'll take good care of her?"

Nancy raised a stricken face to Warner. "Let him think so," it begged. "Tell him so."

So Warner bent to the old man. "I'll take good care of Nancy."

In the presence of Death it did not seem like a lie. It seemed sacred . . . like a marriage.

CHAPTER XXXI

A LEAF FALLS

WARNER went out and sat on the seat under the apple tree at the corner of the porch. In a few moments Nancy slipped out and sat down by him in a burst of youthful grief. "A real father couldn't have been better. One of the first things I can remember was taking hold of his hand and going down the lane road after the cows . . . and in winter. . . ."

Warner would not touch her. It would have been folly. He sat there rigidly, his hands clenched. "Nancy, these things have to be."

She threw out her own hands in a gesture of infinite bitterness. "Oh, what's the use of *anything*?"

Mattie Thomas stayed in the kitchen and cooked things most of the time. Walt brought in wood and coal. Mrs. Nick Denning took charge of the house. She moved about importantly in a striped dress with her hair twisted high on her head as though by taking thought she had added a cubit to her stature.

All afternoon Uncle Jud lingered and far into the night. There was cruelly little more they could do for him. He wished he had some cheese like he tasted once. He and Walt's father had gone on a load of hogs to Postville. It was so near dark when they got there that all they stopped to get was crackers and cheese. He wished he had some of that.

"It doesn't matter," Doc Minnish told them. "Get him anything he wants now."

But when they brought the cheese he had forgotten his momentary desire. "Hell! No!" he said irritably, "what's a sick man want of cheese?"

In the dusk of the evening Nancy asked him, "Did you ever think of the thing you wanted to tell me?" Uncle Jud shook his head. "Too tired . . . to-morrow. . . ."

Aunt Biny, dry-eyed and drawn, did not leave her chair by the side of the bed. He did not take his eyes from her. After midnight, still looking at her, they glazed. The throaty breathing stopped. There was a great stillness in the little room.

Daylight had scarcely broken with all the birds in the trees singing wild pæans to its coming until the country-side knew of the passing. They talked about it over the party lines.

"Jud Moore's dead."

"*Dead?* My . . . my! It was just three weeks ago Saturday . . . no, Friday . . . no, it *was* Saturday because I had my egg-case . . . 'n I saw Jud. I called out to him, 'How you this mornin', Jud?' and he said 'Rotten!' just as grouchy 'n natural like. And now he's *dead!* Well! Well!"

"The last time *I* saw him was that Monday he was in town with the Dennings. He had a sack of salt and a mended bridle; was bragging about how early he was going to do his plowing."

And so they told each other how queer it was . . . that he should have left the spring plowing and the sack of salt and the mended bridle and gone away.

Many people came to the house as they do in country communities. They brought flowers and buns and coffee-cakes and a black veil. What did they do that for, Nancy wondered wearily. She didn't want to see them. She didn't want to see anybody but Aunt Biny and Warner.

Alice came in the sedan. She was gentle and sympathetic. "He was a wonderful man, Nancy. I know just how you will miss him." Nancy was dry-eyed. It did not touch her. She wished Alice would go away too.

Warner came out after the bank closed. "Don't go away," Nancy said, and so he stayed until late in the evening. It was all he could do for her.

On Friday afternoon the whole countryside came. The yard and the lane road and the highway by the cotton-woods were filled with cars. The house was full of people. Men stood outside the door. Aunt Biny let the women fix the black veil over her face apathetically as though it did not matter one way or the other. Somebody put coal in the stove. It sounded crashingly loud in the flower-scented stillness. The presidents looked stolidly down. The preacher, bustling and important with a cold in his head, read cheerfully the text of Aunt Biny's choosing: *He shall be like a tree planted by the river of waters that bringeth forth his fruit in his season . . . his leaf also shall not wither.*

The ground in the cemetery was soggy on the north side of the evergreen trees where the last of the drifts had lain. Part of the dirt that had come out of the yawning hole in the ground was yellow clay. By its side the grave of the little girl that died looked sunken as though under the weight of many snows. Nancy, with her youth and her awe in the presence of death, wept. Aunt Biny, with her crutch and the unnecessary black veil, made no demonstration. Mr. Rineland, faithful to his old pioneer friend to the last, was a pallbearer. Dr. Pearson and Helen Blakely were there. And Marty Spencer, strange looking because unsmiling, was there with Miss Gunn and Mary Mae Gates. Miss Rilla was there enjoying a good cry. Miss Ann had said she couldn't abide a funeral and nobody need try to get her to go. Warner, who knew that his place by every decree of nature was with Nancy, stayed in the background with Miss Rilla.

That had been Friday. Nancy's plan was to stay with Aunt Biny Saturday and Sunday, to leave on the six-fifteen Sunday evening.

Saturday turned warm, a sudden descending enfolding warmth as though spring, having neglected its duty, had rushed frantically to work. The trees over by Tinkling Creek threw out a faint tinge of green under one's very eyes. There was almost a sound of growing things . . . all the little songs that buds make when they are unfolding, all the little tunes that grasses hum when they are stretching.

Aunt Biny did not work all day although the loam and sunshine called to her, every clod and garden tool implored her. Once she limped out to the garden, enclosed by its fence from marauding chickens, and looked over the gate at the freshly plowed patch. "I ought to put in some radishes and lettuce," she said. "But I don't know as I want any of them." Then she limped back and sat down in the chintz-covered chair by the window.

It touched Nancy deeply. To see Aunt Biny uncaring about garden or chickens was to witness a revolution.

All day Nancy did little tasks about the house. She and Mattie Thomas turned Aunt Biny's bed around, hung up some different curtains and put Uncle Jud's clothes out of sight. "Just to make the bedroom seem not quite the same," they told each other.

In the late afternoon Mr. Rineland brought Uncle Jud's tin box out, and read them the will, a simple brief statement.

After supper Warner drove out. The evening was so mild that he and Nancy sat on the seat under the apple tree at the corner of the porch. Everything about them was expanding under the balmy atmosphere. The very buds

over their heads seemed unfolding. They talked of ordinary
and usual things, trivial they seemed, when all the time
there was only one thing in the world worth talking
about.

"What are your plans, Warner? You're going to stay
here?"

"Temporarily at least."

"I wish you'd come out here again this summer to write.
I'd like to think of you here. And Aunt Biny would like
to have you."

"What is she going to do?"

"The oldest Carlson boy is going to live here and do
the chores and go. to school. In vacation he will help
Walt with the regular farm work. Walt is going to farm the
lower eighty on shares and Nick Denning has rented the
upper one."

And then Nancy was telling him about the will. "He
left a life estate in the farm to Aunt Biny, then it is to be
mine. All he had, Warner . . . for me. I'm very glad
about it . . . glad now that they didn't sell. It isn't so
much that I will need it. It's more because he gave me my
trees and orchard and hills and prairie. You know I have a
foolish little notion about that dual personality of mine.
It's a whim, of course, but I like to think that coming back
to the old place sort of . . . brings to life the Nancy
Moore that grew up here."

For a time they sat unspeaking and then Nancy wanted
Warner to walk down to the old cabin with her. When they
had crossed the lane road and gone in they found the interior dusty and unattractive. The two half-packed boxes
upon which Aunt Biny had been working were still on the
table. The doors of the built-in cupboard were swung idly
open. Nancy walked over to it and running her fingers
into the crevice under one of the shelves, drew out the

key. With this she unlocked the drawer under the cupboard and took out the shawl. Closer to it now Warner could see that although it was old and dingy looking, a dull brown in color, it had a rambling intertwining of faded green and blue vine. "This is the shawl that was around me . . ." she shook out its dark folds and its wide wool fringe, "only it was new then. It's all that connects me with *them* . . . whoever they were. Cross-country movers probably . . . gypsies, maybe, and a stolen shawl." She looked ruefully at the old colorless thing. "It's a great heritage, isn't it?" She shrugged her shoulder. "I'm not going to take it with me. This is the place for it here in the old playhouse. I'm putting them away for the last time . . . the shawl and the picture of the Nancy Moore I loved for my mother." She locked the drawer and turned to him. "Write something for me, Warner. Something I can read and know is just for me."

"You know already, that everything I write will be for you."

Time was going ruthlessly. The moments that were to be the last were winged. Dusk was descending on them in the little old house . . . dusk and the shadows falling.

"I'd better go now," Warner said steadily. "It's early but you've had some hard days and the trip back will be tiresome. I think I'll not go to the station with you to-morrow, Nancy. Walt can take you. If you don't mind I'd rather say good-by to you here."

To Nancy standing there in the gloom of the cabin, came the poignant realization that life was passing by and she could not stop it. Can one stop the night from coming on? Or the prairie wind? Her hands flew to her throat to check its throbbing. Suddenly, swiftly it came from her, "Oh, Warner, isn't there *any* way out? We've only *one* life to live. *This* isn't the way I wanted it to be . . .

these aren't the things I dreamed about . . . duty and promises and obligations. I dreamed . . . oh, Warner, I dreamed such *different* things here in the orchard . . . desires that were sweeping . . . love that was enfolding . . . life that was complete. . . ."

With an infinite weariness of spirit, Warner knew that all the strength of will power which was to be used in the parting must come from him alone. Nancy was very impulsive and very young. The things which he loved in her, her youth and her impulse, were the very things he must fight.

He took himself in hand with a grip of steel. "It goes deeper than our own desire. My old friendship for Mr. Farnsworth and my very deep indebtedness to him . . . your own obligation and your honest word to him . . . bind us both. Friendship and promises together make too huge a barrier to surmount. There are always just two ways to take in a big decision, Nancy . . . the wrong way and the right . . . and this is the right."

But even then, when Nancy's hands fluttered out in a brave little gesture of mute acquiescence to the decision, Warner took them . . . and her . . . for the long moment which was their last.

Nancy stumbled up the narrow closed stairway to her room and threw herself in a little crumpled heap down by the bed. She was not given to definite prayer. She so loved life that continually she had sent up unvoiced praise for it. But now she prayed. And her prayer was: "God . . . let me forget him. Let me not remember him through the years to come. All that I ask now is:

> 'Wilt Thou blot out before mine eye
> The little path that he came by?'"

Down in a first-floor room with the bed turned around, and the futile medicines thrown out and Uncle Jud's slippers carefully put away out of sight, Aunt Biny lay with wide open eyes. "I forgot to wind the clock," she was thinking listlessly, "but I don't know as it makes any difference *what* time it is."

Over in Maple City another woman was alone. Genevieve Kendall had been granted her divorce by the judge, and allowed alimony. As she surveyed herself in the glass she was thinking how she wouldn't have to be hounding George continually for money now nor constantly giving him an account of herself. She felt very free.

Across the hall from Genevieve's room Miss Gunn had been reading *Speaking of Operations* by Irvin Cobb. "Nancy said it would improve my sense of humor," she was saying to Helen Blakely who had just come in, "I'm sure I don't know why. I think an operation is a very serious thing."

Down in the front parlor Mary Mae Gates sat at the old grand piano, which the Judge had shipped out from Chicago, and practiced "The Land of the Sky Blue Water." She tried the first musical phrase over eleven times before it suited her. It got on Miss Ann's nerves stretched like fiddle-strings from much house cleaning. She had finished the upstairs bedrooms and would be ready for the storeroom the first of the week. "Sometimes," she announced to Miss Rilla, "I feel like sweeping the boarders all down the front steps with a good stout broom and selling the house and paying off the mortgage. And then with what's left buying a little tiny cheap cottage across the creek by the creamery and settling down to be a comfortable old woman without any financial worries."

"Oh, sister, what would our dear father and mother think to hear you talk about leaving our old home?"

"I think, Rilla," Miss Ann's voice was both sharp and weary, "we've been cursed all our lives with that thing called pride. Of *course* we'd rather work our fingers to the bone to keep up this old barn of a house than to move into a tiny one in a neighborhood where folks as poor as we are live. And of *course* we'd rather put up with the caterwauling of that washing-machine-voiced Mary Mae Gates and the fool jokes of that idiot of a Marty Spencer than forego the doubtful pleasure of entertaining the D. A. R. and the Woman's Club here when our turn comes."

On his way into town, Warner Field was wondering if after all his father's way out was such a poor way to side-step unhappiness. As he passed the Rineland house he could hear the lovely melting notes of the "Barcarolle" from *The Tales of Hoffmann*. Just after his roadster passed, Alice came out on the little iron balcony and looked up at the yellow-white moon. Everything was all right, of course, but she would feel easier and more comfortable by to-morrow night at this time.

CHAPTER XXXII

APRIL SIXTH

SUNDAY morning Nancy was awakened by that familiar sound . . . the first to greet her every morning when she was a little girl . . . the thump, thump of Aunt Biny's crutch on the kitchen floor. Aunt Biny, then, was busy again after her one day of idle grieving, going about her work, taking up her burden alone as cheerfully as though nothing were different. She would take up her own in that same way, too, bravely, cheerfully . . . even alone, in a way, like Aunt Biny. Something was sustaining her this morning. The tempestuous railing at Fate of last night had gone. Although her life was not to be with Warner, she would try to mold the rest of it as he would have her, to make her years very full. She must not let pleasure swamp her entirely . . . society and idle futile things . . . Warner would not want her to do that. She would help Elsa Carlson and Mrs. Bornheimer. Some day, when Aunt Biny became less active, she would come back to get her. Mr. Farnsworth need never be ashamed to have gentle Aunt Biny in his home. If she kept her mind on unselfish things and service to others, she would no doubt grow contented. She felt cleansed this morning . . . was no longer suffering. Last night she had prayed not to be allowed to remember Warner. Now she knew that she would not have it that way if she could. Always she would carry him in her heart but the memory of his strength and stability was going to be helpful rather than one of regret . . . a talisman through all the years to come.

319

She rose and went to the window . . . the queer bay window that looked out in three directions. It was the sixth morning of April and dawning unusually warm. Also it was going to be one of those windy days for which the prairie lover makes no boasts. It is the mid-west's most disagreeable feature. East of her, the sun was coming up over the low rolling hills in a sea of lavender. Little white clouds tinged with shades of rose and heliotrope like mauve-petaled flowers blew across the deeper purple above. The hills themselves were bathed in the light of the yellow-pink sun. Robins in the long maple windbreak were paying their morning homage to its coming, singing their own version of *The Messiah*. There were other notes too . . . distinct and clear: the cheery melodious ones of the meadow lark, the sad plaintive call of the mourning dove, the high sweet trill of a brown thrasher in the top of a cottonwood. Far off across the fields a bobwhite, the ego-maniac of the birds, shouted his own name to the sun. A rain crow added the practical threat of the chronic pessimist.

South of her, the front yard with the old gate, weighted by the horseshoe, lay in the light of the morning. The cottonwoods, tall, straight, full of the promise of life in each sticky bud, guarded the gate on either side. The road, cleansed now from dirty snow, ran brown in the sunshine, little wisps of dust throwing themselves across it in dwarflike whirlwinds.

To the west, the old playhouse sat dingy and shabby with its pealing paint. Beyond were the familiar barn, the stacks, the harness-shed. Walt was doing the chores, bringing in the milk, the brim of his wide hat flapping back from the stiff breeze. How good Walt had been! Beyond the Lom-bardys was his home and in the distance was town. Warner was there two miles away. To-morrow he would be the equivalent of two million. Strangely enough, though, with the thought she had a semblance of peace that she had not felt since she returned to the Farnsworth home. With this suffering she had grown up. For the first time in a care-free life she felt mature. Life was a big thing . . . to be met squarely. In all the years that were past, she seemed to have side stepped it, to have evaded all issues that did not bring her pleasure. Life, then, was not that. It was not to be spent in feeding the desire for enjoyment, in thinking of one's own comfort. It was forgetting self, completely, in service—to do the unselfish things always. In that di-rection, only, lay peace for her. Quite suddenly she knew that there was one unselfish thing to do before she left for good. To-day she could do it. Last night she could not have done so. She was going to see Warner once more for a few minutes to tell him this one remaining thing. It was not so much that it might be helpful to him or that it would influence him, as that the act would cleanse her from her last self-centered thoughts and cause her to leave with no regrets over the wasted opportunity for a generous act.

The day grew more sultry with the climbing of the sun. All morning the hot wind blew. Sometimes it seemed almost like the August winds that blow from off great acres of drying corn, witheringly, blastingly hot. Every one spoke of its disagreeableness. It was the only topic of conversation as the churches were dismissed. Mr. Rineland and Alice, coming out of their own, met Warner. Mr. Rineland asked him cordially to get in the car and come on home with them to dinner. Warner excused himself and Alice, her gentle blue eyes safely upon a passer-by, knew that the reason was not the true one. But she could afford to be gracious and patient. Nancy was going for good. Time binds up all wounds. Just how deep this one was, she could not tell. There were many healing potions one might apply to it. Music was one, tactfulness and serenity were others. Alice was bright enough to know she was second choice and dull enough not to care too much.

Warner ate his dinner at the "Bee-House." It was not a pleasant meal. The wind blew in that hot, disagreeable way. Some ᷄ne raised a window for air and from Miss Ann's newly plowed garden the dirt blew in. Somebody else jumped up and put it down impatiently and they suffocated. To Warner, in the grip of his thoughts, the weather mattered little.

"This is the windiest state in the Union," the Major weighted the statement with the brick of finality. "And our neighbor, Omaha, is the windiest city."

"No," said Miss Gunn definitely, "the government weather bureau says Chicago ranks first. New York and Huron, S. D., are second. Omaha is away down the list at seven miles an hour."

It created an interminable discussion. Dr. Pearson had scarcely finished his soup when Essie called him to the 'phone. Without a murmur he took his bag and left. Warner had always admired that obedience, as from a soldier called to duty. He could see Helen Blakely color a little as the doctor left and he knew that she, too, was admiring that swift response.

Mary Mae Gates was nervously fatigued. "We've added another solo for to-night at the last minute, and of course I have to do it. I see where my Sunday afternoon has to be spent . . . at the piano."

"And I see where mine is to be spent then," Miss Ann said in a savage undertone to Helen Blakely, "down cellar behind the coal bin."

Marty Spencer had a new story. It was about a woman who went into a market to buy a fish. "She says to the man . . ."

Warner tried not to listen. It was all very trying.

Miss Rilla beamed with good cheer shining through her moist eyes. "I certainly enjoyed the sermon."

Miss Ann followed with, "It's a good thing *everybody* doesn't have to run around to get spiritual assistance to live through the week. I'd like to know who'd be cooking the dinners all over town." *Martha, Martha, thou art troubled about many things.*

When they had finished the tedious meal, Warner went up to his room and sat down near the closed window. Dust particles pattered like raindrops on the glass. He picked up Whitman's *Leaves of Grass* but he did not open it.

Down at the Carlson cottage, noisy with youngsters, shaking in the onslaughts of hot wind, Gus and Jen Carlson sat by their east kitchen windows and watched their neat garden with eagle eyes. The tiny lettuce and radishes and peas made a half hundred parallel lines of green against the black earth. Occasionally a wandering Rhode Island Red from the Swansons' would squeeze itself through the fence and, cocking its head coquettishly, advance inquisitively toward the inviting banquet. Simultaneously Gus and Jen would dart out and frighten the explorer to the verge of convulsions.

"I wish every one was in a stew," Jen would call across the garden.

"We'll have the law on Jim and Myrt yet," Gus would threaten loudly. From the messy interior of the Swanson cottage, Myrt, watching the pantomime, would raise the window and call out to Jim at the barn, "Maybe, Jim, we better bring *in* the chickens 'n have 'em set in the rockin'-chairs 'n look at the album."

Out at the Moore farm Nancy was packing her bag. She went at it deftly and cheerfully. "Aunt Biny, I'm going to send you some money every month and I don't want you

to say you don't need it. I don't suppose you do *need* it
but I want you to have it. I want you to get some new
things with it . . . just anything that you've always wanted
but never thought you ought to have. Walt can take you
over to town and you can pick out a new rug for this room
and some new curtains. Get Elsa Carlson to help you. She
has splendid taste and would enjoy it. And I'm going to
leave an order at the greenhouse for fresh flowers every
week for Uncle Jud. Oh, dear . . ." she stopped and
looked out toward the harness-shed where it seemed she
must see him, "after I quarreled so with him! Why don't
we act decently toward people when they're alive?"

At the Thomas farm, Walt cleaned the car up ready to
go into town for Essie. As he was finishing it, an auto
load of people from Postville drove into the yard and
laughed long and hilariously at the pleasant surprise their
presence had perpetrated on Walt and Mattie. Walt was
not unduly overjoyed but Mattie was in her element. While
she was visiting loudly and volubly with them, she "whacked
up" three pies, a pudding, some mayonnaise and a pan of
baking-powder biscuits.

The big Rineland house on the hill stood strong and solid
in the wind. Mr. Rineland, in the privacy of his library,
took from a drawer in his desk the rather faded and old-
fashioned picture of his first wife. Then, with hands that
shook a little, he returned it to the drawer and drew out the
picture of his son. He went through this little reverent
service every year on the sixth of April, the date on which
the young college boy, full of the vigor of living, had met
death in a train wreck on the way home for his spring
vacation. His only son! And people like the Swansons
and the Carlsons had so many!

Downstairs, Alice pulled all the shades to shut out the
light and keep the rooms dark and cool. As she did so she

planned the day. She would rest until five. Then she
would dress. Nancy's train was leaving at six-fifteen.
About six-thirty she would 'phone Warner at the "Bee-
House" asking him to come up to Sunday night supper.
He would be lonely, perhaps depressed. She was still not
sure just how far it had gone. But no matter, she could
manage. She would be gentle and bide her time. She
would play something soothing. Things had certainly come
her way.

When Walt and Essie drove into the yard behind the
cottonwoods Nancy wanted to know if they would take her
into town for a short time. There were a few people she
wanted to see before she left. So the three drove in together. Walt's cheap car was clean and shining. Essie was
shy with him but radiant. Such happiness as had come
to her seemed unbelievable. All her life she would work
hard for Walt. She was glad that she knew how to cook
and sew and keep things clean. Work would be tedious
no longer, but a beautiful task to do for the one person she
wanted to be near more than any other. Yes, a world that
would be drab to one assumes rose tints to another.

The wind blew constantly, hot and disagreeable. Nancy
stopped at the Bornheimers'. Things were better, Mrs.
Bornheimer told her. The children were well and she had
only four dollars yet to pay on the doctor's bill. Mrs.
Rineland, though, didn't bring any more sewing. She
was afraid she had charged her too much. Nancy left
some money. "No . . . don't feel that way, Mrs. Bornheimer . . . I want to. It seems like Johnny still belongs
to me."

At the Carlsons' Nancy talked with Gus and Jen about
Elsa, a shining-eyed Elsa who looked upon Nancy as Joan
may have looked upon the light. Elsa was to come to
Chicago when Nancy would have returned from abroad.

Neither Gus nor Jen would leave the east windows while they talked, for fear they might miss some of the Rhode Island Red intruders. They told Nancy all about it, heaping figurative maledictions on Myrt and Jim Swanson's heads.

She went in to the Swansons', too, for a minute. The children were glad to see her. The omnivorous baby was nibbling bites off a piece of paraffin from the top of a glass of jelly.

Myrt Swanson began right away on her troubles. "The Carlsons . . . they make life so miserable for me 'n Jim. What's a hen or two? Next year I've a notion to raise a lot more, just to spite Gus and Jen . . . such mean things!" What narrow little lives, thought Nancy, the big issues totally eclipsed by the shadow of a chicken.

Then they went to the "Bee-House." Walt and Essie stayed in the car while Nancy ran in. At the porch she met Genevieve Kendall and stopped to talk to her. "Did you know George and I had parted?" was Genevieve's glib greeting.

Nancy did not know whether to congratulate or condole so she said honestly, "I was sorry to hear it, Genevieve. I always liked George."

"It's the queerest thing, Nancy. George is in Omaha to stay. I don't want to tell this to anybody here. But this morning for a minute I thought I saw him coming up the street.. It gave me the queerest feeling. It made me wonder whether I'd do it again if I had it to do over. George had a lot of good qualities about him . . . you know that yourself. And when you've been married . . . I don't know . . . there's just something that can't be unmarried. But anyway I just got to hating him. I guess he got to hating me, too, so it's better this way. But why should I have to feel like I'm still married to him? . . ."

She would have rambled on indefinitely on both sides
of the subject if Nancy had not broken away.

When Nancy went into the house the tin-pan sound of
the old piano and the throaty huskiness of Mary Mae Gates's
voice were filling the Sunday silence with, "There is a green
hill far away." Miss Ann, her face set in grim lines of
stoicism, came out of the old library where Judge Baldwin
had read "The Classmate" to the children on long ago
Sunday afternoons. Miss Ann said Rilla had a headache
and added pleasantly that, what with the air being so pol-
luted with vocal artillery, it was a wonder she didn't have
complete paralysis instead. Nancy would not allow Miss
Rilla to be called, but she asked if Warner Field might
come down for a moment. So Miss Ann called him and
Warner came down. The first thing that came to him on
the landing was how very little the weather was affecting
Nancy. Her slim boyish body in its modish gown and
close fitting hat looked cool, her whole appearance unruffled.

She looked up and laughed while he was still on the
stairs. "You're not rid of me, yet, Warner," she called.
"Am I not a bold maiden to chase you to your lair?" She
had to be gay and natural before Miss Ann. "I wonder if
you will come out and haul me in to the six-fifteen? Mattie
has had a carload of people . . . two layers deep . . .
arrive for supper and she will be serving it just at that
time. So I thought you would do it for me instead of
Walt."

Warner would, of course, although there went through
him the swift fear of the bitter-sweetness of having to tell
her good-by again.

Nancy said good-by to Miss Ann. Miss Ann said good-by
in that constrained way of hers, shaking hands rigidly. "I
hope you will always remember me kindly," she said stiffly.

Nancy could not recall at the moment what particular kind thing she would always remember. As she passed the dining-room door she looked in. The table was set for lunch. There were daffodils in the center of it. She could see that already some one had her place. Life was going on without her. One boarder less made no difference.

At the farm again, Nancy said good-by to Walt and Essie, who were to go on home and face the flippant jests of the company at the engagement. "Essie, you be good to Walt. He's been a mighty fine friend to me."

"Oh, Nancy," Essie burst forth in a little moment of emotion. "If folks were all as kind and lovely as you are! You won't let being awful rich change you, will you?"

Aunt Biny and Nancy ate an early lunch. While they were sitting at the table it clouded and there came a sudden swift dash of rain. But it did not seem to lessen the heat. When the sun came out the dampness accentuated it so that the air was heavy, oppressive. Nancy was cheerful all during the meal. She had that feeling, though, which one has in speaking lines in an amateur play. She was playing a part, not entering wholeheartedly into it, but doing it pleasantly as one must who has been cast in the rôle he did not wish. She would get through it creditably even though it was not the assignment she desired.

So she talked of little things as though she possessed a deep interest in them. "You've plenty of that liniment to last you, Aunt Biny? Now, don't get sick, and above all things be careful about slipping on those back steps." She was speaking her lines, moving about, playing the part, while time was rushing past her like the hot disagreeable wind of the prairie. "I don't know just how long we'll be abroad . . . three or four months anyway. I'll write you from every place we stop. You'll enjoy that, won't you? We're to go up into Scotland a while I think. I'll describe

the places and you can pretend you're taking the trip too.
I'll pick up some little thing for you at each place, so you'll
have packages to look forward to."

It was five-thirty when Warner drove into the yard.
Simultaneously with his turning into the lane from the
main road there came another sharp dash of rain that
changed in a moment to marble-sized chunks of hail. Coming
as it did into the very lap of the heat seemed a most peculiar phenomenon. By the time he was in the dooryard
and stepping out of the the car the ice balls crunched under
his feet.

Nancy was ready. She was dreading the parting with
Aunt Biny who would probably break down. Tears from
the old were so painful. But it was not Aunt Biny who
went tearful. "You're my mother, Aunt Biny," Nancy
held her fresh wet cheek to Aunt Biny's withered one.
"No matter who she was, *you're* my mother. And I wish
Uncle Jud knew how sorry I am for the way I acted."

So after all it was Aunt Biny who had to comfort Nancy.
"Why, dearie, he knows." Aunt Biny's faith was stupendous.

"You'll need some kind of a wrap, Nancy," Warner
called. The cold of the ice balls made as great a change
as though the country had been pitched headlong into another climate. So Nancy opened her bag and got out a
coat.

The two drove out of the yard through the ice with Aunt
Biny standing in the porch and waving her crutch until
they turned into the lane behind the cottonwoods. Then
she limped into the house and looked about her strangely,
almost stupidly. "Why, I'm alone," she said as though
she had not comprehended it before. She sat down in the
chintz-covered chair by the window. For some time she
sat idly in the still room.

CHAPTER XXXIII

FROM THE RIM OF THE PRAIRIE

WARNER and Nancy had scarcely turned into the lane until Nancy said hurriedly, "Warner, there's so little time . . . and there's something more I wanted to say to you before I go. I wasn't unselfish enough last night . . . but to-day I feel stronger and clearer-minded about it. That's why I felt that I must see you again. This morning, when I first woke up, it came to me that all my life I've been utterly selfish, thought of Nancy Moore's pleasure and enjoyment and wishes before everything else in the world. I've always wanted things my own way and most of the time I've had them so. It seems to me that just to-day I've begun to be decent in my attitude toward . . . people that I haven't liked. This isn't so much that it will help *you* . . . that it will make any difference one way or the other with the rest of your life . . . but it's going to make a better person of *me* to tell you before I leave that I hope *now* you will marry Alice. I've just been stubborn and ugly in my thoughts about it. I think if you would . . . it would make her very happy. Alice is a great many things I am not. Your families are friendly. She has blue Mayflower blood in her . . . and mine. . . ." Even then she could not resist an impish, "mine is probably the most scarlet, garden variety of gypsy horsetrader's. She'd do a great deal for you on the social side. In the years to come you're going to be lionized more or less. She's good looking and conservative. . . ."

"And extremely uninteresting," Warner added dryly.

Even if Nancy was human enough to like to hear him say it, she was generous enough to return, "Don't, Warner. Some day, you are going to be very sorry you said that to me. Right now I'm sorry for every little mean catty thing I ever said or thought about her. All our lives there has been a sort of half-concealed antagonism between us. I've probably been more to blame than she. And I'll give her credit for not being tempery like I am. Anyway when you face big things . . . like I'm doing to-day . . . you see things in a clearer perspective. And I believe that you'll find the very unselfish act of making another happy would bring happiness to yourself."

"So you think love is a commodity to be handed over from one girl to another like a package with a 'Merry Christmas' card tied on it?" Their places seemed to have changed. To-day it was Nancy who was strong, Warner who was weakening.

"I think it can grow out of unselfish devotion to another."

"A pretty little philosophy, Nancy . . . as lovely as it is untrue."

"I don't think so. I think if you and I . . . going our separate ways as we are doing . . . would meet a dozen years from now and be honest with each other . . ."

"We wouldn't, of course. We'd be polite and two-faced."

But Nancy did not answer. For there was another on-slaught of hail so that Warner slowed the car quickly as the jagged particles crashed on the windshield. The hail stopped as suddenly as it had come and a great stillness hung over the country. They were behind the long row of Lombardys at the edge of Walt's land.

"Look Warner," Nancy said quickly. "That high smoke . . . there's a big fire somewhere."

Above the trees an immense yellow-black smoke whirled up into the sky, spiraling, rotating, in great volume. But when they came out from behind the first section of wind-break they saw it was no fire but a more cruel Thing. Greenish clouds had whipped themselves into the shape of the bowl of a huge wine-glass . . . a bowl that was twisted and blackened and distorted as though Appolyon and all the powers of darkness were to drink from it with wind for their wine. The stem of the tall glass touched the far horizon, poised there for a moment on the rim of the prairie and then, swaying dizzily, began moving across the open country.

Warner stopped the car on the highway. "We'd better get out," he said quietly. With no word Nancy obeyed him. The two walked away from the car to the side of the road. Fascinated, their eyes never left the restless, erratic, horrible Thing which was charging with frightful mad roaring over meadow and broken field. Warner's arms went around Nancy and he drew her close.

The whole earth seemed to pause in silent contemplation of the uncanny spectacle of the heavens. There was no sound anywhere. No wind was in the trees. No bird sang. No cock crew. There was silence everywhere save in the frenzied heart of the Thing that moved swiftly across the prairie. It boiled and crackled and roared. It was heavy. But it was not clumsy. Gracefully it moved. Almost daintily it picked its way in and out of the farm lands. It bent and swayed and swung. The stem stretched and pulled away from the bowl. But it did not break. It sucked at the ground and whatever it touched, living or inanimate thing, answered its wild call and was pulled up into the cloud glass to make wine for the fallen gods.

Silently the two stood there together. There was no use to move. There was no time to change location. There was nothing to be gained by doing so. For one does not know where it is going. Its birthplace is in the southwest.

Its deathbed is in the northeast. And in its short mad life
between these two uncertain points it stays on no track,
travels no surveyed highway. It is the Tam O'Shanter of
all the storms.

There together Warner and Nancy stood and watched the
Thing, spectators at the wind's debauchery. They themselves seemed safe, its swing an arc of which they were the
hub. They could see the trees and timbers whirling in
the angry wind and dirt. It swept with whirling, rattling
violence past the edge of Maple City near the creamery
district. And then—no longer were they safe, no longer
onlookers at the drunken revelry of the wind. They themselves stood in the path of the Thing. The highway was
plainly to be the arc of its diabolical sweep. It was sucking its way towards Walt's place. It had reached it now.
It picked up his corncribs and flung them lightly aside.
Snarling, it side stepped the house and the windmill. It
twisted the barn around, tore the maples of a half-century
growth, threw the fence posts about like toothpicks and
came toward the two. They could feel the strong suc-
tion of the vacuum. With one sweep of his arm Warner
started to draw Nancy into the field at the left of the road.
As Nancy's hand reached for the fence, Warner jerked her
violently from it. In the brief second taken to reach it,
electric light poles at the side of the highway had snapped
and dropping their death-charged wires across the fence,
charged it with their liquid death. Only the fraction of
an inch had intervened between them and its molten fire.
They were barred from egress into the fields beyond,
trapped between the death-fire of the fence and the death-
wind of the storm. In a few seconds the Thing was to take
them with it . . . like fence posts.

They stood awaiting the verdict of Fate. Whatever the
judgment rendered, they were ready. Once . . . it seemed

a thousand years ago . . . standing on a hillside, Warner had said, "How they must have loved adventure!" and Nancy had answered, "How they must have loved each other." And now they, too, were facing adventure . . . the Great Adventure . . . and they, too, loved like that.

The gods sneered at the two tiny pygmies standing there together in the way of their mad wind-wine debauch and reached out for them. Warner's lips met Nancy's. And then . . . with snarling demoniacal laughter, as though in the act they suddenly recognized the futility of parting these humans, the gods tossed the glass across the road into the field beyond and left the two standing there unscathed.

The stem was bending now. The bowl had become too heavy for the handle. Upper wind currents commenced snapping the glass. It was as though the demons were through with it, had drunk their fill. They bent the stem, twisted it, even knotted it into bows in their wrath. As though the black glass shattered, the bowl broke slowly, splintered into small pieces, disintegrated, flattened out dejectedly, rolled itself in thick gray-black dirt-smoke over the bare cornfields. And the mad orgy was finished.

For a moment the sun broke through scudding clouds in the west. The prairie smiled again. Robins in the Lombardys broke forth into wild singing. A rooster crowed ecstatically. The Thing had gone. Nothing was left of it . . . nothing but the seared trail where the stand of the huge wine-glass had been dragged over the lovely prairie.

Houses would be rebuilt. Trees would grow. Barns would be turned back on their foundations . . . corncribs renewed . . . fences repaired. Only one thing in the slimy trail could never be undone. When Warner Field saw Death coming toward them, riding over the prairie on the back of the wind; when he snatched Nancy from the electric destruction that awaited them both; when he stood facing the Great Force, before which they were to be as leaves of grass, the things which he had not seen were taught him. Neither life nor death was the paramount issue. Nothing in the world or out of it was important but that he and Nancy were one. Wealth, friendship, obligations, debts . . . all the reasons out of which the barrier between them had been constructed seemed no longer reasons but excuses. Warner, his lips to Nancy's, had said, "Don't be afraid . . . nothing can harm us."

And Nancy had said quietly, "I'm not afraid now."

"Nor ever part us."

"Nor ever part us," Nancy had agreed as simply as though the thing were simple.

CHAPTER XXXIV

AFTER THE TORNADO

WHEN the tornado had flattened out into nothing, Walt and Essie, Mattie and the company came up out of the milk-cave. Walt went out to the twisted barn and with great boyish sobs pulled a timber off his best brood mare, talking to her soothingly as one would talk to a woman in illness. Mattie picked her porch rockers and a crock of sauerkraut out of the cherry trees, pulled her clothes-wringer out of the side of the corncrib and stood looking vindictively up at one of her balloonlike kitchen aprons flapping grotesquely from the top of the windmill. With one hand Essie picked up the stripped body of a duck and with the other a bunch of feathers lying near and held them together stupidly as though trying to think of some way to stick them back.

Aunt Biny had just taken down her Bible in the lonely silence. *Let not your heart be troubled, neither let it be afraid.* Then she heard the far-away rumbling sound but thought it was Nancy's train. "Jud and Naney . . . both gone now," she said to herself, "and nobody knows . . . maybe I'll see Jud first."

Over in Maple City the boarders, who had been eating lunch when they first heard the roaring, talked excitedly on the porch of the thing they had witnessed. Some of them still had napkins in their hands. Major Slack in his perturbation had pushed his fork into his belt thinking it was an army revolver.

Miss Gunn remained calm, contributing a few statistics,

336

"It is a well-known fact taken from the weather bureau reports that eighty per cent of the tornadoes take place in the first three months of spring."

Marty Spencer asked, "Did you ever hear the one about the Chinaman who saw a tornado?"

Nobody paid any attention to him.

Mary Mae Gates carried an air of extreme relief, "It's certainly a good thing it didn't happen two hours later with church in session for we've practiced and practiced on our anthems and probably people would have walked right out on us."

Dr. Pearson was already running out his car in answer to a call from the devastated district.

Genevieve Kendall stood a little apart, frightened. She caught herself wondering if the storm had reached as far away as Omaha.

Miss Rilla was openly upset. She wiped her eyes a great deal. "I keep thinking of Nancy," she told Miss Ann. "It happened just about the time she would be out on the road coming in to town to take her train."

Miss Ann had been thinking of it, too, but she would not admit it. "I'm not going to waste any mental emotion over her," she said tartly. "She slips in and out of everything as easy as a greased pig. No doubt she's slipped out of this catastrophe, too."

Down in the creamery neighborhood the Carlsons came up out of the cellar on the east side of their house. Gus and Jen each carried a baby and the frightened older children were all clinging together. Simultaneously the Swansons came up out of their cellar on the west side of the house. Jim and Myrt each carried a baby and the frightened older children were all clinging together.

"All safe, Myrt?" Mrs. Carlson called, hysterically.

"All safe, Jen," Mrs. Swanson answered, phlegmatically.

"Any damage over there, Jim?" Gus Carlson called.

"My God . . . the chickens are gone!"

It was true. The place was bare where had stood the house in which the Rhode Island Reds lived and moved and had their being in those infrequent intervals of being at home. Not even the remnant of a roost clung to the ground.

Jen and Gus Carlson looked at each other for the space of a single inspired moment, then each suddenly pushed a baby into one of the older children's arms and ran out to their own henhouse. Gus took two old squawking hens under his arms and Jen swept a brood of thirteen little Plymouth Rocks into her apron, and hurriedly crossing the deadline, presented them affectionately to the Swansons.

Mr. Rineland had seen the funnel-shaped cloud from the windows of his library. Before running to find Mama and Alice he had hastily unlocked a drawer, taken from it two of his most precious possessions and put them in his pocket . . . the pictures of an old-fashioned, sweet-faced woman and a young man.

Alice Rineland and her mother had watched the death-dealing cloud from the upper balcony with interest but not alarm, knowing that nothing could harm a Rineland in an Italian Renaissance house sitting up on three terraces. When the storm had dispelled itself they went into the house and down to the first floor. Alice arranged the chafing-dish on the tea-cart with some dainty Haviland dishes and a little slender vase of roses. She put a small log in the fireplace, and turned on two soft lights under silken shades. Sorting the music she found Schumann's "Träumerei" and placed it on the piano. Then she arranged the mulberry pillows in the big davenport and sat down among them so that her pale prettiness stood out from them cameolike.

The six-fifteen came in and pulled out. . . .

At six-thirty Alice 'phoned the "Bee-House."

Miss Rilla said that Mr. Field was not in but that she would have him call when he came.

At seven-ten Miss Rilla said no she had not forgotten the message, that Mr. Field simply had not come in.

Over at Aunt Biny Moore's on the seat under the apple tree where the new buds were beginning to swell, Nancy, in the shelter of Warner's arm, was saying, "When I was a little girl, I used to imagine how the man I'd love would look. He was about as tall as you and he had shoulders like you and the back of his head looked like you . . . but I never could see just what his face looked like. And then, the time I saw you by the straw stack, Warner, I knew that he was you. . . .

"That makes me think of what an odd youngster I was. I had the queerest fancies. Uncle Jud gave me a lot of old account books and I always wrote all of my innermost thoughts down in them. I have all those old diaries yet but not a soul has ever read them. Some day . . . when I know you better . . . I'll let you read them. . . ."

CHAPTER XXXV

A BROWN SHAWL

THIS is the end of the love story of Warner Field and Nancy Moore. No, that is not true. It is not the end. They are wrong who count love only as an emotion which touches the high points of existence. If the torrent of love, as of rushing waters, broadens into pools of companionship and understanding it is no less sincere. If it becomes calm in the even places of life's afternoon it is no less love.

Before going East to face Mr. Farnsworth together, Warner and Nancy were married in Aunt Biny's old sitting room with the lumpy couch and the base-burner and the presidents looking stolidly down. Nothing about it was romantic. It was in the morning in time for the train East. Walt and Mattie came over, the whole hurried occasion completely spoiled for the latter because of its lack of time for eating. The preacher, bustling and important with a cold in his head, read cheerfully, "Those whom God hath joined together let no man put asunder." Death and marriage, sorrow and joy, they were all in the day's business.

The neighbors talked about it over the party lines. *"Married?* You don't say! Why I think that's *turrible.* A funeral on Friday and a wedding on Monday *in the same room!"*

"Well, whatever she's going to say to the other man's beyond *me.* Changin' your mind over a man like it was no more'n the trimmin' on your hat. But she was always

340

a little fly-up-the-creek. Never could put your finger right
on her like you could Lena Denning or some of them other
girls."

When Nancy and Warner drove into town to the train
they started early so they would have time to stop at the
"Bee-House" to put up the car and get Warner's bag. As
they turned into the old drive from the Tenth Street side
they could see that Miss Ann and Miss Rilla were still deep
in the house cleaning. There were old-fashioned silk crazy-
quilts over the porch railing and the mink furs that had been
their mother's were on the line behind the house.

"They're the kind of people," Nancy said, "who never
get rid of *anything*. I'll bet they still have every old scrap
of cloth and empty spool they've ever had."

At the house Warner ran up the winding stairs to his
room while Nancy went back into the kitchen to hunt up
Miss Rilla. On the second floor, Warner, catching a
glimpse of Miss Ann through the slightly-opened door of
the storeroom, tapped briskly as he pushed it farther open
and stepped in.

"The Fields have stopped to say good-by," he told her
hurriedly.

It was as though, upon opening the storeroom door, Warner had also opened the rusty-hinged door of Miss Ann's
heart.

She had been crying. Tears from Miss Ann would have
been wrung from the depths. There was an open trunk at
her feet. Pictures, garments, trinkets, all the odds and
ends which people foolishly accumulate through the years,
lay about her on chairs and boxes and the floor. In the
midst of the hodge-podge assortment stood Miss Ann like a
statue of Grief on a shore to which the wreckage of the
past had floated. Startled, she looked up at Warner, her
firm, red-cheeked face drawn and contorted into a harsh

sorrow. For the fraction of a moment she made a motion as though to block his entry into the room, then suddenly abandoned the impulse and broke into uncontrollable weeping.

"Old things . . . keepsakes . . . they always tear at one so. . . ." Her voice cracked in its hoarseness. "Most of these were my little sister's." She flung out her hand to take in the old and odd assortment of things. "She was only seventeen when she died . . . nearly twenty-three years ago . . . broken-hearted for a boy who had hurried home to her but had not lived to reach her."

Warner was acutely aware of the words she was saying but he was staring at a shawl which hung across the back of a chair. It looked bright and new, yet, with the other relics, it had come out of the chest at Miss Ann's feet. It was a warm brown in color with a rambling vine of vivid green and blue and a wide wool fringe.

Miss Ann, standing in the midst of the driftage, cried harshly—loud, wrenching sobs that wracked her.

Silent, Warner stood and stared at the shawl. Although its coloring was fresh and vivid it was unmistakably the counterpart of the old faded shawl which Nancy kept locked in the drawer under the cupboard. It must have been Miss Ann's or Miss Rilla's.

For only a second Warner's mind hesitated, bewildered at the enormity of its thought, challenging its own reasoning. Then swiftly and concisely, like fitting the pieces of a child's puzzle, it began putting together the tragic bits. Miss Ann's and Miss Rilla's young sister had died. Twenty-three years before, Nancy had been left on Jud Moore's porch in a brown shawl. That shawl was old and faded now from much use, but it had been bright and new then. As bright and new as the one lying across the chair in Miss Ann's storeroom.

Miss Ann and Miss Rilla had always dressed alike. Twenty-three years before, they had both possessed new brown shawls with rambling green and blue vines and a wide wool fringe. Could it have been their little sister's child who had been wrapped in one of the shawls and carried to the Moore farmhouse? Could the other shawl have been packed away in moth balls at the bottom of a trunk in the Baldwin storeroom?

Then Warner remembered something. Nancy had told him, that once, when she was a little girl, she had brought eggs to the Baldwin home, trailing her old shawl along behind her. Miss Ann had jumped between her and old Mrs. Baldwin and ordered her around to the back door. In the library Miss Rilla had put tender arms around her and cried over her.

Nancy, then, was the child of Miss Ann's and Miss Rilla's young sister, the girl who had died "broken-hearted for a boy who had hurried home to her but had not lived to reach her." Over twenty years before, O. J. Rineland's son had been killed in a train wreck on the way home from college. Mr. Rineland liked Nancy. Mrs. Rineland, his second wife, disliked her.

Nancy, then, Warner realized, was the child of Mr. Rineland's son and Miss Ann's little sister.

While old Judge Baldwin's clock on the stairs was ticking off a few brief seconds, all the little pieces of the tragedy had shot into their places as neatly as the little pieces of colored glass in a kaleidoscope. The finished solution was here before Warner's mind, as palpable as a material substance. The amazing thing was that it seemed not to surprise him. It was as though he had always known it.

Neither he nor Miss Ann said anything. There was nothing but Miss Ann's harsh crying—as though emotion were painful because of long disuse.

From below Nancy's voice floated up, lovely with laughter. Miss Ann, her hand at her torn throat, her austere face swollen with tears, turned to Warner. "One does what seems best for others," she said brokenly, almost appealingly, as though begging his approval. "My father and mother were proud people. It would have killed t' Old Dr. Minnish understood this and helped me. stood between my parents and my little sister. Afterwards I did what I could to make amends to the child." She was getting control of herself, becoming severe. "When my father died I turned over to the little girl the money he left me . . . it was not large but it was all I had . . . and took the boarders."

"Warner," Nancy called up gayly, "are you coming or am I deserted at the altar?"

Miss Ann stepped hurriedly over a pile of old pictures and put a hand on Warner's arm. "Promise me something. . . ." She spoke low, passionately. "Promise me you'll be good to Nancy?"

Warner Field's arms went around Miss Ann. He drew her to him and kissed her wet, blotched cheek. "As long as I live . . ." it sounded sacred . . . like a marriage . . . "I'll be good to Nancy."

CHAPTER XXXVI

AND NOW

IT was several years ago that Warner Field married Nancy Moore and then went East to tell Mr. Farnsworth that the greatest indebtedness in the world is the debt of youth to youth and that a promise is big but love is bigger.

The Fields have two children . . . David and Phyllis. David came to Nancy in an agony of body so that she knew the intense pain and the relatively great joy of motherhood. But Phyllis came to Nancy because of an agony of girlish mind. When Phyllis was so tiny that she could scarcely comprehend the story, Nancy began to tell her, "I went around where there were babies and babies and they all looked sweet and nice. But when I came to you with your pink fists and your big eyes I said, 'Here's my baby.' You see God sent David to me but I went and *picked you out all by myself.*"

A few summers after their marriage Warner and Nancy, who were living East, came to take Aunt Biny back with them. They said that she had worked hard all her life and now she must stop and take things easy. They wanted to do something for her, to dress her in pretty gowns and let her be waited upon.

"No," said Aunt Biny, "I have to have air and sunlight and room."

They laughed at her. "We don't live in jail," Warner told her.

"There's a back yard all laid out in symmetrical flower

345

beds and it has seats and a little fountain. You'd love it," Nancy explained.

"No," said Aunt Biny. "I've got to see long distances."

Nancy was ready for that too. "The house is high. From one side of it you can see clear across the city. And we take wonderful drives."

"No," Aunt Biny was immovable. "I'm grateful to you both. No." She repeated it stubbornly. Then she pointed with her crutch. "You see out there . . . just beyond the currant bushes this side of the peach trees? Pa and I stopped right about in that spot in our wagon years ago. It was late afternoon. The sun was low and the prairie grass was all a-ripple like a sea. There were wild flowers in the grass everywhere . . . red and orange and corn-flower blue. They sprinkled it so that the prairie looked like figured silk. There wasn't a thing to be seen besides the sky and the grass but some clumps of wild plums and the willows and cottonwoods over by Tinkling Creek. When we stopped a covey of prairie chickens flew up ahead of us. I got out with the baby and looked around. I had brought an ivory-handled parasol with me from Indiana and I reached in the wagon and got it and stuck it in the ground by me. 'Here's our home,' I said to Pa. 'If we can get hold of this piece of land, here we stay. I'm sick of fol-lowing the sun. I haven't got a mite of roving blood in me. Here are you and me and the baby . . . and there's the team and the plow and the seed-corn. What more does it take to make a home? Here's as good as anywhere. Home is what you make it. And I can start a home right here.'

" 'All right,' Pa says, 'I'm willing.' I guess he was glad to have me decide it. It was railroad land. We got the whole upper eighty for one hundred and sixty dollars . . . two dollars an acre. Pa had the money in a little tin chest in the wagon. One of the first things we did was to set out those maple and cottonwood trees."

Nancy and Warner involuntarily looked up at the huge trees that towered like the turrets of some medieval castle. A hundred homes of wild feathered things clung to them. "They were just little saplings that we brought in a wet gunny-sack. I'm like one of them. I was planted here when they were. My roots extend down in the ground far out to the end of the upper eighty and down to Tinkling Creek. If you'd pull me up, the life would just naturally run out of me and I'd be dried up and limp and useless as a hewn maple. No . . . I'm grateful to you both. But I'd rather stay here . . . . where I can look off to the rim of the prairie . . . and see the sun go down."

They knew it was true. So they left her there where she could look off to the rim of the prairie . . . left her there until the sun went down.

Small towns and the surrounding communities do not change rapidly in appearance or characteristics. For the most part our people are still ordinary commonplace people. There has never an extremely rich nor a highly successful person gone out from Maple City. And excepting as Warner Field, in adopting the community, has brought it some claim to recognition, no one famous has ever lived in it.

Maple City is still small and midwestern, which in the eyes of many modernists is synonymous for all that is hideous and cramping. A handful of people, they say we are, knotted together like roots in darkness. Blind souls, they call us, struggling spirits who can never find deliverance from our sordid surroundings. Poor thinkers! Not to know that from tangled roots shimmering growth may spring to the light in beautiful winged release.

There have been a great many changes though among the people. Alice Rineland married the new assistant cashier in her father's bank and they live with her parents in the big house which draws its skirts up from the dust and grime. They have one little sun parlor raised girl whose manners are exquisite and whose snobbishness is deep. Of late years Alice has become a follower of a strange cult which gives her supreme complacency but which no one else among the practical women of Maple City, busy with unselfish service for others, has had time to study.

Mrs. Rineland is thin and sharp-eyed, rouged and enameled . . . a withered old woman trying to look gay and debonair like a rickety house with new paint and shingles. O. J. Rineland is still living, an old man who has had some deep sorrows and many disappointments, but whose philosophy, in spite of them, is fine and sane. His will, neatly folded and sealed, lies in a tin box in the vault of the old First National. O. J. Rineland's business is in order so that Death may not take him unaware. Most of the property is to go to Mama and Alice, but there is a codicil in which is set aside a sum for Nancy Moore Field. Mr. Rineland added it the Monday that Warner Field came hurriedly into the bank to say that he was on his way out to the farm to marry Nancy. After Warner had gone the old banker went into the vault and got out his will. Then he sat alone at his desk in his private office for a long time and remembered many things: his boy's youthful love for the little Baldwin girl, his college days, the letter that said he was coming home, the first news of the wreck, the nightmare of suspense, the crushing certainty of loss. Before the aching pain, like a huge iron hand on his very body, had lifted itself, Ann Baldwin, a figure of stark grief, appearing one evening at the old house across town and demanding

to see him alone. Her tragic announcement of her young
sister's illness. His offer to do anything to help her . . .
with money . . . advice . . . recognition of the child . . .
anything. Her refusal and her grim and stoic acceptance
of responsibility. Her last words: "No, I want nothing but
your silence. I only wanted you to know the truth." How
disturbed he was that night and how he had finally told
Mama that he thought they ought to bring the child home
and raise it with Alice. How Mama had gone all to pieces
over the suggestion, and been ill in bed from it.

Of all these Mr. Rineland thought, that day of Nancy's
marriage, and of many other things: How Ann Baldwin
had carried the child out to Jud and Biny Moore's and
how tenderly they had cared for it. How he had watched
her growth with an infinite yearning to have her for his
own. How often he had seen his boy in her . . . the
brown eyes and a gay, jaunty way she had.

His will lay there before him on the desk. He would have
liked to recognize Nancy as his own flesh and blood . . .
to make her an equal heir. But the pride of the Baldwin
sisters and the pride of Mama and Alice lay between them.
No, it could not be. We could not do with Life the way
we wished. Life was more apt to do things with us. For
a long time he sat there, thinking, and then he picked up
the pen and wrote: "I set aside this sum for Nancy Moore
Field, because, of all the little girls who used to play with
Alice, I liked her best."

Walt and Essie have a new house and the latest model of
tractor and an auto full of little folks. Mattie Thomas
went to live with Aunt Biny after Walt was married. "Walt
and Essie are all right to me," Mattie said, "but there never
was a roof anywhere . . . not even the Kansas City convention hall one . . . big enough to cover two families
without partitions between 'em. The only big one I ever

heard of that covered a lot of relations where they didn't fuss was that Westminster Abbey one."

The "Bee-House" still has boarders, for "men may come and men may go" but eating goes on forever. Miss Ann says quite frankly that she will be sixty-two next month and Miss Rilla, who thinks a woman's age is her own business, has to acknowledge reluctantly that she will too. Only one of the old boarders remains. Major Slack hangs on near the head of the table where he settles all questions as quickly and definitely as the American guns settled the Spanish.

Mary Mae Gates, in spite of her longing for fame, married a clothing merchant in her little home town. When a great wave of longing comes over her to be singing in grand opera, she begins, "Ride a Cock Horse to Banbury Cross."

Miss Gunn has gone to California to play. Some one wrote back that it was quite pathetic, her desire to do funny things in the last of her life. Poor Miss Gunn, not to know that pleasure and work should be so intermingled that no one knows where the one leaves off and the other begins!

Helen Blakely and Dr. Pearson were married. The doctor, scientific and immaculate, with a whole office full of fierce-looking machinery, goes around to his cases. And old Doc Minnish, hands stained with grease, mud on his auto, oats in his pocket, goes around to his. A few of the patients of each die and most of them get well, which does not prove anything.

Marty Spencer, although older in years, is still unmarried, flitting about lightly, sipping at the tips of the blossoms of pleasure.

George and Genevieve Kendall married other people. George is fairly contented, but Genevieve has surprisingly found her second husband also not flawless.

Elsa Carlson is in New York. She changed her name to Elise D'Arlsone and works in an establishment where they charge fabulous sums to make fat ladies look merely plump.

The Carlsons and the Swansons still live side by side, complaining and excusing, quarreling and forgiving . . . the big issues of life clouded by chicken-sized shadows.

Aunt Biny kept her "rendezvous with Death" and Uncle Jud. During her last sickness she spoke of going away as casually and pleasantly as though she were taking the six-fifteen. One grew to think of it as a physical journey. Once she said wistfully to Nancy, "I wish I could take Pa some of the Jonathan apples from the tree at the far end of the orchard." Grant that Uncle Jud's and Aunt Biny's heaven is not one of shining streets and golden harps and many mansions! Make it, Lord, quite humble, and near a meadow where a thrush sings at evening in the maples!

On account of Warner's work, he and Nancy spend most of the year in the East but in the summer they bring the children and come back to the farm that came to them through Uncle Jud's will. Mattie runs the farm and finds great pleasure in trying to outdo Walt with her own crops. When she gets the letter from the Fields giving the date on which they will arrive she lays it aside and hurries, balloonlike, out to the kitchen and gets down all eleven cookbooks.

Warner and Nancy are fond of the farm. Every morning they see the sun rise over the rolling hills and at night they watch it slip back of the rim of the prairie. Warner Field writes of the mid-west. He does not credit it with having in its air either the crispness of the mountains or the salt tang of the sea . . . nor will he discredit the sorcery of the odors of loam and sod and subsoil, of dewy clover, and ripening corn and the honey-sweetness of lavender alfalfa. He does not pretend that it is idyllic . . . nor will he speak of it as bleak and uninteresting. He does not assert that it has attained to great heights of culture and art . . . nor will he sell it for thirty pieces of silver. But in some way Warner Field catches in his writings the gleam of the soul of the wide prairie, dim and deep and mysterious. For here, as everywhere, drama ebbs and flows like the billowing of the seas of yellow wheat.

There is one other thing you will want to know. Did Warner ever tell Nancy about the interview with Miss Ann in the storeroom? And this is the answer:

Last summer the Field children swept out the old cabin for a playhouse. They arranged the chairs and the braided rag rugs, put a bouquet of elderberry blossoms on the table and some broken dishes in the cupboard. Then they tried to open the drawer underneath the cupboard but it would not open. With masculine philosophy David gave up, but with feminine ingenuity Phyllis dug a hairpin into the lock and then a buttonhook and after that a screw-driver. And when not one of these had any effect, she went to the door and called: "Father, come help us get this drawer open . . . will you?"

Warner, who was crossing the lane road by the cottonwoods, came to the little house and stood in the doorway. As he watched his children working with the old lock, he thought of many things: of Alice and her mother in the big house on the hill, of Miss Ann and Miss Rilla in the old decaying "Bee-House" behind the maples and of Uncle Jud and Aunt Biny in their little narrow houses under the leaves. But most of all he thought of Nancy and the joy of living that was hers.

"No . . . let it be," he said with finality, "let the drawer stay locked."

(3)

THE END